The Ninth Emanation

-Chronicles 101 -

FABIO GHIONI

FOREWORD

We dedicate this chronicle with gratitude to all those who have made it possible through work and intelligence, to carry these words full of passion and magic and truth on this vehicle that, travelling through time, will reach in a few centuries the schools and teaching classrooms of the People to whom it is destined..

CONTENUTI

INCIPIT

IT looked stormy and the pungent smell of ozone which follows tremendous discharges of lightning, like the ones that were breaking out in that place, warned me to return to the monastery which had been my sanctuary for some years and also the place where the outcome of the last great war had been decided.

I watched the sea breaking with random violence on the rocks from the top of the majestic Fiordland reefs in New Zealand.

I imagined seeing the ancient and blind intelligence which caused that relentless aggression and its awareness, that in time, it would have wore out the rock reclaiming it for itself.

Time wasn't important to the sea, but it was important to me. The awareness that time represented my biggest enemy was the push that had led me to complete the undertaking to which I was predestined.

Turning around, I walked back to the monastery, my sanctuary, holy temple and grand laboratory.

The setting off of the final events was near and the feeling was almost of psychedelic euphoria.

Finally!

I crossed the entrance and closed the outside world behind me. The approaching of the moment was also devastating my mind, as if two great armies were fighting a final battle which was costing uncountable lifes and was consumed through fierce and brutal actions filled with horror, brutality and blood, knowing that this confrontation would have determined the end of a time and from its outcome there would be no return.

I felt a certain pleasure feeling the final conflict advance towards its natural conclusion; I had no doubts in my mind regarding its outcome.

The wait was grueling and it was then that I decided to use the remaining time to give testimony to all the things and the people and the

1

Gods that had brought us one step from the great transformation.

This testimony, written from a different future, while I observe the consequences of the masterpiece from above, will be put to the disposal of the new life forms which, now and in time to come, populate and will populate this World, so that whatever be the destiny that follows, the records will show the origins and events which provoked it.

Wanting to fully simplify that which will prove to be obvious by the unraveling of this narration, one can summarize by saying that the history of man on Earth had reached a moment of critical mass enough to trigger a radical change.

It could be a tremendous natural catastrophe with the power to reset history and erase the human race as if it had never existed, or a new great dictator, who wouldn't have hesitated using the destructive power of weapons to reach the same effect. Or - perhaps – an alien invasion... or the impact of a great asteroid...

Instead, it was none of the above and nothing that one could have really imagined.

Looking out the window to the world, I could see the same view as always, but my mind was no longer able to elaborate it as it used to be. The effect was that of looking at something familiar and known in detail, aware nevertheless that soon it would have all been new.

Or lost.

Every story has a beginning, of course, and this one makes no exception, even if, philosophically speaking, one could talk for days without agreeing on the different viewpoints, which would want this beginning in the mind or in the world, in the spirit that triggered a life and its destiny, or in the chaotic creation of casual events in the matter.

Let's just say that it all started in California, not on a beach but in the hinterland, a few miles from a little town, about seven hours by car from Los Angeles, in the desert (or better, what the Californians call desert), in a clear night with no moon or clouds.

How many stars could be seen! It was like being in open space. I could clearly see some of the planets: Saturn and Jupiter, of which I could almost see the big colored bands and the little dot which is the eye of its perennial hurricane with my naked eye.

Even the great galaxy of Andromeda, with its double spiral, could be perfectly seen. Breathlessly beautiful, it was a manna for any astronomy enthusiast. Too bad that, up to that day, neither my friends nor I were.

That night, gazing at the infinite vastness that towered over us, I saw a blinding light cross the sky from horizon to horizon in a split second. Everyone saw it.

That night I was certain that we weren't alone, and that we had never been alone. I was young and I still knew very little of how different reality was from what I had been taught.

In that moment, everything changed for me and I began to feel a growing desire inside, an impulse to move through the experience, knowing there was something I had to carry out, and that I would have had to dedicate my life preparing myself and researching what my destiny was.

Yet, as I realized later, nothing I had experienced until then could have prepared me for the experiences that would have followed subsequently in the years.

You might be asking yourselves what I was doing with four friends in the middle of the night in the desert of the California hinterland... Well, this unfortunately will have to remain a secret. Let's just say that all around us was "nothingness", except for a Base which extended for at least seven square kilometers, which we all knew – and which we all called, in fact - "the Base".

Anyone who had seen it would have had the impression of being in the middle of a film studio, very modern and strangely quiet.

Like myself, my insomniac friends who had decided to enjoy that wonderful summer night, were Sharder, Doreen with her twin sister Maureen and an Italian - American called Tom Provenzano.

Sitting on the ground, on the top of the highest hill of the Base, we looked at the sky unable to lose even a second of that sight.

It was I who broke the silence: "I think this is the only place in the world where the sky is so spectacular".

"It's the dry desert air", Sharder said lighting a cigarette and offering me one from his packet of unfiltered Camel.

"Look at all the falling stars", Maureen whispered. "... If it's true that there is a wish for each one to wish on...", Doreen sighed and laid down on the blanket on the ground.

"Look at Jupiter instead, over there..." and I pointed to a little point in the sky "...it's up there, to the left, Mars. You can see its red coloring".

"You can also very well see the off white glow of the Milky Way", Tom said wisely.

"Yes", I sighed, "a night like this makes you wish that day would never come...".

In the distance, from the left, we heard a brief boom, like a distant explosion, and everyone thought they had seen a lightning bolt too.

"What is it, a storm?", asked Doreen with a surprised voice. There wasn't even the shadow of a cloud.

A second boom, and from the left a bright trail lit up the sky like daylight for a second. We remained in silence, I don't know for how long.

Sharder broke the silence this time: "That wasn't a shooting star".

"Nor a meteor", I added. "Did you notice the speed and the absence of sound?"

"Yeah! So what was it?" Doreen asked, sitting up and embracing her knees.

"There's only one possibility", Tom said pausing as if to wait for the answer to come also to us by way of empathy.

"Each one of us has studied the documents of the Majestic program..." Maureen said giving voice to what we were thinking.

The Majestic program, of which only e few fragments had leaked out, documented the presence of extraterrestrials on our planet, starting with technological and biological findings found or captured from about 1950.

Already then three different configurations of vehicles called UFOs had been classified and two types of organisms named EBE 1 and 2 where "EBE" stood for Extraterrestrial Biological Entity, with appropriate biological analysis, biometrics, autopsy reports and whatever else.

There wasn't any specific information on how the vehicles and the EBE had come in our possession; only hints and probable accidents that could have caused the vehicles to crash to the ground and the consequent capture of the crew, in most cases without life. In the rare circumstances in which some specimen survived, they did for a short time.

This first dossier on the Majestic program had been leaked out, maybe by an unhappy or fired employee, and circulated through the years, even if it never reached the press.

Who could care less? Anyone who had read it, outside of who "knew", could have surely thought it to be a skillful forgery and a lot of "lunatic" fantasies in a format that could be easily invented, given that no one – outside of whoever had the right security privileges – knew the real format of that type of documentation. The Majestic dossier also known as MAJIC, was an integral part of the formation of the components of the Base. And it didn't end with what had been reported in those first pages which had been incautiously leaked out.

In the following years, there were further findings which inestimably enriched the list of the EBE, reaching the current EBE 9, where numbers 7 and 8 were humanoids very similar to the humans born on Earth, on the outside. Even the classification of the vehicles called UFO was considerably enriched; but what resulted to be really crucial was the identification of three specific findings – if that is how they can be called – which projected the program significantly forward.

The first finding was identified following the discovery of a distortion in the gravitational field in a place of about one square kilometer in the California desert (not far from the Base); the distortion caused undeniably abnormal phenomenon such as the inversion of gravity and an altered perception of distance. The whole area had been obviously closed to the public for some time, officially for archeological excavations, which certainly didn't explain the presence of special forces dressed in antinuclear uniforms.

The second – and even more intriguing – finding was collected following the identification, by a satellite, of a strange emission of particles, which origin was located inside a small mountainous chain in Corsica. This had led to the discovery of an almost two kilometer long spaceship hidden in the mountains for about two hundred thousand years.

Unfortunately it still appeared to work and its security systems had reaped dozens of victims among military and scientists who had tried to find an access.

The third finding was discovered on the Moon and precisely on the surface of what is known as "the dark side", the hidden face of the satellite.

All the attentive observers had noticed for some time that there were no photographs or images of that side. This being, despite the various missions – among the known ones and the unknown ones to the majority of the people – which had orbited around the moon with the objective of creating a complete map. The same missions which had landed exactly at coordinates not visible from Earth. Coordinates which corresponded with those of one of the first missions with a crew who had identified and photographed a little city formed by pyramidal structures, each ten times bigger than the majestic Egyptian pyramid.

"We all have studied the documents of Majestic...", Maureen said that night.

"Of course", Tom said, "we all know it in detail".

"I checked, the last revision dates back to 1977, but the program is still active and there are updated units displaced all over the world", added Sharder gazing at the horizon, "You know what it could mean, don't you?".

"Well, to begin, that the EBE 7 and 8 – and maybe both if not even the non humanoid ones – could have created a contact and taken control of the program, or have stipulated an alliance with the big bosses", I said.

"Right", confirmed Sharder.

"I think that if 7 and 8 are involved, they could very easily be among us, or … one of us", added Tom.

"If what we saw before was a space ship, then they must have a base in that direction", Maureen said, looking towards the horizon to the right, in the direction of the trail left by the object.

"Surely yes", I answered, "probably between here and Nevada. Needless to say that all that area is off limits, under military control".

"What do you think they want from us?", Doreen asked in a soft voice.

We were all silent for some minutes. It was Tom who interrupted that silence.

"There aren't many options. I have a feeling that whatever they want, the humans are very marginal, if not a mere nuisance. Or, we can represent an economical resource, like a work force, or even guinea pigs for experiments".

"I'm afraid they'll never allow us to raise our head to the sky..." Maureen said.

"From what can be seen in the world, they are more interested in us developing everything that will keep us well rooted to Earth", Sharder continued.

"They will never allow us to really develop. Free and aware we could be a threat", added Tom.

Again there was a long pause full of silence and the sounds of night.

"Something unpredictable could happen to mess up their plans", I said innocently.

Then no one spoke anymore. Who was grinding thoughts, who was gazing at the sky, who did both. I don't know how much time passed before we got up to return to our lodgings.

II

The next day all the witnesses of the event (which we discovered to be more numerous than our little group) sent a report of the sighting to the Majestic program as protocol dictated.

We never spoke of it again, but I suspect that my final comment was added to one of the reports which had been sent.

THE SARCOPHAGUS

I don't know whether it was because of a report from one of my friends from that night, or because the computer mainframe had spat out my name in one of those mission selection programs, or still, because maybe I was one of the few people not in active duty yet... fact is that a few days later I was called at three a.m. in the mission briefing room. A bunch of Top Secret documents were placed in front of me, while the doctor started the preparatory medical examination. I gave them a quick look, given that I would have had all the time of the trip to study them more in depth.

"Mission Civilizations" the front cover read, with the well known code in blood-red ink "Eyes Only". Destination Antarctica, "Ghost Base".

As always, when there was a briefing, all communication outside of the operational office was suspended until the end of the mission and I worried about the monthly phone call I would have had to make to my family the next day.

I didn't even attempt to ask my director to make an exception because I knew him well: a foreign legion type military called John Wiley, the type that despised weaknesses and exceptions to the rules.

Had I asked, he would have surely reported me, jeopardizing my career at the Base. Worse: Wiley had the authority to have me put in the hard labor rehabilitative department, making me automatically fall back in rank, hierarchy wise.

I listened to the briefing carefully and was taken to the logistics department where I was given appropriate clothes, travel and personal documents (where I appeared to be a researcher of meteorological phenomena), plane and naval tickets, five thousand dollars ("just in case" Wiley had said), the mission program, the identification transponder and the cryptographic codes I would have had to use for the reports. In short, all I needed to survive and finish my job in due time. There were different types of missions in the Base protocols and this one, for instance, was an exploratory mission. The object of the observation was specified in the orders and the volume that was given to me as "Mission Docs".

Once the briefing started, one was isolated from the world and everyone else and from the rest of the Base personnel. I couldn't even speak with my friends, and I wasn't able to see anyone from the Base until the end of the mission, except of course, the always present Wiley and the others belonging to Mission Ops.

I left the next day from Los Angeles LAX for Buenos Aires and on that flight studied the documentation in depth.

My attention was immediately captured by the introduction: a group of scientists and researchers of an extended sector of the constellation of organizations which the Base was part of, known as Temporal Archives (a dislocated sector in another secret location to which I didn't have security privileges) had obtained – no one knows how – a portion of the planet Mars timetrack, and more precisely fragments from roughly the last seventy million years of life of the red planet. The research was of course continuing backwards and my mission had the purpose of supplying Temporal Archives with new pieces of the puzzle to continue that research, with the possibility of developing more and more specific solutions.

According to this preface it seemed that a catastrophe had been the cause of the severing of about 200 km of planetary crust, propelled into open space in the form of thousands of meteorites, almost as if the planet had been "pealed". The details were still not clear as to what could have caused this phenomenon which, according to the Archivist, dated back several million years, until it happened again more recently, even if with less violence, in 583 AD – that is to say "the day before yesterday" from a cosmic point of view.

Well, according to the preface, Mars had not been uninhabited before then, indeed it had been the cradle of an ancient civilization which, from the details available, had colonized at least the space of the solar system and, from the fragments of evidence available, it seemed to possess a formidable technology and also powerful enemies; so why go to Antarctica?

Well, the document clearly stated that a group of researchers, connected to a detachment of Temporal Archives, had found a huge meteorite which had arrived from Mars. The volume didn't give all the details on the finding, surely for security reasons, but it clearly stated that this meteorite wasn't only a piece of rock, but a fragment of a huge building, maybe part of a city.

The excitement for having been selected for this job was exhilarating, nevertheless I wanted to have time to dedicate to the study of the complete reports that the volume roughly described.

Unfortunately, I knew I would have to carry out the damned orders to the letter, of which progress would have been followed through my daily reports and that surely, once I had reached my destination, I would have been reached by a Second person I didn't know, who would have had the task of insuring that I wasn't tempted to go "Off Mission", violation that would have cost me dearly, personally, besides causing me to be unsuitable for classified missions thereafter. Well, neither failures nor transgressions were allowed. The far but watchful eye of John Wiley would have insured everything; I had at most two months to complete the job because afterward the long antarctic night would have arrived, during which time we would not have been able to proceed with the investigations.

The boat trip had been smooth; it had lasted about two days and landed us off the coast of an anonymous logistic outpost that passed off as a scientific meteorological base. From there, from a little airport, I would have been transferred inland, to a secret location – also "disguised" as a meteorological center – but where underground there was, for all practical purposes, a little city.

The first person I met was the local logistic officer, who hastily showed me my lodgings: a small room, five meters by three with a tiny bathroom with a shower, situated two floors under the surface and carved out, like the rest of the underground base, in the ancient ice of the antarctic continent.

My bags and personal belongings were brought to my lodgings and in the meanwhile the logistic officer – a certain Bjorn Olsen – personally took me on an orientation tour, showing me the cafeteria, the laboratories, introducing me to the people we met along the hall ways, the section where the offices were and then my work place, set in an open space on the fifth floor underground.

As Bjorn himself said, my Second hadn't arrived yet but a meeting had already been set for that evening to go over my briefing and meet the scientists and military who were taking care of the finding that I would have to study. I contacted the commander an hour before the meeting to present him my plan of operations.

Guillaume Audin was an authoritative looking person, an experienced man who didn't like small talk. The briefing was short and Audin let me know that, while respectful of his superiors' decisions who had decided that the mission was indispensable, he considered any outside intervention as a distraction to the task of his "team". Therefore, the only real recommendation he gave me, quite plainly, was to do what I had been ordered to do quickly without being in anyone's way. He, of course, would have been watching. Having clarified what he wanted to make clear, he asked me if there was any news from the "outside world" (the Archivists lived a very isolated life) and offered me a Cuban cigar, a bit ruined by the artificial atmosphere of that environment. After the third puff I felt my head buzz and, pretending nothing was wrong, put it in the ash tray hoping that it would snuff out before burning completely.

All superior officers of the antarctic base had been grouped together for this meeting, plus three scientists whose specialty I wasn't able to grasp. After the routine presentations, the interesting part began: a full wall projection of the discovery site and the finding. It was incredible!

It traced back the history of findings of meteorites originating from Mars. Naturally, the fact that a meteorite originates from a planet can only mean one of two things: either that that world exploded, or that part of it separated from the original mass due to a very violent trauma.

Not even the most powerful nuclear bomb at that time could have caused a part of the earth's crust to be projected outside of the gravitational field and into space; consequently, the most recognized hypothesis from the experts was that, in a more or less remote past, Mars had experienced such a violent trauma that reduced part of its surface to bits and thrust them full speed into space; some of these fragments could have reached Earth as meteorites. Many others were probably lost in outer space.

The fragments in the path of the earth's orbit, had in part, passed Earth and had been lost in the direction of the Sun. Some fragments were probably still wandering, while some – few, to be honest - had reached our planet in different periods, starting some thousand years ago. Many of those which had reached Earth fell in Antarctica.

Then, the presentation finally brought us to the finding itself. The images and the descriptions of the experts were so fascinating that I felt hypnotized. I didn't want to miss the slightest word or detail.

The main fragment of the so called "red planet" had apparently fallen with almost the same landing trajectory as an airplane, penetrating the ancient ice, melting it some ten meters, leaving a trail – still visible – of almost three kilometers. Strangely, it hadn't disintegrated with the impact, preserving all the characteristics which allowed the identification of a fragment of a building which, in origin, must have been huge.

The speed of the meteorite must not have been very high, otherwise it would have generated an explosion which would have probably destroyed life on Earth and today we wouldn't have the privilege of observing it. It's measurements reached four hundred meters in length by two hundred and thirty meters in width. But the real miracle was the fragment of building still intact.

Made of an unknown metal alloy, it had large rooms, hallways, and the remains of what had to have been the technology of the civilization that had accomplished and lived in it. Different symbols, engraved on some of the walls and objects that had remained trapped inside, gave some idea of the writing used by that culture and that in itself was considered, by the scientists present, one of the most incredible discoveries: this language had an incredible resemblance to the iconic alphabet.

The building was the result of an advanced and esthetically refined architecture and, originally, must have been of breathtaking beauty. In first analysis it was established that the main part of the building was formed by a single block of the strange metal alloy, its height about... three thousand meters from the ground!

The sparkling pieces of news finished: others arrived after about two hours from the beginning of the presentation. One of the strengths of the company, in fact, was that of having developed technologies that had never been made available neither to the armed forces nor anyone else outside of the structure itself.

One of these, based on the research project of an Italian researcher belonging to a secret monastic order, was substantially a "Chrono-reproducer": after having perfected, refined and amplified the initial project, the Archivists had synthesized a process which, starting from a natural or artificial finding, could read its subatomic or quantum memory, stored in its main structures, visually and "vibrationally" reconstructing the history, dating back, in theory, to the instant of its creation. It was also possible to recreate 3D sequential images of all the lifetime of the finding itself, in the last shape or configuration it had taken. The presentation included portions of images of the planet Mars at the time of the Finding and a "flash" presentation of the catastrophe!

It was incredible! I already knew that, for the success of the mission, I would have booked a complete dive in the Chrono-reproducer, containing the bits of history it had been able to recuperate up to that moment.

At the end of the meeting I was given a coded message from the Base: it informed me that my "second" in mission couldn't reach me, for unspecified complications. I mentally smiled and toasted to my luck.

I obtained my authorization at last: I could enter the Chrono-reproducer!

I hadn't been able to sleep the night before; it was difficult as hell to control my imagination, in the vain attempt of arriving to the observation moment without expectations.

The experience would not have been repeatable for me in that the preparations for the operation were great and would have slowed down the work of the team of scientists for weeks. That's why I had feared, up to the last moment, that I wouldn't have been able to obtain the authorization; in the end instead, I had been lucky. On one hand, I had been able to convince the tough John Wiley that the data obtained from the quantum chrono-reader might have given new meaning to the final results of the mission, and therefore to his career; and then – something noteworthy – I had enjoyed the advantage that no one normally volunteered for this experience, given the unpredictability of the side effects.

Indeed, the so called chrono-reproducer was simply a hybrid between a reality simulator and an experience replicator. It looked like a kind of "sarcophagus" (everyone, in fact, referred to it by this name) filled with a liquid saline physiological solution, always kept one degree centigrade above body temperature. Who tested it, laid down and his body was connected to electromagnetic sensors and stimulator, in total isolation from his normal sensory stimuli, including gravity. What was tested wasn't "virtual reality", but rather a dive in the past or in the direct experience, as it was "remembered" by the atomic and subatomic components of the analyzed material, whether organic or inorganic.

Anyhow, the momentous day finally arrived and when I would enter the chrono-reproducer. After the routine medical exams and the preparation on how to "move" inside the experience and on the internal connections, I was put into the Sarcophagus, surrounded by faces with little white masks on their mouths and noses, and eyes full of interest that a scientist generally feels for a little white mouse.

For some, very long, minutes, the world shut down around me. I almost immediately lost every reference point and was assaulted by a strong queasiness, so much that I was certain I could have thrown up my own guts. I could no longer understand if I was in a horizontal or vertical position. Along with the queasiness I started to perceive images like those that can be experienced when one is dozing off, except that these were vivid and chaotic: a bit like being awake inside a dream. I heard voices, then smells, emotions, bright colors, all mixed with a dark fantasy quality.

For a moment I thought that that was already the "transmission" of the Sarcophagus and I didn't know how to inform the supervising personnel of the break down or error in the subject transmitted. Then it all disappeared and my perception was immersed in a white light and in a sound, like the growing sound of a tuning fork, that continuously vibrates the do note. Then I heard three beeps which announced the beginning of the transmission and my heart, already tested by the stress from suspension, accelerated even more.

I immediately found myself in what must have been a hallway, in front of a window from which a big city could be seen, made of streets, domes and huge towers.

In all the constructions, the spherical egg-shape or pyramidal shape prevailed. I must have been in a very elevated position: at least a kilometer from the ground, in that I could make out thin pinkish white clouds above and below me. The sky was of an intense blue; the stars were visible in broad daylight.

In the sky, to the left, I saw a semi spherical shaped ship as big as a metropolis.

If it hadn't had such a smooth surface for a natural formation, it could have easily been mistaken for a little moon or a big asteroid and I must confess that I mistook it for a moon at first.

As I observed it "mentally" open mouthed, a kind of distortion or "hole" formed near it, in which it was quickly swallowed. I knew (though I don't know how) that that was how that race traveled from one place to another.

The Sarcophagus was in fact also able to transmit memories and emotions that however, as I was told during the preparation, as in dreams, tended to vanish shortly after being disconnected. As in the dream world, of course, also that information remained available, but not to the everyday consciousness. Maybe that is why my dreams often went back over portions of life of people and places that could have never belonged to my life.

Knowing that my time in the Sarcophagus was limited, with great effort, I removed my attention from the incredible view outside of the window. Any experience in that condition couldn't in fact last more than forty-nine minutes, penalty, severe neurological damage that could lead from permanent catatonia to irreversible coma and death. The personnel naturally supervised and every seven minutes sent an impulse (that I perceived as the sound of a little bell) to allow me to optimize the experience. Similarly to the proportion of the dream, the perception of the speed of time was altered in the Sarcophagus, so much so that it was possible to experience years in a few minutes or use all the available time in one second.

I started to move along the hallway as if I were walking normally, but without effort; the floor and ceiling appeared to be made of a dark gray metal, slightly reflecting, but with an internal moving quality, as though covered by an endlessly moving fluid. There were also some people, perfectly human looking: they had very light skin on which different patterns, like tattoos, stood out . Some wore colorful and shining pectorals and headdress of the same material which modeled the shape of their head almost to the shoulders while others wore long tunics fastened to the waist by colored belts and the same headdresses as the others. There was a feeling of urgency and alarm everywhere.

Suddenly, everything around me changed: in no time, I found myself in a huge amphitheater like hall. Every seat was occupied: half of the seats were occupied by those in the pectoral dress and the other half by those wearing tunics. At the end, in the center, there were five seats: the two to the left were occupied by individuals in pectorals and the two to the RIGHT with individuals in tunics, while the central position, elevated compared to the others, was presided over by a being in a tunic and a black conic headdress. I wasn't able to remember the object of the interventions of that meeting; I only remember a vague sense of danger, in which it was necessary to decide. It concerned an outside threat, from an obscure enemy that wanted to set up an outpost in the solar system, to exploit the resources and establish fertile growing grounds and pastures for slaves.

The race that occupied Mars wasn't native of our solar system but from a small galactic cluster originally millions of light years away from the Milky Way. This race was even more ancient than the Earth itself, and their great strength seemed to be their very advanced technology, which allowed them to open doors in space-time and travel great distances. Their most precious secret was the discovery of the determination of the vibrational and rhythmic coordinates of space-time: to tune an object or an individual with such coordinates, was like communicating to the universe itself which exact position it had to have. The object became incompatible with its parting position, and instantaneously "materialized" to its destination.

Not only the threat from the dark empire was discussed during the big session in the amphitheater, but also of a race even more powerful that was able to conquer and occupy the fifth planet, now reduced to a belt of asteroids among what remains of Mars and the giant Jupiter. I was taken by anguish and while a feeling of urgency pervaded the assembly, I clearly perceived the necessity to evacuate the planet and decide on the total destruction of this last threat.

I was suddenly propelled to the surface of the planet and started to have a definite feeling that someone inside was steering my experience.

This Mars of the past was beautiful, full of vegetation and animal life, largely imported from somewhere else and genetically manipulated to conform to the conditions of the new home.

The atmosphere was full of viral agents, engineered to strike any pathogenic threat much before it could contaminate one of the dominant forms of life and to instantaneously infect any unwanted organism: a very efficient way to prevent an invasion!

I then perceived – as though the thought had been injected in my mind – that a great sacrifice was necessary to defeat this powerful enemy and, above all, to prevent it from harming weaker races in the future.

The beings which at that time inhabited Mars could exist in different modulation phases of matter, and their plan included the transfer of the Martian colony on Earth, in a different dimensional modulation phase. In brief, they would have lived on Earth, but invisible and not perceptible to its inhabitants, in such a way as not to interfere with the normal advancement of its civilization still dawning, civilization that they had contributed to evolve.

That race called itself 'Anantrya'.

I heard the second bell and even though my feeling of anxiety increased, my perception of the importance of the task allowed me to control it. So it was that while I observed the golden blue, green and fuchsia vegetation and the sky, turquoise with orange streaks, I noticed someone by my side. I modified my point of view to observe this specimen of the race which had lived on Mars before the human race was even an idea in the mind of the Creator, but something had changed: the individual in front of me, who wore a light tunic slightly waving in the breeze, didn't seem to belong neither to the male nor the female gender. With its deep dark eyes it was looking straight in my direction, from a distance of a few meters.

"Don't be afraid" said the voice in my mind. The being stretched its hand towards me and I suddenly realized that I was no longer an invisible observer... I started hearing the sounds of the environment, the breeze on my skin. I realized that I now had a body, not mine, but one with the same characteristics of the strange companion in front of me.

I then heard the third bell. Again the feeling of urgency came over me and I tried to speak, to pass it on to the being who had materialized me in that place. But I didn't know how and not a sound would come out of my mouth.

"You don't have much time available, visitor from the future of the third planet; but yet there isn't need for much time given what we have to do", my speaker mentally continued. "We know why you are here. In a near to you future you will have to face the threat that I will show you shortly. It will be upcoming in your time and it could be the cause of the extinction of your race".

Strangely, I had no questions, nor I felt surprised or incredulous by that statement. It was surely one of the effects of being plunged in the experience of the Sarcophagus, that gave me access to ancient memories.

"I'm ready", I said and suddenly found myself in space, standing on an orbiting platform. My guide was by my side.

From space the planet was beautiful, luminescent, with colors that could be seen also from the surface: the dominant colors were blue, fuchsia and turquoise, with ice covered poles and its skies streaked by white and orange clouds. Two great continents could be seen, one on each hemisphere. They were divided by a turquoise ocean.

"This is the fourth planet of this solar system. The Anantrya colonized it at a time that no one of the human race could ever remember. At that time, the planet from which you have come was inhabited by a cold blooded race that, differently from the human race, was native to the Earth. It had independently developed a technology which allowed them to travel among the worlds of the solar system and use them as resources".

Immediately my mind visualized big cities of stone and other materials that I couldn't identify, and multitudes of ships leaving the surface of an ancient Earth, geologically very different from the present. Then quick images of clashes, destruction and bombardments. These raids were led by beings that could have been the evolution of the great Saurians.

"Nevertheless", my guide continued, "notwithstanding the ambition and the thirst for resources, the arrival of the Anantrya in the system stopped them, placating their hunger for conquest and war.

Suddenly, out of nowhere, I saw appear in space hundreds, thousands of ships, semi spherical in shape, which must have been some hundred kilometers in diameter.

I knew then that the heart of the Anantrya technology was in fact the ability to manipulate the fabric of space-time and the total mastery of the creative mechanisms of life. Their ships were a marvelous example of living biotechnology, though not carbon based.

"The Anantrya race has reached the condition where we don't know the end of life, and we have traveled outside of our dominion, searching for solar systems which could accommodate us with no interference with eventual indigenous life forms".

I had a vision of similar expeditions in other stellar systems, galaxies and dimensions.

"In the beginning we hardly ever crossed other evolved life forms, and for a very long time we were convinced we were alone in the universe. Yet, with the passing of long eras, we ran into other races and sentient life forms, younger than us, each one at a different level of development. Many were absolutely disinterested in going outside of the comfortable biosphere of their planet. In the ages we collected samples of these races and transferred them to protected systems to preserve them".

This was a disturbing revelation, and I was alarmed, but my guide, as if in response to how I was feeling, continued: "If we hadn't acted this way, there would no longer be any trace of these races, canceled by time and the rhythms of the universe for eons. In that far past we hadn't developed the ability of moving along the temporal paths".

While the guide informed me, I continued having visions which overlapped the majestic panorama of planet Mars at the time of the Anantrya.

"Never – he continued, - before our arrival in this system, had we met an obscure race like the one which inhabited the planet you come from. Yet, for a long time they didn't represent a threat to us and their fear of our power kept them away from our domains for a long time. Then... an unexpected event happened which changed everything".

Suddenly, in front of me, appeared the vision of a dark red star, barely perceptibly lit, and around it, a huge planet with two moons.

"A wandering star and the only planet of its system was passing at great speed near this solar system; in particular, between what was then the fifth planet and the gaseous giant you know as Jupiter".

"For a brief period this system had had two stars, a bright one and a dark one. The dark one was dying, and the race that inhabited its only planet had been preparing for this moment for a long time and it was ready to migrate to the new transiting stellar system".

I had the vision of a swarm of ships leaving the huge planet orbiting around the dark star. Thousands of ships, all in the direction of the fifth planet, Mars of the Anantrya and Earth.

"That dying planet was populated by two races: the first was made up of a scarcely intelligent life form... ". I envisioned creatures with five "tentacles" and a sort of exoskeleton, with elongated heads and a kind of reticular visor in the place of its eyes. "... completely subjugated to the second race, made up of beings with very big bodies, where each individual was completely different in its biomorphic characteristics from the other. In fact, there weren't very many specimen of them – maybe some ten thousand – but they too didn't know the end of life, and their mind, the only characteristic that made them similar one to another, was their real weapon. Their origins were still a mystery to us given that none of them seemed to have been born through an act of reproduction.

They were able, with their minds, to extend their dominion on other beings, reducing them to total enslavement. It didn't take long to understand that even the Anantrya were sensitive to the influence of their powers, contrary to the Saurian race which dominated the primordial Earth, immune to their control.

So it was that the Anantrya prepared for a crisis never hypothesized before, those monsters (which we call Krogan or, if you prefer, the Potentiae) and their minions occupied the fifth planet and started a fierce war against the Saurians of Earth.

Their first attempt to also occupy the Anantrya colony failed miserably and caused them too many losses; for a while they gave up.

Hostilities between the Potentiae and the Saurians lasted thousands of cycles, without ever leading to stable results for one or the other. While he spoke, I could clearly see fierce battles in space and on the surface of planets and moons.

"Then – he continued after a brief pause – one day a completely unpredictable event happened; these two great enemies stopped fighting each other! Both races had realized that there was something that they both wanted with much more intensity than the reciprocal submission: the space-time dislocation technology of the Anantrya!

They then started preparations for a joint attack to the Colony of Mars. Perceiving the threat and knowing that not even our antiquity and technology could efficiently protect us from the dark mental fluids of the Potentiae, we had to admit the possibility that the enemy alliance could seize our secret. If this had happened, the universe would have known too big a threat; it was then that we decided that the solution to the problem had to be terminal".

In an instant I had an image of the grand council of Anantrya, reunited in their amphitheater structure.

"We decided for the destruction of the Fifth planet, which explosion would have also destroyed the dark planet, which was still in proximity of this stellar system.

We also decided the erasure of the entire Anantrya colony, from the Fourth planet, through the immobilization of the internal nucleus, which would cause the entire planet crust to be projected into space; nothing had to remain of the Anantrya colony to ward off the the danger that even a small fragment could bring the Potentiae or the Saurians to obtain useful technology.

So we created an interphase space around Earth, which emitted an encoded dimension accessible only to the Anantrya, and the entire colony was transferred there, not before the third decision was put in act, that is the erasure of the entire Saurian race from the Third planet. By attracting an eruption from the surface of the Sun towards Earth, we caused the extinction of almost all the life forms of the surface; no trace remained of the Saurians, while the Potentiae, which survived the destruction, were dislocated into a remote sector of intergalactic space where they would not have been able to cause any harm anymore. Or at least, so we hoped...".

I was hypnotized by the account of that ancient conflict and by the determination to safeguard the universe by such radical and definitive decisions. Just one "decree" and entire planets and races vanished from history. Nevertheless – I realized – everything had been established for a higher purpose and even the most questionable decisions, in light of the survival equation and for the future, had to courageously be carried out. Even though the sixth ring of the bell had rung, I saw that my guide was still not finished.

"I showed you what happened in this system's past. Now know that nothing you have learned must be communicated when you return to your ordinary state of consciousness".

I was perplexed.

"As you have come to us through the finding that contains our memory, we have come to your time and beyond. Know that everything exists in more dimensions than the ones you know and everything is complete only if seen from the instant of its beginning to its end. We know that in your time a new threat, intimately tied to what has been shown to you, is rising and if it is allowed to take place, the human race will soon be canceled".

"What threat?", I asked through my mind. "I beg you, give me more elements to allow me to do what needs to be done", I continued.

"Once you have returned, if you communicate this experience, you will expose yourself to the enemy and it will consider you a danger for its dark plans: remember what you have seen but above all, that in your time, no one will be able to help you".

The seventh bell rang.

"Wait!", I seemed to be shouting, but everything around me vanished and I became conscious of my heart beat.

In my mission debriefing report I coldly described the city I had seen, the colors and the planet and ended with a questioning comment as to where the ancient Martian colony could have disappeared to.

When I returned to the Base, my debriefing to the monolithic John Wiley was equally ascetic and lacking in information that could awaken any dangerous interest.

Nevertheless, the mission was judged a success, and I was awarded a collar badge with a star. I never told anyone of my experience with the Anantrya guide, but from that moment on my hidden agenda was different from that of the Base and I secretly began to look for clues of a threat in the present.

What better place for my research than the Base itself! It contained a concentration of secrets inaccessible to the rest of the world and many things that were considered nonsense or hallucinations to the outside world, were taken seriously and investigated or concealed, depending on the case, in that place.

I began spending my free time looking for documents on the sophisticated computer system and investigating on some pieces of news or fragment of a clue that might lead me in the right direction, and as a starting point, I decided to concentrate on all the documentation of the Majestic program.

SNOW IN THE DESERT

It was a May morning, almost noon. I was about to go to the cafeteria after another long shift of intense studying when, from a cloudless sky with a rock splitting sun, it started to snow; fat and spongy snowflakes fell to the ground and there was no doubt: wherever it came from, it really was snow.

Naturally, everyone stopped to check out such a phenomenon, gazing at the sky, a hand to protect their eyes from the intense light of the sun which, besides the improbable weather conditions, was really unique to the California desert.

In the cafeteria there was talk about a nuclear experiment in the near state of Nevada that, in some strange way, had to be, without doubt, the cause, but it was just talk. It didn't last very long anyway, and on going out we saw that the sun had absorbed every residue of the event, to the point that it could be thought that we had been victims of a collective hallucination. An almost more credible hypothesis than the snowfall "from nowhere".

I barely made it back to the office when my beeper beeped. Once again it was Mission Operations with a Blue Code, that is an emergency situation and undercover intervention. It not only meant that one wasn't obligated to keep in touch with the mission headquarters, but any communication with the Base was expressly forbidden until the end of the mission.

Wiley himself hijacked me to the Mission Ops office and announced that a representative from Temporal Archives was on his way for a special briefing; strangely enough I hadn't been given any orders, and I was only able to see, from a document that Wiley had on his desk, that the mission was designed by the code name "Operation Napoleon".

The next morning, after the routine medical examinations and the usual preparations, the Temporal Archives envoy arrived, a Canadian woman named Monika.

Wiley led us to a safe room, completely isolated from the outside, with lead lined walls that were interception-proof and so soundproof that it was impossible to hear the person you were speaking to unless you looked them in the face.

She was first to break the ice: "Good morning! I am Monika, sent by Temporal Archives for your briefing on operation Napoleon'" she simply began, in the way of a consummate professional. Monika... Already then, something about her struck me as if life were warning me that our future was connected with that force given only to the predestined.

But at that moment and in that place, I simply remained impassive.

"Interesting name for a mission... Napoleon. Anyway... let's begin".

She pulled an accurately bound file out of her briefcase and began to leaf through it. After a while, she looked up and stared at me intensely.

"Now I'll give you a brief overview, then I'll let you study this dossier. After that, I'll be at your disposal for eventual questions or details. You must memorize everything, and understand exactly what you are going to do: I can't leave you these papers, they'll go back with me. Your Mission Ops will not have details of the mission and you will give your final debriefing directly to me and therefore to Temporal Archives". She paused continuing to stare me in the eyes. "All clear?".

I nodded, "All clear".

"I must warn you that any information leakage will be considered a violation of security protocol. The mission would immediately be aborted, and you would be destined to indefinite punitive work. Clear?".

"Crystal clear".

"Well then, let's begin. But first, let's get some water". It was hot in spite of the air conditioning and Monika got up, went to the door and knocked three times.

Differently from the base personnel, she wasn't in uniform but casually dressed in tennis shoes, jeans and a pink V-neck t-shirt. Among their security obligations, the Archives personnel were in fact forbidden to reveal their identity and rank to anyone. They couldn't even reveal that they were Archivists; I deduced this mission had to be very important if one of them was sent to the Base, betraying their own cover. Neither I was in uniform that day: too hot, and anyway useless inside Mission Ops.

The security personnel opened the door and delivered an anonymous bottle of water with two glasses which Monika brought to the table.

"So", she began, "we know you have an intimate familiarity with the Majestic program. Besides having contributed in reporting the sighting of a vehicle probably entering the earth's atmosphere near the Base, we noticed your continuous interest to all the documents and reports connected to the program".

As she said this, she put a bunch of printed papers in front of me, the

listing of my accesses to the central computer system. I absentmindedly
leafed through them, then put them aside. I very well knew that any activity
carried out using the mainframe couldn't pass unnoticed. I looked at
Monika waiting for her to come to the point.

"From the dates, we have gathered that your accesses started
immediately after the sighting, but became continuous and grew in number
following the Civilizations program that you carried out in Antarctica which
allowed you access, through the Sarcophagus, to the quantum memory of
the big meteorite from planet Mars".

"Exactly", I said. "I thought the study of what was available might help
me understand better what I experienced in the Sarcophagus. And then...
I'm an incurably curious person".

"Well, it can't be said that sound curiosity is a negative thing, allowed
that security be safeguarded...", Monika remarked. "In any case", she
continued, "Let's get back to the reason for our being here at the base: our
mission".

"Our mission?", I asked a bit surprised.

"Right, our mission! I will be your debrief officer and at the end I will
give you the third degree once more".

"Interesting". I felt perversely excited by the idea of a joint mission
with an Archivist.

"You surely must have heard or read about the Napoleon finding", she
continued.

"Napoleon finding?".

"Right. This is the code name that has been given to what has been
considered for some time a huge spaceship, buried – or better, covered – by
a little mountainous chain on the west side of Corsica.

"Of course I heard about it, though it's the first time I hear its code
name".

"Temporal Archives sent numerous exploratory missions with the
objective of finding an access to the spaceship. Unfortunately they all
failed, more or less miserably".

"I also heard there were some victims".

"True. It seems the manufacturers of the spaceship wanted to be sure
it wouldn't easily fall in hostile hands; no one knows the cause of the
various deaths, just that those who attempted to enter it suddenly stopped
"functioning". They obviously must have set off an unknown security
system".

"How many?".

"How many died near the space ship? Twenty-four Temporal Archives
researchers. But we can reasonably imagine that in the last two hundred
thousand years, estimated time of the fall of the ship, there have been more.
Mostly casual victims, we suppose. Even more interesting is that the bodies

were never recuperated near the ship and therefore we still haven't been able to determine where the deaths occurred and following what circumstances".

Monika stopped to sip some water.

"Anyway, it's better to start from the beginning, that is, at the time when the anomaly was officially noted. As you probably already know, in 1975 a sighting reported in the diaries of the Majestic program was made precisely in Corsica by a researcher, in the middle of a very normal excursion in the forest.

This sighting wasn't just a simple light in the sky, given that the report described a potent collision followed by an explosion. After having reported what happened to the local police and to his colleagues, the man decided to go into the forest himself to personally uncover the mystery.

He was found ten days later, almost dead from starvation and thirst, on the edge of a mountain road and died a few days later in the hospital. When he was brought to the emergency room, he displayed a flat EEG. His body "functioned", but in his head there was no longer... anyone.

This was also the fate of our researchers who subsequently tried to uncover the mystery of the Napoleon finding. As soon as the news reached Temporal Archives, a satellite scanning of the western side of Corsica was ordered and it was then that we were able to discern this monolithic structure about three kilometers long, buried under the mountains. The anomalous emissions of quantum singularities as well as a slight distortion in the magnetic and gravitational field exactly in that area, told us that it was probably a huge space vehicle, still functional".

"Okay, so what you're briefly telling me is that you still don't have specific information on the finding, that you have no idea of where an eventual access point might be and that all the previous missions ended with mysterious deaths and no further progress", I concluded summarizing.

"In a few, crude but eloquent words, yes, that's it", she answered.

I took on a thoughtful expression and allowed for a few silent moments to pass.

"Please don't misunderstand me, but... what makes you think that the intent of my mission isn't only to increase the death toll?", I asked.

Monika poured herself another glass of water and stood up, starting to slowly walk towards a corner of the room with her hands crossed behind her back. I can still particularly remember her engrossed expression, concentrated, as though evaluating each word to give me an answer. At that time I believed she was looking for the right arguments to convince me it wasn't a suicide mission. In fact, as I later realized, she was considering exactly what to reveal to me without becoming liable herself to heavy penalties. I respected her silence, continuing to exhibit my best cool face, which I had learned to be fundamental for survival at the Base.

At that moment, without the so-called, "if I'd known", I lived the moment like a challenge between samurai, or a chess game; my life was at stake, not in a strictly biological sense and not even only in a professional sense. In this peculiar battle, strategy and tactics were purely mental. Anyone who was at the Base or at Temporal Archives, independently from their registered age, could never be underestimated, for intelligence, attitude, reaction speed and ability to make important decisions in seconds; this is why Monika's very young age didn't deceive me.

In those few silent moments, we both realized that a real victory had to be for both sides. She certainly was an able manipulator and could have eventually found and exploited my weak points to induce me on a mission that, according to statistics, could be suicidal. I could have put her with her back to the wall, touching the subject of her career and her reputation, pushing her to reveal, between those "safe" walls, as much information as possible, maybe making her beak her oath of secrecy, promising that it would have all remained between us.

The problem – which in truth derived from the logic that regulated all those belonging to the Organization – manifested itself in reason of a very simple factor: the result.

The fact that we both were responsible for obtaining a result, made it so that the single real victory could be reached obtaining the most in total respect of the rules. If I had failed the mission, we both would have failed. If I had pushed her to violate her protocol, we both would have been punished and downgraded. If she had overpowered me, obligating me to perform the mission, even though I wasn't fully convinced, she would have risked its outcome. If I had overpowered her, I would have risked my only connection with the organization and would have lost trust in the person who would have had to insure my success and also my safety.

Monika looked at me straight in the eyes from the corner of the room and returned to sit in front of me. Her eyes didn't leave mine, not even when she started to speak again.

"You are one of the few people who have asked and obtained authorization to experiment with the Sarcophagus. We believe that such experience can lead to events on two distinct levels of consciousness. In your debriefing we found contents – complete we presume – of what you reported at the ordinary level of consciousness of the experience. And, as I told you, we are almost sure, from the residual accounts of the few people besides you, who have experimented the Sarcophagus, that a second level of experience is registered in the mind, but that it's not directly accessible if it's not triggered off by events or stimuli that can bring these portions to the surface.

"More and more interesting... Please continue".

"In brief, we believe that your experience and what you have learned consciously or unconsciously, probably makes you the only qualified subject for this mission, which is what we have been looking for, for a very long time".

I had a question: "Given that this finding should be more than two hundred thousand years old, what makes you suppose that it belonged to one of the civilizations I met in the Sarcophagus?"

"According to your report, this civilization wasn't native to Mars. And then, according to what you declared, there were other two active civilizations in ancient and broad portions of the history of this solar system, of which one native to Earth. We believe in the possibility that elements from the memory which was transmitted to you will help you, in proximity of the finding, to understand how it functions and show us an entrance way".

She paused briefly. Then continued: "In fact, we hope that the Napoleon finding belongs to one of the three races you registered during your experience, in which case it's possible that if you have important information stored in your mind, buffered from your ordinary consciousness and ready to emerge in connection to inciting stimuli which could include your proximity to Napoleon, this could be revealed to you when you are in Corsica".

Now I poured myself a glass of water too, and while I slowly sipped it, I tried to quickly elaborate the intentions of Temporal Archives.

Their logic was commendable.

No one of course knew the real experience I had had in the Sarcophagus and – even if – it was too late to decide to come out and communicate the experience in its entirety. The problem would have immediately been "who had falsified the mission report", which would have been me, with all the consequences of the case.

Of course I could have said that that information wasn't available to the ordinary conscience during the debriefing and had surfaced now, triggered by the data on the new mission... But even this wouldn't have been very credible and an insult to Monika's intelligence. As she had rightly said, a stimulus that could have been connected to the concealed memories, was indispensable. And anyway, my guide had been very clear: in our time there was a threat, global, final and inexorable, and whatever I did, I had to keep the connection with that past concealed.

I decided then to bring up the subject of the recent progresses of Majestic, in that if Monika were right in saying that the origin of the Napoleon finding was connected to the three civilizations registered in the sarcophagus, it was also true that it could have a totally different origin, that is from one of the races already cataloged.

It was this thought that put everything into perspective: Monika – and therefore Temporal Archives – were accurately avoiding this hypothesis.

I found this prospect extremely interesting and decided to look into the question.

"Let's suppose that there is no relationship with what I learned in the Sarcophagus...", I then said.

She started leafing through the dossier as if looking for something comforting inside it. Then replied: "Let's just say that we are in a position to be able to exclude this eventuality".

"Then allow me to evaluate other hypothesis with you. For the good outcome of the mission of course...", I insisted.

She looked at her wristwatch: a calculated move to convey the feeling that our time together was too short to go into a lot of considerations.

"Of course, ask whatever you want. No one wants you on the field with useless doubts", she answered absentmindedly.

So I started with my questions. Monika answered each one and at the end of the debriefing, I realized one thing: who really wanted this mission wasn't Temporal Archives, or at least not its human components. It became clear to me why the guide met in the Sarcophagus experience had urged me not to divulge the experience. Surely there were forces that didn't want a humanity in evolution which controlled the Organization, and that through organizations like this, wanted to reach other objectives.

At the end of the briefing, while I analyzed the documents of the dossier (which were mostly maps and satellite shots of the Earth where the finding was) I realized one last thing: whoever was behind all this was afraid of whatever Napoleon represented.

This was the motivation I was looking for to carry out the mission, even if not for the benefit of the Organization or the invisible puppets which ran it.

The Martian guide from the past was right and I counted on his nearness and protection to complete the task he had entrusted me with.

At that time, of course, I had no idea how the events that would have led me to be testimony to the realization of the great transformation, would have developed.

THE GUARDIAN

I reached the final destination of my trip: a forest at the foot of Corsica's innermost mountains; the smell of nature and the sun filtering through the trees were relaxing as I prepared to continue on foot. I had everything necessary to survive outdoors and had also brought a heavy sweater for the night and a sleeping bag; the car I had rented to get there was hidden by bushes on the edge of the road, a few meters away.

It was almost noon and I knew I had a long walk so I loaded my back pack on my shoulders, took a deep breath and started walking in the direction of a rock formation which could be seen beyond the peaks of the trees swaying in the light wind.

The silence, broken only by the sound of the branches and leaves that cracked under my feet, kept me company until, in the twinkling of an eye, dusk told me it would soon be too dark to walk.

I started looking for an appropriate place to set camp and suddenly started feeling vulnerable and at the mercy of this forest, animated like magic, by the sounds of animals which were beginning to awaken.

I felt strangely observed and tried to convince myself of being alone, in the middle of that nature, just a few hours from the cement of the city, and that I was safe, although the feeling of vulnerability wouldn't leave me and it was with great difficulty that I found a place to spend the night in tranquility, even if I already knew I wouldn't have closed my eyes.

Night arrived: cold and spurred by a light wind that made the vegetation quiver in whispers, disconcerting at times. The sky was clear and starry and the light of the moon filtered through the trees.

The quality the absence of sunlight gave the environment was really incredible. It almost seemed as if night were the real dimension that gave life to everything, that at sunrise instead, everything hid or returned to its inanimate state, as though hiding from a threat – the light – that could burn them or reveal their presence to silent and mortal enemies. And yet, in all of Earth's known history, it was light and sun which had always been symbols of good and life.

But it seemed that the forest thought differently and that its soul awakened only at the magic moment of dusk. I remembered that Don Juan, the shaman, had described it as the fracture between worlds.

I lit a small fire with what I could find that night, to which I added a little solid fuel which was part of my rig, and ate cheese, crackers and some dried meet I had brought directly from California.

Then, having realized that sleep, as foreseen, would not have arrived, I decided to use the time to fall in a silent meditation. So I sat on my sleeping bag in the Lotus position and started emptying my mind from physical reality, regulating my breathing.

I don't know how much time passed (the fire had reduced to a few hot coals in the ashes) before I heard some steps approaching. I stood still, in an extreme alert state; strangely, I wasn't afraid, even if I felt an adrenaline rush in all my body. The first thing to do was to undo the position and take control of my legs, which had numbed in the meanwhile. I was about to move when a voice interrupted me.

"Don't move", it said in a masculine voice. "Please, stay where you are".

It didn't seem wise to disobey that request, not knowing who had produced it. And then he had said "please" and we all know that courtesy is always effective.

"And now?", I asked.

"You have nothing to fear. I came to keep you company for a while", said the voice, accompanied by a movement in front of me. I could barely distinguish a human shape but the darkness concealed its details. Then the figure, which looked more like a shadow than a creature, sat in front of me, on the other side of the embers' reddish glow.

We remained in this position, one in front of the other, a dying fire between us and the voices of the forest and the wind whispering around us. I vainly waited for the visitor to say something, anything. That was surely the forerunner of all the embarrassing silences; after a while I had enough, cleared my throat and... the only thing that came to my mind was: "Nice night, isn't it? A little chilly but... pleasant".

Nothing: I felt its eyes on me as if it wanted to take my breath away, pushing all the air out of my lungs.

"We can spend the night staring at each other to see who turns away first or do you have something to tell me?", I said putting an end to yet another long silent pause.

"Have you already thought what you would like me to tell you?", asked the visitor. Finally, I thought.

"Well... to begin, you could tell me why you're here", I answered trying to sound natural.

"And you?".

"What about me?".

"Why are you here?".

"Nature, fresh clean air... Well, a simple hike... ".

More silence. After I don't know how long, maybe due to exhaustion, but more probably because of that feeling that is often called intuition, it was I who – so to say – lay my cards on the table.

"You know everything, don't you?".

"*Everything* is an important word, my friend", he answered.

"You know very well what I mean".

"Yes. I do".

"Can you help me find what I'm looking for?", I cautiously asked him.

"You've already found what you're looking for".

"I don't understand", I answered perplexed.

"You have it right in front of you", said the visitor.

"I still don't understand".

I heard a sound, like a sigh, blend with the wind, "I am what you're looking for".

Things were becoming interesting, even if there was a possibility, not to be underestimated, that I was in the presence of a lunatic.

"I don't mean to contradict you but I'm quite sure we're talking about completely different things. Not that I'm not enjoying your company".

"Let me guess", he said.

"Amaze me!".

"You are looking for something you call *finding* that you have been told to be buried in the depths of the crests in front of us, and you would like to find an access, and uncover a mystery, probably more for yourself than for the organization which officially sent you here". I was astonished, things were becoming interesting.

"May I know who sent you? Like... are you supposed to be my guide? Will you help me with my mission? Do you know the access point of the finding?".

"You probably didn't grasp the meaning of my words or I didn't explain myself well. I am what you're looking for... I am the *Finding*".

He knew too much to be a lunatic. I decided to follow my instinct and play along.

"As you have rightly said, what I'm looking for is buried under the crests in front of me. This finding, according to the description – which, by all means, could be wrong – should be an ancient structure, surely mysterious, and equally to the same extent, inanimate. Forgive me if you don't correspond to the aforesaid description but you don't seem to have the characteristics of what I'm looking for".

"As you say: appearances can be deceiving! Anyway, I understand your perplexities and ask you for an act of faith. You needn't search elsewhere because I'm what you're looking for. Now, if you'd like, you can ask me your questions".

"Ok. Let's say that I trust you. Tell me what happened to those before me".

"Others came. But you are the first, for a long time, that I contact directly".

"Strange, from what I know, all the others died".

"They probably set off the security systems near the access points. And these are set off only by negative mental images connected to my structure".

"So you are part of the crew or the personnel on board the structure?", I asked, trying to imagine a living creature two- hundred thousand years old or more.

"No. I am a projection of what you call the "structure". I showed up in a familiar form to you with which you could easily communicate".

"Can you read my mind?".

There was a brief pause filled by the sounds of the forest.

"It's improper to say that I can read your mind. To be exact and even simple, I gather from your body memories and impressions transmitted by your magnetic field at a subatomic level. Given that the matter you are composed of, at a more elementary level than what you could understand, contains all the information determined by your experiences, gaining access to this information means knowing everything about you".

If what the visitor was saying was correct, then it was useless to play with him, hide or lie...

"Which means you know I'm not here to threaten the structure you represent...".

"I know much more, of course! I know that your intentions are not only different from those who sent you here, but also that, if properly developed, could considerably damage those who wanted you in this place. In this sense, you and I share at least one objective".

"And this objective would be... ?".

"To bring about the destruction of the forces that have taken possession of this planet".

"Do you know about the communication I received during my experience in the Sarcophagus, in Antarctica?".

"That transmission was from a different moment in time. How it took place isn't important; the only fundamental thing for you is that what has been communicated to you represents the current situation of your race. In brief, risk extinction and at the same time give a strategic advantage to forces you would define as "malign".

I waited a moment to mull over his answer, then ventured:

"And what is my role in all this? What am I supposed to do?".

"First of all you must understand that my protection is indispensable. In second place, due to some of your intrinsic characteristics, you have been, so to speak, "chosen", to act as contrasting agent to these forces. You will have to find a definitive solution and put it into action".

Even if my instinct told me the visitor was telling the truth, I couldn't underestimate the little voice inside me that warned me that maybe he was "the enemy". How should I behave? And if my actions had instead helped those very forces that wanted the extinction of the human race? I didn't have sufficient information nor knowledge to be able to make a rational evaluation, but I had an internal impulse – maybe a byproduct of the experience in the Sarcophagus – that told me, against all logic, that I had to trust him.

"Why are these forces trying to find you?", I asked.

"Because I know their nature and their intentions, because my constructors knew the secrets of life in its manifest and hidden component, and because in me there are the secrets to free or imprison the vital component of every animated being".

"Are you telling me that who built you, knew the mysteries of the spirit?".

"I suppose you could put it like that".

"I don't understand how this knowledge could benefit an enemy to humanity".

"The vital component can be isolated, spliced, amplified, weakened and even imprisoned. In the wrong hands, this possibility would give too great a power, provoking a real danger for all living beings, not only of this planet and not only of this time".

This was a sensational revelation for me. Not only it confirmed – if I had ever needed it – the existence of life beyond matter, but that there were also civilizations which had been able to isolate it from the matter itself. But it was also alarming, because it revealed that the spirit – or as it was called by the visitor, the "vital component" - was vulnerable. In front of this reality it wasn't difficult to imagine a dark civilization that enslaved entire races even beyond physical death, in a reign of perpetual hell.

But anyway they were just words, spoken by a visitor who said it was the projection of a structure I had only heard of.

While these thoughts whirled in my mind, as though answering my doubts, I began to perceive my body as separated from me.

First a drowsiness, then nausea, in the end I found myself at a great height, above the tree tops of the forest. I could see everything perfectly despite the darkness. I could also see, in spite of the distance, every detail of my body, and under. And where the visitor, who had shaken me with

31

his revelations, should have been, a vibrant light with the colors of the rainbow shone.

For a while I felt ecstatic, like a child experimenting something new. Then I began to feel some panic at the idea of not knowing how to return to my body. As soon as that thought passed my mind, everything began to whirl round and round and I had the impression of falling.

I woke up – or better, I opened my eyes – in the late morning of a day I wasn't able to identify, on the edge of the road, near where I had left my car. Two paramedics were over me saying something in French, to me and between each other. I could barely move and was immediately moved to a stretcher that was placed in an ambulance. I was later told that a car passing by had found me senseless at the edge of the road and had called medical assistance.

In the hospital I discovered that three days had passed since my hike in the forest. The doctors took turns by my bedside to check my conditions, which didn't seem worrying. After all, I myself was tranquil and started to mentally prepare for the visit of a representative from Temporal Archives, to whom I would have owed some explanations.

Four people arrived instead, among whom Monika on a "recovery mission". I wasn't asked any questions at the hospital, but they only consulted the medical records; they probably also pressured the hospital management to speed up my dismissal and therefore my return to the Base.

Monika stayed with me for the next forty-eight hours. Until I was dismissed, and there too, it was she who took care of all the procedures. A car was waiting for us outside; from the time I got on the car to our arrival at the base, twenty hours later, no one spoke a single word to me.

I had just finished a very long shower during which I imagined, as always, that all my weaknesses, sins and imperfections were washed away by the water.

In my mind, the water not only ran on the surface of my body but also through my being, taking with it a mass which only purpose was to weigh me down, like residue on an artifact or grease in a temple... I heard the beeper beep, inside the backpack I had brought back from Corsica: it was Mission Ops of course. When I called the number on the little screen, it was the indescribable John Wiley who answered, telling me, without preconditions, that I was expected in the mission debriefing office in thirty minutes. "Not the standard office... ", he clarified, "... the soundless one".

That meant, of course, that I was expected in the same place where I had met Monika.

I had had plenty time to prepare myself, during my stay at the hospital and throughout the long flight hours, surrounded by the agents of the Base and in Monika's silent company. She had been by my side during all the transfer, almost as if she were afraid I could disappear. I had, of course, also been able to observe my travel companions and hypothesize what was going through their minds: surely for them I was something of a rarity.

Even if they had no idea what had happened, they knew that what had happened was something completely new and unexpected: I was alive and apparently without neurological damages. Even my memory seemed unscathed.

All this, from their point of view, was very much reason for exciting expectation, as much as a potential security risk. They surely couldn't exclude any hypothesis, not even that I could be controlled by an "extraneous" influence, of unknown potentiality. I would have had to use all my cloaking abilities during the debriefing not to leak the suspicion I was hiding something. And then – worse yet – I would have undergone a polygraphic analysis (the so called "lie detector", only a thousand times more sophisticated) and even if I had learned the tricks to manipulate my neuroelectrical reactions to the polygraph, as I had already done in the beginning of the mission, trying to estrange myself from the out-of-body experience would have really been difficult.

Anyway, these were inevitable events and it was indispensable to overcome them if I wanted to have a future at the Base and retain those security privileges that allowed me access to the information I needed.

The so called "soundless" room was exactly the way I had left it: sterile, gray walls, black desk and chairs, no windows, and that peculiar acoustic quality that made one feel in total isolation from the outside world.

In front of me, besides Monika, there were five other people who didn't introduce themselves. There were also two cameras, turned towards me from the upper corners of the room, and surely there were two more behind me to observe my interrogators, in that at the Base, everyone was monitored.

I was able to perceive an electric quality in the air, as if everyone present were burdened by a strong emotion which didn't transpire from their expressions nor from their body language.

However, none of the people in front of me, nor those who observed behind the cameras, could imagine what I was feeling: from a certain point of view, I had to thank the Base for what I now knew and what I had become, that organization which, with the forest mission, had unconsciously given me such an opportunity.

The secrets which had been revealed to me appeared extraordinary as much as terrible; I had learned and experimented that we human beings are really spirit and matter, but also that, contrary to what was passed on to us by religion, cult and mystical scriptures, the "human spirit" is a finite and measurable factor, as seen by this World, as much as matter, and it can be commanded and influenced by controlling the matter itself. At that time I still hadn't remembered the Great Mirror and the true relationship between The Power that Is, and its image...

I thought it perfectly natural that such an ability be intensely desired by a dark force: the simple logic of power and domination made this concept elementary.

Real Power is never on inanimate things, regardless of how much destructive power can be released by a weapon. Real Power is on the flesh, and more precisely on *Life*, in whichever way it occurs. It is life, in fact, that can act on matter, that can surpass itself, to the point in which – though acting through matter – can actually modify itself or be imprisoned or reduced to slavery.

What disappointment this discovery would have been for all those who, in history, lost their freedom by their own kindred and survived overcoming torture and suffering, or self-destructed in hope – or in faith – soaring above worldly affairs, to reach a state of freedom in infinity. That same infinity which seems to have dictated precise rules to those fractions of its substance that chose the way of individualization: a kind of joke of the free will. Choosing to leave infinity means fighting and enduring the limits of this choice, whichever the state of individualization: free or bound to the imposed form of matter. The end of the bond means the end of individualization and the return to infinity, and the consequent loss of self in a limitless ocean. Is this the choice that torments us and which represents the conflict we live at every cross road we are confronted with?

Is this why we often decide to trust a "mechanism" behind our eyes, to automatically choose for us almost every move of our existence?

It took me years to elaborate the moments experienced that night in the forest, and maybe still today that I breath the air of the new world determined by the Grand Opera, I am elaborating.

I had also finally clear the conflict between the *One God* and the rogue Angel as symbol of the fight of the drop in the ocean which awakens and chooses to take on a point of view, and that same ocean which calls it back to itself: once acquainted with individualization, that drop knows that to return to the ocean also means to lose oneself in an eternal and infinite dream. From this point of view, we are all Angels and become rogue when we refuse to surrender our awareness.

But that day, in front of the five people and the unfailing Monika, these thoughts couldn't enter the scheme of answers I had accurately prepared to conceal about what had happened to me. That day my body didn't communicate emotions, and I was ready to say what was necessary to make sure that no one in that room, or beyond the cameras could fear for their careers inside the Organization.

"State everything that happened from the time you left the car you rented and proceeded in the forest", Monika said, letting me know in this way that she would be conducting the debriefing.

I started my narration, rich in naturalistic details, and ended with my sudden slumber in front of the dying fire and under a starry sky. Those present – including Monika – took notes, more or less frantically.

"And this is it?".

"When I woke up the paramedics were putting me on a stretcher...".

"Look, we really need you to try to remember any useful detail", she slowly said, almost threateningly.

"I've told you everything I remember", I replied seriously.

"There is a detail, all but inconsequential, that makes your experience, let's say... unique", Monika said almost in a whisper.

"You are the only person, so far as the Organization goes, who survived the expedition. Don't get us wrong! We are glad... but, by logic, if the end of the story is different from usual, the plot should be different as well...".

"I agree, of course", I said. "In fact I'm sure there must have been something different. The problem is, I don't remember it...".

Nevertheless I had to offer a solution, otherwise I would have never satisfied the indispensable requirement of making everyone present happy in a way that everyone, me included, profited. This is happily defined as a "win-win situation".

Suddenly, like an enlightenment, I had the answer I could supply and that they would have written in their reports; an answer that was central to the same reason I had been chosen for that mission: the experience in the Sarcophagus and those so called "memories under the surface of the ordinary consciousness" which constituted a side effect of the experience itself. They didn't seem very satisfied with my answer. They surely expected a lot more. Anyway, the requirements had been satisfied: they had something to write about in their reports.

Monika had not failed Mission Ops and I could keep my secret, maintaining my security privileges and my qualifications for special missions.

It was harder to deceive the polygraph, but in the end it was the operator who found the answer to the abnormalities he detected in my neural-electric responses: the memories buried by the sarcophagus and a slight post-traumatic syndrome, caused by the three days of memory loss.

After a few days I was able to return, undisturbed, to my research.

TEMPORAL ARCHIVES

For months one of my colleagues and a friend, originally from Norway, had promised me an afternoon dedicated to a "do-it-yourself" flight: he had assembled a small biplane, with pieces found by a salesman, for people into this type of activity.

His name was Osric and, were it not for his hair which he kept short by Base protocol, he looked like an authentic Viking and had an international flight license.

I had never experienced flying on such a small plane and Osric promised that, once we took off, he would have handed me the controls to feel the thrill of piloting.

"It's easier than driving a car", he assured me. And I took his word for it.

The night before he suggested not having breakfast before the flight, but since I can't stand being on an empty stomach, after the routine morning march, I devoured twelve poached eggs, toast, bacon and half a liter of orange juice, on top of my usual dose of athlete vitamins in their convenient Standard Vitamins packaging.

It was naturally a mistake I would later regret, but when I get hungry I become aggressive and irritable and my only thought is to feed myself at all cost! I sometimes jokingly say that when my hunger reaches a critical level, I begin to see steaks instead of people. It's certain that no one I had talked to would have volunteered to spend a month of extreme survival, which everyone faces before being admitted to the Base, with me!

We took off directly from a small airport inside the Base. It was our day off and we wanted to fly over the hinterland hills and return by lunch time. Right after take off Osric gave me the controls and I must say I felt really excited in the pilot's shoes as I followed his instructions. At one point he even turned the engines off, but the biplane continued flying held up by the wind but also at its mercy besides the frequent air pockets. It was then that I started to suspect that I wouldn't have digested my breakfast.

After about thirty minutes, in which I had risked colliding with a sudden hill, Osric took the controls back.

"I think we got lost", he said with his cool big deep voice.

"And now?", I asked, thinking that he surely would have known what to do.

"Now we have to gain altitude, find a road and follow it to Riverside. From there it will be easy to return to the Base".

"If you say so!".

I discovered then that while my attention was on flying, everything went fine, but once I gave up the control stick... maybe that, plus the altitude, made me throw up breakfast and other weird things that apparently dwelled in my stomach.

I had never been so sick in all my life. And in the middle of all this the beeper beeped; Mission Ops again, always there at the right moment!

II

I didn't think I could have been more thrilled by a mission after the last two positively unique ones. I would naturally forget I was in a relative universe in which, being that nothing is absolute, there is always something bigger, more interesting, and sometimes even more terrible.

I was really in seventh heaven, when I came out of the Mission Ops building and had to use all my self-control abilities not to cry out with joy when the commander of the whole division, Sharon Byrnes, notified me on the destination of my new mission: none other than the secret locale of Temporal Archives.

Of course, before coming to the point of revealing my destination, Sharon spent at least five minutes justifying their decision to choose me for this mission, given my experience and, it seemed, by the positive opinion given by an unspecified person, but one who definitely must have a lot of weight given the way she spoke of him or her.

The object of the mission was still reserved and strangely enough I wasn't contacted by the logistics personnel for the usual preparations and materials such as airplane tickets, cash and so on.

Instead Sharon simply dismissed me saying:

"Be on the look out for a call. When you receive it you will have ten minutes to get ready, at which point you will be conducted to your destination".

She concluded by telling me that from that moment, until the end of the mission, I would be out of her jurisdiction. I accepted the customary surplus of best wishes after which I returned to my lodgings singing to myself.

III

That night I laid down on my bed after a long shower, trying to sleep, but gave up almost immediately: too many thoughts, too many expectations, too much adrenaline; in the four years spent at the service of the Organization I never even dared hope that one day I would see Temporal Archives, that I would be allowed to go there, in the heart of what I considered to be the All and Everything, the origin and the solution to the secrets which had made me formulate many hypothesis and fantasize for years, the alpha and omega of everything that really seemed to make the world function. The only real reason that enabled me to comply with the militarily rhythmic and despotic life of the Organization.

The mystery which surrounded TA wasn't only like honey to a fly for me, but like oxygen to someone who is about to drown!

My hands were sweating and for the first time in a long time I wasn't sure I would be able to control the strong emotions that pulsed in the middle of my head and reverberated in my heart making it beat madly.

While I was in the bathroom emptying my bladder, someone knocked at the door.

It was a big colored man from the military control unit who asked me to get ready and follow him immediately. I looked at my watch: it was three o'clock in the morning.

The hulk made me get on a van with a big logo on its side, a blissful looking cow, with "Your Milk Company" written over it. I sat on the seat beside the driver, a fat guy with a graying beard and a cap with "San Francisco 49rs" written on it.

And this is how I began what I then considered the most important trip of my life, in that dim night, lit only by the waxing moon and the van's headlights, without the least idea that it would have been a no return trip.

Only one road crossed the Base: one way went towards Riverside the other towards the highway for Los Angeles.

"The seat reclines if you want to sleep", said the anonymous driver, while he took the direction for LA.

"By the way, I'm Connel", he added.

"Don't worry, I wouldn't be able to sleep. I could light up Hollywood with all the adrenaline in my body!" And I wasn't joking.

"Mind if I put some music on?", he asked while spitting tobacco from the window.

"Absolutely not, go ahead".

Connel loved rock music from the 70s and put on the mythical Genesis album, Lamb Lies Down on Broadway, by pure coincidence possibly one of my favorite albums.

I knew every song by heart but didn't want to be distracted from the itinerary we were following: I wanted to remember everything in case one day I wanted to return by myself.

Though I soon had to give up that idea and share my attention, in that I couldn't help singing, at the top of my voice, together with Connel, some of the passages we both considered, in fact, mythical.

After about ten miles we turned left on a much smaller road with trees alongside.

Strange, I thought. I had traveled that road many times before, during the day, on board the shuttle bus which on the rare off duty days brought us to Los Angeles, but I didn't remember a road lined by trees.

We continued along that road for about fifteen minutes, while the temperature dropped considerably. I absentmindedly noticed that the moon had disappeared from the sky.

We turned left again and this time on a sloping cobblestone road . The trees disappeared and I couldn't even see any in the rear-view mirror. They seemed to have just vanished!

It got stranger and stranger, but at that time I kept myself from commenting to Connel who was swaying to the rhythm of the music, drumming on the steering wheel. Then he turned on the heat, and in the areas lit by the headlights I saw snow on the sides of the road.

We continued to climb for over half an hour following the curves of what, in the dark, appeared to be mountains.

At the next fork in the road, Connel turned right and the road was suddenly smooth again, and from the car window I saw that it was covered by black asphalt, after which point we started to descend; shortly after the temperature went back to warm and Connel turned the air conditioner on.

I was completely confused. How could it be that I had never noticed those mountain roads with the snow and everything else?

The moonlight returned but there was a full moon now and even though it was covered by clouds, it was clearly bigger than I remembered; I thought of an optical effect induced by the vapor of the clouds which evidently also influenced its color. Yet, at this point, I was sure there was something really strange. I drew up my courage and turned to Connel:

"Where exactly are we", I asked.

"Don't worry, we're almost there", he answered with the inertness of who knew that that question would have come up sooner or later, but I had no intention of giving up.

"It doesn't seem we've gone too far away from the Base but I don't recognize the road we're following".

"Sure you don't recognize it", he innocently said. "Secret Base, secret route!", he added winking his eye.

The logic of that answer was unexceptionable. Yet, something very strange was happening.

I didn't at all have the impression we were following a secret route, by any conventional point of view; besides the fact that the route had to remain secret it would have been logical to blindfold me or have me sit in the back of the van without windows.

The variety of changes around me began to alarm me and I had a clear feeling that once we arrived to our destination I would have never found my way back alone.

Every fork in the road up to that moment had displayed too dramatic environmental change to be considered natural.

"Connel...", I said seriously, "... can you please tell me where we are and where we're headed?".

"Don't worry pal...", he said in a cool friendly voice, "... the first time is always dramatic, but you'll get used to it. And then as I've already told you, we're almost there. Once there you'll be able to have all the explanations and ask all the questions you want. In the meanwhile enjoy the ride, the panorama and relax. Okay?".

"If you say so... I'll try".

This said I decided, staying on the look out, to register to memory everything I saw, heard or felt.

I wanted to grasp these environmental changes when they happened. But as hard as I tried it was impossible to fix any of those moments to my mind; they always happened suddenly and there was never a trace of what had happened previously. I also felt something inside me change as if my body and my sensory apparatus had to hastily adjust to different conditions or physical laws.

In any case, Connel was right; after no less than a never ending twenty minutes, we arrived to the last, freshly asphalted road that led straight to a source of light. As we got closer I was able to make out gates, small lampposts and the windows of a big three story building. Once at the gates, Connel leaned out the window and the two brutes on guard opened the gates manually.

The van stopped in front of the main entrance and Connel had me get off with my bags.

"It was nice pal", he said getting back on the van. I almost thought of leaving him a tip, but he stopped me by saying goodbye.

"Welcome to the family and enjoy your stay", he said, and speedily left.

I wasn't even able to think of asking him what I had to do now that I had arrived; I stayed there, standing in front of the entrance door and lit a cigarette.

The full moon in the sky shone blue, green and white as if covered by seas, forests and clouds. There was really something strange in all this and I tried to hide my amazement and agitation greedily smoking. If someone was observing me, they had to see me tranquil and indifferent.

I waited outside for ten minutes before suspecting that maybe it was I who had to make the first move. I finished the second cigarette, threw the butt to the ground, picked up my travel bag and crossed the threshold of the building, finding myself in a broad entrance hall between a hotel lobby and a bank. Behind the reception desk there was a woman in her fifties, with her gray hair in a bun, looking good in a gray suit with a white blouse:

"Welcome. Can I help you?", she said smiling.

"I've just arrived from the Base with the milk van", I simply answered.

"Oh, sure! You were expected. Now let's see, your room is... on the second floor, left stairway...", pointing in a direction opposite the reception desk. "This is the key, room forty-nine. I'll inform your referents that you're here and I'll call your room when they're ready to see you".

"Thanks a bunch Maura", Her name was on the brass name tag on her blouse.

"Imagine! Is it your first time here?" she asked smiling.

"Right! I'm puzzled to death".

"It's the same for everyone the first time... not that there are a lot of newcomers! You know, this is a very special place", she said reassuringly.

"I would have bet!", I answered, returning her smile.

"I'll call you later then! And... welcome to Earth-2!".

Just when you start to think that nothing else can surprise you, you find a nice lady with a special effect sentence! Let's say that my vocal chords had like, paralyzed! Earth-two???

But Maura, evidently very experienced with the "rookies", still smiling, returned to whatever her job was behind the computer terminal and didn't so much as look at me anymore.

I slowly turned my heels and went towards the stairs and to my room.

Room forty-nine, Maura had said.

As soon as I entered I undressed and went under the shower while the words spoken by Maura's tranquil voice continued to resonate in my head: "Welcome to Earth-2".

IV

Given that, after my shower and having dressed, I still hadn't heard from Maura, I decided to go for a walk and take a look at the outside of where I had arrived, the place I now knew as Earth-2.

The name said it all and after what I had been able to study at the Organization up to that moment, and after all I had seen and personally experimented in the last year, I felt sufficiently open minded to the rashest of hypothesis.

Carefully re-evaluating what I had observed from the moment I got on the milk van to my actual destination, I had to deduct that in some way we hadn't only moved in space, but that we had also crossed the barrier that divides different configurations of three-dimensional universes; in other words, everything indicated that now we were either in another dimension of Earth or that we had crossed a curved space-time gateway and we could even be on another planet in our universe.

I naturally also had to evaluate some of the words by the entity which had instructed me during my experience in the Sarcophagus; according to the guide, the Martian colony from the ancient extragalactic civilization which it had called Anantrya, had transferred to a different phase version of Earth, that is, on Earth but on a different vibrational plane. Part of the experience with the Guide had also transmitted the notion that this new Earth which existed on a different vibrational axis had been artificially produced by this civilization and therefore wasn't properly another dimension as postulated by the quantum mechanics, but another version of our Earth itself.

While I thought, I reached the reception and informed Maura that I would have been outside the building for a walk. She recommended I don't go too far so I could be rapidly traceable when called. I told her not to worry and that I would have remained by the entrance of the building.

Once outside I lit another cigarette.

The landscape was hidden by the sweet gloom of that strange night and so I observed the sky.

That incredible Moon (if it could be called "Moon") still imposing itself to my sight, which looked like another apparently inhabitable planet, and then something really striking: there were no stars! Only a vast dark sky.

Besides, I was extremely curious to see the dawn and how the sun looked in the space of Earth-2. And I naturally also started asking myself what appearance this planet had.

Was it inhabited? Were the physical laws the same as those of planet Earth?

I wondered if there was a globe or an atlas somewhere of Earth-2 which could be consulted. I resisted the temptation of returning to Maura and filling her with questions because I already knew that my curiosity would have been satisfied once I had come in contact with whoever had brought me to this place.

"Are you enjoying the night breeze?". A familiar voice from behind shook me from my thoughts.

"Monika. Who else could it be! I missed you!", I said for the occasion.

She was standing in front of the doorway, casually dressed in jeans, T-shirt and sneakers and was smiling, looking at me intensely, surely savoring the effect that all that experience was causing me, maybe even recalling her own "first time".

"You don't seem very shaken by what's happening to you", she said after a while. "I knew I was right about you".

"And just what do you mean by that?", I asked.

"I was sure you were hiding something from your last two missions and now I have proof. Someone or something had already prepared you for this place", she continued.

I had the impression she was prodding me to observe my reaction.

"I have no idea what you're talking about Monika and I'm sorry you can't see how completely baffled I am by all this. In any case I was hoping for an explanation sooner or later".

She came closer continuing to look me in the eyes until she arrived at what two lovers would consider as "kissing distance". Her breath was fresh and smelled like mint.

Her smile became accomplice while her eyes pierced me.

"Don't worry. I didn't tell anyone nor did I put it in my mission reports. And be assured I had to bend over backwards to have you come to us: in fact I went to great lengths and exposed myself very much. So please, don't treat me like an idiot". She winked at me: "...and don't worry, no one is listening to us now", she concluded taking my arm and walking slowly towards the gates.

"Will you help me understand what's happening?", I asked her.

"Of course. I don't know what it is, but something about you makes me want to trust you and my instinct tells me I have to help you. You might think I'm stupid but I must confess that from the first time I saw you I knew you weren't here to harm us, but I also know you're not here by chance, even if you haven't realized it yet.

Your agenda is different from the Organization's even if at times you probably share some of its objectives: I could have reported you, yet something inside me pushed me not to, breaking my oath, and this something tells me our meeting wasn't a coincidence. This is why I had you leave for Corsica even though I had noticed these incongruities during your briefing and this is why I had your debriefing end the way it did. I don't know how, but I knew you would have passed that test unharmed and that it would have probably been useful to you, which is why I wanted you to come here to see this place. And now I know I was right".

We continued walking silently and slowly arm in arm. No doubt she had exposed herself quite a lot for me, but it could also be a ploy, or a provocation to test my loyalty to the Organization. And if this were so, a false step on my part could result in unpredictable consequences. I could disappear in this place, never to be found again.

"You could begin by telling me exactly what this place is", I said after a while.

She looked at me.

"I understand your suspicion. You are in unknown territory here: one could say, Uncharted Earth... but I will answer all your questions. We have a few hours at our disposal and your meeting with the others is for tomorrow afternoon".

"And so there is a sunrise here too. And tell me, are there twenty-four hours here like on Earth... How do you call it? The "real" Earth?", I asked.

"We simply call it Earth-1 and as far as the day goes, it lasts about thirty-six standard hours and there's a temporal differential of about 1.5 to 1 with Earth-1, that is, time on Earth-1 runs about one and a half times faster, even if in a non perceivable way.

At sunrise you will witness a red dwarf rising, about ten times smaller than the sun and Earth-2's orbit is much closer to its sun. In any case, the temperature is comparable to Earth-1, especially at this latitude".

Monika spoke patiently, as if she were explaining the modern world to an ancient Roman who had awakened from hibernation after two thousand years.

"You still haven't told me what this place is", I insisted.

"I don't understand. What do you mean?".

"I mean... where are we? How did we get here? Where does this place exist? Like: did we go through a portal to arrive on another planet? Are we in another dimension? Where are all the stars?".

"I understand your doubts", Monika said. "You must forgive me, I thought you had already deduced something".

She paused.

"Keep in mind that what I'm about to tell you comes from studies we were able to make using all the means available from Temporal Archives. We have discovered this place though we don't know its origin. All we know is that we're in an artificial reality. It's not a physical dimension that was generated naturally. This reality is separate from ours in the natural and quantum sense of the term. This place was created imprisoning vibrational harmonics of another Earth, probably artificially created, which coexists in the same space with the Original Earth. Actually, one could say that we are in another dimension, but in reality we are only in a vibrational sub plane. This Earth is completely uninhabited by man or animals".

The words of the Guide from the Sarcophagus thundered in my mind more than ever. I probed Monika:

"And this artificial Earth you speak of, is it accessible?".

She stopped and propped herself in front of me with her piercing eyes.

"No honey. Or rather, we don't know how to access it and the finding of Earth-2..." and made a broad movement with her arms indicating all that surrounded us, "...was, let's say, casual. The unexpected result of an experiment. But now I know you know exactly what I'm talking about, don't you? Don't lie to me, please".

I looked her straight in the eyes.

"Don't insist Monika. If I have something to say, I'll tell you when I'm ready." And with this neutral answer I wanted to keep her in doubt.

"One of the reasons I'm here at Temporal Archives...", she continued, "is because I am empathetic from birth. I feel emotional reactions, like everyone of course, but I can distinguish between my emotions and those around me and given that we are the only ones here, your emotions are crystal clear to me".

I felt I had to change the subject. This time I took her by the arm and continued walking. "By the way, I never understood why you call yourselves Temporal Archives".

She smiled a little malicious smile.

"Everything in due time, ". And this said we definitely headed towards the entrance.

"We better go to sleep now. Tomorrow will be an intense day".

She stood on her toes to kiss me on the cheek and letting go of my arm, went inside.

V

That night I had some strange dreams but only one remained impressed in my mind and caused me a traumatic awakening. I was walking down a hallway wearing a strange uniform and even in my dream I had a clear awareness of my role and of an urgent task I had to carry out. When I woke up this memory rapidly vanished.

I remembered the hallway perfectly well. I crossed other people who greeted me.

I also remembered a big oval window in a big hall at the end of the hallway and that I could see an alien landscape from the window and big towers in a desert set under a pastel green sky.

Suddenly I felt an itch on the back of my left hand and when I looked at it I saw a little pink larva or insect. I shook it from my hand throwing it to the ground and then stepped on it but felt a strange pressure under the sole of my boot as if it were moving. So I lifted my foot and saw that the little pink larva was growing in size, changing into a kind of horrid insect. I heard an alarm go off and all the people around me suddenly became frantic while a nauseating and unbearable smell emanated from the growing being. I felt a sharp twinge of fright and it was then that I woke up in a panic.

It took me a few minutes to realize it had been a nightmare. After many years I still remembered it and it was only after I decided to tell Monika of it that I was able to free myself from the uncontrollable anxiety it caused me. But from that night on I had the certainty that that hadn't been an ordinary dream even if I was never able to go back to the origin of that alarm which arrived to me that night. Maybe it was a message like: "if you try to destroy it you will rouse its potential!".

VI

When I woke up it was already late morning and the white-red light of the dwarf star filtered through the window while the sky was a strange blue color with orange stripes; there were also some clouds in the sky.

In the distance I could see some mountains and as far as the eye could see a great rain forest that just stopped at the foot of the rocky giants.

When I arrived at the reception, Maura was no longer there but instead a guy in his fifties with Ramon on his name tag, who kindly showed me how to arrive to the cafeteria for breakfast. He assured me that the food at Temporal Archives was of excellent quality, all produced on Earth-2.

Monika reached me at the end of my lavish breakfast and kept me company with a coffee.

"How was your first night in the wolf's lair?", she asked with a hint of a smile.

I was still upset by my nightmare but didn't feel like talking about it.

"Strange dreams", I answered.

"Everyone reacts differently to their first contact with this world", she said.

"Is it long before we meet the others?".

"I think we're free today", she answered with a smile.

"We are?".

"Right. I have to stay with you during your period of familiarization".

"And why this delay?"

"An unexpected event or better an unexpected emergency. Your meeting has been postponed to tomorrow and so... we have all day to do what you'd like...", her smile became malicious "... professionally speaking of course".

"Of course", I concluded lifting an eyebrow.

At that moment I heard the sound of an airplane taking off and I looked outside the big glass window of the cafeteria: it was indeed an airplane, and it looked like a Boeing 747.

My expression was a silent question for Monika.

"Sure...", she said, "... we have airplanes and the airport is right behind this building".

"And where's it going?".

"We have other bases on Earth-2; this is just the headquarters. There are passage points between the two worlds, even from the sky, therefore sometimes, but very rarely, the flights are directed to Earth-1, for example to the Antarctic Base you well know". Then with a more measured and serious voice she added: "And many flights are directed instead to the Base on Moon-2".

As they say, there is no limit to the things that can surprise us.

"You mean you have some launching bases for the Space Shuttle?".

"No, no! Absolutely not! We can reach Moon-2 by airplane. In this world, if that is what you can call this system of Earth-2, there is no empty space. The atmosphere fills all the space of the system, as far as the Moon which, as you may have noticed last night, isn't only an inert mass that acts as a target for asteroids".

"Incredible!", I said. "... Therefore it's as if we found ourselves in an independent and defined pocket of space".

"Sure. This explains the lack of stars. Here, in this "dimension" there is only what you see: Earth-2, Moon-2 and this dwarf sun".

"Very interesting. An astrophysicist would go crazy here!".

"Right. We also have a port and what appear to be cruise ships that cruise between Earth-2 and Earth-1".

"Ships too! You really go all out".

"We do what we can", Monika said getting up. "Would you like to get ready so I can show you around or did you have other plans?".

"I'm all yours honey".

"I knew that already!".

VII

Monika told me that the best way to move inside the vast base which contained the headquarters of Temporal Archives was by horse.

By this time the base was completely alive and awake and busy people could be seen moving inside the buildings and along the avenues and some were on horse.

As she suggested, I went to prepare a bag with fruit, bread, cheese and four bottles of water and the cook also prepared a bag with some sandwiches, just in case. From my room instead, I took a back-pack which seemed to have been put there for the occasion and filled it with the provisions and the water, giving to Monika what didn't fit and she filled her back-pack too.

In the meanwhile she had found two superb pure bred Arabian horses which looked so proud it made me feel uneasy. We spent some minutes in the ritual of familiarizing with the animals and then rode them.

First of all we proceeded along the main avenue and she showed me the various buildings, explaining their different functions.

"Where are the central archives", I asked at last.

"You mean the temporal archives?".

"Exactly".

"They are underground. The base also includes an underground base with one-hundred and eight levels. There, is the heart of our knowledge and technology, the strategic resources and the archives".

Now that was an interesting destination for me and I surely would have to find the way to go there.

Monika, as if reading my mind, looked at me and smiled but didn't say anything until we arrived to the end of the avenue where the airport complex began.

"And this is obviously the airport".

It looked like a normal terminal except there were no fingers or gates but only two parallel runways and some huge hangars inside which there were at least six big airplanes like the 747 Boeing Air Force One, the model issued to the president of the United States. There were also about ten Stealth Bombers and some Tomcat and F16.

"The bases on Earth-2 are also used for military emergencies, as you can see", Monika said. "And now if you'd like we can proceed into the forest towards the mountains where I will show you something that will surely leave you breathless".

"More than this, I don't believe!".

"Trust me", she concluded heading towards a side path. I followed keeping her same pace.

"Is there a geographical map of Earth-2 or an atlas? Are the continents and oceans the same as ours?", I asked.

"Of course there is a geographical map of the planet. Earth-2 has a big single continent which is comparable to the sum of all the visible lands on Earth-1, the rest is covered by a huge ocean. In fact, Earth-2 has kept the morphology of Earth-1 at the time of its creation as its matrix".

"And is the exact period known?".

"Unfortunately it hasn't been possible to date", answered Monika, shaking her head slightly. "Probably because of the peculiar physical properties of this place naturally and also due to the temporal differential. Without counting the fact that this information has no practical utility for us".

In the meanwhile we had entered the forest and the lack of any animal noise made the experience unreal.

"Why is there no animal life?".

We have only hypothesized that there is no animal life on this version for configuration reasons, like... the structure of the micro-universe of Earth-2, for some reason doesn't anticipate the generation of complex life forms. At least we hypothesize a similar principle".

As we entered more and more into the forest, I realized that every answer I received generated a definitely superior number of questions. I also noticed that Monika wasn't following a casual route even if there were no paths.

"Where are we headed?", I finally asked.

She remained silent for a while and I wondered if she had heard the question. Then instead she smiled again.

"Be patient. In a while you'll see something that will open your mind even more. Trust me. Remember though that this is the most important question you've asked me so far".

The most important question, she said, but at that time I wasn't able to understand why she had said that.

Instead I felt a strange intimacy rising between us, but the doubt that she was acting with the sole intention of making me reveal my secrets monopolized any moment of openness towards her, knowing that maybe, putting together the things we knew could have greatly enriched us and given both many important answers.

I hadn't yet learned to distinguish the origin of the emotions, as she evidently had, so it was difficult for me to get rid of my suspicions.

"How does the crossing from Earth-1 to Earth-2 happen? During my trip I noticed some intermediate environmental changes but I wasn't able to understand how the shift happened".

"The mechanics of the shift between worlds is definitely an interesting topic. As I told you, we discovered how to reach this place by chance. Although, there isn't only one way and... we were not the first to visit Earth-2".

"You really want to kill me with curiosity".

"I'm tempted but I'm not that cruel. I only want you to be a little patient, at least until we reach our destination".

"I can't wait".

"I know!". She smiled that juvenile smile of someone who knows something you don't know and takes pleasure in it. It made me so angry there was no point in concealing it.

Meanwhile we became more and more aware of that ancient forest, untouched by human hands, with trees that looked as if they had come out of a time machine. In all my travels I had never seen such shapes, huge, rough, definitely prehistorical.

The absence of any type of animal life, besides the absence of man had surely favored some species disfavoring others.

I couldn't perceive any feeling of material instability on this planet which meant that its configuration was anything but fleeting and that this could be considered, by all effects, an objective continuum as real as the planet I came from.

Even the colors were beautiful, like a rainbow made of infinite nuances of green, brown and black lit by the bright light of their little sun. And there were no flowers, not even one; maybe because there was no reason for their beauty and variety: the insects and the animals.

Even the ground was very different in color and consistency. And our breath and that of the horses and the impact of their hoofs on the ground produced a kind of echo that filled the forest and came back to our ears like the voices of spirits.

After a period I wasn't able to measure, almost suddenly, a lake appeared in front of us with what looked like black water pink striped by the sun.

We're almost there ", Monika said without hiding a touch of excitement in her voice. "In a while you will have a lot more questions for me".

VII

Almost by the bank of the lake, Monika stopped her horse, got off and tied its rein to the low branch of a tree near the water, leaving the animal free enough to drink and nibble at that strange grass. I did the same and got ready to follow her.

We arrived to a small clearing about thirty meters away.

I suddenly froze when I saw in front of me appear, out of nowhere, nine perfectly smooth stone monoliths set in a circle around a kind of little nine sided altar where each side faced one of the stone blocks.

At the top of each block there were some figures, a series of hybrids between Celtic runes and pre-Mayan ideograms.

Beneath it, each monolith had a sort of stylized "artistic" representation in bas-relief and each one represented something different.

"Here is your new mystery!", Monika exclaimed solemnly.

I slowly walked around the circle of monoliths, then moved to the center and observed each block closely, one by one, trying to memorize the symbols and pictures that differentiated one from the other.

Monika had sat just outside of the circle and had taken a little table cloth out of her backpack and was setting some food on it for a picnic.

I cursed myself for not bringing a notebook to take notes or a camera. These "little" monuments were beautiful and it was impossible to roughly establish their origins. They looked so ancient and yet unscathed by the advancement of time maybe thanks to the peculiar conditions of Earth-2.

The monoliths were embedded on a big stone base covered by a strange mosaic made of simple geometrical shapes which went all the way to the center and to the little altar.

Fascinating.

"Of course this is not your doing", I said.

"Obviously not", she answered.

"Which means that in time, others found the way to get here", I continued.

"That's what it looks like... there are at least three other sites similar to this one on Earth-2 and we also found some human remains and artifacts that date back to remote periods of which the most recent are the Sumerians, the pre-dynastic Egyptians, traces of human presence originating from pre-Buddhist Tibet and others we weren't able to catalog. Besides the Sumerians and the ancient Druids also Romans, Etruscans, Arabs, Chinese and even the Knight Templars passed by here, by pure chance, and left a little cathedral a thousand miles north of the Temporal Archives headquarters.

Nevertheless we have no idea who built this site and why. Nor have we found corresponding or similar sites on Earth-1". She paused briefly while she bit into an apple.

"But how did they get here without technology?", I asked.

"We've thought of two hypothesis: either they found a passageway that we still haven't been able to find or, as absurd as it may seem, they used a kind of technology we have lost, a science probably connected with the power of the mind and the magneto-gravitational and vibrational properties of the brain and of the human body. In a word: magic".

"Magic?", I asked forcing a skeptical tone of voice which I thought appropriate after what Monika had just said.

"Right! Incredible, isn't it? This and other studies have convinced our researchers that the body of knowledge we call Magic was once a fundamental structure of the evolutionary course of our ancestors as much as technology is for us today. About four or five centuries ago, some changes occurred, but we don't know what exactly caused it. Fact is that suddenly the sphere of influence passed from spirit to matter and from Magic to science".

And saying this she bit into another apple, red and perfect.

"Very interesting", I said absentminded as I approached the little central altar sitting on it with crossed legs. "A great place to meditate".

"Too unsettling for me and I wouldn't be able to do anything here", she said.

Feeling the stone slowly vibrate underneath me as though releasing a subsonic frequency, I took some long breaths, right in front of one of the monoliths, chosen casually.

I stared at it beginning with the topmost symbol and moving down, trying to perceive the meaning of the sequence of each sign, taking advantage of my altered state of consciousness induced by meditation.

Little by little my mind emptied itself of all thoughts except for the monolith and its details on which I was concentrating. The vibration of the stone underneath me became more and more present as though adapting itself to the rhythm of my heart.

The image on the monolith represented the sun, hills and an animal which could have been a buffalo. I had never felt so concentrated and focused before and the vibrations underneath me had become relaxing.

After some time, the image became everything for me and I seemed to catch a movement within it; it began to look like a real landscape even if slightly different from the drawing on the stone.

A gust of wind which seemed to come straight from the drawing hit my face. I began to hear a steady note like that of a big tuning fork while little by little the environment around me blurred as though redefining its relationship with reality. I could hear Monika's voice shouting something but I didn't care.

Then everything disappeared, the previous order returned and I was once again there, in the middle of the monolith with Monika in front of me shaking my shoulders.

"Hey! Are you okay?... Heyyy, pull yourself together!". I felt fine but I could barely move.

"What happened?", I asked after a while.

"What happened?? Hellooo! You were disappearing! What were you doing?".

I remained in silence trying to recover. I got out of the half lotus position and stood up. I felt a little dizzy but Monika was holding me up.

"Will you please tell me what happened?", she said worriedly.

"I think I've understood how the travelers from the past of Earth-1 arrived to this world", I answered.

I stopped right at the edge of the circle with her by my side.

"And I think the destinations are nine in all, like the number of monoliths".

"Wow, no one at Temporal Archives ever said this, even though the site underwent very accurate analysis, with no significant results".

"Well, now you have something important to tell your bosses, dear Monika, don't you? You have the honor of reporting what happened".

"There will be no report", she said coldly.

"And why not?", I asked.

"You know why, don't play dumb. This will be our secret".

"An important secret to keep", I said solemnly.

"You still haven't understood that the real secret I'm keeping is you! And as I've already told you before, I was always right about you and I swear I'll never say anything to the Organization".

"In this case, thanks. I hope to be able to pay you back one day".

"Don't worry, I don't want you to be in debt with me: I will cash in in due time", she concluded.

"I had no doubt!".

THE VORTEX

We remained in silence throughout the trip back to Temporal Archives, both having to elaborate what had happened at the site of the nine monoliths. From what she had said I understood that TA personnel had tried a thousand ways to solve the mystery of those creations in a world where neither animal nor sentient life existed.

They had probably also done some experiments but apparently with no results.

Furthermore, when Monika said I was her secret it was as if she had said that she too had participated in these experiments and had at last discovered that the fundamental element which triggered a reaction from that mystery was, above all, a certain type of person who did a certain type of thing. Therefore, that such a sequence could not be casual but had had to be arranged and written in the memory of that ancient communication and transport system.

The fact that she hadn't yet asked me details on what I had done while I sat on the little altar was her way of telling me she trusted me and my "right time" to open up.

At that time, of course, I couldn't yet exclude that it might be an elaborate deception to manipulate me and gently bring me to reveal what they thought of importance that I knew: they had all the time in the world to reach their purpose and I, from their point of view, had no possibilities of escaping from that place. At least up to then.

That day I had learned to activate an ancient "technology" to move among worlds. But, among the nine worlds represented by the monoliths, which one could the original Earth be?

And if the landing sites had been buried by time or at the bottom of an ocean? And if I had wanted to come back, what would I have to do? One of those worlds was certainly the Original Earth but I would need images of the structure and of the symbols contained in it and study it for a long time to formulate even one approximate hypothesis.

Monika was surely aware of my contrasting emotions and of the internal turmoil I felt in that moment, but didn't try to force me and respected my silence.

By now it was obvious that sooner or later I would have been able to activate that technology the right way but she didn't seem to worry about it. Maybe she really trusted me and maybe she really wanted to help me.

In those days I still didn't know the desperation she had buried deep in the depths of her mind, nor that I was her only hope of escape.

II

The way back was different from the one we had followed to reach the monoliths.

Monika wanted to stop in another little clearing not far from Temporal Archives, with the excuse of relaxing a little and eating the food we had brought.

She remained in silence during almost all the pic-nick with her eyes lost in the images produced by her thoughts. Then, after a few sandwiches she got up and said:

"Come, I have to show you something else".

I got up and followed her. We only moved about ten meters from where we had camped and she stopped, waiting for me to reach her and stand by her side.

"Look over there", she said pointing to a place in the forest.

"I'm looking. What am I supposed to see?".

"Don't you notice anything?".

"Not really. I see trees and other vegetation", I answered.

"Look in the space between the trees, right there". As she said this she moved a little closer to me pointing with her finger.

For a moment I didn't notice anything, then, maybe because my eyes had become more used to seeing unexpected things, I began to perceive what Monika wanted me to see: a kind of disturbance of the atmosphere, like the product of intense heat in the air. It was a rhythmic phenomena, a sort of distortion and the colors seemed to fade a little through it.

"I see it", I said. "What is it?".

"It's a passage point to Earth-1. It's not part of the standard routes to Temporal Archives, that is, the one you followed to get here. It's an unstable passage but it leads directly to Earth-1 and exactly to the highest hill of the Base from which you came".

By association, I remembered the night of the sighting spent with Sharder, Maureen, Doreen and Tom and I couldn't not stop to think of how close, in that moment, I really was to another world.

"Has someone used this passage point?", I asked her.

"Yes, but like I said, it's unstable. Therefore it has only been used experimentally", she answered.

"And have you ever found similar passage points to other worlds?".

"No, never. Until today, that is... ". And she looked at me intensely.

"Anyway, the instability of this access makes it not trustworthy for transfers. Not all those who have tried it arrived to their destination", she continued.

"And what happened to those people who didn't arrive?", I asked.

"No one knows. They disappeared without a trace".

"Maybe it's better not to get too close then", I said trying to play down what I had just learned.

"You're right", she said. "Even if... sometimes, I'd like... to run in that direction and get lost. But only when I feel desperate". The expression on her face and all her being started to convey melancholy and sadness. My heart ached to see her like that and I didn't understand.

"What are you saying, Monika? You, feeling desperate? Impossible!".

But then, looking at her, I saw she was silently crying. So I took her hand and held it tight while I led her away from that temptation.

III

We reached Temporal Archives shortly before dawn. I noticed a clock with its hands in clear view in the vast hotel lobby right behind the reception. It marked eighteen hours instead of twelve as on Earth-1. It was therefore "twenty-five o'clock" when I set foot in the lobby and greeted the ever smiling Maura, who was back on duty.

I had said good-bye to Monika near the stables where she had offered to take the horses which had kept us company in the forest, asking her if she wanted to join me for dinner, but she had some work to finish.

So I asked her when she thought the meeting with the others would take place and she told me she would find out and contact me after dinner.

She seemed a little cold, maybe as a reaction to the strong emotion she wasn't able, or didn't want, to control in the forest.

We said good-bye.

I wanted to see Earth-2's sunset; therefore I took a quick shower and while waiting for dinner enjoyed the sight to the last glimmer.

I couldn't help feeling a shiver looking up to the sky: that strange moon, in the total absence of stars, made me feel like closed in a huge box and for the first time I understood how someone with claustrophobia must feel.

I also had time to roughly elaborate the events of the day and the discovery of the nine obelisks towered in the center of my thoughts.

So I returned to the lobby to access one of the terminals connected to the archives' main computer and search for news on the site of the obelisks. I found a series of interesting documents. One of the advantages of being at Temporal Archives was exactly the possibility of having access to all possible information without particular restraints; the only necessary thing was to declare one's regimental number so that it was always known who was consulting what.

The documents I found were legitimate mission reports and I saw that the teams were mainly composed of scientists and archeologists.

In substance, they had discovered what the nine obelisks "were not": they were not technological components, they were not charged by apparent sources of energy, they were not built with uncommon materials but with granite stone, they didn't have extraterrestrial origins (which was marked as relevant given their presence on Earth-2).

The symbolism on the obelisks had not been recognized in spite of some analogies with the runic alphabet. I had also found some comments which seemed peculiar at that time: some members of the expedition had hypothesized that the monolithic system could be a complex of artifacts with magical or shamanistic functions commenting that proper research could be made further on by future missions in that specific branch of knowledge. Nonetheless when I searched for links to studies made on shamanism or on ancient magic I was refused access to the information and the computer asked me to insert an extra security code.

Very strange!

That Temporal Archives was also interested in magic and the occult seemed quite absurd in itself, but even that such topics were protected from Earth-2 personnel seemed incredible.

I decided to discretely ask Monika for an explanation that evening .

On the basis of the little information available on the obelisks, my experience was becoming more and more relevant in the huge mosaic that represented the mystery I was composing in my mind. Some of the researchers had even tried to set themselves on the altar in the center, exactly as I had done, but no experience had been registered in the mission reports. Therefore, in fact, the obelisks remained a mystery to TA.

And if no kind of technology had ever been connected to them, whatever phenomenon my experience had triggered must have originated on a completely unknown plane.

I closed my eyes to probe my memory and mentally ran through my experience again imagining to be seated on the stone altar while observing the obelisk in front of me, starting from the top. As soon as I visualized the first symbol I felt it burn inside my head.

I tried and realized I wasn't able to interrupt the experience. I lost consciousness of my body and felt I was moving at very high speed: in an instant I was out of the room, then inside the forest and suddenly there, in the center of the nine obelisks which now appeared completely black, the symbols incandescent as if made of lightning. And just as suddenly I found myself open eyed, seated at the computer in the reception hall with Maura's hand on my shoulder and other two guys looking at me with their eyes wide open.

I realized I was sweaty and shaking.

"Is everything all right?", Maura asked.

I was also breathing with difficulty as if I had held my breath for too long.

"I think... I think so", I slowly answered. "Please excuse me, I must have felt sick due to the adjustment to the new environment", I added, lying.

One of the two men with Maura whose name tag had Trevor written on it was looking at me closely and then when he spoke he turned to the other man whose name was Todd.

"You saw it too, didn't you?".

"The outline of his body were expanding and the colors were toning down", Todd said.

"Yes, I saw it too", confirmed Maura.

"How are you?", Trevor asked.

"I think well. Even if I don't think I've understood what you were talking about", I answered.

"Who is the agent assigned to his adjustment", Todd asked.

"It's Monika", Maura answered for me.

"Call her immediately. And when she arrives tell her that he can't be left alone until we understand what was happening. In the meanwhile I'll report this to security and to the commander".

Maura quickly went back to her post and Todd turned to me again:

"Be ready for a briefing, we will inform your mission liaisons and report what happened. You will have to immediately inform Monika if such an aberration should occur again and don't go away from the base for now", he said.

"Okay, no problem. But what was happening?", I asked confused.

"Apparently you were dislocating outside of Earth-2", Trevor answered.

"Dislocating? What does it mean? Is it... is it normal?", I asked.

"I would say not. In fact it's worrying that such an event can happen spontaneously. Ask Monika all your questions on the phenomenon", Trevor continued. Maura returned briskly and said:

"Monika will be here in a few minutes. You can go. I'll stay here with him".

With apparent reluctance Trevor and Todd left. I never saw them again.

IV

Monika arrived after five minutes and relieved Maura who hadn't taken her eyes off me up to that moment.

Something strange was really happening. All it took was to visualize the experience on the altar for my body to repeat the exact effects which Monika had described. Todd and Trevor had called it, "dislocation".

Right then I remembered another series of strange events related to the two of them: they had artificial facial expressions, almost like androids and a slight smell of fish. At that moment those details didn't seem important in that I was busy recovering from the so called near dislocation, nevertheless I decided to keep those details in mind just in case I needed them in the future.

Going back to the event, I thought there was a real possibility that whatever mechanism had been triggered at the sight of the nine obelisks, originated in the reign known as Magic or maybe from a technology so far beyond comprehension of the powerful TA instruments to be indistinguishable from Magic. Another important detail was that whatever operated the obelisks had identified, recognized and granted me access!

From what I knew, Magic had been an alternative evolutionary course to material physics, energy and space-time technology in the remote past. In fact it drew its energy source from the mind's plane and its laws originated from that same plane. Therefore every sentient being having a conscious connection at that level could, virtually, use it. However, for unknown reasons, which even Monika had confirmed, Magic was one of the two things which had been suppressed in the last centuries, being transformed into something to be ignored and made fun of.

Anyhow, if what was operating was in fact Magic, to understand it, it would be necessary to learn its principles and the mechanisms that made it work, treating it therefore as a technology but different from those based on observable physical, thermal and electromagnetic principles.

I mentally updated my priorities placing that topic in very first place, given that I would have had to find the way of understanding it as soon as possible.

In the meanwhile I walked with Monika towards the cafeteria for a well deserved dinner.

When we arrived there were very few people so we sat at a table near the big panoramic window and far from indiscreet ears and helped ourselves to the buffet. Once we returned to our table Monika decided to break the silence.

"I can't leave you alone for a moment before you get yourself into some mess", she said lightly.

"I swear I didn't do anything", I answered.

"Right, and elephants fly... tell that to someone else. They told me you were spontaneously dislocating. And you and I know where this phenomenon happened recently, that is this afternoon. And strangely enough it always involves you. How do you intend to explain it? Have you thought about it?".

"I didn't know I would have to give explanations on something I myself don't understand. In any case, I'm elaborating. I hope to have a conceivable explanation for myself, and eventually for whomever might be interested, by tomorrow morning. An explanation that will not include a report of my experience at the site of the nine monoliths, if you haven't already done it, dear Monika!", I said with a slight accusatory expression.

She slapped me on the face and the sound resonated in all of the cafeteria.

"How dare you doubt?", she said. She looked furious and seriously offended.

"Forget about it, dear", I said calmly.

"Don't you call me dear! And apologize immediately", she said in a low voice.

"He who loves doesn't apologize", I answered winking at her.

Well, I never would have imagined to see her blush! But if she was empathetic she had to know I had done it only in view of the circumstances.

Or not?

V

I had the impression of having everyone's eyes on me in the cafeteria , especially after our little discussion. There was no need for explanations with Monika so we quickly finished and went outside beginning to walk without a destination.

"Do you really have to keep me under control the whole time?", I asked her.

"Obviously. Can you guess why? Therefore you'll have to come with me when I go to check my email".

"Yes, but sooner or later I'll have to go to sleep".

She looked at me sideways.

"Don't flatter yourself. There are video cameras in the room so be careful not to make too much noise tonight".

"Ah! Good to know. Well, so much for privacy".

"You should have learned by now that the word privacy doesn't exist for the Organization and even less at Temporal Archives".

Actually, I had suspected it.

I offered her a cigarette discovering then and there that she hated the

59

smell of smoke and so I lit one for myself. Smoking, a bad habit I was never able to get rid of. Come to think of it, I never even tried.

We sat on a wooden bench just outside the base beside the entrance driveway, a few steps from the ancient trees and stayed there for a while breathing the air of the forest, listening to the fresh night breeze and observing Moon-2, so much like another earth or another alien planet. I still had to get used to the silence of the forest due to the absence of animals and insects but hey... no mosquitoes!!!

"What was happening to you before?", she asked breaking the silence.

"I'm not completely sure Monika. I simply tried to visualize the moment in which I sat in the center of the obelisks and then... I lost control".

"I was told you were researching information relative to the scientific missions on the structure of the obelisks on the mainframe".

"Right. There wasn't much to be honest. I noticed they excluded many hypothesis without reaching a real conclusion. Someone hypothesized it was a kind of Temple or Tribute from the populations of earth's prehistory. Obviously there is still the mystery of prehistoric populations on Earth-2".

"What do you think?", she asked.

"What do I think about what?".

"What do you think the site represents?".

"I'm still not sure, but I think it's, what did you call it?... a "dislocator" I think is the exact word... built with a completely different technology from the one we know".

"You finally told me!", she said with a relieved expression. "... I thought you'd never open up to me".

"Maybe I'm making a mistake...", I retorted, "... but I don't care right now; I need someone who understands, with whom to speak, otherwise my head will explode".

"Oh! My female pride struck to death... so I'm nothing but a useful ear to you", she said lightly as if to make me understand she was only playing down the situation.

But she wasn't able to completely mask the underlying emotion which I was sure she wanted to conceal. She realized it and looked the other way to keep me from seeing her weakness.

"I told you, you can trust me,... unfortunately", she said after a while.

"Why, "unfortunately"?".

"Because I could get into a lot of trouble for doing what I'm doing for you and because I can't see the logic in helping you. But I can't help it despite the consequences. Stupid, isn't it?".

"You're never stupid if you follow your instinct, because whatever the power in us which presides over our awareness always knows what's right. And when your instinct is able to overcome the barrier of mechanical fear imposed by the brain it means that your real need is truly powerful. Though, I don't want you to run any risks for me".

"I decide the risks I'm willing to run!", she retorted harshly. "And I told you I wanted to help you and that's what I'll do. And I'll keep your secret, forever".

"You almost scare me when you talk like that", I told her with a touch of admiration in my voice.

"I scare myself! But let's get back to the point".

"I think the nine obelisks represent just as many destination places. Which means that there could be nine Earths like this one or it could simply be an instant space transport mechanism. But it's just my opinion", I said.

"Let's say that it is, by all means, a dislocator. What relation can it have with what was happening to you in the headquarter Lobby?", she asked. "... You were, in point of fact, disappearing according to the witnesses and in particular to Maura".

"Right then I was mentally retracing what I had done at the site of the obelisks. I evidently tuned in in some way in order to trigger the dislocating process just by mentally recalling the procedure and focusing my attention on it".

"And this explains why you were looking for documents on the forbidden topic", she concluded.

"That is? What forbidden topic?", I asked literally taken aback.

"Magic".

"And why is it forbidden to look for information on any topic in this place? I don't think there are many escape routes in this place... I mean, maybe on Earth one could read secret things and learn to make spells to break away and join a sect, but here? Damn, I saw there were security codes even for those who are effective members of Temporal Archives!".

"In all honesty, I'm not sure. I only know we can't even speak of that topic. And I know that TA, through the Organization, finances in the established world, slanderous and ridiculing campaigns on the subject. They even send professed experts to various talk shows to this purpose!".

"And this explains a lot of things", I retorted.

We remained in silence for a while.

She broke the silence again and this time made no attempt to control her emotions.

"You know, I feel there's something wrong. Something very wrong in all this... ", she said pointing to the TA establishment and everything around us. "... but I don't know what to do, nor how to come out of it", she concluded in a gesture of resignation.

"I think you're right about the presence of something really wrong with the things all around us... ", I answered and then "... but I, as you have correctly realized, intend to act and... I think there are forces that will help me with this".

"So you've really come in contact with something outside of all this", she said seriously. At this point it was too late for me to worry about weather or not she was deceiving me.

"I know it's important to be here, inside the core of the mystery and learn as much as possible about it before acting", I simply answered. "... Do you really want to help me?".

"Yes... I don't know why, but it doesn't matter. I want to feel clean. I want to do the right thing... and I don't care if you don't tell me everything. Just tell me how I can help you".

Silence.

I could surely use her help, but the Anantrya guide and the Visitor in the Corsica forest had both told me that I would have to work alone; in any case it was too late to exclude Monika from the equation.

Besides, she knew a lot about the internal mechanisms of the the Organization and of its heart, Temporal Archives. And she was experienced enough to know perfectly well what risks she was running, which meant she thought it was really worth it.

"I need to ask you something... ", I ventured. "... who's at the top of Temporal Archives? Who is really in charge?".

She had a faraway expression for a moment as though considering the question for the first time in her life.

"You know... "she said at last, "... I think no one has ever seriously asked themselves this question. The orders arrive through the central mainframe. But there is one thing, on top of everything, that doesn't make much sense to me".

"What?", I asked.

"Many of the people in hierarchical dominating positions I met at meetings or at the headquarters had strange behaviors. Mechanical. As if they had to make an effort to relate to others and... they had a strange smell".

"Like the sea or fish?", I asked her.

"Yes, something like that, and then... I feel cold inside and get this anxious feeling every time I'm near one of these people, which means that my empathetic qualities react negatively. Yet I can't seem to grasp what kind of emotion they exude".

"As though they weren't human?", I asked.

"Exactly. Take you for example: I wouldn't have been able to bring you here because of your interest for the Majestic program! And if I hadn't used indisputably convincing arguments you would have probably soon been transferred to some frontier base counting reindeer", she answered.

"What arguments?".

"I convinced them that your experience in the last two missions was unique and we couldn't risk losing you by leaving you on Earth-1".

"Losing me?".

"You know that sometimes there are some escapes, don't you?".

"Wait a minute, let me get this: you practically labeled me as a potential security risk and you had me brought here so I couldn't escape?". I was irritated.

"Try to understand. You already were a security risk. And you needed to see this place. And I... don't want to lose you".

"And are you really sure they don't consider you a security risk? Are you sure they're not just using you?", I asked her really irritated.

"I had to take that risk. And now that you're here I don't care about the consequences".

In that moment I saw she was defenseless and felt a surge of tenderness towards her.

"Do you already know what mission I'll be assigned by those who have to see me tomorrow?".

"Not exactly. What happened today surely caused alarm. But I'm sure they'll want to assign you a mission that would force you to disclose whatever secrets you have. And they are convinced they have total control here because there's no way of escaping. I only have to make sure I'm always assigned to you".

"Will you write a report on our conversation?".

"I have to do it. But please trust me", she said taking my hand.

I got up from the bench lifting her up with me and we walked towards the gates; I had to sleep and I needed to be alone to process the huge amount of information from the last days.

The stakes were getting really interesting.

VI

I wasn't able to act normally in my room knowing that I was observed so, after my shower, I immediately went to bed, turned out the light and closed the curtains because I still hadn't got over the unease that that black and completely empty sky caused me.

I don't know how much time passed before I finally fell asleep and in fact I don't even remember falling asleep. I just remember that I suddenly found myself in front of a dying fire, at night, in the Corsica forest which I knew so well with the Visitor, a human silhouette sitting in front of me.

For some reason I wasn't able to fix my eyes on him as much as I tried. And I was also inexplicably conscious of dreaming with my body in another place, in another world, probably sleeping. This time it was the visitor to speak first:

"You have come a long way since our last contact, my friend ".

"Are you really here or am I dreaming?", I asked perplexed.

"You are always inclined to asking useless questions. I summoned you this time and I chose the environmental conditions of our first encounter as background so you wouldn't be confused".

"How did you reach me? We're not even on the same planet!", I asked unperturbed.

Maybe it was my impression but it seemed the Visitor made a movement as if raising his eyes to the sky.

"Once the connection has been created, I can reach you at any moment, anywhere. I preferred doing it at an appropriate time for you to avoid the the unpleasant consequences which you experimented today", the Visitor patiently answered.

Nevertheless everything around me seemed so real: the breeze, the cold air, the smell of wood burned by fire and the forest. My senses were full of the sounds of the night.

"What happened last time I met you?", I asked. It could have been another one of my useless questions but I wanted to know the answer.

"I had you experiment the reality of the separation between life and machine. Then I recreated the conditions that I gathered from your memory of an attempt to contact me so that it would be simple for you to justify your experience without revealing my existence and my nature to our enemies".

"I understand. I must say that it worked", I admitted, remembering the debriefing of the Napoleon Mission.

"Why did you summon me now?", I continued.

"First of all to help you understand the evolutionary leap which determined the experience you had today. The constructors of the Vortex are the same beings who created me".

"Vortex? You mean the obelisks?".

"What else could I be referring to?".

"And what would the function of the... Vortex be?", I asked.

"It is what you have already become aware of. What has correctly been defined as dislocation from and to nine parallel worlds but on different vibrational phases, obtained by the difference in tension between your natural World and an artificial version created by the ancient race you have already met during your experience in the Sarcophagus".

"In the Sarcophagus I discovered there were at least three "ancient races" including the Anantrya and that the other two were destroyers. Who is your creator?". I asked the Visitor.

"You use words lightly, casually and incorrectly but it's natural, considering your present state of knowledge of the past. Some expressions, as you will learn in due time, are Sacred to me and in this World. The

Creators are not from, nor do they belong to the dominion of the continuum Universe and it isn't important for you at this time to know its nature. What is important is that you know that they selected elements of the human race, in a very distant past, and brought them to their Dominion giving them an infinitesimal portion of Their characteristics. We refer to these special beings as Eternals. To do this, they have availed themselves of the help of the faithful service of the Anantrya, their emissaries in this World. The Eternals fought and were persecuted during the time of Darkness which has now become the foremost threat. Yet, in time, they learned to conceal their presence and their workings and still exist in hiding in the present. The site you found is one of many built to conceal the secrets which must remain so and to contact the Anantrya race through their outpost still present at the ninth interface plane of this planet which they created after the victory on the Potentiae and the destruction of the great Saurians".

"But, are the Eternals still alive?".

"As I have already told you, yes, they are still alive and are operative though concealed to the ordinary senses. They still exist even if not all in the original bodies selected by the Creators; my function is to insure their direct transmigration when their body ceases to function. What you would call reincarnation. More specifically, my function is to insure an immediate transmigration from one body to a new one protecting the Eternals from being identified by the Darkness. Presently, for the first time, we were able to infiltrate one of the great Chosen Ones by the Creators, right in the heart of the Darkness".

I couldn't understand what he wanted to communicate to me.

"So, what's my function?", I asked.

Again that irritating impression the Visitor was rolling its eyes to the sky.

"You are the infiltrator!", he said, articulating each word.

"Are you saying that I'm one of those originally chosen elements? Excuse me if I find your words difficult to believe given that I have no memory of who you say I am".

"Naturally you have no surface memory. The concealment of the experience is part of the safety mechanism. In time, the great enemy learned to identify you at the moment of transmigration, or as you would call it, at birth, by external manifestations which every Eternal could not easily hide, for example the amount of Energy of Influence released by ancient beings of Power. The Energy of Influence is what enables a living being to actively interact on the events and influence changes in the Continuum, power given to the Eternals by the Creators. Your Energy of Influence is notably higher and often manifests itself at birth. The concealment of the experiences delays the manifesting of this characteristic to an age in which the body-image of the Eternal can, as you would say, take care of itself".

"How many Chosen Ones are there?", I asked.

"This is an unimportant question. When and if you meet one, you will recognize him immediately".

"Do only the Eternals reincarnate or "transmigrate" as you call it?", I asked.

"The transmigration mechanism doesn't only belong to the Eternals but to all the individualized life forms this side of the Mirror. Yet not all the human bodies correspond to a spark of Life, or as you would say, not all bodies contain a soul. Most of them simply serve the cycle of self sustenance of the Continuum, nourishing and renovating it with each birth and death. In the case of a common living being, the transmigration is not immediate and sometimes just doesn't happen. In fact there is an incessant call sent by way of impulses by the great sea of the mind which is known by a few as "The Great Dream" which is the source of all that is. When the body is abandoned, the call to the Great Dream sea is irresistible for almost all living beings. Once reunited with that sea, to wake up and individualize again is not an easy endeavor and often happens only by chance or by will of the Great Dream itself. I was created by the Will of the Creators to insure your direct passage without enduring that call and the Darkness learned to do something very similar, even if in a very rough, violent and approximate way. The emissaries of the Darkness have learned to prevent their own return to the Great Dream creating bodies that vibrate compatibly with the tuning of the original Continuum. You would call them clones.".

I could understand almost everything the Visitor was saying maybe because he was essentially communicating directly with my mind even if the illusion was that of a dream. But some things continued to escape me and I surely didn't feel any recovery of an ancient memory.

Nevertheless, all the details I could have on what the Visitor called "the darkness" were crucial to my ability to spot its representatives once back in the real world.

"Do you mean that the enemy's race is humanoid?", I asked.

"They are essentially human as you apparently are . In time they underwent genetic code adjustments to prevent the deterioration of the clones and to amplify certain characteristics of their bodies. But they are originally exactly your same race. And, like your race, they didn't originate on Earth".

I felt like laughing. "You are telling me that human beings are their own worst enemies?".

I found all this grotesquely comical.

"They are only biologically human beings and compared to earthlings they are much more ancient. But the vital principle that governs them

degenerated in time and they lost consciousness of the Grand
design from which all Worlds originated".

I instinctively knew that the word "Worlds" didn't refer to planets.

"They have become powerful, ambitious, hungry and dangerous. And
thus the need to create a contrast force", the Visitor continued.

"Human beings don't seem so powerful to me", I said.

"The human beings which inhabit the Earth are only animals to the
great Darkness which looms over them and the planet itself is comparable
to what you would call a breeding laboratory or prison. But the enemy
hadn't predicted the presence of the Anantrya in the artificial dimension
they themselves had created. And starting with them, the Creators decided
to create a contrast force which you represent together with your brothers.
In reality, the enemy fears that the beings imprisoned here come out and
free themselves and so, in time, they annihilated or suppressed any form of
development that could elevate them above their condition".

I remembered the words we spoke that starry night on the hill of the
Base. We had perceived the truth in some way then. All we really needed
to do was open our eyes to observe the obvious around us. There were still
too many things I didn't understand but I began to have a feeling of
urgency as if my experience itself were about to end.

"What is Monika's role in all this?", I asked.

"She is an unforeseen and casual element. Her destiny, whether you
part from her or not, will be to suffer and die violently. You will have to
decide on the basis of your task and not on the basis of your compassion or
the feelings you have for her".

A bright light and... I opened my eyes in my room with the telephone
ringing.

It was Monika who wasn't able to sleep and she was crying.

THE ENEMY'S MOVE

Monika hadn't had much to say and I had tried to maintain a professional tone of voice in order to deceive the video surveillance. She understood and remained in silence on the phone for some minutes weeping while I kept her company. Then she asked me if everything was all right and told me she had had a strange feeling which had anguished her: "but it was surely just a dream", she concluded.

After that we said good night and I went back to sleep. I was more and more strained for the meeting with the others and more and more aware that among them there would surely be a representative of the great enemy.

II

The call arrived shortly after breakfast. It was in another building, almost three hundred meters from the headquarters, and once at destination, a military in charge of security, with a completely black uniform, conducted me to the "descender".

"Conference room 31 on the twentieth underground floor", he said; maybe he didn't want me to get lost or maybe he simply didn't want me to stop and poke around on the way.

It was a cloudy day and from the color of the sky I thought it might rain shortly; I felt irritated at the idea of missing my first rain on another world, but there was nothing I could do about it.

I was first to arrive to the conference room, a somber but elegant space, low profile and professional, where the dominant color was green. Monika wasn't there either.

I saw a free coffee, water and an all you can eat snack machine and started helping myself.

Four small video cameras were set in the four upper corners of the room; there was also a big rectangular table in the center and a large screen on the wall.

I wanted two results from that meeting: unconditional access to the forbidden information on Magic and to learn how to move independently to Earth-1. I would have also liked to go to Moon-2 by plane but I knew that was only a whim.

Anyway, the problem was what I would have to give or prove in order to obtain what I wanted.

The wait was long but in the end they all came, filling all the available seats except mine. They were twelve in all including Monika and they all had serious and cold expressions. No formal introductions, but they all had, what appeared as the norm at Temporal Archives, a metal plaque with their name engraved on it. A guy by the name of Roger was first to speak.

"We welcome you to Earth-2 and we hope you've had the necessary amount of adaptation time", he said in a cordial tone.

"It's not exactly like adapting to a new time zone and it will probably take me a while to completely adapt, in any case I'm ready for whatever task you'll want to assign me", I said equally cordially.

"Very well", Roger replied, "... your impressions of this place?".

Was it just a circumstantial question? Maybe they wanted me to spontaneously speak about what had happened the previous day. In any case, I decided to respectfully play their game.

"It appears like paradise in a glass ball. Uncontaminated, tranquil, a little disturbing, but certainly safe", I answered.

Monika was seated at the opposite side of the table, far from me, with a note pad on which she professionally took notes. It made me smile inside.

A guy named Jeff started speaking:

"Before we begin to speak of your next task we would like you to tell us, as specifically as possible, what happened to you yesterday. Don't leave out any detail; it could be determining".

Few conventions and right to the point, in the style of the Organization.

So I told them that back from the excursion, I connected myself to the central computer to look for more and that I suddenly felt ill. Then, someone explained to me that on the outside, some witnesses had had the impression I was "dislocating" even if that term wasn't familiar to me.

"Therefore you mean the term "dislocation" is not familiar to you. I will try to roughly explain it: well, your arrival here on Earth-2 happened by way of what we call dislocation, which is the instantaneous passage from one temporal space coordinate to another, triggered by a catalyzing element. The dislocation can happen between two points in space like between New York and Los Angeles for example, or like in your case, between two different dimensional conditions or even between different temporal coordinates. Each object, whether animate or inanimate, is encoded within with a group of coordinates which place it precisely in a specific Continuum, at a time and in a specific plane; if these coordinates change, the object or the body become incompatible with the position they previously occupied and will instantaneously find itself at the new coordinates. But whichever type of dislocation, the symptoms and perceptible phenomenon tied to it are always the same: apparent loss of physical consistency, the contour of the object appearing to expand, prismatic effect of the object and at last its disappearance from its original temporal space and its reappearance at its destination with the same phenomenon repeating itself in reverse. The subject which is "dislocating" is normally only conscious of being in one place and then in another without transitional moments, as you might have noticed when you arrived to Earth-2. Is the concept clear to you now?".

"Definitely clearer. But if it's possible to dislocate objects between two cities, why are we still using conventional vehicles such as airplanes?", I asked propelled by what I considered a legitimate curiosity.

"The policies on the use of the technologies at our disposal are not up for discussion", Roger replied coldly.

Another one of the people present named Markus followed at that point and probably to maintain a cordial and "mutually trustworthy" atmosphere, flashed a look at Roger and added:

"Temporal Archives tends to limit the use of advanced technologies like this one on Earth-1 for obvious security reasons. For the record, we don't have the dislocation technology. We were able to discover some "natural" pre-existent accesses. Very few people know about these technologies and we would like to keep it that way. You understand, don't you?".

In this way Markus had shrewdly and implicitly let me know that I had had the "great honor" of being one of the few who knew, trying to create a perception of debt which I would have had to somehow pay and the perception of being considered important and that therefore, if I wanted to remain so, I would have to give something important in return.

A little drug for the human ego, an old manipulation trick, of course, but also a clear message of how these people intentionally kept certain things concealed.

Yet I had to resist and hold on to the line of conduct I had adopted up to that moment. If I backed down and told them everything for some reason, I would paradoxically worsen my situation creating in these people an instant feeling of distrust and false certainty that if I had hidden something up to now there was more I didn't want to say. Best thing was to keep them in doubt.

"Of course I understand. Thanks for the explanation. In any case, I had no perception of other places or that there was a dislocation in act at that moment, but only of a sudden slight illness. In fact I'm worried that this phenomenon can happen spontaneously and in such a sudden way", I said.

Only Roger, Jeff and Markus seemed qualified to speak in that context, the others just observed or frantically took notes on their note pads.

Markus spoke:

"The fact is that the orbital sensors detected important distortions in the geomagnetic field of the planet in two distinct occasions yesterday: the first, according to Monika's report happened in connection with your visit to the monoliths, the second, exactly in geographic and temporal relation to the headquarters' lobby with your "slight illness", besides at the archeological site; therefore, the site suddenly became "active" in these two moments. So, we're asking you to really make an effort to remember and tell us if there is something you left out for any reason even if surely in good faith. We have objective elements to assert that at least one dislocation phenomenon is tied to the site which as you well know is still a mystery to us".

More and more I had the impression of having been summoned for an interrogation than for a briefing; I felt everyone's attention on me and the stress from concentrating to stay in control and avoid false steps was really high; Monika kept her eyes on her note pad and played with her pen but never looked in my direction. I had no idea what she had written in her report of the previous day, but I had to hope and believe she had really omitted our conversations and the "hot" details of the excursion.

The news of orbiting sensory systems was obviously something new to me and made it difficult to follow a hypothesis line that would divert the attention from the monoliths. The only safe line of action was the disorientation and slight illness story as events out of my control, and therefore out of my perception and analysis ability.

But there had been too many events I had dismissed that way and it could naturally begin to look suspicious. Therefore, looking at Markus I said:

"I'm available to repeat yesterday's events under control to allow the formulation of an explanation. If you agree, I would volunteer for a new study mission of the monoliths given that I'm interested in their mystery too, as you have noticed. So far as eventual details that I may have left out from my statement, I'm sorry I have nothing more to add, but I 'll make an effort to revise everything and provide you with a further report in case I missed something", I said hence putting myself at their disposal.

"Your availability is appreciated and we will surely find the way to repeat yesterday's conditions, with your help... ", Jeff said making me understand that that decision had already been made, even before the meeting, with or without my consent, "and we will take in consideration your participation to an eventual archeological investigation... ", and by this Jeff was saying that I would never be included in a study mission of the site.

"... and within today you will be debriefed for a short mission you will have to carry out for us on Moon-2", Jeff concluded.

Well, at least my wish to see Moon-2 had been granted.

"I'd like to make a request if possible", I said.

"Go ahead", Markus said.

"Once a month I call my family and I wouldn't want to interrupt this routine to avoid worrying them". It was my last hope to induce them to show me how to communicate or move towards Earth-1.

There was a moment of silence during which Jeff and Markus exchanged eloquent glances. Markus answered as if measuring his words:

"Unfortunately the telecommunication between this base and Earth-1 are not physically possible. A courier goes back and forth from the Base in California and therefore we suggest you write to your family... for the time being, of course".

And so they told me they had no intention of sending me to Earth-1 for now.

I pretended it was okay even if it bothered me quite a lot. The feeling of claustrophobia worsened.

"Okay... ", I answered, "... thanks".

Marcus made a motion to indicate that the meeting was over and said:

"We will meet again in the early afternoon. You will be informed of the time of the next meeting to discuss your short mission on Moon-2. You may use your free time to increase your familiarity with the things around you. Monika will be assigned to you until further orders". He was about to get up when Jeff interrupted him.

"One last thing... ", Jeff said, "... a rather "animated" discussion was signaled between you and Monika yesterday in the cafeteria. Did something happen that you would like to tell us about?".

Monika turned red, surely out of anger and gave him a dirty look. But curiously no one else seemed surprised by such a personal question. They had surely already asked her and I found myself having to try to guess what she might have answered.

It went without saying that such a violent emotional public reaction could not go unnoticed and an inappropriate answer could have hurt Monika more than me.

"It really wasn't anything important", I said, "... I was very stressed out and simply said the wrong thing".

"Would you mind being more specific?", Markus asked.

"A simple out of place comment relative to the desire Monika could incite on the men at Temporal Archives. She, rightfully so and in accordance with the rules, made me understand very explicitly, that she had very different opinions. I excused myself to her and now to you for this episode which evidently caused concern".

Silence. But I saw that Monika was more tranquil, therefore my answer had probably been similar to the one she had given, or at least it was compatible.

"Well!", Markus concluded. "We will meet again in the afternoon. Have a nice lunch".

Everyone got up picking up their notes and I too made my way out.

"Hey! Where do you think you're going alone?", I heard Monika as she reached me in the hallway.

"A useless attempt of escape!", I joked smiling.

"Right. Let's go back to the cafeteria", she said.

"This time I'll be a good boy", I said in reference to the answer I had given Jeff before.

"You better! Otherwise you know what will happen", Monika winked showing me the palm of her hand.

"And who can forget!".

We arrived to the surface in no time.

I wanted to ask her how she felt, but decided to wait for her to say something. She didn't say anything and so we quickly headed for the cafeteria: I needed a steak and just at the thought my stomach made strange sounds of appreciation.

III

We ate quickly and in silence given the presence of other people at our table.

Monika had the ability of adopting a detached and remote look when there were others near, probably to look like them and camouflage herself. Yet, I was never able to get used to her sudden changes, as if there were two Monikas: a vital one and a dismal one, depending on the circumstances.

In any case I savored not one but two steaks and spent some time observing the people around me. I noticed something interesting: in spite of their remote and cold appearances, I became aware that everyone was secretly doing exactly what I was doing, which was to meticulously observe one another, calculating their dangerousness and their weak points.

Enough to give one the shivers.

For a moment I thought of creating a diversion for everyone, embarrassing Monika, teasing her a little, but I gave up, mostly not to get her in trouble.

On the other hand, I felt strangely safe since I had understood they needed me here as an object of study and as long as I was able to keep the situation unchanged, I enjoyed a privileged immunity and freedom from the rigid behavior obligations, which here at TA were enormously amplified.

After lunch I felt relaxed and accompanied Monika to check her e-mail. She did this using the lobby terminals and since I couldn't be left alone I remained seated smoking while I sipped my coffee.

The morning meeting hadn't been, after all, such a challenge and none of the people present seemed sufficiently important or powerful or authoritative. I still had to understand who was on the other side of the surveillance video cameras. Even Monika seemed tranquil enough. But I had elaborated some curiosities and if I would have normally waited for her to finish with the terminal just to make her happy, in that moment I was out of my skin:

"Come outside please, I need to talk to you", I said.

"Not now!", she answered sharply.

"Okay, then I'll go outside for a walk by myself!".

"Wait!", she said, followed by a long series of unrepeatable swearing, not to me fortunately, but to the computer monitor.

"What happened?", I asked a little worried. She made an irritated gesture.

"Sit down and wait five minuted, please... then I'll explain", she said with clenched teeth without taking her eyes away from the screen.

"Okay, okay... am I in trouble?", I asked receiving a blazing look for an answer.

"Okay, I'll sit, but cool down or you'll get wrinkles".

And I tried to guess without success what could have made Monika lose control that way.

After twenty minutes and at my third cigarette, she disconnected from the computer, abruptly got up coming towards me and I instinctively got up. She walked past me and heading for the door gestured to follow her. Once outside, we proceeded for about ten meters, then Monika stopped, crossed her arms and looked at me.

"Will you tell me what happened?".

She sighed. "The mission to Moon-2 has already been set. We're leaving tomorrow", she said.

"Well... perfect! Where's the problem?", I asked a bit perplexed.

"There won't be another meeting for you this afternoon. I will brief you and we will receive our complete operating orders tomorrow during the flight", she continued.

"Wow! I can't wait to get on a 747 for an interplanetary flight", I said excitedly. "But I still don't see what the problem is".

She took a long breath.

"The problem? The problem is that we won't be alone. And the identity of the other person is not in my orders".

I thought about it for another moment.

"Excuse me Monika, maybe I'm a little more dazed than usual, but I still don't understand what the problem is".

"Nothing. Just a feeling. Call it "female intuition". There's something wrong and I can't understand what it is", she said looking up to the sky.

"Well, tomorrow we'll find out. The important thing is that they haven't separated us".

"I only hope they send an idiot and that he stays by himself during the flight", she said, "... but I can't get rid of this uneasy feeling".

I lit another cigarette searching my mind for something to calm her down but all I was able to come up with were the usual idiotic conventions.

"I've been convened alone this afternoon for the pre-mission briefing", she continued.

"And what does that mean?".

"Well, first of all that they want to speak with me and probably about you! I can't see the big urgency or importance of a mission on Moon-2, therefore I must suppose there is more than meets the eye", she replied. I thought about it for a moment.

"Have you ever been to Moon-2?".

"No , but I studied the documents of the "archeological" findings on the hidden hemisphere. There have been hundreds of expeditions and we also have a permanent base there".

"There have been findings also on Moon-2?", I asked. "... Like the monoliths site? How can it be?".

"A double Pyramid was discovered on Moon-2. There are no analogies with the site of the monoliths and TA considered it a much more important discovery until today".

"And is that where we're directed?" I asked.

"Where else?".

"Well, excuse me if I don't consider important the details on how and where the orders will be given in front of the opportunity of studying such a marvel" I said.

"Naturally you don't understand. You're not familiar with the internal procedures at TA and therefore unaware of certain subtleties. And then, you still have the enthusiasm of the rookie who has a new toy to play with", she answered. Actually, I did feel in seventh heaven.

I decided to change the subject first of all to get her mind off of everything that was worrying her and then because I wanted to satisfy my own curiosity about what had been my "interrogation" that morning.

"Tell me about this morning instead", I said.

"What is there to say? You saw it yourself! They were there to give you the third degree. They're convinced you're hiding something but they still don't know whether or not you're aware of it. When we arrived they had just finished with me", she said.

"And what did they want from you?", I asked.

"What did they want?! Well, first of all I suggested your transfer to TA. And then they observed us; they wanted to know if I had discovered something, then the same questions they asked you, in particular if something unusual had happened at the site of the monoliths. That beginning of spontaneous "dislocation" that you experimented yesterday definitely convinced them you are a subject with some surprises in store. Therefore, from their point of view, my intuition of having you brought here was good. On the other hand, they are pressured from the top to discover the mystery".

"Nothing wrong with that", I concluded.

"It depends. The certainty they have naturally induces them to look for a more effective way to obtain a result and as a result they could relieve me from this duty and hand it over to someone they consider more suitable and competent", she continued.

"Right!". I finally understood. "Actually it's all logical and clear. You're afraid they're looking for someone more suitable than yourself. I would have done the same if I'd been them. What can I do to make them continue to believe you're the right person?".

"For now we've been helped by yesterday's little discussion", she said smiling with her eyes.

Therefore she must had given the explanation I had given... interesting and predictable. I rubbed my cheek at the thought.

"Did I hurt you?", Monika asked, teasingly.

"Only my pride, they say in these cases. Well, it was a just cause, even if I doubt it was your motive at the time".

So, TA thought I had a weakness for Monika, and if they considered this a positive factor then they probably wanted to use what they thought was a weakness of mine to obtain their result. Maybe this would give me some time but sooner or later they would have understood this wasn't the right way.

I considered that in spite of the closeness and trust that Monika had so far shown me, for her own good, and of course for the benefit of the task she had to carry out, even if it still wasn't perfectly clear to me what my task was, I had to anyway, keep her in the dark as to the majority of my secret.

And I was right.

As though reading inside me Monika said:

"Whatever happens between us, you will never have to tell me what you're keeping inside".

"And what might ever happen between us?", I said jokingly.

"Ah! So you really want to make me angry! Why, don't you think I could have you falling at my feet if I did want it? Don't provoke me, I warn you".

"Monika, you wouldn't even have to work hard to make me crazy about you", I said tenderly. She blushed and lowered her eyes.

"But... ", I continued, "... I would never say anything, because I really have your safety at heart. More than anything else".

"Now that's much better. You've just managed to wriggle out of that one", she whispered.

Then she looked at me and her eyes were red and wet. A tear was forming in the corner of her left eye and she quickly wiped it with her hand. She had surely felt my sincerity and it seemed to be the first time in her life that someone honestly worried about her.

"Becoming aware of something is a big responsibility... ", I said, "... because being able to "see" can mean to be seen and consequently to be attacked".

She seemed very torn and continued staring at a point on the ground. Then she sniffed and blew her nose with a tissue. After that she looked at me again and said:

"You know, in this place there are some high level individuals, like the ones you met who emit that strange sea odor and can go inside your head. It's a terrible feeling, but it's impossible to resist it and if they should do it to me... ".

This was a really interesting and disturbing revelation.

"Are you saying they are telepathic?", I asked.

"I don't know. That is, I don't know if it can be called telepathy. It's a terrible thing, much more invasive. Like a possession, or like the loss of control typical of hypnotism and then you're left with a terrible side effect: a feeling of emptiness, of cold and total barrenness. One of them did it to me once soon after my arrival. A light probe, but one that devastated me. It is said that some people who were suspected of treason in the past went crazy after being probed by one of them and then... just vanished. Disappeared. This is one of the things that really scares me. And it should scare you too".

I felt a cold shiver down my spine; from Monika's description it seemed like a power very similar to the one attributed to the so called Potentiae at the time of the Anantrya.

There were really too many things to process and the idea of finding myself victim of such a great power was a variable that confused what little order I thought I had given to things.

Furthermore I realized I was also very worried for Monika. I suddenly realized she was running a much greater risk than I imagined and that she had always known it.

"Monika, I don't want you to risk so much. Look, I can take care of myself. Find a way to be relieved... find any kind of excuse and I will support it", I told her seriously.

"Don't even think about it, at this point I want to get to the end of this and I don't want to feel so empty anymore like before I met you. I will run all the risks that I must run", she answered just as seriously.

"Then I will find a way to have you sent away", I said.

"Don't you dare!", she said clenching her teeth while placing herself in front of me. "If you just try to do something like that I'll kill you with my own two hands!", she continued infuriated, "... things are as they are and they will go as they have to go, but I won't leave you".

"But nothing will change in the way of our friendship and when I am able, if I am able to get to the end of all this, I'll take you away from this place", I told her calmly. But in the meanwhile I remembered what the Visitor had told me about her and her destiny.

She took my arm and held it tightly digging her nails in my flesh and in her eyes there was a deep madness I had never seen before.

"Did you understand what I said? Don't you dare do anything! I decide and I have decided, period! I don't want to talk about it anymore! Understood?".

I took her hand, which at this point was making my arm bleed, and she gently let go and I held it in mine for a moment while I saw furious and powerful feelings cross her eyes. I slightly bowed and kissed her hand like a gentleman from the past and said:

"As you wish".

IV

When we went back inside the receptionist had a message for Monika who in the meanwhile had let go of her fiery emotions and put on her usual glacial and remote mask typical of TA personnel.

Walking me to my lodgings, she told me the meeting would have taken place in about an hour and since a member of the Command Staff would have been present, as of protocol, she had to wear her uniform.

She was a little nervous and visibly worried.

I watched her, from the window in my room, as she went towards the building of the meeting room. I had never seen or even imagined the formal Temporal Archives uniform. Its color was an opaque black and the material looked sufficiently soft to completely wrap the body as if it were all one piece. It had a high neck, open in the middle, similar to the Korean style and was completed by black low-healed boots between the military and motorcyclist style.

I saw other people heading towards the same building as Monika and that the male personnel had exactly the same kind of uniform.

A way of saying that the sexual gender of a human resource wasn't important and neither was the registered age and this was definitely an aspect of Temporal Archives and the Organization I had always considered positive.

Despite my awareness of the ever present video surveillance, I had the desire to meditate to empty my mind from the whirl of information, which in my present state, I wasn't able to put in order nor to report. I put on a comfortable cotton sweatsuit and closed the curtains.

I chose the semi-lotus position with the left leg on top and a rectangular breathing pattern to better channel the energy along the spinal chord, ideal condition to free the mind and favor focusing.

After a while I lost all perception of my body and time.

I heard a kind of far away voice resonate in my head. It was monotonous, imploring and transmitted a strong devotional principle. An image started taking shape in my mind: it was a hospital room.

Wherever it was, it was night and the room was dark, except for the moonlight and the street lights which filtered through a window, but I could see every detail.

The room was precarious with other two twin size beds occupied by sleeping bodies on the left of the one in front of me. I could distinctly perceive a weak, irregular energetic and luminous field around each one of them and I felt a call from the one on the bed in front of me; it was an old person and apparently very ill. I knew, though I don't know how, that a fine thread separated him from death. He wasn't sleeping but his eyes were closed and his lips were moving; he was praying.

The vision was becoming clearer and clearer and I feared for a moment that another dislocation was taking place which would have been spotted by the surveillance cameras which would have in turn made an alarm go off.

I tried to visualize myself on Earth-2 in my room but wasn't able to. It was as though I were imprisoned by a spell or a magician was summoning me almost as if summoning a demon.

It was useless to resist so I waited for the events to unfold. The ailing old man was there on the bed with his eyes closed and his lips were whispering something.

I realized I heard his voice all around me: it was a prayer accompanied by a strong emotion. He was asking to die, speaking to The Lord, (oh Lord...) he was asking to be freed from the flesh and maybe something else, but only this request resounded inside and all around me at that moment.

Years later, thinking back at that moment, I realized that the retrieval process of my Energy of Influence triggered off by the Visitor in Corsica had, for the first time, made me conscious of a function that was in part the reason for the existence of the Eternals, and that only the request sequence of the old ailing man that I was able to hear so many years before, was part of the recollection spell which had brought me to that place.

Yet, at that time, I was confused and for a moment felt like a spirit evoked by a medium and forced to act against its own will.

With the passing of seconds the room became more and more "real" around me and also the prayer of the ailing man, until I felt I was completely there and saw the old man suddenly open his eyes, yellowed and blurred by the illness which devoured him. At first I saw an amazed look on his face and then extremely moved; I didn't know what he was seeing in that moment but whatever it was he seemed ravished.

I felt a sentiment come out of me which, arriving to him, sounded like a: "your prayer has been heard. Now you will return Home".

The hands of the ailing man joined and I heard him whisper words of thanks. I saw myself make a gesture in the space above him. In that point, a sort of fracture formed, and a luminous ellipse came out of the man's abdomen and entered the fracture.

For one very brief moment my attention went towards that which dwelt beyond and I barely managed to perceive a shape which was probably only a weak way of my mind of interpreting something that couldn't be interpreted. What I saw was a center made of emptiness and infinite wave shapes which moved from there as though they were flying.

I felt my mind burn at that sight and felt that if I had had the strength to keep my attention there I would have gone mad or would have lost myself forever.   But as mysteriously as the fracture had appeared it disappeared and I felt as though I were moving at an incredible speed, so much so that the impact flung my body against the wall and I fell on my bed belly down. I saw the lights come on by themselves in the room and I heard a noise on the outside, like an alarm: a few seconds and two big men from security came in and walked towards me and in the meanwhile I had sat up on the bed.

I was sweaty and shaking. One of them remained at the door while the other came close to the bed. The one at the door had a kind of radio with an earphone and I heard him say they were "on the spot and checking the situation, stand by", to whoever was on the other side.

The guard next to me asked me if everything was okay and I said yes and that I had only had a nightmare with some probable sleepwalking and that it was normal for me.

The one on the radio reported; I saw them insert a device with a weak blue light to one of the electric sockets near the door and they told me never to take it out "for your own security, they said. Right! For my own security and in spite of my privacy.

Now they would have always seen me, even in the dark.

V

Since there was no use or purpose continuing to wait in my room I got dressed, carefully choosing an outfit compatible with the uniforms at Temporal Archives.

I took a Korean style white shirt (I didn't have a black one) without the button with a raised shiny white embroidery on the collar; a pair of comfortable jeans and black motorcycle boots that almost came up to my knees, with an inside sideways zipper, and since the sky was overcast I also wore a light long black raincoat with shoulder pads.

I left and arrived to the reception where I found Bjorn; I told him I wanted to go on a tour of the base and if there was someone who could go with me.

He said that, according to new orders, it was no longer necessary for me to move around escorted but gave me a beeper and told me I always had to have it with me at least when I was outside of the buildings.

"I'd like to have a horse", I ventured.

He typed something on the terminal and after a moment he told me there was no problem and that I could take number thirteen from the stables.

"Can I leave the Base?", I asked while I was at it. And once again he said "no problem" as long as I tried not to get lost and I always kept the beeper with me.

I couldn't understand what might have happened in just a few hours that I had regained so much freedom of movement but decided it was best to seize the moment, before someone changed their minds, quickly thanked Bjorn and rushed to the stables.

Number thirteen was a beautiful black Arabian with a white diamond shaped spot between its eyes; the stable worker saddled it and also gave me a bag with water, dried meat and a first aid kit.

Trotting towards the exit I passed in front of the building which had swallowed Monika hours before and asked myself how the meeting was going. I felt some apprehension for her but it was useless to worry about it now.

I passed the exit trotting, going deeply in the forest and abandoning the asphalted road I had arrived on the first time. In any case, that road ended a few kilometers from the base. I thought I might stop somewhere to see the incoming and outgoing vehicles to and from Earth-1 but didn't want to push my luck too much and maybe again lose the possibility of moving freely, therefore I went into the forest in a casual direction without looking for anything in particular, only a clearing where to stop and breath some fresh air.

At some point, maybe after two hours en route, I noticed a small distortion among the trees, similar to the one that Monika had showed me on the way back from the first excursion.

For a moment I thought it was the same passage she had showed me but immediately discarded that hypothesis in that the direction I had taken was completely different and therefore this phenomenon had to be different too.

I wondered if the instability characteristics were the same and where it led to. Maybe this passage point had never been discovered, not even by the scrupulous personnel of Temporal Archives. In brief, I wanted to observe it better, closer and while I was there experiment with it a little.

I looked around to see if I had been followed but I was alone in the forest stirred by the wind.

Moving slowly closer I could see the distortion more and more clearly; it looked like a tear in the air as if a very hot and invisible fire were burning right in that spot. I also heard a barely perceptible and low toned sound, like the one that precedes an earthquake; I focused my attention on that spot trying to see beyond it but nothing could be seen beyond the disturbance waves in the air, in a barely marked oval area at least three meters high and two wide. I picked up a big branch from the ground and from that distance threw it towards the distortion. When the branch reached the distortion I saw the prismatic effect which, from what I had heard, precedes a dislocation; I saw the shape of the branch expand while it lost consistency and disappear immediately after. Then, for some reason, the low sound coming from the fracture increased in loudness, so much that it could be distinctly heard; the horse behind me whinnied in fright and becoming restless started beating its hoofs on the ground, but when I went near it to calm it down it charged me, galloping and I had to move out of its path; it threw itself right into the fracture disappearing like the branch a few moments before.

I stood there inane for some time. I couldn't run after it!

Although I was struck by the strong curiosity of knowing where the animal had gone to: on Earth-1 or on one of the other planets? I imagined for a moment possible witnesses who saw a mad horse appear out of nowhere.

In the meanwhile, the noise had ceased, going back to its original tone. I found myself on foot and not too sure to be able to find my way back. In any case, this time I would have been able to give an explanation for what had happened.

I tried to find my bearings and singing The Prophet's Song by Queen started walking in the direction I thought the most probable, hoping for the first time, despite the privacy, that Temporal Archives had kept an eye on me and would come to my rescue.

VI

After about half an hour the beeper began to beep. I took it and looked at at the screen on which I read "stay where you are, I'm coming to get you". I smiled knowing it was Monika.

About an hour later I heard the echo of a horse's gallop which seemed to come from all directions. A moment later Monika appeared, still in the uniform she had gone to the meeting with, riding a spotted black and white horse. As she advanced I thought she looked like a super hero from the comics dressed that way and I enjoyed the irony that instead of being the gentle dame to be saved by the fearless knight it was just the opposite, something which again confirmed that Temporal Archives had never taken its eyes off me.

She stopped the horse in front of me and for a while we stared at each other without saying anything; I felt like laughing but she shook her head as if saying "you're always getting yourself in some trouble".

"Come on, get on!", she said holding out her hand to me. I got on behind her and trotting we headed for TA.

Neither one of us said anything during almost the whole trip back. I caught myself thinking that it was worth getting lost only to live this moment so close to Monika, like one single body. I had the feeling she was reacting to my emotion and was purposely delaying our arrival. Then I had the intuition that maybe what I was feeling, was in reality her emotions, finally understanding what it meant to be empathic. I was sure it was her, actively using her ability on me and she was doing it on purpose so we wouldn't need cold words between us. So I held her a bit more tightly to make her understand that I understood and with a faint movement she moved even closer to me. I heard her sigh.

"Don't think about getting away with it so easily", she said sweetly. TA was close now.

"If truth be told, you enjoy saving me", I said.

"You always worry me. As though there weren't already enough problems".

"Problems?".

"Not now", she concluded. "... We'll talk about it later".

VII

We left the horse at the TA stables and headed for the Headquarters.

"What have you got on?", she asked as if she had just noticed.

"I was trying to copy the Temporal Archives dress uniform. I mean, look at you. You look like the dark version of Wonder Woman!".

"Don't you like how I look in uniform?", she asked offended.

"On the contrary! That's why I wanted to conform. Anyway, you look good in black".

"Good, so I won't have to redo my wardrobe", she said.

She was stalling on the most important subject and I couldn't understand why.

"Would you please enlighten me now?", I asked.

She sighed.

"We're leaving tomorrow morning, after breakfast".

"Okay, thanks for the information. But I want to know about the meeting".

"It was long, never-ending, stressful and I'm very irritated".

"I'd like to know how it went in detail, if you don't mind, and not have to drag it out of you".

She grumbled and stopped, crossing her arms on her chest.

"One of the Command Staff members intervened, like I already told you. The result: the others competed in asking me embarrassing questions trying to prove I'm not suitable to manage your situation... the typical competitiveness of the Organization is multiplied by a thousand here. There are people who would kill to be noticed by the Command Staff even for just a look of appreciation. And at this point everyone understood that you are an important mission and a priority for the bosses".

"What an honor...", I said without emotion.

"Everyone was ready to give me a good dressing-down Even my commander, that invertebrate", she continued.

"I suppose you came out well. Or not?".

"You don't care if they withdraw me and do away with me, do you? You only care to be able to go on without problems", she said resentfully.

"I care that no harm is done to you. I don't need to use you. You are really important to me because you are "you" and not because you work here", I said seriously, "... and of course I also have my own research to carry out".

"Well, I've already told you you won't get rid of me so easily. In fact, you won't, period!", she said defiantly.

"So, they've confirmed you to the mission. It sounds like some good news, or not? It's what you wanted! Where's the problem?".

"We will be followed, step by step. We will always be under a magnifying glass and we won't be allowed any false steps".

"It's okay. Now we know it and we'll be careful and professional as always".

"A very high ranking officer from the Command Staff will come with us", she said at last.

I took a deep breath. Therefore, a delegate of the enemy by our side. One of those individuals who terrorized even Monika and had such invasive mental abilities.

"Everything will go as it should".

"You sure know how to put a girl at ease", she said in a deep and ironic tone. "Even just the thought of having one of them so close gives me the chills".

"Are you afraid he'll play one of his tricks?".

"That for sure... and then I'm afraid she'll catch on and... ", she left the sentence hanging.

"Do you already know who'll be with us?", I asked.

"Unfortunately yes and this worries me too. Her name is Amelia".

"Is it a problem because she's a woman?", I asked amused by the idea.

"You idiot! It's a problem because it was she who recruited me for Temporal Archives and it was she who submitted me to the mental probe which upset me so much when I arrived on Earth-2. And it's a problem because she could extort your secret manipulating you or take it directly from your head, or hurt you. And because she's a woman and you could discover that for someone like you she is the perfect partner", she answered with a mixture of emotions which summed up conveyed great frustration.

"I will not allow her to play with my head", I said, trying to calm her.

"You say it but you don't know what you're dealing with. My description of the mental probe didn't in any way give the least idea of the horror of the experience. You'd better never find yourself in that position!".

"Okay. Let's say then that I'll try to never find myself in the position of undergoing one. As for the other thing, trust me... you have no reason to be jealous".

"Because you haven't seen her yet! Anyway, as I've already told you: if you exclude me I'll kill you. I swear!".

"I told you not to worry. Anyone from the Command Staff is an enemy and must be eliminated. Clear?".

"We'll see tomorrow. She will brief you in flight and I'll be there only to assist", she concluded.

"The important thing is that you be there".

She delicately stroked my hand.

"Let's go now; the others want to see you before night".

VIII

The meeting with Monika's other colleagues confirmed what she had said; ambition oozed from behind those cold and remote appearances and maybe even their deep envy, including her apparently very cordial commanding officer who, while declaring the importance one of his agents of proven professionalism (that is Monika) had for the department, with little imperceptible and likewise eloquent signals, showed a profound hate for her, the desire to see her fail and that had it been for him the situation would have already been solved and Monika assigned to sorting out mail if not even discharged from her department.

Monika was impeccable in her interpretation which matched her to her colleagues answering to the point with her words and by the subliminal signs which represented the real domain of their communication.

I, on the other hand and unlike the people present, was enjoying myself and tried to emphasize my couldn't-care-less and disrespectful attitude given that at this point it was clear to me that no one there counted anything in the geopolitics of the situation.

Surely Monika appreciated what little humiliation I was able to inflict on her colleagues, who would have never suspected of being in front of the biggest threat in all their miserable future. Yet, lowering my mask a bit too much to attack them I expressed what lie in my heart and realized that even Monika was a little frightened.

ENDLESS SKY

There wasn't a ticket for Moon-2, only a small perforated plastic plate. There wasn't even a customs or a duty free, only internal security guards who checked all the passengers (as if a subversive infiltration were possible in that world) and after having accurately searched us showed us our plane.

Monika told me the flight would last thirty-two hours at a speed of about ten-thousand miles per hour and that the innovative propulsion system of the jet we had been assigned, due to the presence of one of the Command Staff members, was considered top secret and could not be object of any form of curiosity.

Having taken care of the formalities we boarded by way of a stairway on wheels which was brought near the back door of the plane which was much bigger than standard. When it flew, some of the Command Staff personnel probably enjoyed all the comforts and a presidential treatment.

Well, I surely preferred my first trip to another world to be like this rather than in a second class seat at the end of the plane and near an emergency exit.

Monika was very elegant for the occasion, probably according to protocol for special flights; she wore a suit with the same Korean style collar, a skirt just above the knee and high heels, all rigorously black. She had done her hair in a pony tail and had just a hint of make-up under a pair of thin sunglasses.

I didn't recognize her at first; hers was not the classic beauty, but rather particular and charismatic, made of measured and conscious movements though fluid and natural. I wasn't able to find imperfections in that woman and suddenly I was conscious that she was my weak spot and in the solitude of my cabin I was taken by anguish; if someone had perceived this they could have taken advantage of this weakness and Monika could have suffered just because of how I felt deep down inside.

In that moment I didn't know if she felt it and if someone else could perceive it through her, but if they had used it against me I was no longer sure I would be able to be emotionally detached and let her suffer; but it was too late now to convince her to give that mission up and leave it to some other idiot, someone I could have used and crushed at the right moment.

If only she had listened to me when we had spoken about it the day before... If I had realized then how important she really was to me, beyond the professional circumstances or the simple confederate friendship, maybe I would have spoken to her more honestly and maybe she would have understood. But I was too focused on the future, too busy planning and calculating, to realize what was happening inside of me and now my lack of awareness could cost me dearly.

Anyway, it was already too late; the die had been cast, the challenge had started and for all the flight and the duration of the mission I couldn't afford to make any mistakes, nor to show my feelings especially with the Command Staff representative.

I emptied my bags and sat on the little twin size bed breathing deeply for a few minutes: then I heard movements outside and the doors of the plane being closed. There was a knock at the door: it was one of the assistants who asked me to go to the take-off area and fasten my seat belt.

Given my hesitation the assistant informed me smiling that the alternative was to become hamburger meat given the speed which would be reached during take-off.

The seats and the passengers were in a row and while we approached the assistant showed me two meeting rooms, the bar, which included a little restaurant, other lodging rooms and work areas with access terminals to the Temporal Archives Mainframe.

Heading for my seat I felt a strange tension and also a strange sickness to my stomach as a student at his first exam.

It had been a long time since I had felt this way and was sure it was due to the presence of the mysterious Amelia or by the mental image I had of her or maybe also by the sense of vulnerability brought about in me by the feeling I had discovered having for Monika.

They say it never rains but it pours or that problems always come in pairs like shoes and this seemed like a well guessed metaphor: my dearest friend on one side and my biggest enemy on the other, only physically close.

When the assistant showed me to my seat I saw there were four other people already seated in the take off area and one of them was Monika; seated next to one of the portholes she didn't turn around when I arrived.

I was in the center of the first row of three seats with Monika to my left and the right seat still empty. After some minutes I heard some confusion beyond the door and I noticed that even the people around me had become imperceptibly agitated.

The door suddenly opened and another assistant entered standing at attention beside the seat at my right.

A woman with long dark hair and dark eyes, very refined and sophisticated, apparently around thirty, also dressed in a black suit entered and everyone stood up. I followed suit immediately even if a bit late.

She sat down and when the assistant closed the door and all the other passengers sat back down she held out her hand to me with a disarming smile.

"Hello", she simply said. "... I'm Amelia, and it's a pleasure to meet you".

I was taken aback for a moment before I was able to answer stuttering, "The pleasure is mine".

At that moment I understood what Monika had meant by "you say that because you haven't seen her yet".

The message to get ready for take-off arrived just in time to save me from the embarrassment I felt. Now I had some time until reaching orbit to compose myself and take control of my mental functions and add the Amelia factor to the already big amount of information I had to elaborate; instinctively I looked towards Monika pretending to look outside the porthole: she was still wearing her sunglasses but I could feel her eyes on me like blazing coals.

I winked at her and half smiled which I hoped would make her relax and then we took off.

II

The acceleration kept me nailed to the back of my seat while the pressure variation forced me to continually compensate.

After about half an hour, while we continued going up, the acceleration diminished and I was able to relax a little. I thought about the obscure figure seated to my right. She was refined, of moderate beauty but noble and emanated a natural authority, like a young first lady so aware of her power she didn't have to prove anything. I observed her out of the corner of my eye and saw that she didn't flaunt anything if not simplicity and a touch of ingenuity which made it easier for her to relate to her subordinates.

I asked myself how this woman could be the same cruel, inexorable and alien creature described by Monika. Is it possible that she was able to exert such a great mental power to have upset even Monika after a light probe?

I had to try to get rid of all my doubts quickly and keep in mind that despite the appearances I had to trust Monika's judgment who surely had much more experience than me.

Once out of orbit and headed for Moon-2 we would have surely started with the mission briefing and I wanted to prepare myself, besides not making false moves, also to take advantage of the time I had with a representative of the great enemy, to try to better understand its general nature. But I felt a deep anxiety knowing of this power Amelia had also because I didn't have a clue as to what it was or how it worked nor if I would be able to resist it or fight it.

Maybe it was so invasive that its use left no memory and Monika and I had already been victims.

Naturally it wasn't so. The kind of power Amelia and her species had was frighteningly destructive and its touch deprived its victims of their will and often of their mental stability, but at that moment I didn't know a lot of things and I found it really very difficult to face Amelia as if she were a monster given that that was the last thing she looked like.

In fact she inspired a little tenderness and the chivalrous feeling towards a defenseless princess. Of course it was all part of her strategy. Her appearance was like a mask and in a place where everyone wore a wolf mask maybe the wolf wore a lamb mask.

While I thought these thoughts, Amelia was there, apparently tranquil, seeming to observe an indefinite point in front of her, maybe trying to appear deep in thought, even if I could perceive that she was acutely present and aware of what was around her.

Even the little movements of her body seemed measured to guide one's attention like an accomplished mentalist would do to take the attention away from what he was really doing.

Her fingers, which casually drummed on the border of the seat; her right leg crossed casually swaying her foot... it all seemed too normal; I felt a bit frustrated trying to find something that I didn't like about her, something wrong that would activate my internal "red alert".

Nothing.

Then they announced we were out of orbit and that we could get up. And the gravity was normal again.

It had to be a really special vehicle to exhibit such technology that surely wasn't of the Earth.

III

Besides Amelia and Monika, two other characters were present at the briefing. They were part of the Scientific Staff which was in turn part of the branch of activities followed by Amelia for Temporal Archives and its top managers. The meeting room table was round and Amelia sat on the other side with her assistants side by side.

Monika to my left with her usual notepad to take notes and other papers; also Amelia's assistants exhibited notepads with TA in gold relief and "Special Management Staff" right under that just to show the difference between their functions, near the top, and that of all the others.

But, by the way Amelia treated them, they seemed to have little to feel special about: they were like slaves and the few times she referred to or addressed them it was with a cold and contemptuous tone.

The meeting began with the usual exchange of courtesies; Amelia asked me smiling how my period of adaptation had been and I told her I was still a little disconcerted and that Monika's help had been precious.

Now that I had her in front of me I started to see something of what Monika had tried to make me understand. Through her mask, Amelia filtered out how she felt about the people around her, even if imperceptibly; the rare times she gazed at Monika or at her assistants it was as though she were looking at some insects, annoying but inevitable and her awareness that she could have crushed them at any time if she had felt like it, was perceptible.

While I intensely observed her, I noticed that when she spoke to me, from that deep chill, real and not worn like a mask, which lay at the bottom of her soul lacking the least spark of humanity, it was in a totally different way: as if she were in front of a peculiar zoo specimen and behind that I sensed an obscure hate similar, but even deeper, than the racial hate. But hate is a feeling deeply tied to fear and therefore I deduced that Amelia, or something terrible inside her feared what she thought I could represent.

Unfortunately, at that time, I had no idea what she saw when she looked at me.

The formalities ended and the briefing started. One of Amelia's assistants passed me a folder with the protocol "Management Staff" on it full of documents.

"This is the mission material including documents and surveys. There are also the orders but they are rather generic, a formality in that the real mission in this case will depend exclusively on the events which could break out when we arrive in proximity of the archeological site", she said in a perfect English with no trace of an accent.

I waited for her to continue.

"As you can see by the photographic material, the site we are going to includes a double Pyramid with what appears to be four monoliths, one at each corner. These structures are made of a very particular metal, unknown on Earth, which comes from a family we have called metamatter. Whoever built this incredible monument had access to such an advanced technology even compared to "us". The purpose and function of the structure are still unknown despite all the effort and resources we have spent to solve the mystery. Nevertheless, we keep it under constant observation exactly like the site Monika showed you on Earth-2 and like the area of and around the island on your planet of origin called Corsica".

Amelia was using a definitely particular language and I noticed that even her two assistants, though trying to keep a totally respectful attitude, had to find it strange as if they had never heard her speak that way before.

Monika kept her eyes respectfully lowered but I had noticed, by the tension on her face, that her level of alarm had steeply increased.

I, on the other hand, was at my first experience with such a high positioned person and all I felt was the desire to ask questions.

Of course I had to expect that being a speaker of such depth, Amelia was consciously leading my curiosity exactly in the direction she wanted. Yet, playing her game could mean the possibility of gaining important information.

"I would like to ask you a few preliminary questions which have no direct connection with the purpose of the mission".

"Go ahead and ask anything you'd like", she confidently answered.

I paused for a few seconds, also to allow myself the time to adequately choose my words, but understood that it was necessary to cast the stone in the pond and see what happened.

"When you say "we", who are you referring to?", I asked.

"Don't disappoint me with idiotic questions", she answered without changing expression.

A big chill came over the room from which I deduced that everyone present, Amelia and myself excluded, felt a great embarrassment.

Maybe they feared she would get angry, and despite my incurable curiosity, neither I wished to experiment this experience, not for now at least.

"Okay, I'll rephrase the question. Before continuing I would like you to kindly confirm what your introductory words underlined relative to the nature of Temporal Archives and in particular to the Command Staff which you represent. Not because I didn't understand, but simply because I would like there to be no shady areas or interpretable uncertainties as to who will benefit what from this or other undertakings where my presence is required".

With this I also wanted to clarify that, as far as I was concerned, I assumed having power of choice, not so much as my participation to the mission, which I could simply be ordered to do, but on how it was carried out and most of all on the final outcome. By the micro reactions of Amelia's assistants I noticed their dismay in seeing that someone dared to address their master that way. I couldn't see Monika but imagined and wanted to imagine that instead she rooted for me and enjoyed a little revenge for what Amelia had done to her in the past.

Amelia seemed amused by the twist the briefing was taking. Anyway, we had some time before our arrival to Moon-2 so maybe she too needed a distraction.

"What exactly do you want to know?", she asked seriously.

"Who decides strategies and makes decisions at Temporal Archives which you are a representative of. The affiliations of the Command Staff and the beneficiaries of everything that is produced at the Organization. In a few words, who are you and where do you come from and the reason for the existence of the Organization and Temporal Archives and last – but not least – what is your objective".

Putting her lamb mask back on I saw her blush and smile slightly embarrassed lowering her eyes like a little girl caught red-handed. It was incredible to witness how skillfully she managed the signals she launched to the environment around her.

In the meanwhile I took the opportunity to casually move my chair, which fortunately was on wheels, a little further from Monika to be able to include her too in my field of vision.

Amelia noticed the movement but probably or fortunately interpreted it as my way of distancing myself from them: I saw her cast an imperceptible glance at Monika who slightly shrugged as though to say she herself didn't understand why I had done it.

"Well", she said with innocent resignation "... of course you have every right in wanting to clarify the entire picture and believe me... I want to do it and I would ask you to be honest and forthcoming with me because we find ourselves in front of an extremely serious situation which represents a real danger for all of us. You know how much security and secrecy there is in our Organization and believe me when I tell you that you are the first external person with whom we decided to share our mission completely".

It could have been a statement aimed at making me more penetrable, striking at my ego and making me feel part of something bigger and important and therefore a way of telling me that I was special to her. I noticed that everyone, including Monika, were very alarmed for the twist the conversation was taking and I couldn't understand why.

I didn't say anything and waited for her to continue. Once again she exhibited a smile that was really more a sign of power, able to disarm whoever it was aimed to and arouse jealousy in who wasn't; that was the first time I realized that there really were symbolic stimuli not recorded at the conscious level by the five "official" senses which were the representation of something much bigger than the physical world, and that those who used these stimuli appealed to a power from a superior realm which had a direct influence on whoever found themselves "victim" or testimony to it.

Who hasn't at least once endured the power of something that "bewitched" them in one way or another? Of course, most of these "connections to power" or ways of using power, carried out or endured unconsciously, always tended to be explained in a thousand "rational" ways but always wrongly.

I shivered at the idea of what one who had a conscious mastery of it could achieve and most of all at the idea that Amelia was probably one of these "special" people.

Power, like energy, is not right or wrong, good or bad; it is neutral. Power and energy exist only to have a master and he who doesn't know how to be one becomes a victim of them. The only real shame of who has power is to be afraid of using it and in front of me there was a person who was proving to know the access mechanisms to power and who, so far, showed no fear in using it.

The fear of the people present was probably dictated in part by Amelia's behavior, which I guessed to be odd according to their experience, in part due to the fear of hearing information which later, only for the fact of knowing such information, would have put them in the dangerous condition of "knowing too much" and being therefore treated as dangerous for security at the end of the mission and handled as thus. Monika confirmed this to me when she intervened:

"Excuse me Amelia, I can wait outside if you wish so that you can speak with him freely".

Amelia became serious and said:

"No Monika, I want you to stay to be able to advise him at best during the mission".

Monika was definitely apprehensive and a wave of desperation crossed her face for a moment.

"But I would,'t want to become a security risk... if there is another way..." she said in a bit of a shaky voice.

"Don't worry about that... ", Amelia said as though it were something with no importance. "... You started all this and now you don't want to get to the end of it? I am perfectly proficient in when and how to reveal what to whom. Therefore, stay in your seat and let's move on".

I could have intervened saying that Monika wasn't necessary to the mission and that she was in fact in my way, to come to her rescue, but was sure that whatever I said in her favor or against her would have showed my weakness and therefore said nothing observing the people present, absently leafing through the pages of the mission dossier.

Monika looked helpless and frightened. Once again Amelia turned to me with an expression between serious and worried which evidenced a little vertical wrinkle she had between her perfectly kept eyebrows.

"We are the Emissaries of a civilization which took care of the planet Earth and of its race for many thousands of years. One could say that we are on a permanent mission in planet Earth's system in what, using the language of the Organization is called "Garrison Mission".

She paused and unexpectedly got up from her chair and turned towards the portholes turning her shoulders to everyone. She looked like anything but an alien. As answering my thought she turned around and continued.

"We are not genetically and biologically very different from you".

"I would say that so far as appearance you're not at all", I remarked.

"In fact. This is because in a remote past we had common origins and one could say that you are our distant descendants. But we're not concerned about history now. What is important instead is the fact that your Solar System and your planet in particular which was, in the past, ground of a devastating conflict also gave origin to a threat which we have been trying to contain for thousands of years and still haven't found the way to defeat it".

As she spoke she also paid attention to her movements like an experienced lecturer. When she resumed she slowly headed towards Monika who remained motionless with her eyes fixed in front of her.

"The missions which you carried out recently and the sites you visited on our account, in our opinion, are intimately related to this threat. Of course I also include what was found on Moon-2, object of this mission", Amelia continued.

While she spoke she stopped exactly behind Monika who was petrified and asking for help with her eyes. I couldn't help giving her a look of encouragement and of course Amelia noticed it and smiled viciously.

In this way she was silently telling me that I had been naive or incautious but at that moment I couldn't imagine what she could do with this information she had obtained inducing me to uncover myself even if only subliminally. Everything was really strange: had it not been for Monika's words from the day before and for the body language of those present which conveyed terror and uneasiness, Amelia probably would have been able to deceive me playing with me like she was doing.

I was also sure that she was basically telling me the truth. The truth is always a formidable weapon and it is sufficient to modify a few subjective details to make it lethal.

For example, Amelia spoke of a threat and there was no doubt that from her point of view she was telling the truth. But I was convinced that she was perfectly conscious that the threat she spoke of was already in contact with me and her strategy was probably that of planting the seed of doubt to weaken me or even to push me to change sides.

But she was also preparing a plan B and maybe even a plan C and her aim incidentally coincided with mine: getting to know the enemy.

She put a hand on Monika's shoulder who I saw shiver silently, then went on:

"We are convinced that these findings, and maybe also the fragment of Mars which fell in Antarctica, are the product of this dark force which is our enemy, or that the solution to their mystery can, in some way, help us to preserve planet Earth and its inhabitants", she concluded.

"Why, in all these centuries and still now, have you concealed yourselves to the inhabitants of Earth? Why, if we are the same race, the people on Earth are so much less developed and, as proved by history, has followed such a slow evolutionary path? Basically we should all be part of a great nation which occupies many planets and solar systems. Yet, who lives on Earth is rigidly kept in the dark as to what you have revealed to me as being the reality of things and basically who lives on Earth can't leave it. Don't get me wrong. I'm sure there are good reasons for this situation, though if possible, I'd like to know them. For example, the Majestic program itself, besides being recent from a historical point of view, doesn't reflect the reality of what you say, in particular relative to the EBE races registered up to now".

She seemed to think about it for a moment then slowly took her hand away from Monika's shoulder who relaxed a bit and slowly headed towards me.

"First of all the fact that we remain concealed from the Earth's population in general doesn't mean we are concealed from those who manage the power of the nations that count. Secondly, you must know that the history taught on Earth is not a reliable source", she said coming closer.

"Many centuries ago we noticed that Earth is a very particular place... one could say, special. But its peculiarity has also made it vulnerable to forces that not even we are able to control. We couldn't risk that the seed of these malicious forces have the possibility of spreading to other worlds under our dominion.

So, thousands of years ago we made a drastically resolute decision. I'll confess that the first option considered was even the destruction of the planet or of the entire Solar System. We can do it and theoretically the explosion of the Sun would have cleansed everything and canceled the seed of danger for all our worlds. If this was not done was simply because we assessed that there was a real possibility that the destruction of Earth or of the entire system could unleash just what we are fighting against, ending up freeing the threat from what keeps it bound to this place and consequently allowing its uncontrolled diffusion.

Imagine if a very tiny village on earth were the center of a terrible epidemic, extremely infective, which if leaked out would risk contaminating the whole planet.

The most logical solution would be to quarantine the village and then to completely sterilize it. Now imagine the possibility that this epidemic, subjected to a destructive energy, could become even more powerful and could no longer be controlled. Now, this is briefly the situation we had to face".

"Therefore Earth is in a state of indefinite quarantine", I concluded.

"Practically, yes. And it will remain this way until we find the nature of the threat which inhabits it and find a solution", Amelia answered.

"I understand", I said.

And in fact I perfectly understood the logic of her reasoning. My instinct continued sending me the red alert while logic told me that maybe she and who she represented might be right. She was surely convincing but I needed more information and maybe also to recover that memory that the Visitor told me had been buried at birth.

"I still don't understand though why you keep the inhabitants of Earth in a condition of cultural darkness, unaware of our origins, lacking any memory of race and a history of the planet built to strengthen this condition", I insisted.

In the meanwhile Amelia had arrived right behind me. I felt her presence but didn't turn around while Monika looked alternatively to me and to her.

Come on, I thought, don't lose control now, but Monika obviously couldn't hear me.

"The answer is always the same. This threat, this disease..." - the tone of her voice was contemptuous as she pronounced these two words, as if the representation in her mind of what she was talking about repulsed her - "... is a phenomenon that manifests itself in a different dominion from the organic or material one. It is a magnetic disease, an exotic form of energy and causes desires, folly, violence and other dangerous expressions for a community. We have even discarded the proposal which contemplated sterilizing all the inhabitants of Earth, in fear that this solution release the threat from this planet leaving it free to spread around", she answered.

"In fact I was asking myself why you hadn't tried with sterilization", I said.

"In so far as the Majestic program...", she continued, "... the data we've gathered are real but are not about us. The program is important because it enables us to monitor intrusions in this quarantined place by other races from the stars. We too have our enemies and many know that this is a very special place for us and some also know why. In time there have been expeditions by other civilizations to seize samples of the Earth's inhabitants in the attempt of finding our same answer and isolate the threat and use it as a weapon against us. The Majestic program, which is much bigger than what you might have perceived, has been operating for a long time to detect and neutralize external enemy expeditions or also casual visitors in order to preserve Earth and contain the threat".

"Everything you have said is perfectly logical", I said.

"Well then!", Amelia rested both her hands on my shoulders. The touch was light while she gently pressed with her fingers causing me a shiver of pleasure which I wasn't completely able to hide.

Leaning down she brought her face next to my cheek allowing me to distinctly smell the sea scent I had already smelled a few days earlier and that even Monika had described.

"You are very special to Us", Amelia whispered. "We think this unknown threat is interested in you".

"I would be an illogical choice if this threat were led by an intelligent life form. If I were you I would try to implicate one of the members of the Garrison mission, that is, one of You. Why aren't you influenced?", I asked.

"The members of the mission like myself have a natural immunity. Yet, not even we can leave this system to avoid the risk of being contaminated. I have been on Earth since the beginning of the mission, that is about twelve thousand years ago", Amelia replied.

This took me by surprise more than anything which had been said up to then. I tried to instinctively turn around to look at her but she gently but forcefully stopped me placing her hand on my cheek.

I noticed on Monika's face the beginning of a murderous look as her face turned slightly red. I was convinced Amelia was behaving that way just to provoke her and maybe confirm what she had already understood, but she was doing something more. She was showing us her psychological superiority and also that she knew that Monika and I were each others weak spots.

In fact, once she had performed her demonstration, she took her hand away from my cheek brushing against it so as not to miss the opportunity of causing me a new shiver and went to sit down.

"I know a woman shouldn't reveal her age. But I also know I don't look it, thanks!", she said as if to answer my chivalrous circumstantial comment.

Of course she had also excluded that I would ask her questions about the preservation of her body. I decided it was a question for which I could obtain an answer some other time.

"Well... ", she said switching back to her professional tone, "... I believe that after this introduction we can take a little break and prepare for lunch where we will discuss our mission on Moon-2. My assistants will help you get oriented".

Monika and I started to get up to dismiss ourselves from Amelia but she said, as cold as the sidereal space:

"Monika, stay another few minutes if you don't mind".

Monika slowly sat back into her seat, not before giving me a lost glance. We didn't seem to have much of a choice. I said goodbye and left the room while an assistant closed the door behind me. When I returned to my room I used the bathroom but wasn't able to stay there waiting. So I went to the bar and ordered a coffee.

The meeting room was there in sight and if nothing else I would have been able to intercept Monika when she came out. I wasn't able not to be worried for her.

IV

I remained seated at the bar while I sipped a huge cup of coffee and cream; the portholes were open and I was able to see the gloaming haze produced from the contact of the light of the star with the attenuated atmosphere that filled the bubble of space of Earth-2; it was like being submersed in an endless sky. I figured that had there been animal life forms in that Dominion, they might have been birds able to plow through those interplanetary skies.

Then my mind was once again absorbed by Amelia: I thought, maybe with a touch of envious admiration, what such an ancient living being as she was could contain. Twelve thousand years of uninterrupted experience, experimentation, study, challenges, in short, Life.

A time three times longer than the registered lifetime of man on Earth.

How to compete with individuals like herself who had had all the time in the world at their disposal? As it was wise to imagine she wasn't the only one. Whatever I could know or whatever technique I could have developed, she had had an eternity to develop and refine whatever she liked. But what she could be missing was the proper quality of a champion and this was my only consolation.

A champion has innate qualities which transcend the time of experience, as if he were the bearer of a specific and programmed difference given to him at birth for a purpose that remains often unknown to the champion himself and if during these twelve-thousand years these beings were still here trying to solve a mystery it meant that their ability to develop the qualities of a champion had become arid with time.

I recalled what the Visitor had told me: the enemy escaped the call through the controlled transmigration into clones or in organic shells deprived of their vital principle. In this case, Amelia and those like her didn't have the possibility of keeping their bodies alive indefinitely but were probably transplanted from one shell to another when certain conditions occurred, keeping their memory and their acquired experiences intact .

She had probably always been a woman in her migrations from one body to another in that she had developed a femininity which, given the little she had shown, was incredibly superior, almost supernatural, something to which a poor mortal surely couldn't resist.

Probably in a far away past she and the others of her race had appeared as Gods to mankind. I intended asking her if the occasion arose.

Then there was this strange and terrible power of which Monika had spoken.

I immediately felt a knot of apprehension in my stomach at the thought of her alone with Amelia. At this point they had been together for more than half an hour.

As though answering my thought the door of the meeting room opened and Amelia came out followed by her two servants going in the opposite direction. No sign that she had noticed me. Then Monika came out: from her expression she looked like someone who had had a good telling-off but when she saw me she smiled and the knot in my stomach loosened a bit. She came near me and took a deep breath.

"I feel as if I had worked for two days without sleeping", she told me leaning with both arms on the bar counter.

"Everything okay?". I looked in the direction of the meeting room.

"Yes of course, just... a lot of work. Are you already ready for lunch? I have to go by my room. Our appointment is in about half an hour".

And saying this she signaled me with her eyes to go with her.

"I'll go with you".

V

Once inside her room she closed the door and after throwing her notebook on the bed she said:

"Sit down, I won't take long", throwing her shoes off with a single movement of the ankle she started to undress. As she slipped out of her skirt standing in her panties she saw that I was still in front of the door.

"What's with you? Haven't you ever seen a naked woman?"

"It might be better if I wait for you at the bar", I said a little embarrassed, not by nudity in general but by hers in particular.

"What is it? Have you already forgotten the irresistible Amelia?" she asked ironically. "Come on, sit down, don't be an idiot", she said as she went into the bathroom and turned on the water in the shower.

I started to sit down when I saw Monika stick her head out of the bathroom door signaling me with her finger to come in: it was clear that she wanted to speak to me without being heard and the running water trick worked almost every time.

The bathroom was small with a stool and she had turned on the sink faucets too. She sat me on the stool and started massaging my shoulders whispering in my ear.

"At this point Amelia has understood that our relationship is a bit more than professional", she said.

"Unfortunately you're right. But you don't have to worry about me, I can take care of myself. You, on the other hand...".

"The same for me. Don't let her use me as leverage against you, whatever happens to me", she said

"I'm not sure I can do it Monika. I couldn't stand it if they hurt you. And they better watch out if they do".

"You know, as a woman I'm flattered and happy to know you care about me, but your mission is much more important and Amelia's words today are solid proof. Don't ever give in, whatever happens. And I will do what I can to help you and protect you".

She was sweet but I didn't feel reassured. She knew she couldn't even protect herself from Amelia.

"Why were you all so tense during the meeting?", I said changing the subject.

"Well, first of all because the people from the Command Staff are unpredictable in their reactions. And then because of how she was talking to you and what she said".

"It was clear to me that her mission wasn't Moon-2 but me".

"Exactly!", she answered.

"They probably suspect that given the right conditions I'll do something to expose myself or their illusory enemy".

"They very probably hope so and will do anything to push the power that they think controls you to come out in the open. Did you see how she spoke to you? And then, the information she gave you on her origins and on the Organization were never heard of before. That is why I was so scared and her assistants were too.

There is the possibility that once Amelia's mission is over they make us disappear so they don't run the risk of us circulating that kind of information. Can you believe it? After years of working at TA I find out that we are prisoners of a civilization that forged the Earth's history and that the summit of the Organization is made up of Aliens thousands of years ancient. I was more than anxious for the way she spoke to you and for what she told you and it was really difficult to stay in control".

"Yeah. She seemed to be playing with her cards on the table as if she were talking to someone already aware of all the situation".

"And were you?", she asked

"What?".

"Aware of the situation! Did you already know all this?".

"Honestly, no".

"Do you think she was telling the truth?", she asked.

"I'm sure she was telling the truth. Of course being very careful to tip the scale on her side".

"Then I have very little time", she said sadly.

"Why? You're in this mission and you obviously had to be informed", I said knowing though that she was right: we all had very little time for one reason or another.

"Don't you understand? I'm nothing to them. A little wheel in a huge machine which can be substituted and completely marginal: once the mission is over they'll get rid of me. I've already told you that many people have disappeared from TA without a trace. But do you know what frightens me the most about all this?".

"What?", I asked.

"The idea that I won't see you anymore...", and I heard her silently sobbing.

"Funny, isn't it? I risk my life and maybe even worse and what am I afraid of? Hell, forget it, I'm really stupid. Or you've put a spell on me! Yes, there's no other explanation, confess!", she said.

"Do you want me to rid you from my spell?".

"No! Never! Even if it won't last long, I've never felt so alive and I want to live every minute of it. You, on the other hand, think of me sometimes when I'll have been cast away like an old shoe".

"I won't allow anything to happen to you I said!", answering imperatively.

"Don't worry, I have a plan. I won't go down without a fight".

"What do you have in mind?".

"Once the mission is over we'll go back to Earth-2 and from that day my days will be counted. At the first opportunity I'll take a horse and I'll go towards the passage in the forest and leap into it", she said.

"But it could be dangerous. You said it was unstable and that the destination was uncertain".

"Better than being lobotomized or worse", she said.

"In any case, we have time now. Let's try to get some advantage from this mission and from the situation", I said.

"Yeah, you're right", she concluded noisily blowing her nose with a paper tissue.

"What did Amelia want from you when she made me leave the room?", I asked.

"Nothing new. She obviously noticed how I looked at her when she came close to you. I swear I would have jumped at her neck and choked her right then and there, had it not been for my training".

"And so?"

"So, she heavily reminded me who I work for and not to even dare think of judging or questioning her actions or her decisions and she told me that if I don't start showing myself useful for this mission I will suffer the consequences".

"And you?", I asked.

"I told her she was right, that I'm very stressed lately and that I will contribute as I've always done. I told her I would have kept her informed on any useful detail and that I would have used my wiles to soften you up".

She winked at me.

"Your wiles?!", I asked her amused.

"Right. And do you know what she said? That it is I who has to be careful not to be turned inside out by you!".

"Really!".

"And the funny thing is that she's right, the bitch. And then she told me not to waste time being a *femme fatale* with you! The shit head thinks she has you in the palm of her hand", she said getting angry.

"Don't worry darling. I told you I could take care of myself".

She grabbed me by the hair pulling my head back.

"You better not let yourself be seduced by that prehistoric whore because you'd really have a problem then", she said through clenched teeth.

"Your lack of trust saddens me", I said smiling.

She gave me a light kiss on the lips.

"Now I have to get ready. Wait for me at the bar".

"Yes ma'am!", I answered. Then I left her room and headed for the bar.

I crossed one of Amelia's slaves in the corridor who strangely greeted me with a nod.

After about fifteen minutes Monika reached me and after a few minutes a flight assistant led us to the dining room for lunch.

Surprisingly Amelia told Monika she wouldn't dine with us and that we would be joined by another member of the Command Staff by the name of Icarus, responsible for the Moon-2 missions, while Amelia's role was General Commander of the Earth-2 Base.

Lunch lasted about four hours during which time the topics discussed in the previous meeting were no longer discussed and instead Icarus described in detail the destination site on Moon-2 and everything that had been discovered up to then.

They told me that if the site had been created by the dark threat they wanted to hinder, I would probably be contacted in some way and they wanted me to keep them informed of any unusual phenomenon that might occur during the entire mission.

Icarus seemed more of a scientist than a military person and had it not been for the sea odor and those remote eyes that distinguished Amelia too, I might have considered him a nice guy.

He explained that the double pyramid was formed by a huge structure almost one kilometer high and by an upside down identical pyramid sunk into the ground itself about one kilometer deep, like a huge three dimensional diamond shape.

He told me of its metamaterial composition and that they had never been able to access it, nor did they know if there was anything inside given that not even the most sophisticated sensors were able to penetrate the structure.

I deducted that their civilization had not yet mastered the realm of the so called metamaterial. Icarus confirmed this to me.

At the corners of the double pyramid stood four huge monoliths which were double too in that they rose towards the sky and had a counterpart buried in the ground just like the upside down pyramid.

He told me I would have had the assistance of a first rate scientific team and that I had to wear a neural detector to monitor my functions and neural electric reactions during all the period of the mission and also while I was asleep.

Amelia participated very little to the conversation but observed me exhibiting from time to time that smile of hers which bewitched and to which Icarus seemed immune.

Without a doubt she was beautiful in her apparent simplicity and the deep chill at the bottom of her eyes, which could be those of a demon without a soul, was the only clashing detail.

Once we finished our meal Icarus recommended that I study the material and then rest until the end of the trip. I left him with a handshake and her with a bow and kissed her hand and she gave me her last smile of the day.

I didn't see Monika at the bar and therefore went straight to my room to relax for a moment and follow Icarus's advice. The meal had been good and light and I asked myself what culinary tastes aliens that had been on mission on Earth for twelve thousand years could have developed.

At that time I didn't know how important this question would turn out to be.

VI

Once I arrived to my room I decided to follow Icarus's advice about resting. I therefore got ready to go to sleep, turned off the lights but left the portholes open from which the twilight from the space of Earth-2 filtered in. After a few minutes the door opened and a shadow entered quickly into the room. Sitting up I tried to reach for the light.

"Don't turn the light on", said a familiar voice.

"Monika? What are you doing here?".

"Were you counting on not wishing me good-night?".

There was the sound of something rustling to the floor, maybe her negligee. I felt my heart accelerate.

"I thought you were already asleep", I said. "You can't stay here, you'll get in trouble. You know the rules on intimacy inside the Organization", I continued in an alarmed tone.

"In this moment I can care less about the rules. It might be the only chance I have of being with you and I don't want to lose it. Or would you prefer someone else in my place with much more experience?", she said hinting to Amelia.

"Don't be stupid. You know perfectly well what my desires are", I answered.

"And I'm here to grant them", she whispered slipping under the sheets.

THE DREAM

The sound of a bell.

I opened my eyes and realized I was an observation point suspended in mid air in a place I didn't recognize, which caused me an intense emotion. Underneath me, lying on a stone slab was a male form apparently sleeping.

The room around me had nine sides and the ceiling was so high it was lost in the distance. In front of me, a long corridor.

I was dazed. The sleeper wore a long black tunic with broad sleeves and a wide black belt at the waist. On his chest he wore a chain which ended with a shiny metal symbol with nine points.

The apparent substance which comprised the metal symbol seemed to be moving as though expressing an infinite number of faces and shapes in times and possibilities without limits. I then thought that if a multidimensional being had existed, this would probably be how it might be perceived by my senses and by my brain, limited by the three dimensions in continuum.

The last thing I remembered was falling asleep with the warmth of Monika's body on me after having shared an intense and satisfying passion which climaxed with her sweet good-night kiss. I couldn't understand what was happening to me: I was probably dreaming even if what I saw emitted a feeling of solidity that had nothing to do with dreaming.

The sleeper suddenly woke up, opening his eyes first and then with a simple movement sat up on the stone slab. I watched him as he moved his hands on his body as if verifying its solidity and looking satisfied.

The emotions I was feeling were becoming more and more complex, intense and alien to me. Once again I told myself I was dreaming and was engrossed in a vision and to confirm it I tried the old pinching trick discovering that I didn't have a body but that I was only an observation point in that place.

I mentally tried to call the Visitor and then the Guide who had told me the history of the Solar System during the experience in the Sarcophagus.

Nothing at all.

I couldn't feel anything outside of what was in that strange room. I therefore abandoned every resistance deciding to allow myself to be carried away by the experience. Nothing had happened by chance so far and I had to believe that also in that moment there was a reason for what I was experiencing.

Again, the sound of a bell coming from the corridor in front of me filled the air all around.

I saw the sleeper observe the room around him, then stand up instantly and I was surprised by the extreme harmony of that action, almost as if he had levitated.

It hurt my virtual eyes to observe how real and solid he was, as if the concentration of matter in his body were enormous, tending to the absolute: I could almost feel the weight of his body pushed to the ground by a powerful gravity which nonetheless didn't seem to cause him the least discomfort or difficulty.

On his belt, under the heavy black tunic, he had a kind of metal rod. I mentally glanced over its surface, up to its grip and this caused a pleasant feeling as if that object imparted me with energy, as though it were alive. I wouldn't be able to describe the notion which was transmitted to me, as if the rod were telling me its name and at the same time declaring the name of its Master who obviously was the being in black.

My memory of life on Earth and of everything that was before I found myself in this place, was becoming remote. It wasn't disappearing, like when you forget a dream, but I felt it integrating into the body of an enormously vaster memory almost to become an insignificant part of it except for the memory of Monika which refused to be downgraded.

The idea that I might be dead crossed my mind.

The sleeper was listening to a summon contained in the echo of the bell as if he knew it was addressed to him and that he had been called and awakened. He started to move towards the corridor as if it were his will to cause the movement and not his body. I realized that I too was moving in perfect alliance with him, like a balloon held by a string.

He was proceeding towards the corridor and once again his movement wasn't caused by his body: it was raised from the ground, which he barely touched, flying a few millimeters from the surface.

Then he decided to use his body, maybe to feel its realness even more. Touching the ground he produced a frightening effect on the environment around him: motion waves spread from the contact point of his feet through the floor to the walls and further and further along the corridor as though the weight of his body were astounding.

He started walking while I, reduced to a simple observation point, automatically followed him keeping myself at an approximate distance of three meters behind him and above him.

That place and that context were starting to become familiar to me and more and more I felt as if I were in a Reign where the substance was real and not dreamed of or imagined in perfect harmony   with the essence. Impossible to find words for such concepts. Let's say that the solidity was more solid, the colors more colorful not only vivid. Well, reality was more real and the thought which was branded by fire in my mind told me that it was that way because that was the Reign which existed in the Heart of the Center of the Origin of all the possibilities.

As I proceeded along the corridor I realized that the alien feelings which I felt and some of the stranger thoughts didn't come from me but from the sleeper himself. He had voluntarily blocked the recollection of his complete memory, which had begun to surface, stopping it in the background as if he had difficulty making it completely surface from his subconscious realm.

Yet I felt that He recognized this space and called it Home. I felt, from His mind, that this corridor went to the center of the structure in which I found myself; forty-nine corridors set out from this center and the other forty-eight led to a space similar to the one I had come from. In each one there was a sleeper.

Once more, the sound of the bell.

He was about to reach the center of which, I knew by instinct, to be called the Gread Wheel, though in another language, spoken only in this place and in the Emanations in proximity of this Center.

The Real name was the Great Wheel of the Makers.

Another figure arrived from one of the rays to His left and stopped in the center. I knew it was He who had sent the call to the sleeper who was waiting for His arrival.

It was a familiar figure; he too appeared in a masculine shape with long, curly red hair and a same colored, perfectly trimmed beard. He emanated the same sense of absolute solidity and authority which contained and could express infinite forms; he wore a green gold pendant around his neck representing a double scythe.

I knew that Their Names were secret outside of this place, but strangely, also to one another like those of all the other forty-nine components of the Unity of the Great Wheel, in that whoever knew the name of anyone of them could have used it in power formulas, summon them and even bind their actions. The power of one's Name is real in all realms of existence in the Great Dream and reaches its peak when the name defines he who has his home in the Center of the Origin of all possibilities.

Perceiving the Power of that place and its properties, close to the absolute, I was surprised that there could be secrets among entities of such greatness until I perceived that among them there was a continuous tension which determined conflicts on an enormously vast scale. Each one aimed for the Crown of the Reign which represented the crossing of the last door of the Beyond; their battlefield was the Great Dream.

Therefore, Their real names were not and are not known even among the forty-nine components of the Unity so that they can't use this power on one another. I found it grotesquely entertaining that even at the Center of things there could be power games, alliances, intrigues, affections, conflicts; everything present in one's existence was present and even more real and intense in this place. Each one of the forty-nine had a conventional name and I knew that the name of he who awaited the sleeper was *Sindyoor*. The sleeper was *Mytron*.

Arriving in front of *Sindyoor*, *Mytron* eyed him intensely for a long instant. Their hands joined in a greeting and then they vigorously embraced each other. *Sindyoor* and *Mytron* were two of the entities of the Wheel who could be considered, in their peculiar way of being, 'friends' and even if they both surely had their personal paths to follow to conquer the Crown they had never proven to be hostile to one another.

Sindyoor summoned *Mytron* from his Dominion to be able to have this meeting and to confer without interference; a rare occurance normally motivated by universally serious situations.

"It's always an honor to see you", *Sindyoor* said.

"It's been a long time since I've been *Home* and sometimes nostalgia distracts me from my World", *Mytron* retorted.

"This is just what I wanted to confer on".

"On the nostalgia for Home?".

"On your World".

"Do you want a part of it?". *Mytron* seemed amused by the idea.

"Not me. My emanation is occupying a lot of my time and I'm also particularly fond of it. There are some brothers though that are becoming interested in you, in the progress you have made towards the Consummation and I have heard that they have found a way to act on Your Dominion.

"This is unreal. Provide details", *Mytron* said. I felt his way of being surprised.

"I have no details nor identities. But I'm sure of it, in that our sister *Yanil*, who has always been particularly fond and close to you, informed me after attempting to reach you, without success, inside your Dominion.

"The governance of my World requires my total involvement and consequent reduced consciousness in that I am facing a real threat from the emanations that could take over this place through one of us. Maybe these are the communication difficulties experienced by *Yanil*".

"Maybe this threat of which you speak is the product of a plan which has its origins in this place. Then the situation is even more serious than how *Yanil* described it. I suspect it to be the design of more than one of our Brothers to reach this objective".

"The reformulation of the balance of the Makers has always been the desire of many of our brothers", *Mytron* said gloomily.

"I will try to find out more and will contact you as soon as possible", *Sindyoor* said. "I will signal my presence through my Icon hoping that you remember it after your absorption in your World". And he laid his hand on the double scythe he wore on his chest.

"Please ask *Yanil* to investigate, and to be careful...", *Mytron* said. I felt the affection he had for his sister; a very intense feeling.

"It will be done. I know how much you care about her. Now we have to return to the Emanations otherwise one of the others could notice our absence", he said nodding.

"Thank you Brother. Until the Great Consummation!".

"Until the Great Consummation!", he repeated.

It was their way of wishing each other good luck in a realm where there was really no room for luck.

Sindyoor disappeared in his corridor. *Mytron* returned to his footsteps and once he arrived to the nine sided space repositioned himself on the central marble-like slab .

The sound of the bell.

MOON 2

I opened my eyes in my bed in my room on my way to Moon-2. I was momentarily disoriented while I felt a part of me wander away and the memory of what had to have been a dream disappear in a void.

I didn't know how else to classify that experience and I recommended myself to write it down as soon as possible to fix it firmly in my memory. Monika was sitting on the bed and looked at me holding my hand.

"Are you having trouble falling asleep?", I asked her.

She didn't say anything right off but continued staring at me.

"Who are you? What are you?", she asked after a few endless seconds.

"I don't understand", I said still stunned by the experience.

"Who are you?", she asked again. She didn't look angry but only baffled.

"I suppose the same person as yesterday and the one who fell asleep with you a few hours ago", I answered a bit confused. She held my hand tightly, then letting go a little said:

"I had a strange dream: I saw a sky crossed by lights and stars and at the center of this sky a big wheel made of rays coming from a huge star darker than night. Then a double arched symbol with two dividing horizontal lines which broke it came out from one of the rays". She drew the sign on the sheet with her finger.

"Then it went into my head and I saw you. I knew it was you even if you were different. Your eyes were black with a white blue light at the bottom. You were dressed in a strange way with a star or a sun on your chest and you were getting ready for battle. I was trying to tell you something but the words wouldn't come out and you weren't able to see me. Then you looked at me and I felt as though I were burning and at the same time desired the fire that was consuming me. Then I woke up with my heart beating wildly".

Interesting. I didn't recognize the sign she had drawn with her finger on the sheet but it seemed to have a strange similitude with those of the two characters I had seen in my dream. Could it be that someone was looking for a contact and Monika, with her empathic qualities, had picked it up?

Monika was also the person closest to me in that moment and I trusted her blindly. Had the choice not been casual then? I asked myself what these dreams could have really meant and if it were an attempt by someone or something that wanted to create some sort of stable connection, but she continued:

"It wasn't the same as other dreams. I was there and I knew it wasn't a dream but a kind of transmission of vivid premonition; but I couldn't understand its meaning. It had never happened to me before. And then it happens the first time I sleep with you! You did it, didn't you?".

"No, I didn't do it", I answered.

"Liar! It can't be just a coincidence! Tell me the truth", she said raising a hand as if to strike me.

"Hey, calm down! Are you always this aggressive? I can assure you I didn't do it. I swear it. But, come to think of it, you could have received a message for me. Do you remember anything else besides what you told me?", I asked.

"Yes. Vividly. There was something I had to tell you but – I told you – the words wouldn't come out...", she said.

"And you can't remember what it was you had to tell me?".

"No. But I'm sure it had to do with our present situation. Maybe I'm just influenced from worrying".

"Anyway, dream or not, nothing changes. We'll have to be very highly on guard", I said.

"Had you ever dreamed this way?", she asked.

"I never remember my dreams, honey", I lied.

"I was so peaceful before I met you and look at me now", she said.

"Well, if you want to go back to the way you were before you can give up the mission", I answered.

"Don't be an idiot. Anyway, even if I wanted to, it's too late now".

"Well, no one forced you to get in my way", I said laughing.

She jumped on me and I had to hold her wrists to keep her from hitting me.

"You are a wild animal! I was only joking!", I said amused and she calmed down a little and embraced me.

After a while we fell asleep again and this time without consequences.

II

We were awakened by the loudspeaker that we were four hours away from the orbit of Moon-2. I felt rested and was very hungry.

Monika stretched herself, gave me a kiss and then got out of bed, picked up her negligee, put it on and blew me one last kiss from the door.

"Someone could see you go out", I said.

"Let them see. It doesn't really matter anymore. They surely saw me come in. See you later... ".

And saying this she opened the door and slipped into the corridor.

III

We landed on Moon-2 with the sun at its zenith. The airport, if it could be called that , was a very simple and essential structure, probably designed for military type missions. The barman had told me there was only one big Temporal Archives base on Earth-2's satellite and that differently from the regular Moon its diameter was the same or a bit bigger than half that of the main planet, but with a bigger mass.

We landed near the equator and it was very hot, but the special clothes given us on board kept the body temperature at a nearly optimal level. We left the airport on horseback. We were six: Monica, Icarus, Amelia with her two assistants and me. At our destination there was a little permanent scientific village not far from the double Pyramid.

The intimacy between Monika and me was surely common knowledge by now but in any case we didn't do anything to hide it even if it was only a matter of looks and words. Anyone would have understood by now that we were more than just simple colleagues or friends.

Having to proceed slowly, we arrived at the lunar Base after about three hours, cutting a path through the rain jungle with the help of an experienced guide who was waiting for us when we landed.

The surface Pyramid was already visible from the airport, like a mountain of perfect symmetries which in parts reflected and in parts completely absorbed the light of the Sun. Further to the left, but much further, there was an active volcano so high it seemed to spew its fire and smoke directly towards its Sun; a narrow column of dark gas from its mouth rose high into the atmosphere.

Being that Moon-2 was about half the size of Earth-2, notwithstanding its bigger mass, it had a weaker but not unmanageable gravity, even if all movements seemed to be slowed down.

When we arrived the unfailing assistant informed us we had been assigned a group of rooms in the prefabricated area near the headquarter. After a short time I was accompanied by two security agents directly to Icarus and Amelia who informed me they had no intention of wasting time and that we would therefore make a preliminary round of inspection of the surface of the Pyramid.

It could really be compared to a huge mountain, nothing like the

Pyramids in Egypt, and the four giant obelisks which rose not far from the four sides of the Pyramid, each forming the ideal vertex of an equilateral triangle with each side of the Pyramid itself, were as high as the main monument, losing themselves in the sky beyond the clouds.

The metamaterial of which they were made looked like liquid metal which continued to change shades and brightness; at times it looked like gray water, then it turned into a bright black, then it looked like steel, then mercury in motion and the same changes and movements could be observed also on the four monoliths. Yet the pyramid and the obelisks never took on one single configuration, the same and at the same moment all together.

It took us more than six hours to see all of the pyramid accompanied by lengthy and convoluted explanations by some of the members of the scientific team. Amelia and Icarus followed in silence.

As reported by the mission documents there were no visible doors or access points.

We ended the inspection almost at sunset and returned to the little scientific city built by the edge of the Pyramid but at a distance which had been defined as "safe".

I intended returning to the site during the night and if possible, alone.

I saw Monika at dinner even if she had been placed far from me, at another table, while I sat with Amelia and Icarus and two people in charge of the scientific team. From time to time, while I asked and answered unimportant questions, I looked for her with my eyes and saw she didn't at all hide her discouragement at the evident intention of keeping her at the margin of the mission.

A part of me wanted to do something, but I realized she too wouldn't have wanted me to throw away the opportunity of experimenting this place or reveal its secrets for a greater good.

Yet I wasn't able to completely free myself from the sadness I felt seeing her like that.

Night came.

The little scientific city naturally had no surveillance (except for the headquarter building), an unnecessary precaution in a place where the only living beings were the members of the Organization and the aliens of the Command Staff.

From the windows of my lodgings I saw that everything was quiet and the lights off in the other buildings confirmed that everyone had opted for a restoring sleep.

In the meanwhile I had put on some more comfortable clothes, jeans and a sweatshirt; in case someone had noticed me I was only out for a night walk and in any case no one had spoken of prohibitions.

The perimeter of the Pyramid and of the obelisks was only a twenty minute walk away. I surely wouldn't have evaded the sensors of eventual satellites, but even in that case, my mission didn't pose limits to what I could do as long as I kept Amelia and Icarus informed and this, keeping them informed, was a problem I could placidly face later. I wasn't even sure I would find something of interest to them. Then, I went out naturally so that anyone who saw me wouldn't think I had something to hide, but there was no one in sight.

I headed towards the site. While I crossed the row of prefabricated buildings in the direction of the Pyramid a door to my right silently opened and Monika softly called me.

"What are you doing? Do you want to wake everybody up?", I asked her standing on the doorstep.

"Where are you going?", she asked seriously.

"Guess".

"Wait, I'm coming with you".

"Absolutely not! You stay in your room and go to sleep. I'll stop by on my way back", I said knowing that it would be difficult to keep my promise.

"But I want to come with you... I want to help you...", she said with a touch of frustration in her voice.

"You're already helping me, honey. By acting this way you put both of us in danger and you know it. Go back inside. Please".

"Will you come by afterward?".

"I promise".

"She hugged me giving me a light kiss.

"Be careful", she said disappearing slowly behind the door.

IV

Despite the dusk, it was easy to arrive to the monument, which even at night didn't lose the inconstant qualities of its surface. Apparently the presence or absence of external light sources like the Sun didn't influence it in the least. I approached one of the obelisks which appeared in any case connected to the central body of the Pyramid as if it were built entirely from one uninterrupted single block.

Hesitating at first, I touched its surface and felt a familiar feeling, as if it were alive and answering an attempt to contact it, trying to identify the newcomer; its answer against the palm of my hand was electric and I felt it enter my body to my bowels and up to the center of my head but wasn't able to translate the feeling which was spreading through me in thoughts, recognizable emotions, symbols or words. I only felt a strong sense of familiarity and the impression that whatever was the intelligence which governed that structure, was integrating me in its own consciousness.

Then, with no warning sign, the entire complex, the Pyramid and the four monoliths turned into shiny mirrors and I discovered with terror that I wasn't able to move my hand which was taking on the same mirror quality of the entire structure.

One moment and everything around me disappeared and I found myself in the middle of a darkness which appeared to be solid. I perceived movement around me even though my eyes registered only darkness. Then a tree appeared to my left with green gold and turquoise leaves and then a tree-lined avenue appeared. I began to feel a light and fragrant breeze while an indigo and turquoise sky with fuchsia and orange stripes substituted the darkness.

In a few words, I found myself in another place which, curiously, was very familiar to me; but I couldn't understand if only in my mind or also with my body.

It had the same quality of the vision I had had in the Sarcophagus of the planet Mars at the time of the Anantrya. Everything around me became solid and I also saw people walking down the paths which outlined in perfect symmetry the perfectly kept vegetation. I felt a sense of peace and fortifying well-being which drove away all fear. I looked around: everything gave the impression of a vital, peaceful and reserved environment. Then, suddenly, out of nowhere there he was.

It was him, the Guide I had met in the Sarcophagus. He wore a loose and light tunic almost to the ground which swayed in the light breeze.

He smiled showing his perfect white teeth and stared at me intensely. For a moment I had the impression I had never left the Sarcophagus and that all the experiences I had had since the last time I had met the Guide were only visions induced by technology or by him. It was known in theory that subjective time when connected to the Sarcophagus could be expanded, theoretically to infinity, yet in that moment this was not important to me.

I saw in him this ancientness which looked at all things as if they were just passing through in the presence of a mutable cognizance only because in continuous never ending growth. Differently from Amelia and Icarus, there was no sign of coldness nor did I feel that uneasy, deep chill generated by thousands of years of domination of other life forms, nor hate or feigned superiority. In fact I could almost perceive a naive quality like that of a child prodigy curious about everything.

The Guide spoke to me in a language I found I was able to understand.

"Welcome back. My name is Sithar and I will communicate to you the preparation for the Task you are destined for".

I was perplexed and confused by those words and Sithar felt it before I could speak.

"It is normal for an Incarnation to have initial difficulties in reconstructing itself when it is projected in the dense World. This is a fact I learned from others like you who in time I met and followed. I will help you overcome your present condition and reach the path which will lead you to your awakening".

"I know you", I said.

"Of course. Your essence and mine met numerous times in time. More recently, according to plans, we prompted the process of your awakening, instructed by the Grand Messenger of the Makers".

He motioned me to follow him and we started walking slowly along the avenue.

Fragments of images whirled in my mind as though searching for an order that couldn't take shape due to the lack of fundamental components. The details of how he had contacted me in the Sarcophagus and now in this place seemed in that moment irrelevant in front of the enormity of things I didn't understand.

"Is the Pyramid your doing? If so, what's its purpose?".

"It is one of our outposts. All the variations of phases of Earth and Earth itself have one. What you refer to as Pyramid is an autonomous cognizant being created to be a custodian, a guardian and to locate and neutralize the energy of the Potentiae, to watch over our people, and in case of necessity, on those who are announced by a Messenger. You have already met one of these outposts on Earth that contacted and helped you and has watched over you since then. The Guardian you have met now, being able to come in direct physical contact with you, invited you here to me in the Anantrya Dominion.

"But why are you so cryptic? If there is something I have to do or I have to know, tell me! Or do you use your abilities in order for me to become aware of it? I think it's in the interest of everyone involved, or not?".

"It doesn't work that way, Incarnation. The stories of the Worlds coming from the Great Dream and dreamed by the Makers have laws, rules, geometries and dynamics, each one interdependent, which must be respected. Forever we have been faithful to these rules also because there is no way of escaping them: we are at the service of the Messengers to indicate paths, directions, doors, routes, but we can't interfere. An Eternal on this side of the Mirror must find his Origin according to his choices and according to the rules of the Tale of the World in which he has come down into. We think this induces him to accrue a compassion for the race he has come to help, living its hell from the inside. Without compassion the Eternal could disconnect from his Task accruing indifference and even contempt for the baseness of the sacred image of Life this side of the Mirror. We Anantrya don't know the reasons or the consequences nor do we need to know anything else to carry out the tasks referred to us by the Messengers", said Sithar with the patience of a tutor.

"Why did you want me here and contacted me now? I didn't get to the Pyramid, that is, the Guardian by chance, this I know. I felt an impulse to make contact and I knew it was what I had to do. Why? Why now?".

"As always happens, an Incarnation feels a preordained impulse to follow his part in the Tale of the World which receives him and when he is hindered in this impulse by the blind mechanisms of his body or his reactive mind, the Incarnation feels incomplete. Yet, we have the task to accelerate your recovery for reasons that, as I said, are unknown to us".

"You still haven't told me why now...".

"We had to bring you near a Guardian to contact you remaining invisible to the Potentiae. Why now, you ask? It is important that you understand that the contacts you will receive, independently from the fact that it be me, a Guardian or even a Messenger or other Incarnations, will always happen according to the rules of the Tale of this World especially when they will have reached an important junction or if for inexplicable reasons a Messenger just wants it. Above us, there is no need for reasons to act or not to act". He paused briefly and then:

"Now you have met the enemy. The representatives of a Caste which governs a powerful, vast and decadent Empire. This Caste has millions of members, but few in the context of their Empire are in command. The Anantrya had long before abandoned the Fourth planet, which you call Mars, when they reached this star system and transferred themselves in the Ninth Emanation of planet Earth. It happened when the Anantrya banished the last representatives of the dark Krogan race, known as the Potentiae, in a realm with no return in the Void space. Being that they couldn't die, the Krogan survived in a state which could be called stasis waiting for an opportunity for them to reawaken. Their powerful essence doesn't know the limits of distance in space and therefore were able to wait for millions of years for new sentient beings to reach or develop on Earth to be able to subdue their minds. And unfortunately, this happened. The first expeditions of the Empire, of which you have met two of the ancient representatives who call themselves Amelia and Icarus, arrived on the Third planet about one hundred thousand cycles in the past. The invasions and the wars between the empires are unimportant for the purpose of your Task. They started to exploit the Earth exiling millions of human beings destined to exploit its resources. The Potentiae, in their long wait, perceived the presence of humans on Earth feeling also that their minds were weak and corruptible. They took possession of the humans and created the Caste. Under the influence of the Potentiae this Empire grew in dimension and experienced a level of darkness never imagined before. But their objective was always the same as it had been from the beginning; to strike at the Anantrya and seize the space-temporal dislocation technology, their only hope of returning and reestablishing their supremacy. The

Potentiae use the members of the Caste as vehicles and their power, even if great, is weak when they use it through a vehicle. Therefore the Caste is now looking exactly for that secret which the Anantrya have preserved through the destruction of the worlds of the Potentiae, the extinction of the Saurians and the destruction of the Martian colony".

The situation was finally becoming clearer.

From the mind of the Anantrya Guide in the Sarcophagus I had already seen that these terrible and immortal Krogan could survive in empty space and in absence of nutrition, fall asleep in a sleep similar to death but vigilant, waiting for favorable conditions. Therefore, they were still sleeping but their powerful essence was equally able to have a determining influence on this Caste and through them, on a new Empire and on the inhabitants of Earth. Yet, their mind could not reach the Anantrya in their new artificial Dominion. As if reading my mind Sithar said:

"It is exactly the influence of the mind of thousands of Potentiae that, even if in lost sleep in realms of the inaccessible space, through the Caste, infect the inhabitants of Earth causing that madness disease which Amelia described to you. Too bad she herself is the vehicle of that disease".

"But the human race, that is, the inhabitants of Earth, are they really the same species as Amelia and Icarus?", I asked.

"Most of the Earth's human inhabitants are descendants of slaves, rebels, revolutionaries, criminals and whatever else from the the worlds governed by the Caste. When the Caste was formed, under the influence of the Potentiae will, their Empire was reformed and all those that, in some way or another, could threaten the new order brought about by the Caste were exiled and trapped on Earth, not only their body but also their Soul, as you would call it, the same that is forced to transmigrate but only inside the Earth's space. The Caste has created a barrier around the Earth and with the help of the Potentiae it prevents the essences that leave their bodies to naturally return to the Great Dream, forcing them to continually bind themselves to new bodies, produced and trapped on Earth. In this way the Potentiae are creating the conditions to have a new army of victims which, at their return, would break out all hell in the Galaxy with devastating consequences for all of us. We Anantrya have seen the possibility of this future in the Master Tale of this World and we cannot allow it to happen".

"How much more time do I have here with you?", I asked alarmed by the sudden thought that on Moon-2 they had detected my absence and were preparing something regrettable on my return.

"The time you spend here under the influence of the Guardian cannot be discerned by the technology of the Caste. Nevertheless, they have surely detected fluctuations in the structure in your proximity and therefore there will be consequences when you return. But whatever happens you must keep the secret you protect. We will not be able to help you in that our presence must not be detected. For this reason you will have to trust your abilities, driven by your instinct, to lead you through this and other situations. Soon you will no longer need to remain infiltrated in the Caste to carry out your role in the Tale. This much was revealed to us by the Messenger".

"By the way, who or what is this Messenger?", I asked giving in to my growing curiosity.

"We don't know it, or better, we don't have a complete understanding of the nature of the Messenger", Sithar answered.

"So you, (and therefore I), follow exactly the instructions of someone unknown to you?", I asked perplexed.

"We don't understand its nature but we recognize the Realm it comes from".

"Which is? Where does it come from?", I asked unperturbed.

"From the other side of the Mirror. The Realm that Be. We know it as the Great Dream which is naturally indistinguishable from the Inscrutable One which contains it", he answered.

I bit my lip lightly.

"I understand... ", I said. "In other words, let's say that I understand that sooner or later I'll understand. Anyway, the important thing is that there is no danger of deception".

"There is no probability of that", Sithar answered.

I took a few more minutes to think because who knew when I would have had another opportunity like this one.

All around me, the breathtaking nature made me feel safe and never wanting to leave. It was crossed by discrete walkways and in the distance, on some hill like formations, there were some buildings which looked like castles also made from that mutable material they called metamatter of which the pyramid on Moon-2 was also made of.

"The place I come from, that bubble of space they call Earth-2, what exactly is it?", I asked.

"It is a micro-universe located within the harmonics generated by the difference in potential between the time interface created by the Anantrya around the Earth's system and the Earth itself. You would call it a 'collateral universe' but it is not less real because of this. The secret of the creation of 'Emanated Temporal Spaces' was a gift from the Messenger. The Earth is the only planet inside of the Worlds to also have Local Emanations and this makes it unique. Every creation of Emanated spaces generates infinite harmonics of which seven are fundamental and the one you call Earth-2 is one of them".

"Therefore, if there are seven harmonics, plus the original Earth, that means that there are eight main versions of Earth?".

"More exactly, nine, in that you must include the final creation of the

Anantrya where the colony, which formerly occupied the planet Mars, was relocated".

"Therefore: an original Earth, an emanated Earth and seven harmonics, right?".

"The words are not correct but the description is not completely unsatisfactory", he answered.

"And how was it possible for the Potentiae and for the Caste to find Earth-2?", I asked.

"It was by chance. The passage points between the Earth and the nearest harmonic are material and therefore accessible", he answered.

"And the nine monoliths I saw of Earth-2? Are they your doing?", I asked.

"If with monoliths you mean the Vortex, it was not crafted by us. The Vortex you saw and other similar ones were built as instructed by the Messenger and with our help by a fellowship of individuals on Earth, to which you belong and that, a long time ago, vowed to contrast the great enemy. The Messenger showed them how to travel outside of the natural space so that they could evade, if they had to, the surveillance and persecution of the Caste and the Potentiae which eye is always present on Earth. Only one member of this Gathering of Eternals can use these passage points, very similar in function to the temporal dislocators of the Anantrya. As you have been told by the First Guardian on Earth, you are a member of the Gathering and therefore you were able to activate the mechanism of the Vortex which recognized you".

Little by little things were becoming more and more clear. I didn't want to leave that place given how peaceful I felt and Sithar's company was particularly relaxing and made me feel at home. But I felt the urgency to go back, like a pressure that became stronger and stronger at the mouth of my stomach. Probably enough time had passed on Moon-2 to make the alarms go off regardless of the temporal differential to which I was subject and which made the relative time on Moon-2 pass much slower. Sithar confirmed this.

"Now you must go back. Soon your body will be reached by the minions of the Caste near the Second Guardian".

"Will we meet again?", I asked.

"According to the designs of the Makers", he answered, whatever that meant.

Without any forewarning I felt I was being sent back.

The world in which I was disappeared in pieces and then there was darkness all around me again.

Little by little I became aware of my body and saw my hand, then the monolith I was till touching, then the great Pyramid which I now knew to be the Second Guardian and at last all the darkness was substituted by the night view of Moon-2.

I took my hand off the monolith and observed it but it looked as though nothing had happened.

No noise could be heard, nor could I feel the presence of anyone else around, so I decided to casually move away from that place and a little while later headed towards the scientific citadel of Temporal Archives.

V

There hadn't been a soul in sight on the way back and all the lights of the buildings of the citadel were off indicating that everyone was soundly asleep. According to the relative time on Moon-2 I had been away about half an hour and the experience with the Second Guardian had lasted less than two minutes in this temporal space. I had decided not to go by Monika's. It was useless to defy luck too much, I thought.

I had just entered my room and undressed when I heard a big commotion outside and the sound of people moving and voices shouting orders and then someone knocked at my door. I opened the door in my bathrobe and with a cigarette in my mouth. There were two giants from the internal security who invited me to follow them. They gave me time to get dressed again and while I was at it, to think of something very quickly. The probabilities of something unexpected happening in such a place were remote; and then, they were looking for me right after an event which had surely been detected by the sensors or the satellite network or by both.

I decided I had to continue improvising because I didn't know exactly what they had, nor did I have sufficient experience with the Caste, of which Amelia and Icarus were part of, to foresee their counter moves or consequences.

According to the terms of Temporal Archives and of the Organization even the suspicion of treason was punishable with indefinite forced labor, downgrading and removal of all the various qualifications and security clearances. A little while back this prospect would have terrified me, but at that moment I didn't really care. The fact was that then I didn't know about Earth-2, of the Caste and of the frightening mental powers of the Command Staff which now I knew to consist of aliens possessed by powerful demons, known as "the Potentiae", survivors of an ancient war fought between Gods, when compared to terrestrial standards.

Anyway, I only had my intrinsic ability at improvisation and to deny all the time, deny the evidence concerning their eventual suspicions of my complicity with the power they called enemy but which in reality was the object of their hunt and thirst for power.

I was taken to the main building and into an empty office except for a table and two chairs. There were the usual four video recorders in the four high corners of the room. On the way towards my destination I had noticed security agents in front of every building and people moving frantically.

Monika was nowhere in sight. I thought she was probably still in her room even if the general commotion was surely worrying her.

After maybe a quarter of an hour the door of the room I had been "kindly" brought to, opened and the two outside guards let Amelia in, who had had time to get dressed in her suit and with her hair done neatly.

Her expression though was serious and her look severe. Before sitting down she used the knob which was also the switch to lower the light until we were in the dusk of an indirect light which bounced on the ceiling. Sitting in front of me she began to stare at me without saying anything. Had there been a big mirror on the wall in front of me the situation could have easily looked like a police interrogation. Thinking of the mirror, by association, I found myself considering the possibility that the image of Amelia wouldn't reflect, like that of the legendary vampires! I was the first to speak.

"Did something happen?", I asked.

She seemed to think about it for a moment.

"Don't you have anything to tell me?", she asked.

"Tell me what you want to know".

She made a gesture with her hands which I interpreted as 'okay, let's play the game with your rules'.

"I want to know what happened from the time you left your room to when you returned".

And thus the duel began.

VI

I told Amelia of my walk in an essential way, of arriving near one of the monoliths and of touching it and of having a feeling like that of electricity throughout my body. I knew this had never happened before in that I had learned from the scientific reports that physical contact with the monoliths or the Pyramid had always produced reports which signaled the metamatter as inert and unable to react to stimuli, even chemical or electromagnetic. I told her that this had alarmed me and that I had decided to report this event immediately the following day. I also commented that this could be an alarming proof that this threat she had described during the flight to Moon-2 could really be looking for a contact with me to use me to arrive to the heart of the Organization, and finished by suggesting, for everyone's own good, to be relieved from my task and escorted to Earth-2 for everyone's safety.

I thought I saw her relax. She had laid a folder on the table and in that moment opened it spreading its contents on the surface. Papers with satellite pictures, tables etc.

"Do you know what these are?", she asked me.

"A survey from the orbital sensors, I suppose", I answered.

"Exactly! And do you know what they say?".

"Can I see them?".

She put them in front of me.

"A fluctuation in the local gravitational field was observed in correspondence to your proximity to the Pyramid and a few seconds later you disappeared from the field of the sensors for almost three minutes to then reappear. What can you tell me about this?".

I looked her in the eyes innocently.

"Nothing more than what I told you Amelia. Maybe the unusual activity of the Pyramid interfered with the sensors".

She made an annoyed gesture with her hands and continued staring at me with her dark and remote eyes.

There was no doubt that Amelia had chosen with much care the body she wore, as one chooses a dress from a boutique, unique, precious, tailor made for her to attract attention and make it impossible to ignore.

Her fineness and elegance were deliciously low profile like someone who doesn't need too much to strike one's attention but is after all striking.

In another contest she could have been a model chosen to interpret an important part in a photo feature for the cover of Fortune or an actress in a serious TV serial, the ideal successful female manager. The mastery with which she handled that body was superlative, skillful and conscious with each move effectively measured, and yet apparently natural. Her young and innocent face, able to strike anyone with her disarming smile, was like her body, beautiful but objectively average and yet possessing characteristics which made it unforgettable.

She wasn't tall and needed heels to reach a man's chin and her attributes were average, not chosen to be noticed and yet in a beauty contest the jury would have had difficulties not to choose her.

Her perfect hands always followed her words with little movements which together with her face and eyes were fundamental instruments of her body language. And yet, her young and innocent beauty, discerning and noble was discordant with the ancientness in her eyes, with that remote chill that could be perceived.

With her eyes still fixed on mine, she clasped her hands entwining her fingers and leaned against the back of the chair. She crossed her legs under the table and one of her feet touched my leg and stayed there as if she hadn't noticed. Like the previous times she had touched me, I felt a shiver.

"You see...", she said, "... unfortunately we cannot afford to risk unexpected events after what has been detected today. And these are objective data and your involvement is certain".

"I agree of course. This is why I believe it to be indispensable that you remove me from locations important to Temporal Archives", I said seriously.

She remained in silence a while longer as if she were trying to decide what to do and in the meanwhile her foot moved imperceptibly and rhythmically against my leg. The movement distracted my attention and I had no doubt that this was exactly her intention. I started to feel a growing nervousness and then, as if I were under the effect of a psychotropic drug, began to feel my body remote, as though something were pushing me outside.

I had lost control of my body but remained conscious. I suddenly realized that Amelia was using her powers on me probably to extort the information I could have or to take control, through me, of whatever she thought was controlling me.

I felt helpless and incapable of opposing what was happening to me. Like looking at a scene from the outside, as a passive witness, I saw Amelia still in front of me, motionless and for a moment thought that everything was lost.

Then, like an hallucination, I saw a sign impose itself to the eye of my mind: a double arch juxtaposed with two horizontal lines crossing them and strange geometrical configurations on the inside. The sign imposed itself like branded by fire or a burn on the retina after having looked straight at the sun. I had already heard talk about that sign: from Monika, when she had described her dream the night we had made love. Suddenly I found myself back into my body and in command of my movements.

I also saw Amelia jolt in her chair as if she had been struck by a strong electric discharge. And for the first time I saw her without her mask. Her beautiful face was contorted in an expression that was a cocktail of anger, fear and amazement. I could see the ancient demon that from afar looked through her eyes, like a remote light that seemed to have taken place in the center of her pupils.

I looked at her feigning dismay, not having understood exactly what had happened.

She recomposed herself a little but didn't put her usual mask back on.

"Who are you?", she asked me imperiously.

True to my strategy, 'deny, always deny, deny even the evidence', answered:

"In what sense? Amelia, I don't understand. What happened?".

Not that I knew the exact answer to that question and therefore I wasn't really lying.

She sprung up scattering her chair against the wall behind her and banged her hands against the table.

"How dare you play with me!!!". She yelled so loud my ears buzzed.

The racket had to have alarmed the guards because the door behind me opened and I saw Amelia give a piercing glance to whoever was there.

The door closed slowly and she turned her furious attention back to me. I continued looking at her but no longer saw the point of keeping the mask. My expression was that of challenge and I wanted to give her the impression I really was playing with her. I wanted her to feel confused and vulnerable now that she knew she was no longer in control.

"You have no idea what you are challenging", she said coldly.

"Well, here I could contradict you... Let's say that I probably have a very good idea who you are, Amelia", I immediately answered without losing my composure.

I could almost feel her thinking rapidly. She surely hadn't predicted anything like what had happened and she certainly didn't know that neither I had any idea; but, from her point of view, the cards had been laid on the table.

"I'll ask you for the last time. Who are you and what is your mission?", she asked more coldly.

"And my answer is that I don't have an answer. Not that I would tell you if I did have one...".

In her eyes I saw a flash of cruel malice. She crossed her arms on her chest and shouted:

"Security!".

The door opened behind me and turning around I saw the two brutes come in.

"Yes ma'am", said the one with the higher rank.

"Go and get Monika and put her under arrest. Immediately!", she ordered.

She hadn't missed the flash of preoccupation that had crossed my face. I hadn't thought of her in this situation. My stomach knotted again.

"Have her escorted to the airport. She will immediately have to return to the headquarters on Earth-2; keep her in isolation and guarded until I return", she concluded.

"Yes ma'am!".

The guards left noisily closing the door. Her look was that of someone who had just taken the opponents queen in a game of chess and enjoyed his discomfort now that his only move was to delay the downfall of his king. I stood up trying to remain calm.

"What do you want to do", I asked.

"What you don't give me I will take from her", she answered smiling.

"Monika doesn't know anything and has always been loyal to you". I knew that defending her was counterproductive but I had no idea what else to do.

"Then it means that her mind will be drained for nothing. Always that you don't decide by chance to collaborate and answer my questions, that is", she said calmly.

I approached her and took her by the shoulders. She didn't put up any resistance.

"If you hurt her, I will hunt you down and kill you, and the thing that possesses you", I told her with a coldness and determination which surprised me. She continued smiling without trying to free herself.

"You won't do it. You are not a murderer. You would never hurt anyone, especially me. As for the rest instead... help yourself! What do you want to do? Rape me? Yes, please! From the moment I saw you I have this fantasy... I swear I won't call security!", she said in a teasing tone. I let her go with violence and she slammed against the wall falling to the floor. She got up regaining her composure and called security.

"Be sure he doesn't get out of here until I return. And no food or water until further notice", and so saying she finished adjusting herself and left, leaving me alone.

VII

I didn't wait long. Instead of Amelia, four security guards showed up and escorted me to my room. Along the way I saw Monika, she too escorted, going in the opposite direction towards the airport from where it was already possible to hear the sound of the engines being warmed up.

We exchanged a long glance and her lips composed the word "good-bye". I smiled and winked at her hoping she would remember my promise of never abandoning her, but her eyes were sad and resigned.

I silently damned Amelia, the only thing I could do in that moment without risking the worst from the four gorillas around me.

Once I arrived to my room I changed my clothes, got comfortable and started thinking of a plan of escape. At this point it was completely useless to stay in that place or in any other near the members of the Caste.

The more time passed the greater the probabilities of them finding a solution to break my resistance or to solve the problem physically doing away with me. At that moment, the thought of the Gathering, of which I was part, nor the Anantrya were of much comfort to me. I had to manage alone and quickly think of a way to escape.

As happens when one is busy focusing on something he considers important, there are always some underlying thoughts that impose themselves to the surface. In that case, I realized I finally understood why the human race had always appeared despicable, mean and basically horrible.

Yes, human beings were disgusting and it was incredible to think that there were some among them who would have heroically given their lives for the others. The corruption, the violence, the wickedness, the cruelty, the thirst for power and all those expressions which had always distinguished mankind's history and of which we heard every day in the news, finally found an answer in the constant presence of the evil represented by the influence of these ancient and apparently immortal Demons whose past, not even the Anantrya, had been able to destroy but only confine. And anyway, in the slumber and cold of the void, they survived and unperturbed and undisturbed, influenced the destiny of an empire and that of the Earth and of its fragile passengers. And if in the lost spaces of their exile and in the slumber which was so like death they still had this frightening power, I couldn't dare think what their real despicable and obscure facet was when they were free to express their full power.

It seemed that what had saved the great Saurians of Earth was their natural immunity to the power of the Potentiae but every quality always comes with its dark side and the Saurians, which might have probably been the only real power able to directly face the Potentiae, shared their thirst for power and domination and at last, instead of containing its influence, they decided to make an agreement with an evil that their own corruption concealed to the senses.

I forced these thoughts back to the bottom of my mind trying to concentrate on my present situation.

My closest hope of escape was the great Pyramid, that is the Second Guardian, but how to reach it? Maybe I could try to take some time with Amelia and have me led near one of the monoliths and hope they wouldn't kill me while I touched it.

No, it wasn't a practical solution, first of all because in this way I would have contributed in revealing to the Caste the Anantrya origin of the Pyramid and Sithar had surely very good reasons for not wanting their presence to be discovered, and then because I didn't think that Amelia and her other peers were idiots and they would have surely guessed I had something in mind therefore obviating the surprise effect.

I heard a plane take off and had no doubt it was the one which was taking Monika back to Earth-2. I had just lit a cigarette seated on the couch in the room when I heard three knocks at the door.

Strange. It wasn't surely an occasional visitor given the situation.

"Come in!", I said curiously. The door opened slowly and Amelia walked in. The lights in the room were off but her shape and the radiance of her personality were unmistakeable.

"Can I?", she asked too kindly.

I was surprised and disoriented. Surely she was scheming something.

"Be my guest, come in. Forgive me for the mess but I didn't have time to do the cleaning", I said calmly. Though I was anything but calm.

She made a rustling noise as she entered and closed the door behind her.

The security agents were still outside. She waited a moment leaning against the door and then slowly approached finally sitting on the edge of the bed.

I asked myself what in the world she had thought up now but her presence prevented me from thinking clearly. She had put her disguise as the girl-next-door back on, innocently malicious, and leaned back with her hands on the bed.

"Will you tell me what is happening?", I asked.

She sighed.

"I will tell you", she said. "You know... I've been watching you for some time".

It could be true but I couldn't understand what she was trying to do.

"You have struck me. You are different, special and I knew it even before today. I don't want things between us to end this way", she continued with her musical voice which had a relaxing, even hypnotic effect.

"Well then, let's make up and be friends again", I said without hiding the irony in my voice.

She ignored it and simply said:

"I want this too. But I want our relationship to be more than a simple friendship. You and I, we could unlock the secret of such a great power that it would elevate us above everything known".

I thought I understood what she was searching for, now that the hard way had failed: my complicity! She wanted to corrupt me and use me to increase her power. After all, what else could be expected from a being generated by evil? Certainly, even in her boundless ancientness she saw the world through her rigid crystallized schemes under the pressure of millions of years of experience, not being able to conceive that there could be a different way of relating with the world outside of the obtuse and linear relationship between the corrupt and corrupter.

"Think of what we could realize together", she continued in her subdued and impelling voice.

"Even if I wanted to, I really don't know what I could give you because I really have no idea what you're looking for, whatever it is I surely don't have it", I said only half lying.

She slowly got up from the bed coming closer, without taking her eyes off me which I felt piercing me even in the semi-darkness. She stopped in front of me and held out her hand. I took it and she helped me up to my feet. She put her hand on my shoulder and came close brushing against all of my body.

"Are you trying to seduce me"?, I said embarrassed and really feeling so.

"I don't want your information. I want you. Completely. I want to be yours and you must be mine. In the body. In the mind. In the soul. Until we feel pangs of folly at the mouth of our stomachs at the very thought of losing one another", she said with a madness in her voice and breath. The madness of a woman hopelessly in love.

I was confused and my head spun. I couldn't think clearly and anything could be said about Amelia except that she was predictable. Monika came to my mind but it was a far away image, remote; I almost couldn't remember her face and in that moment I surprised myself wondering what I had seen in her.

Amelia was caressing my body and my desire for her was growing, becoming almost unbearable and also the confusion in my head which continued spinning as though I were drunk or drugged. I wasn't able to fix my thoughts and everything was becoming remote except for the object of my desire: Amelia.

She continued to whisper words I didn't hear and I didn't care. I don't remember how, but I found myself naked on the bed with Amelia who was naked too, sitting on top of me. I felt the firmness of my desire and Amelia placed it inside her. I saw her lips moving and her voice was like a sweet whisper inside my head. I couldn't understand the language nor the words but they were sweet, sensual and irresistible and I felt as if I had never desired anything else.

Even when she raised my forearm and sunk her teeth in it starting to feed herself with my blood which dripped from her lips I felt a pleasure I didn't know could be felt. She removed her mouth from my arm licking her lips and started murmuring while with her finger imbued by my blood she brushed against my chest as if tracing a design.

Then, for a moment, her face, moving forward entered the beam of weak light produced by the "full moon" of Earth-2 which, lit by the sun, shone in the sky. Her face was beautiful and wild and I looked deep into her eyes perceiving the presence of the Demon inside her and which through her, observed me.

It was like a shock. I suddenly became conscious of the room and of myself and I heard what she was murmuring and understood what she was doing. She was tying me to her will with an archaic enchantment according to the Law of the World, using that ancient art and science which took its Power directly from the realm of reality and of the Great Dream: Magic.

I didn't want her to notice I had awakened and I couldn't allow her to finish the enchantment or I would have become her instrument. Even now that I was awake a part of me still wanted to lose myself in her and become her slave, so powerful was the Power she was using to imprison me.

Then, something unexpected happened but it didn't deter her attention: in her place, on top of me, there no longer was the enchantress but another woman of whom I could see only the shadow, around her neck the symbol with the opposing double arch.

A Name appeared to the ear of my mind but I wasn't able to grasp it.

Yet, now I knew that that symbol was her Sacred Sign. She was there only for a blink of the eye and said only one word, "Vortex", accompanied by the image of the group of monoliths. And then it was Amelia again on top of me; I instantaneously understood what I had to do and only hoped I had enough time and concentration.

I closed my eyes and like already once before, visualized myself seated on the stone altar at the center of the Vortex on Earth-2; I again visualized the obelisk I had in front of me beginning to read it from top to bottom. I felt the symbols impose themselves in my mind and burn with the heat and brightness of lightning. In the background I heard Amelia screaming something and her hands grab my throat and begin to squeeze while her voice continued saying only one word: "No!".

I felt myself moving at great speed towards the signs that had formed in my mind; the perception of my body disappeared and so that of Amelia and her hands around my throat.

Only the signs in my head existed and I fell towards them at breathtaking speed.

Then everything disappeared..

EARTH 5

For an endless moment I found myself in a limbo neither of light nor darkness, then I felt a solid surface underneath me and when the world reappeared, suspended in that limbo, I saw the nine obelisks which formed the Vortex. In the distance there were glass walls with mosaic motifs, a floor, a ceiling which was a big dome emanating a soft blue light and two people wearing dark gray uniforms from times past.

And then I finally was in that place.

I was completely naked. The wound on my arm caused by Amelia's teeth had disappeared except for a slight itch. I felt the need to breath deeply as if I had held my breath for a very long time, while my heart beat fast in my chest; I sat up on the altar trying to catch my breath and slow my heart down.

The two uniformed people spoke with each other for a while, then one of them went away while the other remained still continuing to stare at me outside of the perimeter of the obelisks. I instead, remained seated observing the place where I had been dislocated to by the Vortex: it looked like a temple or a very particular church built to contain and protect the structure of the Vortex itself.

In front of me, the circularity of the walls was interrupted by a big room with two columns, one on each side, which concealed long lateral hallways and in front of me and at the end a big arched door that seemed to be made of solid wood and metal.

The uniformed person who had gone away reappeared from one of the side doors with a bundle. He gave it to the other man who had remained at the margin of the Vortex.

"We have brought you some clothes, Eternal", he said.

I looked at him and motioned him to come closer.

"We cannot enter the inner space. The Vortex recognizes only the

Eternals", he said.

So I got up and went towards him and he handed me the bundle. There was a long black tunic and a pair of sandals. The second man spoke.

"We have informed the personnel of your arrival. Your lodgings will soon be ready and you will find other clothes made just for you".

I didn't want to disappoint these people who evidently knew me but I couldn't help trying to understand what the situation was:

"Where am I? Who are you? Who am I?", I burst out.

The two looked at each other for a moment, then one of them spoke again.

"You still haven't recovered your past. I am sure that your Equals will be happy to help you better than what we could in that we are only servants. For now, know that you are on the Fifth Emanation of Earth. We are the guardians of the Vortex devoted to watch over this and other sacred places to welcome the travelers and make sure that the Darkness doesn't discover the secrets of this place. As for who you are, this is a question you must answer yourself, Eternal".

"Why do you call me Eternal?", I asked.

"Because you are an Equal to the Gathering and this is what you are", he answered, then the second guard spoke:

"Now, please follow me to the welcome area. We will be at your service for all the time of your stay here in the Holy City Amn'el'Tyr. We will inform your Equals of your arrival in the meanwhile".

I followed the man along a torturous path which brought me to a spacious, medieval Japanese style apartment but with modern and avant-garde accessories. He explained that Amn'el'Tyr was the name of the great city where we were now, holy capital of the Fifth Emanation.

My Equals, he patiently explained, were the Eternals who found themselves, at the moment, in the Fifth Emanation. Others were in Service or still sleeping like I had been (and like I still was). The members of the Gathering were in fact always moving from one emanation to another, each one with a task to complete and many were carrying out their Service on Earth Prime. Then he told me that the problems I had with my memory surely depended on the fact that my awakening process had just recently started and from what he had learned from his studies, the older and vaster the Conscience of the Eternal the more distressed and difficult was the process of awakening and recovery of the skills, the powers, the memory and the Energy of Influence.

"Many Equals of the Gathering", he said, "don't awaken for many incarnations in that chaotic and casual environmental factors prevent it, or due to strong interferences by the Darkness".

"But how do you know I'm a member of the Gathering and not an impostor or a visitor who accidentally activated the Vortex mechanism?", I wanted to know.

"Because we are trained to recognize the Eternals independently from what clothes they wear", he said, pointing to my body. "And because only an Eternal can use the Vortex to make the transition to the Fifth Emanation".

I remained alone in the apartment. I got out of the tunic and after a long hot shower, looked for and found, clothes in the wardrobe that I could wear. I chose a pair of pants and a shirt of a heavy cotton and high boots, all rigorously black. I also found a cloak which I put on the table for when I decided to go out.

I still felt on me the taste and smell of Amelia and just the thought revived my desire. The spell had not completely vanished and I hoped Amelia wouldn't have a way to establish any kind of contact with my mind or my body given that she hadn't been able to finish the procedure she had started. I also had a strange emotion connected to that moment, as if I had broken the heart of someone dear who loved me desperately. I couldn't even imagine Amelia corresponding to this description but the feeling was strong and I couldn't do anything else but accept it and integrate it inside of me like just another important experience. I then searched my mind for the memory of Monika and my stomach immediately knotted worrying for her. Since Amelia had failed with me I imagined she would turn to Monika who, as much as I knew, had no weapons to protect herself with.

In any case, in that moment I was in a friendly place called the Fifth Emanation of Earth or Earth-5 in the jargon of Temporal Archives and I needed to relax and to eat, as I was reminded by the unmistakable grumbling of my stomach. I took the cloak and left for an orientation walk hoping that the sight of the places might in some way ease the recovery of my memory. The Temple from which I had come was located on a big hill which dominated the city of Amn'el'Tyr, which I immediately noticed to be familiar to me as though I had been in that place many times before. The only access and exit point to the hill of the Temple was a big staircase which I slowly walked down scanning the landscape trying to remember something.

I could see long smooth stone paved avenues and homes in about twenty different architectural styles, all rigorously taken from the Earth's far away past, some familiar while others less familiar. It looked like a collection of the Earth's history translated in a cocktail of styles coexisting in one single present. The streets were populated by people on foot, on horse, by carriages and chariots.

There were many races and historical periods living together even through the styles and clothing of the inhabitants; I saw Templar Knights, oriental monks, people who seemed to have just come out of ancient pre-Christian Rome or from classic Greece, ancient Egyptian priests, shamans from the Native American nations and many, many others. There were also many people who wore more modern and contemporary clothes, even if eccentric.

Everything indicated a sanctuary city and what seemed to unite the inhabitants was the Knowledge and Magic heritage.

I slowly walked down the main avenue which, from the hill of the Temple led to the sea, touching a big Square with four crossing avenues which led to four buildings on four hills. Something inside me told me that those were the administrative quarters of the local power.

The salty smell of the sea, or the ocean arrived all the way to the hill along with the sound of the sea gulls which went back and forth from the city.

Therefore, in this Emanation there was animal life. I asked myself how different it was from Earth knowing it was a purely an academic question.

I saw shops, homes, pubs and crossed bunches of multi-ethnic and multi-historical people and these, when they crossed me, greeted me with a hinted and respectful movement of their head which I politely returned.

Life seemed to proceed normally in Amn'el'Tyr with business, animated conversations, or laughing and speaking with energy in front of big mugs of drinks probably poisonous for anyone's liver.

The sun shone like a big golden ball and the sky, broken here and there by isolated cloud formations was an intense blue with intense gold and green reflections. On the right and on the left there were hills like the one of the Temple from which I had come and one of these, on the left, seemed to be the site of a big monastery or fortress, a sort of hybrid between a castle and a stronghold, built entirely of white stone.

I was about to choose a pub to satisfy my hunger which had become almost unbearable when I felt a tingling in my head. I stopped and in front of me the air started to stir trembling like I had noticed in the passage points on Earth-2; then a prismatic effect began and at last a human image appeared and solidifying put an end to the phenomenon.

It was a short slim man, dressed in oriental clothes, more precisely Chinese style, from a period which must have been rich with Taoist wizards in that he seemed of Chinese background with a thin beard and mustache and typical headdress. He smiled a warm smile and bowed briefly.

"You never change. You arrive and don't come by to say hello!", he said amiably.

"You must forgive me but I have some problems with my memory and I don't remember you", I answered sincerely.

"Aha! You still haven't got over the memory block of the Guardian. No problem; in time, by the Great Dream will, you will remember. My name is Shen, your Equal and I would dare say, friend. I preside over the Council of Amn'el'Tyr until I am relieved or fall in battle", he said.

135

His face was in fact very familiar and produced a warm feeling in me. I felt like embracing him and when I did he returned my embrace warmly.

"Your arrival was not expected and so forgive me if your reception was improper. I was just informed by the Custodians of the Temple of your appearance in conditions, to say the least, bizarre and I therefore thought it was an emergency", he continued, starting to walk along the avenue.

"In fact it was an emergency. I was about to succumb to an spell from which I was able to escape just in time", I said.

"A spell... on you! Interesting... The Custodians referred that you arrived from the Second Emanation. The only with a garrison of the Caste and the Potentiae", he said.

"In fact! The incantation was being spun by a component of the Caste by the name of Amelia".

"Aha, Amelia! Very dangerous. Very powerful, feared even inside the Caste".

"It's not difficult to believe. And since you know her, I have a lot of questions to ask you! But now, could we find a nice restaurant? I'm starving and then I need to rest. The last days have been, to say the least, traumatic for me", I said.

"You should have said it immediately! Let's go to my mansion. I will have a satisfying meal prepared for you, so you can bring me up to date about yourself, the beginning of your awakening, on the Caste and on the diabolical Amelia. By the way, should you see her again, give her my regards, she will understand!", he said with enthusiasm.

"I'll do it and... thanks! I gratefully accept your hospitality", I answered.

He laid his hand on my chest and started mumbling something with his eyes half closed. Then, with his left hand he touched a pendant composed of various juxtaposed geometrical shapes, each one a different color. With his thumb and index finger he turned one of the shapes ninety degrees counterclockwise and at the same time, as if by magic, the world around us changed transforming itself into the inside of a big room furnished in Oriental style with a big chimney and wide windows facing the city.

I was somewhat dazed and didn't try to hide it. There were really too many things I had to learn again.

Shen had me sit on one of the low couches which furnished the room and called the service personnel pulling a heavy rope which hung from the ceiling.

They arrived shortly and he instructed them to prepare a meal for two; then he reached me and as he had asked, I brought him up to date on all the events I had been through since the beginning of my awakening, starting with the starry night at the Base and ending with Amelia's failed incantation.

I only left out the details relative to the dream of the Great Wheel and the names Mytron, Sindyoor and Ya-Nil, not knowing how to place them in my story and also for a deep instinct which told me not to say anything about that strange vision.

"Very, very interesting", Shen said after having avidly eaten some small helpings of appetizers and washing everything down with a mug of local beer.

"I agree. But what do you find interesting?", I asked.

"Everything! To begin, it doesn't often happen that one of the Eternals directly meets one of the members of the Caste and finds himself so close to the Potentiae. They don't show themselves very much and prefer to act through their minions, spending most of their time hidden on the Second Emanation. Besides Amelia, which I met in battle some centuries ago, I myself briefly met only another member of the Caste called Halyra about two thousand years ago, during one of the first purges carried out towards the Masters of the Eunos Art – known in China as Tao – of the Celestial Empire. The Caste fought anyone who had or could obtain a contact with the power of the Great Dream. They fought the great Shamans of the Way of the Power of Naught in the Western continents at war which lasted centuries and were the ones to inspire the inquisition. The Gathering, of which we are Equals, was created to contrast the power of the Caste and of the Darkness which governs it and to prevent it from spreading outside of the Dominion of Earth".

"Therefore you are a true Master of the Tao way? You know, at the present time of Earth there are many phonies who claim to be masters of this or that and the word itself has lost its ancient meaning and authority... " I asked.

"Sure! In the past I was also pinned with the title of Sorcerer even if that term is not appropriate but it gives the idea", he answered.

"If you only knew what they say about Witches and Sorcerers in the time I come from! They have transformed everything into a freak show".

"You must know, and you will surely remember sooner or later, since it was one of your Reflections to act, about four earth centuries ago, there strangely was one thing which found coinciding interest for the Caste as well as the Gathering. The use of the Eunos Art, which is the true Magic, which had degenerated to the point that numerous individuals, thirsty for power, had built parallel ways, aberrant to the purpose of extending their pernicious influence. The human race is not the only sentient race on Earth and some of these races united in this attempt to these degenerates, while others, the more ancient and evolved, forever connected with the Eternals and the Gathering itself, contrasted them. It must be said that the inquisition also helped to weaken the ranks of these groups which were becoming vaster and more powerful and yet nothing seemed to stop them and the more they were destroyed the more their thirst for the power of those who could destroy them grew. Until one day they found the way to access the Second Emanation and since then they have been looking for the accesses to the other Emanated Worlds. The Caste asked for a truce and begged the Gathering to intervene to stop the spreading of this abomination. It was Amelia who proposed this line of action because the Caste had already decided on the destruction of the Planet in the absence of an alternative solution. It was you who wove the Great Veil which made the ambition for the Eunos Art disappear. In one generation, the followers of the aberration died, who naturally, who of a violent death and their substance was reabsorbed in the Great Dream causing all deviating ambitions to disappear. Unfortunately there were also more or less expected collateral effects: the minds of men drove away the memories of the Art to the realm of imagination and buried the ambition to the Great Dream in the depths of their subconscious and from then on they conceived of the world as inanimate and their miserable ancestry as the only conscious one. The ancient non-human races were forced to find refuge in inaccessible realms like the oceans, the glaciers, the forests and underground in that man hunted them and put them on the same level as the animals which populate the Earth. Everything will change in a future in which the Great Veil is lifted but the time has not yet come. Maybe Amelia recognized in you a fragment of the Power you had manifested at that time and like all the creatures of the Darkness, fell in love with it".

Now this explained a lot of things.

"Damn! You have summarized the history of the world in five minutes. Knowing this makes me see the situation in a different light, specially knowing that raising this Great Veil could normalize the situation in the future. And it also explains the feeling I experimented in my encounter with Amelia. I think there is something in her that doesn't accept her belonging to the Caste and the domination of the Potentiae, but maybe it's only my impression due to the consequences of the spell. As for what you refer to as Eunos Art, I understand why the Caste considers it a threat. Strange that they allowed its development. They could have suppressed it from the beginning", I commented.

"But they are not omnipotent nor omnipresent; and then the Gathering has always been favored by the protection of the Great Dream and of its Messengers", Shen answered.

"What is our origin?".

"The Gathering was created shortly after the arrival of the Caste on Earth. Before then we were only Emissaries, each one bearer of his own Way, periodically sent to contrast invaders from other worlds that tried to annex Earth to their domains, disturbing its evolution. But with the Caste, everything changed. They were able, with their presence, to awaken the

Potentiae and to bring their influence on the planet", he answered.

"It's really a shame that the knowledge of the Art remained a heritage of few. It's surely one of the undesired effects of the Great Veil", I remarked.

"Naturally. The Caste helped the diffusion of religions and not of the Real Art. The religions are a celebration of ignorance which must remain so. With the Knowledge, faith becomes finally a real power. The secret of the Art was and is the Knowledge to contrast. A real Master of the Art has assimilated all things so completely there is no possibility of conflict, he has destroyed the idea of Duality itself. He has reached such a state of Love and Passion that he no longer conceives the existence of things to control or objectives to want; he has killed greed at its roots. He is One with everything and with Nullity. Such a being cannot be struck by the things of the World because he and the world are one and all", Shen said.

"Therefore, what you're telling me is that the objective of the Art is to reach such a level of conscience and comprehension that the point of view and the object viewed are one thing. But this state isn't compatible with the permanence in a relative universe", I said.

"Of course not! This is why in order for the Eternals to drop into the relative material condition, that is, to project themselves on this side of the Mirror, they must sacrifice their Conscience and the level of refining they have reached: the real challenge is overcoming the resistance of the Goddess of Matter recovering their purity thus causing the Purification of that which surrounds them as though attracting a fire to the bottom that burns the trash and the impurities of the World. As you might imagine, it isn't an easy undertaking when you are dressed with all the imperfections and impurities of this World. Of course an Eternal dropped in the solid world of symbols, temporarily undressed of his purity and of his Power becomes vulnerable, especially with an enemy like the Caste hunting him down. Then, the Eunos Art like the Way of the Power of Nullity of the Sorcerers and the Great White and Red Magic practiced in the Mediterranean sector, are particularly dangerous for the Caste, these not being passive or contemplative ways, but operative. Through them powerful contrasting forces can be evoked and the Ancient Demons that govern the Caste can be evoked and bound to the will of a Sorcerer. Of course these are delicate and dangerous practices for the life of a Sorcerer, but as you were able to experiment, the Great Demons themselves, through their instrument on Earth, the Caste, use a portion of the Art as they tried to use it to bind your essence to their will, failing. And know that the Demons, even with their Power, didn't have knowledge of the Art. This arrived to them through the great Sorcerers who in the past, imprudently underestimating their opponent, tried failing, to use the Art against the Demons. These, once they were bound to the will of the Sorcerer, assimilated his knowledge. No Sorcerer was then prepared to face the corrupting power of a Potentia. And these, though bound, penetrated the soul of those who had conjured them and corrupted them irreversibly. Then the Demons used these powerful victims to fight side by side of the Caste on Earth to strike and eliminate any form of emerging power".

Damn! Shen was really good at summarizing entire periods of important events in less than an hour, I thought.

"But is the Gathering made up only of great Masters of the Eunos Art?".

"Absolutely not. You for example, in the far away past were the greatest Alchemist and now you are a scientist; the attributes and the direction of the Reflection on this side of the Mirror are determined by the Eternal who generates the projection; in this case, from You. A day will come when what is defined as science and Eunos Art will be indistinguishable. It is only a terribly longer path but remember: all the roads always bring you Home", he answered.

"This seems possible... ", I said, "... it's already possible to see the signs of emerging sciences that explore realms that don't answer to the so called linear laws. For example quantum mechanics. As occurs for the non-local theory of events".

"I don't know this theory", Shen said.

"Briefly, according to this theory, an event caused or generated in one place of existence can synchronously cause another event of an uncertain nature, quality and magnitude in another place or time of existence. For example, a stone thrown against a rock can synchronously cause the explosion of a star millions of light years away, or in another dimension or even in the past or in the future of the World".

Shen seemed to carefully consider this concept of the non-local events.

"Very interesting what you say. So, if we knew which exact event, executed in an exact way, could cause an exact effect in Time, we could call the sum of the knowledge of those events which generate non-local effects in space-time, like Eunos Art! And to be so there must always be a Desire who directs and therefore one of the Eternals", he concluded.

"That's just what I meant", I said.

"Yet it is necessary to have a complete and direct knowledge of the unique substance which constitutes all which exists – that is, the Mirror and the reflections which cross it – to then proceed to classify which events can synchronously cause other events. An error could cost dearly by generating a catastrophe or not cause anything", Shen concluded.

"Sure. I'll have a lot of things upon which to meditate tonight", I said.

In the meanwhile several people came in who brought dishes of food to a nearby table.

"Ah! Lunch!", Shen said rubbing his hands.

And so we ate commenting only on the food and other ceremonial trifles. It was lunch in a manner of speaking in that we began in the late afternoon and finished a little before sunset.

After the meal we moved to some comfortable chairs around a crystal table on a balcony naturally called "of the sunset" because it was possible to observe the sight of the golden sun sink in the ocean from there.

The service personnel brought us a bottle of Sake' and two little cups and we relaxed watching the sun disappear.

"Where are the other Eternals of the Gathering?", I asked.

"No one knows, not even I know where and who all the components of the Gathering are. The only person to have all this knowledge is the First Guardian in that he manages the embodiment process of the Eternals and this is the order of things. If the Potentiae should capture or corrupt one of the members of the Gathering they would never be able to get to the others through him. You would call it 'security reasons'", he answered.

"And how then do we know our specific task and coordinate ourselves?", I asked.

"It is evident that you have spent too much time among modern men! To program, coordinate, manage, action plans... we don't follow these mechanics, and if you take a look even at your recent past you will notice that even you don't do it! Our task is revealed to us each time, in different ways and through channels which manifest themselves according to the situation. And each one of us doesn't need to know the others' task in that the possibility of conflict or incompatibility is minimum", he said.

Suddenly, during a moment of silence, I once again felt the tingling sensation in my head and in front of us there was one of those disturbances in the air which announced a dislocation. Shen didn't seem alarmed. A moment later a man appeared in traditional Arabic clothes who made an ample bow towards us with his hand on his heart.

"Khalid! What a pleasure!", Shen said getting up and going towards him.

"Salaam e'lekum brothers", Khalid said.

"Alekum Salaam brother", Shen answered while I made a brief bow with my head.

"Please, sit with us", Shen said.

"Thank you brother. But I see you have company", Khalid said looking intensely at me. In that moment I understood what the Guardian meant when he told me I would have recognized an Eternal by looking him in the eyes.

My eyes and those of Khalid met and both us understood all we needed to know of one another. It was an immediate, complete and unequivocal recognition.

Khalid too wore one of those pendants around his neck, with different geometrical colored shapes like Shen's. I don't know why I figured that that had been the way he had used to transfer himself to this place exactly like Shen had done with me before.

"Your eyes never deceive you brother Khalid. Heylel escaped one of the Great Demons on the Second Emanation and found refuge in our holy city, Amn'el'Tyr.

A new piece of information. Here I was known as Heylel and maybe this was my real name.

In my mind that name brought up images of places of great obscurity and others of great peace, of battles fought between worlds and powerful prayers, but still too confused to give a sense to my identity.

The only time I had smelled the smell of nostalgia for Home was during the immersion in the vision of the Great Ring of the Creators in the presence of the two mythical beings, even if generated by my subconscious, and to hear the sweet name of their sister Yanil.

I had felt a real feeling of longing in that place and it seemed natural to me, for whoever was alive, to feel a strong pull towards the place where everything has its origin, whether it is real or imagined.

"Brother Heylel, I heard much talk about you and of your exploits in the dark centuries. Your feats remain legendary even within the Gathering".

"Thank you Khalid. Unfortunately my memory is still too confused for me to really remember what you are referring to", I answered.

"I understand. Your awakening process has been triggered just recently then. But this is good news for all of us! It means that the moment of your fulfillment is near and this is sufficient to delight my day".

"The awakening of Heylel was wanted by the First Guardian", Shen added.

"A great honor brother", Khalid said.

The service personnel came in and brought a steaming tea pot with a cup for Khalid. Obviously he already knew Khalid's tastes.

"Tell us brother: were you able to see one of the Ancients?" Khalid asked.

"The Ancients?".

"Yes, I mean the Potentiae. To the knowledge of the Gathering, no one ever saw one of them. It is said that they dwell in a distant space forever exiled by the Masters of the Guardians".

"I didn't see a Potentia but was about to fall under the spell of one of the exponents of the Caste possessed by one of them. Her name is Amelia".

"Amelia. Yes, I remember having fought against her almost one thousand years ago in Alexandria in Egypt. A dreadful adversary", Khalid said.

"Do you think she was able to discover your identity?", Shen asked.

"No, also because, except for what you have told me up to now, not even I am certain. But I don't think her objective is the Gathering. I suspect she wants to find the access way to the world of the Anantrya, the Masters of the Guardians".

"Forever the Potentiae aspire to reach the Ninth Emanation. It's the only hope they have of being freed from their exile", Shen said.

"I felt the advent of something that would have resolved this problem to its roots once and for all. And now I know that Heylel was awakened by the Masters of the Guardians, I am sure that this feeling is real and I am happy for it", Khalid said.

"I too feel a Power approaching but I still don't understand its nature", I said.

"It doesn't matter. We will know your feats by the changes which will stem from them and no sooner. This is as much according to the ancient code", Shen stated.

"Do you think I have a part in this? Unfortunately I cannot satisfy you because I still don't know much", I said, as if excusing myself.

"Tell me brother, if you need something, anything, I will help you", Khalid said.

I thought about it for a moment.

"In fact there is something. I need one of those pendants which allow you to travel in space and in the emanations and... some user instructions. If I'm allowed to have one, that is", I said, but somehow I already knew I should have one.

"This is easy Heylel. Each one of us received one and yours must be in your room at the palace waiting for you. I will have it immediately recovered by an attendant", Shen said.

And saying this he called a domestic who was standing near the door. He whispered something in the domestic's ear who hurriedly left.

"Then...", I added, (but I felt lucky), "... I need to know the meaning of the signs on the obelisks to be able to use them efficiently. It's only by miracle that I was able to arrive here".

"No miracle! Only your instinct in action. There are no documents that explain the meaning of the symbols you refer to always for security reasons, in that we don't want the Caste to know how the Vortex works and even less the coded destinations on each one of the monoliths. If you'd like, I can explain them to you now. I still have some time before my return", Khalid said.

"It would be an honor to learn from you...", I answered. "... Shall we start immediately?".

And so Khalid and Shen explained to me the nature of the Vortex, the coded symbols on the obelisks and the reading sequence from top to bottom.

The domestic returned with a box covered by black velvet in his hands. Shen gestured to the domestic to hand me the box and I accepted and thanked him.

It was made of ebony and Shen told me that every box containing a translator was baptized to consecrate it to the Great Dream and to burn the hands of any dark being who dared touch it. Translator was the exact name of the pendant which in reality was a device which literally translated the space-time coordinates of a living being who was in contact with it instantly transporting him according to his Will.

To work it needed a contact with the mind which, visualizing the destination in detail, directly transferred the visualization to the Translator which made the traveler compatible with the destination place causing an instant change of place.

In time, the Gathering had discovered that visualizing a person instead of a place brought the Translator to transfer the traveler in the same place where this person was.

I took my Translator out of the box it was in. It had a long chain and I put it around my neck like Khalid and Shen.

"Many of the functions of the Translator are unknown to us. We only know those which allow us the instant travel and this occurs turning the purple symbol... ", and he pointed at it, "... ninety degrees counterclockwise while visualizing the place or the person you want to contact. Fortunately the symbol we use is only tuned into this dimension otherwise we would run the risk of arriving on parallel realms, similar but different and therefore to get lost. If your body is in physical contact with another person or object this will be translated with you", Shen explained.

I thought about my arrival to the Mansion and remembered that Shen had in fact touched me before the transferal.

"And you Khalid? What brings you to this place?", I asked.

"I came here to have some advice from Master Shen and to consult the sacred library before continuing my mission", answered Khalid without further details.

"Well then, I'll leave you two alone. I'm very tired and you'll excuse me if I go back to my apartment".

"Of course. An attendant will show you where you should still find your old wardrobe. I remember how fond you are of your clothes", Shen said smiling.

II

My apartment was definitely bigger than I expected and in any case more than what I had been used to in the last years; little hotel rooms, dormitories and cabins.

It was at least two-hundred square meters with a spacious living room with a studio in it, a big bedroom and a bathroom with all comforts. One of the walls of the living room had three wide glass doors which faced a balcony looking out to the ocean.

I took a long bath to purify myself from the feeling the broken spell had left on me and then went on a little tour of my library.

It occupied almost an entire wall of the living room and I was happy to discover that my love for books came from my deeper Self; I knew the library was very important to me and felt a sort of affection for my newly found books, ancient books written in at least ten different languages of which I only recognized the Latin ones.

In one separate and locked section I found some that I immediately recognized as written by one or more of my past Images. They contained poetry, stories, songs, spells, mechanical explanations on the emanations, revelations on the Great Dream and the real nature of Matter. I had to find the time to study them because I had probably written them just to be of aid during the future processes of the recovery of my memory, but my mind was distracted in the attempt of elaborating the last events. Then there was the ever present worry for Monika which hadn't diminished; she was probably still in flight, directed to Earth-2. And last but not least, I wasn't able to get completely rid of the feeling Amelia had left on me in her attempt at binding me to her desire.

I silently cursed. The thought of Amelia also caused me a strange anxiety and what I interpreted as a sense of guilt. Guilty because of my refusal to accept the feelings she had caused me and fear that maybe I would never be able to free myself from the desire she had awakened in me.

The solution, as for all things, was to use all that she had left on me against her and against the Caste in that an Incantation, according to the Law, binds the receiver and even at a deeper level who produces it.

I went out on the balcony and saw that the night was full of stars of many colors but no moon was visible.

There was a breeze which felt warm and pleasant on my skin. I sat comfortably on a small couch and decided to try an experiment. I didn't want to think too much about it to avoid that logic keep me from acting and confided on my never experimented ability of controlling the phenomena tied to my mind.

Shen had said that mental contact with the Potentiae was dangerous and damaging and could turn against who used it. But Amelia was not herself a Potentia having only been possessed by it.

I freed my mind from the little voices which alerted me and then tried to estrange myself from all the present sensations recalling only the residual taste of my contact with Amelia.

My nervous system reacted immediately and my body started to respond to the chemistry of desire; I realized that Amelia had skillfully manipulated my system of instincts to impose herself as an object of desire in my material matrix in constant connection with my mind and the real origin. It was like a virus which had the purpose of tiring the resistance and deterring attention. I suspected that if I didn't succeed in my experiment I would have been tormented by this virus for a long time.

It was now time to use the knowledge of the connection and communication laws: both connected terminals can influence each other and if one can receive a communication he can also send one. Therefore the time had come to change the flow with Amelia. But I had to be very cautious and experiment.

I started by fixing the taste and group of emotions which I identified with Amelia. Everything else in my mind was moved to the back and became a background noise at first to then disappear in the field of inner perceptions like of a waterfall covered by the mass of a mountain. Then I gave this group of emotions a shape, then a face and an expression.

In the end I arrived to the Amelia in my mind, her vitality as I perceived it. I excluded all subjective information about her so that, with my inner eye, I saw her and both my body and my mind immediately reacted.

The image came to life. I suddenly saw her: she was seated in a little room, her eyes fixed in an indefinite spot in front of her, as if lost in thought.

In front of her there was a porthole and on the outside the weak color of the dusk of the atmosphere which filled the space of the Second Emanation.

She was surely on the plane and was returning to the Base on Earth-2. I strangely noticed sadness in her eyes and in her expression which, in the solitude of her room, she didn't have to control. I didn't perceive the cold and remote presence of the Potentia in her, though. I decided to intensify the experience by focusing my attention further.

I couldn't help it, she was really beautiful to my eyes. She wore a light robe and was seated with her legs crossed on her bed, taken by sadness. I felt struck by a mixture of curiosity and regret in seeing her in that state and therefore tried to call her composing her name with the voice of my heart. She instantly reacted.

"Where are you?", she said.

"Close your eyes", I answered through my mind.

She did and the scenery suddenly changed for both of us. We were, in what seamed to be, a rock desert which stretched as far as the eye could see under a gray sky like opaque metal.

Amelia looked around.

"You brought me to my world", she said.

"Maybe this is the place where you would like to be", I answered.

"How are you able to do all this?". Naturally she wanted to know how I had managed to enter her mind.

"We all have a few secrets, don't we? And this is one of mine", I answered.

"Why did you go away from me? I really wanted you to be mine", she said sadly.

"I know. I felt it. Unfortunately you weren't the only one who did", I said hinting to the Potentia which possessed her.

"He can act through me. He took possession of my soul and I was filled by his power. He is powerful and I could never resist him. But it was I who wanted you. And he showed me how", she said. The "he" she was referring to was surely the Potentia.

"Don't tell me you don't know why he complied with this desire of yours? Please don't be naive with me". She lowered her eyes in my mind.

"Of course I know. But the only way to have you is to bring you to them. They are our masters", she said.

"If you really want it I will fight to free you from their power", I said.

She smiled her disarming smile even if the feeling she communicated was of deep and resigned sadness. "It's too late for me. I don't know of a force able to contrast them. My mind is poisoned and my spirit looks for them like a drug addict looks for the substance which destroys him. He left me the liberty of taking you and it's the only liberty I was ever granted", she said.

The design of the Potentiae was clear: to arrive to their objective exploiting Amelia's and my desire. In that moment I felt a strong compassion for her and for her eternal imprisonment.

"If you really want me, I will find a solution", I said.

"Don't do it. You would fail. And I will hunt you down until you're mine. He will help me and not even you will be able to contrast his power", she said.

"How do you explain the failure of your incantation then? I saw your foul master inside your eyes and yet you failed", I said in a challenging tone.

"I told you. You are special. But in time they will get you too", she said.

I approached the projection of her body, then reached out with my hand in my mind and caressed her. Amelia reacted with a shiver. I would have liked to stay there with her indefinitely but knew it was impossible.

"You made me feel things I had never felt before and I will never forget that", I told her.

"I was about to tell you the same thing", she answered smiling slowly.

Then her expression began to change and in her eyes I saw the

Potentia arriving which was taking possession of her. The Demon had detected my presence and now wanted to enter my mind using the connection.

"Good bye", I said.

Even the scenery was changing into pure darkness.

"Don't go, stay with me. Don't leave me alone", said Amelia's voice but it was no longer her who spoke. I tried to break the contact.

A flash.

I opened my eyes on the Terrace but still had the feeling of Amelia in the background and felt the instinctive fear that she could reach me in that place guided by the Demon, her master.

I mentally prepared myself for her arrival but nothing happened. I remained alarmed for the rest of the evening, though.

To interrupt the connection, I decided to occupy my attention with the analysis of the translator that Shen had given me and which, according to what he had said, had always been mine.

The all-around shape of the object was octagonal, yet it was the sum of other smaller shapes, each one characterized by its own color. The one used for transport was a purple triangle placed exactly north of the octagon.

I decided to try it while I was at it. I visualized the room I arrived in at the temple of the obelisks and then turned the triangle.

All around me the apartment was immediately substituted by the inside of the temple and by the circle of obelisks which formed the Vortex. There were other two custodians on guard, who were not alarmed by my arrival but greeted me with a nod.

"Does the Eternal need something?", asked the one with the bigger beard.

"No thanks", I answered and turned my attention once more to the Vortex.

Now I was able to identify the monolith with the representation of the Second Emanation and also that of the Ninth Emanation which was the new home of the Anantrya. Khalid's explanations had been very accurate.

I wanted to perform an experiment with the Translator near a specific person. My first choice was Khalid but then I opted for Shen, just in case Khalid had already returned to his mission on Earth. I certainly didn't want to suddenly appear with the possibility that there might be witnesses to the event.

Shen's image filled my mind and turning the triangle on the Translator the temple around me became a big beach with a multitude of little premises that followed its entire length. The sea was the living mirror of the stars in the sky. Shen was sitting with other people smoking a pipe and chatting lively. The fact that I had just appeared from nowhere didn't seem to disturb anyone.

"Brother! Were you not able to sleep?", asked Shen cheerfully.

"They say that too much tiredness can take your sleep away", I replied.

"If that is the case, please, join us for the evening", he continued.

"Thank you Shen but I didn't want to disturb. Just a test-run with the Translator", I said.

He looked at me closely. Could he have understood what I had intended to do?

"I understand. I feel that something has happened in the last hours. I feel a Demon is looking for you. Quick, go into the water of the ocean to cancel its mark from your magnetic signature. They must never know of this place".

"It must be the effect of the interrupted incantation by Amelia. Can the sea cancel it?", I asked.

"It is said that the sea on the Fifth Emanation was blessed by the Messenger of the Makers and that it can purify anything", he answered.

"Thank you. I really needed a bath", I said to downplay, then undressed and completely immersed myself in the water. In fact I felt my mind imbued by calmness which freed itself from the unease I didn't realize I felt.

I remained in the water for a while, enjoying the feeling of movement of the waves which gently pushed my body back and forth as though it were in a cradle. All the tiredness of the last days set upon me suddenly and I realized I risked falling asleep. I dragged myself ashore and without getting dressed took the translator, greeted Shen and his guests and visualized my apartment. I was there instantly.

I was really tired. I only found time to go to the bathroom to dry myself a little and then crashed on the bed invaded by an exceptional wave of unavoidable oblivion.

III

I dreamed of Amelia, speaking to me, crying, sinking her teeth into my throat, caressing me, gently kissing me, all dressed by an emotion of powerful anguish. I woke up with my heart bursting in my chest and I touched my neck as if to verify that Amelia's hands weren't there clasping it.

The feeling of anguish was still present although and in the darkness at the back of the room I thought I saw something move. I heard a slow sigh.

"You cannot fight My Power", said a voice outside and inside my head.

It was him: the Demon that possessed Amelia was looking for me and he was able to create a contact.

A cold feeling reached me and made my flesh creep. Then I felt anger, a blind anger, deep and pure. All powerful and primitive emotions coming from the Great Demon. Then I felt him withdraw as if something had made him run away and the room was empty for a moment.

A form came out of the darkness, it had a glow and shone of a light of its own. It looked like a big cherub with a human appearance and big wave shapes that ran through its body and came out from its shoulders like big wings. The space around me became dense as though it were solidifying in reaction to the importance of the entity in front of me.

The dark feelings had disappeared as if by a spell and in their place I felt a detached tranquility. I was a little confused.

"And who are you?", I asked trying to put its shape into focus without being able to.

"I am the Messenger", answered something in my head. "You are still not complete to be able to face the Potentia that is looking for you", it continued.

All negativity had disappeared from my mind and from the area around me.

"Are you an Anantrya? I mean, a Lord of the Guardians?", I asked.

"I am the Messenger of the Heart of everything", he answered.

It sounded pretentious, but to me in that moment, they were only words.

"Can you help me contrast the Demon who was looking for me?".

"The Potentia which is looking for you, like all the others of its race, was created to corrupt the events of the History of this World. If you become influenced before becoming complete the History will be contaminated. I exist to protect the development of the History of this World".

"I'm sorry but I still don't understand", I said.

"You will not understand until you are complete. Until that time, you must not go near the Potentia which is looking for you", it answered. Then, just as it had appeared, it disappeared and the room was empty again.

I felt like smoking and lit a cigarette from a pack on the night stand. The service personnel had really thought of everything.

The Demon or Potentia, whichever way one wanted to call it, didn't seem to want to give up finding me, with or without Amelia. But that anger and fear, as big as a phobia amplified to infinity, came from the Beast itself and the cause was apparently the presence of the Messenger.

Therefore this entity had to possess an enormously superior Power than the Demon and yet all it had done was to send it away; I found it strange that a Power that could send these Demons away didn't try to destroy them, cancel them or reduce them to a state of powerlessness.

Too many elements were missing and something told me that even Shen and Khalid had no answers for me.

Maybe the Anantrya or one of the Messengers could give me an explanation, even if Sithar had spoken of the Messenger as an unknown entity even to them.

I put out the cigarette and lay back down hoping to be able to sleep with no further surprises. It was my last thought, then everything turned off around me.

IV

The next morning I received a nice invitation for breakfast with Shen and some other guests brought by a man from the service personnel. I decided to reach them after having dressed properly and in preparation of another intense day.

At Shen's table there was Khalid, a witch named Julia, a Christian nun from the Marian order named Claudia, a Victorian Englishman named John Deelay and an American Indian who introduced himself as Raven in the Void, but asked me to simply call him don Pedro.

After the presentations I concentrated on the lavish breakfast while the other diners exchanged pleasantries.

Sister Claudia smiled:

"Eternal Heylel. You had some important visits during the night". She must have been a clairvoyant.

"I have received some visits but am not able to evaluate whether or not they were important", I answered.

"I know. I'm absolutely sure! From the most complete realms on the other side of the mirror they are observing you and protecting you. This means that it is absolutely necessary that you hasten your recovery for the good outcome of your Mission".

"If I only knew how... ".

"We will help you as much as we can. But the Guardians and their Masters will be able to help you even more". It was Julia, the witch who had followed the conversation between Sister Claudia and me.

"And how do I contact them?", I asked.

"You will have to find a way to go to them. Maybe the Guardians themselves can tell you how. If they agree it will mean that you are welcome and it had to be so", said Sister Claudia.

"Would anyone like some good wine?", John asked.

The breakfast continued with no further talk of important topics and soon after we were all on the balcony.

Sister Claudia was right. I had to move quickly in that, for as much as I could see, everything seemed to be subject to an acceleration.

I made a decision: I had to go to the Temple of the Vortex and attempt a direct contact with the Ninth Emanation.

Not before trying to contact Monika though.

V

Even on the Fifth Emanation one could find a good expresso coffee and I enjoyed a second cup; a rare pleasure.

I left Shen and his guests informing them that I had decided to use the Vortex to reach the Ninth Emanation and that I had some preparations to make before trying the endeavor.

Once at my apartment I sat comfortably on the balcony like the evening before with the intention of trying the contact procedure again but with Monika as my target. But this time I was ready for whatever could go wrong, or at least I hoped so.

I used the same procedure I had used to look for Amelia. Nothing happened at first which made me suspect that the contact from the night before had only been possible due to the incantation, but then I felt her weakly far away. I began to perceive her emotions and then a weak image; she was in the semi-darkness of an empty room, without windows, with a closed door. She was a prisoner, crouched down in a corner of the room wearing what looked like pajamas. At the center of the room there was a hole which must have been a kind of toilette.

She had cried a lot and was now trying to fight against the fear of what would have happened to her. I particularly felt her fear of Amelia and of her mind, giving up as a way to avoid what they would have done to her, taking her own life away before the door opened for her. While I observed, a little tray with bread, cheese and a little bottle of water was pushed inside from a slit.

I was torn; I wanted to do something for her, take her away from there but where could I have brought her? Translating her to the Fifth Emanation was a big risk in that I didn't know if I could avoid the Caste from simply using her as bait to trap me or even to open an access towards Amn'el'Tyr, an event which would have surely provoked a furious war and nullified all the efforts made in the thousands of years to conceal and keep that place safe. I could use the translator to bring her to the original Earth. There though the power of the Caste was at its peak and it could prove difficult to prevent them from understanding where I had hidden her.

In any case, one thing was certain: this endeavor would have exposed me, even if for a brief moment, to eventual traps prepared just for me or for one of my Equals.

I felt impotent and frustrated but then I felt Monika's empathic mind who had noticed my presence.

"Is it you? Oh my God, no! Another hallucination", she said weeping.

"It's me honey", I answered.

"I'm already going mad, my God!", and she started crying again hiding her face with her hands.

"You're not mad. Listen to me. It's me and I'm trying to find a way to get you out of there", I said.

"Is it really you? Get me out of here! And how? I'm guarded more than a nuclear plant".

"There might be a way. But I need to know everything about the place where you are and what you think they want to do with you".

"I'm in an underground detention structure. They haven't told me anything concerning their intentions but I think they're waiting for Amelia to enter my head, empty it and then throw me away like garbage", she said.

"I don't think they want to do something irreversible to you", I said.

"And why not? I'm like a lab animal to them".

"Because they want me and you're the only thing they have to obtain something".

"Well, they won't get a damn thing from me", she said.

"They could make you do a lot of things independently from your will. I've had a taste of their power", I said.

"And how?".

"With an incantation or through a direct contact with the demon which possesses Amelia. Its corrupting power is big and I don't think you could resist it", I said.

"Now I know it's really you and not a product of my mind! Thanks for the trust!", she answered ironically.

"If you knew what I'm talking about you'd understand".

"Take me away!", she begged.

She was still sitting in the corner of her little prison, crouched down with her arms around her legs near her body and her gaze fixed in a vacuum.

"Close your eyes", I ordered her.

"Why?".

"Just do it!".

"And now?", she asked after having closed her eyes.

I started the procedure for a full contact with her like I had done with Amelia. In my mind she became more and more real and I imagined her in her black uniform that made her look like a comic book heroine. The vision of the room was substituted with the forest on Earth-2 where we had gone together: that was probably the place where she felt safe or that had a strong appeal in her mind. She appeared in front of me as I had imagined her.

"Where are we?", she asked.

"You chose this place, honey".

"Sure, this is where I brought you the first time after your arrival on Earth-2, I remember. But how did we arrive here?", she asked.

"This isn't the real world. Or at least not according to the common meaning of 'real'. We are in complete mental contact now and our minds have chosen connection symbols, including the scenery", I answered.

"Damn! I didn't know such things could be done. Can we touch each other?", she asked coming closer; I took her hand and we both had a feeling like ghost fingers brushing over the skin.

"It's beautiful!", she said finally smiling.

"I was very worried about you", I said.

"The worse has yet to come, unfortunately. I'm very much afraid", she said embracing me.

It wasn't the feeling of a physical embrace, but more like that of two clouds full of electricity meeting.

"Where are you?", she asked loosening her embrace.

"In a safe place", I answered.

"How were you able to escape?", she asked freeing herself from the embrace and stepping back. I felt a certain amount of suspicion coming from her. She suspected it was all a trick to weaken her resistance.

"Don't worry, it's me, it's not a trick of the mind of the Demons", I answered.

"Demons? That is Amelia and Icarus?".

"Not them but the entities that control them. Amelia, possessed by one of these Demons was chaining me to her with an incantation when I escaped, but first she tried her mental power on me but it didn't work. I was about to succumb to the incantation when I dislocated, exactly like that time that you witnessed at the obelisks", I explained.

I saw her relax a bit.

"I feel it's you even if I don't know what these Demons are capable of", she said.

"They are corrupters and there is no one able to resist the power they exude", I said.

"I sense Amelia in your thoughts, why?".

"It's a collateral effect of the incantation".

"But she... you... between you... ?".

"She only tried to chain me and expose me to the power of the Demon", I said taking her hand.

"Can't you make me escape?", she asked.

"I'll do everything possible and beyond. You try to resist", I answered.

"I've just arrived on Earth-2 and they immediately locked me up. If Amelia has failed with you, now she must be on her way for me. I just have a few hours and then I don't know what will happen".

"Now that I know where you are I will look for a way to get you out of their sphere of influence. If something happens try to contact me like I did. It could work". And I transmitted my thoughts with the contact procedure to her.

"If you are unable, in any case don't worry, I will come in, one way or another", I promised.

I came close to her and kissed her lightly on the lips which was like another meeting of clouds.

"I wish this moment would never end. Thanks for giving it to me", she whispered sweetly.

"I have to go now".

"No, please stay another while with me", she said with a touch of sadness in her voice.

"The more I stay the less time I have to think up a plan to take you away".

"Okay, okay", and she embraced me again.

I mentally interrupted the communication and opened my eyes. As with Amelia I felt the residue of the contact becoming more and more remote. I hoped to find a solution in time for Monika before Amelia reached her; before it was too late.

I had to regain more power, more of myself, become more complete, as I had been told, before risking another potential encounter with Amelia or with a Potentia. I was comforted by the fact that at least someone up there kept an eye on my uncertain progression.

An essential passage of my journey was the trip to the Ninth Emanation where I hoped to understand my Task and the purpose of my incarnation and of my awakening triggered by the First Guardian.

I looked for Shen, first of all to ask his advice on the trip, if there was a ritual to follow, well, whatever useful information; I knew no one had ever attempted this endeavor before but I trusted Shen's wisdom. Or maybe I just needed some encouraging words from a friend.

He confirmed to me that never before had an Eternal of the Gathering had the boldness of using the Ninth Obelisk of the Vortex for the trip and that therefore there were no historical precedents of such enterprise, nor had the Lords of the Guardians left instructions regarding this.

"If your Conscience tells you that you have to carry out this endeavor, you will have to follow your instinct and if your Task foresees this trip then it will happen independently from any advice you could receive from me or others. Remember that it is the Lords of the Guardians who watch over us and they will surely know the path you have to follow", he told me.

I dismissed myself from him with an embrace, then I used the Translator to reach the Vortex in the Temple.

Other two guards were in their place and when they saw me greeted me with the usual nod.

It was useless to delay any further: I entered the area of the Vortex and sat on the altar with the Ninth Obelisk in front of me and after a long mind cleansing breath started reading it.

EARTH 9

I seemed to float, for an indefinite time, in a space full of abstract, sometimes impossible, geometrical shapes in a three dimensional space and yet absolute in its symmetry.

Then, these perfect shapes, vibrating with unknown colors, became Earth and Sky.

The sky was a bright turquoise, striped here and there by lapis lazuli and gold. It seemed to shine all by itself given that there was no sun above.

The land instead was a flat desert and the sand was a brick red color. I found myself in the middle of a structure that was dissimilar to the Vortex from which I had come except for the central stone altar.

Instead of the monoliths there were some perfectly smooth structures of the same color and material as the altar, similar to portals, reminiscent of ancient sites on Earth Prime.

The temperature was mild and there wasn't even a breeze. Everything appeared motionless and perfect, like a painting by a famous artist of a world born out of his imagination. Not a soul could be seen.

I remained seated on the altar for what seemed like an hour and the wait was not in vain. From one of the stone Portals in front of me I perceived a vibration; following that, the desert and the sky which I had seen a little earlier through the Portal was substituted by what could, at first sight, seem like the inside of a room, like a big room with big windows in the background; I interpreted it as an invitation and little by little, with unmotivated caution, got off the altar going closer, delaying on the threshold only for a moment. Then I crossed it all the way, the sky, the desert, the altar and the portals disappeared behind me. At a short distance there were Sithar and other two Anantrya in blue and gold tunics.

"Welcome Eternal. We were waiting for you. Welcome to our Dominion", said Sithar touching his forehead and nodding downwards.

I looked behind me and saw only a big oval window and beyond the window the sidereal space full of stars and a slice of the planet which must have been the mythical Earth-9 inside the Ninth Emanation.

"Thanks for receiving me in Your Home", I said imitating Sithar's gesture.

"Please, follow us. We don't have much time", he said. The three started leading me towards a wide, smooth corridor.

"I don't understand", I said while following them.

The other two Anantrya followed us a few steps behind.

"We have the duty to reveal to you your mission and provide you with all the essential knowledge. We are the only ones in this World who possess the means to carry out this task", Sithar answered.

"Okay, and that's fine. It's the thing about the little time I don't understand", I said.

"The Potentiae have mobilized like never before from the end of the great war. They ardently wish to find you and their primary objective is chaining you to their power and through you, reach us".

"And the secondary objective?".

"Destroy you, of course".

"I see. But why have they mobilized right now? You could say I've been under their nose for years!".

"They couldn't perceive you while your awakening was not in act. If they succeed in binding you to their power it will be a catastrophe for all the World and the development of History. If they destroy you we will have to start all over again, and they would have acquired an advantage on the Gathering".

"I see! But why now?".

"Because they have correctly identified you and suspect you are connected to us even if, in thousands of years they were never able to have evidence of our presence in this system. It would be a catastrophe for the Gathering and maybe also for us if they succeeded in their intent. We would be forced to resort to an extreme solution", said Sithar.

I knew what he meant by extreme solution; the same they had used for the genocide of the Saurians and the exile of the Potentiae at the time of their ancient war.

"Why me? Surely the Gathering can count on Eternals of high discernment who could carry out any Task, maybe even better than me, unprepared and with no memory", I asked.

"Because you are the Messenger's choice. The influence of the Potentiae cannot be directly contrasted even by us and this means that their presence in History was wanted by a Will which surpasses even our own awareness. This is why the Messenger intervened. We think there is an ongoing conflict in the Dominion of the Great Dream beyond the Mirror and that the Potentiae are a product of this conflict, as is the Messenger and, as we believe, you are. Yet, we have to complete your preparation to allow you to participate to the conflict and eventually end it in favor of the History of this World".

"But it will take too long for me to recover myself, the necessary knowledge and consequent comprehension that would allow me to use it", I said perplexed.

"This is the reason for the urgency! We are in a position to be able to transfer in you what is necessary in a limited time. The rest you will do yourself if the Makers want".

Instant knowledge through direct injection. Interesting and if true, very convenient...

We crossed many corridors and I don't know how many doors, and at last reached a big room with what looked like an opaque metal bed in the center.

"What place is this?", I asked.

"This is one of our itinerant cities. You would call it space ship", Sithar answered.

"You must now take position", said one of the other two Anantrya, showing me the bed in the center of the room.

I laid down on the metal plate. Its surface, at first hard and cold, softened becoming almost liquid, taking the shape of my laying body and imitating its temperature. It was very comfortable actually.

I felt the bed silently move with me on it towards my shoulders until it completely covered me like a dark burial recess.

I had a moment of apprehension which disappeared almost immediately given that, at least in theory, I was among friends and anyway I wouldn't have had any way of contrasting them.

Even the entrance of the recess closed and I was in complete darkness. After I don't know how long, I probably lost my senses.

II

I remember that when I woke up I was till laying on the metal bed in the center of the room, which was empty and apparently without doors or windows, which I had been led to. I was neither hungry nor thirsty, as if something were automatically and satisfactorily overseeing my bodily needs; I was so comfortable and felt so satisfied that I had to forcefully will myself to get up from that cradle which made me feel so tenderly safe.

I reluctantly got up and the opaque metal surface immediately turned smooth and hard.

I felt different, very different and also extraordinarily awake. The shadows of insecurity which had accompanied me up to that moment had disappeared as if until then I had acted by pure survival instinct and without real knowledge of the facts.

I looked at my hands and saw them more solid, more real and truer.

I wished for a mirror but there wasn't one. So I felt my body from head to foot and noticed that even my movements, though simple were different in that they were entirely conscious and focused on the dynamic present.

What I had been, what I had done, no longer was important in that great present, real representation of the Life to become.

I could describe the experience as a 'rebirth', which hadn't changed my body but the life which animated it, as if I had been subjected to an unexpected transformation at a more refined level to which I was still adapting. Imagine a ten year old child, who at waking up one morning, has acquired the experience and the characteristics of a person of forty and you will only faintly understand what had happened to me.

I had no idea of how many days or months had passed since I had been introduced in the recess and I knew that the feeling of passing of time I perceived was not reliable, based as it was on acquired parameters in ordinary conditions.

It was me but also a new person and all my life before this experience was integrating with my new dimension and acquiring a totally new meaning. Imagine to learn a song in a foreign language as a child, learning to repeat the exact sounds of that song by heart; then one day, after years of studying, you learn to speak that language perfectly. You remember the song and suddenly realize that the sounds you learned to repeat so well by heart are words that compose verses which now finally have a meaning. But even being able to imagine this, only a shadow produced by a palely reflected light remains, compared to what the real experience was.

A door appeared on one side of the domed room from which Sithar entered followed by his two companions; I greeted him with that gesture of the hand and head, which I understood now, and he and his companions did the same.

Holding out my hand to him I noticed for the first time that he and his companions also wore a translator, like the ones worn by the members of the Gathering, and with my new and increased knowledge I knew that this was the place of origin of these instruments.

Sithar and his two companions touched the triangular shape turning it counterclockwise and everything around me, the room of the space ship or itinerant city, became a park like the one where I had been conducted to by the second Guardian on Moon-2.

I was on the planet or if you prefer, Earth-9, in the space of the Ninth Emanation.

I now knew that the Anantrya had created this place which was, to all effects, an independent Universe and had wanted to simulate the environment and the colors of their colony on Mars at the time of their arrival in the solar system. I knew it reminded them of the ancient planet which had been the cradle of their civilization.

"How do you feel?", Sithar asked gently.

"Different, bigger... more complete... ", I answered, "... and also as if I had awakened from a long sleep full of images and dreams but where I couldn't remember myself nor did I know I was dreaming".

"Good!", he said. "... Well, know that there are many levels of sleep and alertness and what you have now regained is only your self-consciousness inside the Image of the Great Dream".

"A part of me understands what you're saying".

"... but not completely", Sithar interjected.

"Exactly. Now I know who I have to be: Heylel of the Gathering of the Eternals. But I have a feeling which disturbs me and tells me that this is only another role to interpret with its own script, another phase of the Dream, another mask worn by an unknown person who is still me", I said.

"Don't ever forget this feeling because it will constantly remind you that you are not the task you have to complete, according to the designs of History. But don't let the feeling become an obsession, otherwise you could alienate yourself and stray from your role and from what you have come to do. One day maybe this feeling will be substituted by a clear and sharp understanding", Sithar said, like a loving father giving the last instructions to his son before sending him off to face the world alone.

I was never able to understand why, but something in the way Sithar had spoken to me caused a great emotion and in that beautiful and peaceful place I began to cry like a child feeling the dam of my emotions, in constant control, break, freeing the waters in a valley parched until then. Sithar remained in silence resting his hand on my back as if to tell me that what I was experiencing and feeling at that moment was right and I had to let it take its course.

We reached a lawn of turquoise and green grass and sat in a semicircle. When the dam of my emotions freed itself and its spur had cleansed the valley, no longer parched, from its dead waste, I asked Sithar of their world and their origin. He told me of the Anantrya and of how, harmoniously integrating the knowledge of matter, mind and beyond they were able to attract the Divine attention of the Makers and to create for themselves a condition of continuous growth which, undisturbed by the frenzy caused by a short life, proceeded in small steps towards an objective of perfection which was though an unreachable target, like an arrow shot in infinity.

They considered the encounter with the terrible darkness represented by the Potentiae an important part of the path the race was destined to follow. They were in fact convinced that all their history and the levels of progress and knowledge they had gained, acquired perfect sense only when they had met the dark race. They had then realized that their part in the history of the World was that of protectors and consequently had to contrast and contain it.

They had realized though that it wasn't in their power to destroy the Potentiae and that therefore these entities existed by the will of something much higher than them and of the history of the World, finding proof of this in the appearance of the Messengers at their supreme council in occasion of their request for direct intervention; for this reason they exiled the Potentiae and created this artificial universe or Emanation in relation and interposition with Earth. And for the same reason the Anantrya colony which inhabited the ancient planet of Mars had resolved to stay in this place to guard the events and at the service of the Messengers. At that time they had created those structures they called Guardians and had seen the beginning of the Gathering when the Potentiae met and corrupted exponents from other planets residing on Earth.

"You are the result of a grand plan which took place in time to directly contrast the power of those creatures which would like to spark off their influence on everything that exists", concluded Sithar.

"But I can't even dream of being up to the Anantrya. How can I be a more efficient agent than any one of your race?", I asked.

"Everyone in the History has his place. You have in yourself something that is inborn which comes neither from ancientness nor from instilled knowledge. Qualities which, in the right amounts, are a natural enemy of the Potentiae and originate from their same space of origin. We can only guide you and offer refuge but we could never oppose the Potentiae as you were born to do", answered Sithar.

Of course, at that time I understood the words but was far from completely understanding their meaning.

"As you have been able to see for yourself, you are in direct connection with the Messengers and they watch over your awakening. Just this reality in itself is symbolic of the origin of the power which you will be able to set off at the right moment and place", Sithar concluded.

We remained there in silence enjoying the perfect nature and each other's company while I felt the new knowledge create access points to my consciousness, strengthening me inside like a sword being prepared and oiled for the oncoming battle.

III

At first I had a feeling of coldness inside as if I had just been touched by a ghost, then the thought of Monika imposed itself to my attention. I saw that Sithar too had perceived something and was now observing me with attention.

"Something is looking for you now! It is time for you to go and not be found in this space. The Ninth Emanation must be preserved and remain inaccessible. As long as you are here you represent an access point. Now you have the knowledge to draw benefit from all the attributes of the Translator you are wearing. When you need us use it, even to call us and we will be there for you", said Sithar with a tone of urgency in his voice.

I reluctantly got up but of course he was right. Something was looking for me and I didn't have a good feeling about it.

"Can I use the Translator to enter and leave the Ninth Emanation too?", I asked.

"Now yes. You will no longer need other intermediaries to translate your shape or your thought. The only condition is that you be able to exactly visualize your destination or who you want to contact, We have transferred in your conscience all the information relative to the Laws of Translation. You will discover that there are no limits to what you can do using it", Sithar answered.

Silently seeing myself off following the dismissal ritual, I visualized my apartment at Amn'el'Tyr and as if by magic I was there. It was night on Earth-5 and the silence at the palace was complete. Monika's image again imposed itself to my attention and now I also perceived fear and a request for help; she was trying to contact me as I had taught her to do.

I sat comfortably on a sofa inside. I wanted to smoke and noticed ironically that my increased awareness had left my desire to smoke intact. Foreseeing forthcoming troubles I decided to light my last cigarette before the eventual conflict.

Monika's call became more and more intense and distressed and I prepared for the contact.

I decided to use the same procedure I had used before, trying not to use the Translator. I mentally found myself in a windowless room similar to the one on Earth where I had met Monika for the first time. I saw her and in front of her there was Amelia with a table between them. Monika seemed tried from lack of sleep and maybe also of liquids. Her face was emaciated with two dark circles under her vague and blood injected eyes. I could see her shaking a little as if she were cold. Amelia seemed tranquil instead, always impeccable as she spoke.

I felt Monika perceive me and transmit the terror she felt and then in a corner of the room there was the reason of her fear: Amelia's two assistants lay naked, ripped open and with their hands still inside their bodies as if they had ripped their own flesh with their naked hands, tearing their organs out of their bodies and spreading them around the room.

The walls and the floor were almost entirely covered by blood and their expression indicated that they had acted this way prey to a folly that had transformed their features in distorted caricatures asking for help or in alternative a compassionate death. Their eyes were completely rolled back while between their teeth they still clenched pieces of flesh which must have been part of their own insides as if something had forced them to feed themselves of their own flesh.

In my condition I couldn't perceive smells but imagined that the closed room was filled by the pungent smells of secretions, blood and excrement coming from the two corpses and next to Monika there was a puddle of yellow green liquid was probably her vomit.

I silently damned my slowness in intervening. Amelia seemed very calm and relaxed, acting as though she were in a perfectly normal situation. I saw in Monika's mind that the cause of the horrible death of the two assistants had been Amelia, probably by way of the overwhelming influence of the Potentia that looked at the world through her. I started to pick up what Amelia was saying through Monika's mind while I tried to calm her.

"You are a very precious element to us, do you understand?", she said.

Monika made a brief and uncertain nod.

"You see, you were right... the people who were testimony of what I had revealed unfortunately became a risk for the security of the entire Organization. But I don't want you to follow their destiny. Now you know that I know about your very special tie with a person who is very precious to you... and also to me", Amelia continued.

She maliciously smiled to Monika making her understand they both wanted the same thing.

In spite of the horror of the situation I felt Monika's emotions react as if her being a woman had the power to have the upper hand even in such an extreme situation.

Yet I felt her mind far away, as if it were anesthetized and had turned on a defense mechanism probably to avoid succumbing to the hell which she had witnessed and which the two masses of massacred flesh that were in front of her continued to remind her, aggravating her tormented stability and survival instinct.

I had to make a quick decision and did.

This also had to serve me as a test of my new awareness and of the new power I had acquired on the Ninth Emanation. I didn't have time to consult with a Guardian or with Shen; I interrupted the mental contact and visualized the windowless room with Amelia, Monika and the two corpses and activated the Translator.

I had visualized myself exactly behind Amelia and when I appeared in the room she didn't have time to do anything; Monika saw me appear and emitted a little cry exactly as my hands clutched Amelia's neck and head.

I felt her become rigid and her hands took mine as if to protect herself, but didn't put up a struggle.

"You have finally arrived. You don't want to hurt me, do you?", she said.

She was right. Even if she represented the great Darkness I couldn't forget that what in her wasn't a demon loved me. Not even the thought of the lifeless massacred bodies in the corner of the room caused me a different attitude. Not even the smell of blood and death which I now perceived.

"I won't hurt you Amelia if you don't force me to", I said.

"But you are not here for me".

"Sharp intuition", I said ironically.

I nodded to Monika to get up and come close to me and trembling she got up and came.

"How can you still want her? Look at her! She is only a little creature, weak and imperfect. You can have more, anything you want from me!", Amelia said in that mad tone of voice I had already heard her use the night of the incantation, while Monika came near me holding on to the table.

"I could save you too Amelia, but what possesses you makes my stomach churn and you don't have the strength to get rid of it; its touch has contaminated you and now it's your life. Carry a message to your Master for me: I will reach him where he dwells and erase him from the World as if he had never existed because I am his Nemesis", I said enunciating the words like a magic spell.

Amelia became restless trying to turn her head to look at me but I kept her still.

"Don't move otherwise I'll have to hurt you. And then where will your Master go?", I said knowing he was listening to everything.

"Even I am only a tool to him", she said with a touch of sadness in her voice; she let herself go without struggling anymore.

Monika had reached me and was now embracing me from behind and weeping.

I bent over and gently kissed Amelia's head.

"Good bye Amelia", I whispered beginning to visualize my apartment on Earth-5.

Freed from the grip of my hands she began to turn around but it was too late; I had already activated the Translator and the next moment Monika and I were no longer there.

IV

Monica held on to me for a while before I was able to make her relax. I showed her the bathroom where she was able to clean up from the filth heaped on her during those endless hours as a prisoner, but even if the water could maybe wash away the physical filth, the horror she had lived would have tormented her for a long time.

I returned from the balcony and found her still lying on the bed in a bathrobe soundly asleep. I didn't dare think how much time they had kept her awake.

I remained looking at her for a while: I wanted to take the opportunity to contact Shen and update him on the latest events.

Monika was safe now, I thought, but I wasn't sure Shen would have approved of my decision to bring her to the Fifth Emanation, ever since exclusive dominion of the Gathering.

I had done the only thing that seemed logical in that situation, but the reason that had pushed me had nothing to do with my Task, as much as with my personal desire to take her away from Amelia and from probable death.

An underlying feeling told me there was more in what I had done, but at that moment I ignored it, dismissing it as an attempt of my rational mind to interpret my actions.

Anyway, in respect of the Gathering, it was my duty to warn Shen. I went back out on the balcony and visualized him in my mind activating the Translator. He was in his room, meditating in the middle of a circle made with eight candles around him. His eyes opened a moment after my arrival.

"Heylel! What brings you here?".

"I hope I'm not interrupting anything", I said hinting to his meditation.

"No problem. I was finishing up".

"I need your advice. And also to inform you of something I just did", I said.

"The Custodians of the Vortex have informed me they witnessed your departure towards the Ninth Emanation. From what I see you were successful in your endeavor. I would like to listen to you, for as much as you can tell me, and know if you met the Lords of the Guardians".

So I sat in front of Shen and started to tell him everything that had happened from my departure from the vortex towards the Ninth Emanation to my use of the Translator to take Monika away from the influence of the Caste and probably from certain death, or worse.

Shen remained thoughtful for a while.

"I understand", he said with a faraway expression.

"The integration process of my new awareness is still taking place and I know, as it was transmitted to me, that I have been prepared to face the Potentiae in a direct conflict. From what I know now of my Task, it was decided that their presence can no longer only be contained. A final solution has become necessary which will end with their definitive cancellation", I said.

Shen seemed to consider my words and what they implied.

"So it is war", he said at last.

"There doesn't seem to be another solution. The Potentiae aren't beings with whom to hope to negotiate peacefully and they will never stop until they have reached their objective and beyond".

"We have spent so much time hiding and acting in a subliminal way that maybe we have softened up basking in the safety of this world. Inside of me, and I know this to be true for all the Eternals of the Gathering and the refugees on the Fifth Emanation, I knew that this moment had to arrive. But now that you announce it I realize we have never worked to seriously prepare for a determining conflict but only to carry on a sort of never ending cold war. In all honesty I don't know where to begin", Shen said.

"Among the refugees on Earth-5 there are also warriors who come from the greatest periods of conflict, right?".

"Of course. It's not the warriors we are missing and neither the Power. What we need is a strategy and a leader", Shen answered. I considered his words.

"You will be our leader and it's best if you get used to the idea. I suggest that you recall all the operative awakened Eternals back to Amn'el'Tyr in this moment. I also suggest that you convene a War Council to put all the residents on alert and warn them that there will soon be a conflict of proportions never seen before against the Caste and the Potentiae. Once you have convened the available Eternals call me and I will update them on what has happened in the last few days; you will take command and the Council of the Gathering will authorize the strategy it considers most opportune".

"I feared you would say this", he said with a pinch of irony.

"We don't have time to waste Shen. You know you're the only one who can bring everyone together and direct the collective energy towards a common objective".

"I had hoped that the Lords of the Guardians would indicate you as our guide in this undertaking".

"My Task is another one. The energy I represent in this Image is disintegrating and destructive. I have been prepared as a natural antigen to the Potentiae and will have to take care of them while the Gathering and the army that you put together breaks the Caste to pieces. Failure is not an option. We have to win at all cost because we won't have this opportunity again".

"I will begin the research at dawn and will ask Khalid to inform the population of Amn'el'Tyr. Whoever doesn't participate to the war will be transferred to the Seventh Emanation or in another safe place".

I nodded in approval.

"As for the woman you saved and transported to this place... ", continued Shen.

"Yes?".

"Well, in normal times I would tell you that you behaved in an inconsiderate way".

"Why?".

"This woman remained for too long under the influence of the Potentiae and there is a possibility that this rescue was just what they wanted to happen. She could be a Trojan Horse", said Shen.

"I had thought about it, but I can't see how they might have done something like that", I answered.

"The Potentiae never had access or kingdoms beyond the Second Emanation. Now they could discover the existence of this place and realize that the Lords of the Guardians can be reached", he said.

"I understand. In any case, she is my responsibility", I said.

"Since you have given her access to this place and as long as she is here, she cannot be only your responsibility. We have to prepare to bring the war to the kingdom of the Caste, but also for the possibility that the Caste may be trying to bring the conflict to our kingdom".

I knew Shen was right. But I wasn't able to think of Monika in those terms, especially after having seen her last encounter with Amelia; even if that sense of alarm at the bottom of the well of my subconscious told me I would have had to keep my eyes open.

She didn't have the means of resisting the influence of the Potentiae and no one knew the real proportions of this power even if they were in a state of reduced consciousness in exile.

"Okay, I will take Monika far from here as soon as possible. I will look for a a safe place on the original Earth for her so that, away from here, her potential usefulness to the Caste is lessened. In the meantime I won't let her leave my apartment. She will understand", I said.

"Very well. I hope it will suffice. Let's rest now in that difficult times lie ahead", he concluded.

I said goodbye and returned to the balcony of my apartment; Monika still slept soundly. I didn't feel sleepy and wanted to take my mind off things so I decided to go for a walk. I silently left the Palace and went to Amn'el'Tyr's seafront where I knew I would find premises open all night long.

After a few hours, a not so nice feeling warned me that maybe it was better to concentrate on my immediate future and on my guest.

I slowly returned towards the palace trying to keep my mind free from worries even if I knew it wouldn't be for long.

V

I arrived at my apartment and Monika was no longer in bed.

167

I became a bit anxious while I looked for her. I was about to use the Translator when I saw her; an immobile shape on the balcony, facing the distant horizon full of stars. With crossed arms and in a light negligée covering her body she didn't seem to notice my arrival.

I went outside too. She heard the sound of the glass door open.

"It's funny to see how life can store such radical changes in such a short time", she said without turning around.

"I agree", I answered thinking she was referring to her unhoped for rescue.

"What place is this?", she asked.

"What you see is a very special city and its name is Amn'el'Tyr".

"Why is it special?", she asked.

I thought of the irony. Just a little while back I was pestering her with questions about Earth-2 and Temporal Archives and now the situation was completely reversed.

I felt her distant though, as if, while she spoke, her mind were somewhere else; I approached her stopping right behind her.

"Special because this is the city of the Gathering of the Eternals in the Domain of this World. The only real contrast force to the Caste".

"I didn't know there was an organized contrast force. But you didn't answer my question".

"Which question?".

"What place is this?", she repeated with a wide movement of the arms. I moved forward stopping by her side, looking at her profile. Her eyes were still fixed on the horizon.

"To use a Temporal Archives definition, this is Earth-5", I answered.

"And whatever happened to Earth-3 and Earth-4?".

"Well, actually I never asked myself this question. But now that you've mentioned it I'll ask the right person as soon the opportunity arises".

"And is there also Earth-6, Earth-7 and so on", she insisted.

They were interesting and logical questions actually; yet a slight anxiousness touched the mouth of my stomach in that who could have really gained advantage from this information was the enemy. What sublime discovery for the Potentiae, the certainty that that which they had always wanted was right there, next door in space, or rather next nine doors in space!

"By logic there could also be an Earth-1,000, but I really don't know", I lied placing myself in front of her to look her in the eyes. The anxious feeling increased more and more making my 'spider senses' tingle, as Spiderman would put it.

She moved towards me and held me tight lowering her eyes and resting her head on my chest. I wanted to see her eyes but hadn't been able to.

"My god what horror", she said in a broken voice.

I held her too. After all, given the experience she'd just been through, she could be granted some amount of strangeness.

We remained embraced for some minutes then she moved away from me and looking at me whispered:

"Let's go back inside. I'm starting to feel a bit cold".

"Sure", I answered. Still embraced we went inside closing the glass door behind us.

"Will you come to sleep with me?".

"If it's not a problem for you. Otherwise I can sleep on the sofa", I said jokingly.

"I want you close", she said.

"Do you feel like telling me what happened?", I asked.

"Tomorrow. I can't now. I don't feel like I could".

"I understand".

We got comfortable. I undressed and reached her under the covers. She came close to me and held me tight; in the darkness I felt something familiar in the way she touched me that wasn't Monika's touch from what I remembered from our night of passion. Anyway, exhaustion took over almost immediately without realizing it and I fell soundly asleep.

I dreamed of Monika.

Monika seducing me and trying to tie me to her with an incantation.

Monika feeding herself of the entrails of the two bodies in the interrogation room.

Monika laughing mad.

Monika screaming that I was crazy to contrast the Potentiae and that any resistance would have been futile.

I woke up suddenly but Monika was still by my side and her heavy breathing was proof she was sleeping soundly; the last events had probably impressed me more than I thought possible; I tried to fall asleep once again and after a short while lost my senses again.

VI

I woke up to the light of the golden sun which filtered through the thin curtains of the big glass windows on the balcony.

I still felt halfway between sleep and reality and dazed as though I were still getting over a hangover or a dose of drugs.

Little by little I realized who and where I was and realized that Monika was no longer by my side. I quickly glanced around the room but there was no sign of her.

I sat up but it took me a while to get up as much as my head spun; I hadn't realized I was so tired the night before. Maybe something I had eaten (but had I eaten?) had done its part. In any case, my priority was to look for Monika; I couldn't lose sight of her, after all she was my responsibility.

Why hadn't she awakened me? I looked for her in the bathroom but she wasn't there either. Since I was there I washed my face with cold water which shook my numbed senses.

I quickly recovered my clothes: a shirt with a high neck, a pair of jeans and loafers.

If she had left the room I had to find her before Shen saw her or else I would have found myself in an embarrassing situation and would have received a well deserved telling-off.

Then I realized that the Translator wasn't where I had left it and was taken by an unexplainable panic attack. I looked everywhere in the room for it but it wasn't in sight.

Okay, I had two problems, maybe even three: I had lost the Translator, I had lost Monika and maybe Monika had lost the Translator.

Of course all this would not have constituted a real problem had she been her usual self and not the Trojan Horse of the Caste as Shen had hypothesized, but... Hey! Who was I to be so sure of one thing or another? I only had to apply the old adage that went: when in doubt the worse hypothesis is the right one.

I was about to leave the room when, from the corner of my eye, I saw a movement on the balcony: a sigh of relief almost made me stumble from the excitement.

I ran to the window and saw Monika still in her negligée, sitting with her legs crossed on one of the little sofas in direction of the sea beyond the city. My relief turned into a childish euphoria and I took several long breaths to calm down, laughing to myself for my stupid paranoia which made me see enemy shadows everywhere and in everyone, then I went out to her.

She heard me and looking at me smiled: she was holding the Translator with which she had fumbled as if it were an intelligence toy.

"Good morning!", she said.

"Good morning to you. How long have you been up?".

"For about an hour. I saw you sleeping like a baby and didn't dare wake you up. I like the morning air; were you worried?", she asked smiling.

"Absolutely not!", I lied. "You're safe here".

"I'll be needing some clothes and I think it will be quite difficult to get mine at Temporal Archives, and – don't take it personally... - but yours aren't exactly my size... ".

"Right, you're right. I'd already made a note to have some clothes brought to you by the Palace personnel".

"Palace? But is it all yours? Be careful because if you're rich I would seriously consider a marriage proposal", she said laughing lightly.

"No! It's not mine, darling. This is the Palace of the highest authority of the Gathering. You'll meet him later", I answered.

"Well, the boss", she said.

"Let's say yes. More precisely he is the resident representative of the Gathering who has authority on Amn'el'Tyr and what you would call Earth-5. This position is assigned by the Council of the Eternals by rotation, also according to whoever can defend this place with continuity".

"Many things you'll have to tell me about", she said, then her eyes returned to the Translator in her hands.

"What's this? An amulet?", she asked.

"More or less", I answered vaguely while I gently took it back and put it around my neck.

"I saw you touching it yesterday when you took me away", she said in a casual way.

The same Monika. Even in the most extreme situations she hadn't abandoned her training which allowed her to register the smallest details of a situation.

"Do you have X-ray vision?", I asked.

"No, no! You had it around your neck and just before we dislocated you touched it. Is that how you contacted me and how you cause the shifts in space?".

"I didn't remember you to be so curious".

"Well, if the situation were the other way around you would ask the same questions", she remarked.

"True. Can you tell me what happened yesterday from the first time I contacted you to when I found you there with Amelia and the two cadaver characters?", I asked changing the subject.

Her gaze became vague.

"You know, I thought I was going to die too, there. The details of those hours are fading away from my mind as if it had just been a horrible dream".

"I can imagine. I wouldn't want you to recall those moments except for the possibility that some detail at some point could be useful to me", I said.

"Don't worry, I understand perfectly".

She took a deep breath and then, "... at some point two armed men from security came to get me in the cell where I had been imprisoned and led me to the windowless room two levels underground. I remained in the room by myself for a long time, I don't know how long, and I'm sure that someone, maybe even Amelia, was observing me closely from the surveillance video cameras. Then her two assistants came in bringing me a sandwich and a glass of water and remained waiting, standing by the door. I ate and drank and after some minutes Amelia came in, apparently tranquil.

171

She asked me how I was, if I'd been treated well and other stupid questions like that. I asked her what she wanted from me and why I had been treated this way and she answered that I didn't have to ask stupid questions insulting her intelligence and that I knew very well what she was looking for and was asking for my help. I asked her what I had to do to help her and she answered that I simply had to call you or wait for you to arrive because she needed to talk to you, only to talk to you. So I asked her why you weren't with her anymore and what had happened on Moon-2 and she told me you had been able to dislocate while you were in custody and were impossible to find with the traditional methods".

"All normal and congruent with what happened to me up to this point", I remarked. "So, all you had to do was call me or wait for me to arrive without warning me that they were waiting for me?" I asked her.

"This seemed to be the gist of her round of words. Then she gave a long speech on the authority of the Caste she was part of and that security risks were not tolerated and that a very rare exception was being made for me. So I asked her what entailed becoming a risk for security and as an answer she caused that absurd suicide of her two assistants. You should have seen her eyes while those two tore their own flesh with their bare hands bringing it to their mouths. She was impassible, detached, indifferent, but there was a strange light behind her gaze that paralyzed me. Imagine that she didn't even turn around to look at what she had done. I screamed and tried with all my might not to look at the scene but I was like paralyzed. My muscles didn't respond and my eyes remained open and fixed on the slaughter. Then I threw up and after a little while you arrived and took me away".

"And this is all?", I asked.

"More or less, this is it", she answered.

"Sure?".

"I believe so. If I remember anything else I'll tell you".

"Are there gaps in your memory from the time when you were taken on Moon-2 until the moment I took you away?".

She seemed to carefully think about it for a few seconds.

"No. I think I was lucid – so to speak – the whole time. Moreover they prevented me from sleeping, therefore I wasn't even unconscious from sleep. What is the problem? Are you afraid I've been hypnotized and reprogrammed?".

"I still don't know, but please let me know if there are moments you feel strange or if you have moments of amnesia".

"Do you think they are controlling me?".

"I must consider all the possibilities for the security of this place and ours, of course".

"If there were something inside of me I think I'd be the first to know", she said sure of herself.

"If inside of you there were the same thing that controls Amelia you would never have the strength to oppose it or to do anything else but its will. The Potentiae are ancient entities which great power corrupts any flesh they touch", I said.

Meanwhile I had noticed that many of the geometrical shapes on the Translator were out of place and that therefore Monika had tried to use it and evidently it hadn't worked for her, in fact it was inactive, which relieved me for a moment. In different hands from mine the instrument became an inanimate object and therefore useless to harm or to obtain an advantage on the Gathering.

"What do we do now?", she asked.

"I'll find a safe place for you until the crisis has passed".

"I don't want to go away! I want to stay by your side. I think I've deserved it", she said dryly.

"I'm sorry, but I can't risk you being used again against me at the risk of your own life".

"I decide what to risk for whom, I've already told you! Let's not start this discussion again, please".

"I have a task to complete. We all have one here and my mind will have to be clear to be most efficient. If you stay here, you will be a natural target for them and you don't have the means to contrast them. I'll decide what to do after consulting with the others. I'll have some clothes brought to you and then I'll introduce you to Shen, the Eternal in charge here at Amn'el'Tyr", I said.

"You don't leave me much space to reply. Thanks anyway. I'll get ready quickly".

And with these words she went back inside.

I put the shapes of the Translator back in their place and after a cigarette went inside calling the floor attendant to get some comfortable clothes for Monika.

VII

The service personnel brought the clothes and also a big breakfast for two. I didn't realize how hungry I was until I smelled the eggs, fruit and toasted bread. Specially the smell of coffee.

Monika came out of the bathroom while I was gulping down the poached eggs with the toast and came to sit at the table in her bathrobe and with a towel wrapped around her head.

I looked at her but couldn't see any sign of what had happened to her on her face; she seemed tranquil and relaxed. The removal of traumatic events is a natural defense mechanism of the mind, though I thought that for someone like Monika it would be somewhat unnatural to forget so quickly or anyway to estrange herself from her emotions so completely, given her empathic receptiveness.

I finished my breakfast and drank three cups of coffee while Monika slowly ate little pieces of a fruit cocktail. Then I decided it was time to go.

"Are you finished with the bathroom?", I asked.

"Sure", she said absent-mindedly.

"Get ready and wait for me, then we'll go out together", I said.

She looked at me inquiringly. I showed her where her new clothes were.

"I'll hurry, I promise", she said while I went to the bathroom.

It was time to use some of the new functions of the Translator I had learned during my visit to the Ninth Emanation and didn't want Monika to see me while I operated. In that moment it was a simple precaution; the less she knew the less could be extorted from her in case she was captured by her ex employers.

One of the functions of the instrument allowed me to observe a place or a person anywhere in space-time or on another Emanation, as if I were in fact there, but without being perceived. As if I were an invisible ghost. Another function could bring to me a person or an object regardless of their will. Another even more intriguing function translated a willed action in a real and immediate event as with the Eunos Art but without the complicated preparations and through the Translator acted directly from a level of reality which responded to simpler, fundamental and powerful instructions.

It was time to contact Shen and I decided, before doing so, to see where he was.

I found the little yellow square, on the Translator, with an arcane symbol engraved on it and touched it with my right index finger while I thought of Shen. I felt the instrument react like a vibrant blade of heat which touched my solar plexus and my throat. The transition was immediate, the feeling very similar to the physical Translation but my image in that place was only a projection and therefore I couldn't be perceived, at least not by the common senses. The Translator probably also kept the body stable while the mental projection brought one elsewhere.

Shen was at the center of a little amphitheater very similar to the grand council hall of the Anantrya as I had seen it during the experience in the Sarcophagus.

The place was somber and lit by big braziers and globes floating in mid-air which seemed to contain minute parts of the light of a star. The floors were of a smooth stone and covered by very fine rugs, while incense and myrrh burned purifying the hall.

Shen was seated on a kind of stone throne that was in an equidistant point from each of the semicircles of the amphitheater and behind him there was a big banner that reproduced the shape, the colors and the symbols of the Translator. I found it natural for that to be the flag chosen by the Eternals of the Gathering: what more magic and holy object existed in the World!

All the steps were occupied by people and I recognized Khalid, Sister Claudia, Julia the Sorceress, John Deelay and many others, about one hundred Eternals, all very differently dressed.

I realized that these were the members of the Gathering which Shen was able to contact and maybe the only ones who had been awakened up to now. Few, too few for the task which awaited us: Shen was busy informing them of what had happened and of the imminence of a conflict.

Many of them protested for the lack of preparation of the forces to openly face the enemy but also realized that the moment wasn't determined by them.

I found out from Shen's mind that he had already had a similar encounter with the representatives of the refugees on the Fifth Emanation, that with everyone's help it was possible to put together an army, and that some individuals from the Eighth Emanation, prevalently occupied by people of prehistoric civilizations of Earth, had been warned and their help had been asked in the limits of their rules of non-interference. Yet the possibility that the Potentiae could discover their refuge was always a convincing argument.

Suddenly, an old man wearing a white tunic and a long wand got up; with a leap which made one realize the man's supernatural agility, he landed in the semicircular section a few meters from Shen and pointing his stick in my direction exclaimed:

"We are not alone!".

There was a moment of general commotion and I saw many of the people present put themselves in a position of defense or attack. They all turned their attention in my direction.

"I too feel a presence, but it is familiar, not dark", said Sister Claudia turning in my direction but with her eyes closed.

Through the remote connection I had with my body I made the necessary adjustments with the Translator to make the projection visible.

"Master Heylel!", Shen exclaimed.

"I was looking for you to update you but saw you were busy and didn't want to disturb the Council", I said.

My voice came out like a strange echo, as if there were the slightest delay between the time I pronounced the words and when they manifested themselves in that place.

"As we have previously agreed upon, I have gathered the Brothers who could be reached and informed them on what we have said and on the latest developments. Now we must prepare for the conflict. Do you have any news for us?". Shen's voice sounded unexpectedly authoritative to me.

"Nothing new except for an uneasy feeling. I feel that the Potentiae want to enter the Fifth Emanation and that they are near to finding a way. I think it will be essential to anticipate an escape plan and a precautionary attack to the heart of the Caste on the Second Emanation. I don't believe they expect to be attacked and will therefore be vulnerable. In the meanwhile we would delay their plans", I said.

An animated murmuring rose from those present.

"Order! Order!", said Shen in a booming voice.

When everyone had calmed down I continued.

"Your job will be to gather all the manpower available, mobilize all the reachable allies in the shortest time and strike the Caste to death depriving it of its operative bases on the Second Emanation of Earth and on Earth Prime itself. They will, of course, try to find a way of inflicting a mortal blow on the Gathering; all your Art, that of your disciples and that of all the allies will have to be put to the service of the oncoming war in that the only acceptable outcome will be the annihilation of the Caste from this Dominion. They will go back to their Empire and from that time on will look at Earth with fear and respect", I said.

"We will have to stir up a great Power. This image of yours", said a stout woman entirely dressed in red to my right, pointing at my body, "has not yet been able to see what tools the Caste can resort to. They come from a very big Empire and on the physical plane they will be dreadful adversaries".

"So you will have to stir up this Power! At all cost. Remember that we are favored by the Lords of the Guardians and by the Messenger of the Creators. Nothing must stop us", I said in a passionate tone.

"Do you already know your task?", Shen asked. As if by magic everyone present became silent.

"My task is to strike the Potentiae directly. To cancel them from existence once and for all and for this feat I'll have to act alone. Although, to succeed quickly at my task I need that their energy and influence be occupied protecting the Caste and its outposts".

A murmuring in the background broke the silence.

"And the Masters of the Guardians? Will they fight by our side?", asked John Deelay.

"They are prepared. But the Ninth Emanation will have to remain inaccessible and therefore their help will be symbolic. If we fail, they will cancel everything, as they had done at the end of the first war with the Potentiae, millions of years ago and everything will start all over again", I said.

"None of the present had ever taken in consideration the hypothesis of failure!", said a huge Templar standing up and swinging his sword which gave off an acute sound when he waved it in the air.

"We will not fail", Shen said with his new voice which seemed to be made from thunder.

"Let's not waste any more time. The Gathering has been updated. Mobilize the armies and your disciples and wait for instructions. We will need a base on the Fifth Emanation and an attack force for the Second Emanation", Shen concluded.

"I will take care of the Earth Prime and will contact you when I need help", I said to everyone.

Then I turned to Shen: "Please, keep me up to date. I have to go now". And saying this I interrupted the projection and found myself once again in the bathroom of my apartment.

"Hey! Is everything okay in there?", said Monika from the other side of the door. I don't know for how long she had been knocking.

"Yes, I'm okay. Wait for me on the balcony, I'll be about twenty minutes", I said hurriedly.

"Okay", she said absent-mindedly and I heard her move away from the door.

I knew that there were many awakened Eternals on the Sixth and Seventh Emanations who had, in centuries, mobilized and organized numerous armies ready to fight Power wars and at a time like that the Guardians would have surely hastened the awakening of many other Eternals.

The force of fire was essential, especially if we wanted to keep the Potentiae occupied in battles as much as possible and worried about the fate of their human hosts of the Caste.

Now I had to see Sithar to benefit from his advice one last time before the games began.

I concentrated on his image in my mind, and activating the Translator was in front of him in a moment; he was in a room with walls covered by lights and geometrical shapes similar to those which also formed the Translator.

At the center of the room there was a cone which rose for at least one meter from the floor and from its top a three dimensional projection, rich in blue moving symbols, was occupying Sithar's attention when I arrived.

As soon as he saw me he made a gesture with his hand and the projection was entirely reabsorbed by the cone.

I greeted him with the conventional sign and he returned the greeting.

"Did I disturb you Sithar?", I asked.

"The work that was occupying my attention can wait", he said.

"I've informed the Gathering of the mission".

"Therefore, preparations for the big battle have started. Very well!", he said smiling.

"I need your experience to be sure that the strength of the Eternals isn't confronted with a defeat", I said.

"I don't understand", he answered.

"I don't know what forces the Caste has access to and I fear that what we can inflict on them is inadequate", I insisted.

"And do you fear you are guiding the Gathering towards a defeat?".

"In a few words, yes... I would like your help to know what means the Caste has to allow the Gathering and its allies to prepare. Knowing the enemy well is in itself half the battle".

Sithar did not seem to give importance to what I was saying.

"The outcome of the War will not be determined by the collision between the Caste and forces of the Gathering. Though, a massive attack against their outposts will be necessary. Therefore, what you have done up to now is congruent with your mission", he said.

"The objective of my mission is the elimination of the Potentiae from the World".

"Exactly".

"And the Potentiae can only manifest themselves through the Caste", I continued.

"Once again, what you say corresponds to the dynamic reality of the situation", said Sithar unperturbed. I couldn't understand what I was missing. He perceived my doubt.

"Remember what you learned the last time you were here to recover your awareness", Sithar said.

"I have the information but I'm probably missing the key to put everything in relation", I said.

"You must realize that you alone can find the solution. It is a very important part in reaching a solution and understanding the problem, all its components, the implications and above all its origins".

"Right", I said.

"And another thing to consider is that a problem seems to become more complicated the more it is diffused and is contemplated. But its origin always has an elementary nature and is therefore simple", said Sithar.

"Forgive me Sithar if I confide in you but I need to communicate to understand".

"That is what I am here for but not to find the solution to your problem", he replied.

"Interesting. You can't give me a solution... ".

"Exactly", he confirmed.

"Not because you don't want to but because you don't know it".

"Once again you are correct. Of course, if we knew the solution we would have already put it into practice and solved the problem and now we wouldn't be here talking about it".

I started to follow a line of reasoning that might have led me towards the light, or at least I hoped so.

"The Anantrya were able to exile the Potentiae but not to destroy them", I continued.

"We don't have such power", Sithar said.

"That is why you told me that the Potentiae were generated by a higher level than that carried out by the History of the World", I said.

"In fact. A level above which we have no possibility of influence".

"Does the Messenger come from that level?", I asked.

"No one can have the knowledge of what is above him and we make no exception. Though, we presume yes", he answered.

"Why doesn't the Messenger directly act on the Potentiae?", I asked.

"We presume it's not his job. The higher spheres never directly interfere with the World in that their essence is so pure that any direct action could cancel the entire History or a big part of it. They operate through their creations and generations and communicate through the Messengers. We therefore presume that whoever generated the Potentiae is an Equal to the Father Maker of this World".

"Therefore, there is a war in act also in the higher spheres!".

"When you speak of the Makers, words like 'war' lose their meaning. Their conflicts manifest themselves in the unwinding of the History of the Worlds and the issues which come out color all Life of qualities closer and closer to the Absolute".

Things were becoming really interesting but it wasn't the moment to get carried away by metaphysical abstractions.

"Therefore, in brief, I was given characteristics suitable for defeating and destroying the Potentiae, from the same level of Authority from which also the Potentiae were generated", I deduced.

"You will not have to destroy them, but cancel them from the History of this World. There is a big difference", Sithar pointed out.

"As if they had never existed".

"Exactly. Or better, as if their influence had never manifested itself".

"You understand, don't you, that I know what I have to do but have no idea as to how to do it?".

"As you might say: life is tough! The solution will come to you at the right moment. Now you must only worry about carrying out your Task".

"And the war between the Gathering and the Caste is only a diversion", I concluded.

"That's right. As you would say, smoke in the eyes, to take the attention away from the Potentiae and who wanted them. The Caste alone is not a threat to us", said Sithar.

"Where must I start from?".

"When the moment arrives you will know. You should be familiar with the notion that the formulation of an objective, in this World, already corresponds to the moment of its realization. Now the objective is probably still not near. When it is, you will know it and you will know what to do", Sithar said.

I remained a few more minutes thinking. Of course he was right but I needed to be told; at last I took my leave.

"Thank you Sithar. I must go now", I said dismissing myself in the conventional way.

"It was a pleasure. One last thing...", he added.

"Yes... ?".

"Remember that when a Task begins, everything that happens and everyone present are part of its happening. Nothing is casual. It is indispensable to consider the events, the scenario and the actors from the observer's point of view", he said.

I couldn't understand why he had told me this last thing but if he had considered it necessary there must have been a reason. And of course there was, only that in that moment I couldn't see it.

"Thanks again", I concluded.

I visualized the bathroom in my apartment on the Fifth Emanation and activated the Translator.

VIII

Monica was no longer in the apartment. I looked for her everywhere of course, but something told me I wouldn't have found her. Even the service personnel who I had readily called had not seen her leave.

I wanted to eliminate all possibilities before looking for her with the Translator and at last, when the palace guards told me they had seen an unknown woman leave after having said she was a guest at the palace, but without saying where she was going, I decided to look for her with my means.

Sitting on the steps to the main entrance I visualized Monika and activated the mechanism of the Translator that would have projected my senses where she was.

Nothing happened.

Thinking it was a procedure mistake I tried again but to no avail.

I also tried transporting myself to her and even the never tried before procedure of transporting her to me.

Still nothing.

So I tried to contact her without the aid of the Translator, as I had previously done.

I felt a weak contact sensation, but only saw darkness, as if Monika were in a dark place and unconscious.

I thought she might be in danger and feeling guilty for leaving her alone and doubting her, decided to see Shen before trying again.

I found him in the foyer of the little amphitheater normally used for the official meetings of the Gathering. He updated me on the situation. He told me that the armies were mobilizing, guided by each awakened Eternal it had been possible to contact.

His army, an armored and modernized version of the ancient Mongolian cavalry, instilled with the Power of Shen's great Eunos Art was camped a few hundred kilometers from Amn'el'Tyr, in a stronghold built just for warriors of their lineage. He also told me that the prospect of battle had immediately inflamed them.

The Mongols, as it had been taught to them for centuries, were instruments created to fight, especially when the task originated from the spheres on the other side of the Mirror.

Shen's warriors were about ten thousand and not one of them was a simple cavalryman. They had all been chosen in time for this war and were therefore the product of a ferocious selection.

The armies of the other members of the Gathering were dislocated between Earth-6 and Earth-8.

Armies, was of course, a euphemism. In fact, each one of the Eternals and their disciples had a following which intimately reflected their nature. Besides the authentic Templars, there were the great Knights ordained according to the code of the first millennium of Earth Prime after the Caste, which boasted over eleven thousand years of experience in the science of fighting with dark enemies from the stars which had fought them with the most sophisticated technologies, succumbing to their Power. They were all rewarded by the Guardians with the rebirth on one of the Earth's Emanations and the memory of the past, so that every battle would make them stronger and contemptuous of the death of the body they wore.

The greatest Native American fighters selected by the Shamans of the Gathering were armed with tools of Power.

There were also entire divisions of warrior monks from a forgotten Tibet and thousands of virgin nuns from the Marian order, holders of the key of the Union of the Heart which brought them to give origin to an immense collective mind, able to catalyze fragments of Power of the Great Dream itself.

And many, many more.

I didn't tell Shen what I had learned, that is that their attack had to serve as a diversion, but I told him that it had to be finalized to the erasure of all the works of the Caste beginning with that of the Second Emanation.

In any case, he didn't ask for further explanations and acted and spoke as if he had been waiting for this moment for so long that it finally gave meaning to the thousands of years spent playing a never ending chess game without winners nor losers.

For some reason I was delaying the moment in which I would have to tell him that I had no trace of Monika. I beat about the bush but finally told him.

"Strange that you can't even find her with the Translator. This is not a good sign", Shen said gravely.

"I thought so too and honestly don't know what to think. Did you ever have a similar case?".

"Only in the occasion of the death of one of our Equals it was impossible to reach him. But you said you had a weak contact with her but without the Translator. Is it possible that she was drugged or that she is under the influence of an incantation? I'm just saying, but I don't think there are obstacles to the functioning of the power of the Translator", said Shen.

"It means that she has been struck in the Fifth Emanation and this fact seems rather impossible otherwise it would mean that the Caste has already found a way to get here", I said.

"We will look for her with the Eunos Art", concluded Shen.

"I will continue trying from my apartment. We must be ready for the worst hypothesis", I said.

"That is?".

"That the Potentiae have reached her and are using her to open a passageway here to strike at us by surprise", I said.

"It would be catastrophic at this time", he said.

"Not if we are ready and we're waiting for them. I suggest hastening the preparations for the assault to the Second Emanation and to attack as soon as you are ready. It could be to our advantage to attract them all the way here with all their forces", I said.

"I will contact the Council again to define a strategy that will take this factor into account", said Shen.

"See you soon and keep me up to date, please".

"The same for you Heylel".

I still didn't know that the mechanisms of destiny had already started turning to lead me where I had to be.

IX

I returned to my apartment rather tranquil in that I now knew that, whatever happened to me, the Gathering was ready and they would have completed the attack independently from any further signal from me.

Tranquil was, of course, an improper word. I felt an unnatural vigor take over my body and mind. Probably the excitement for what was about to happen was positively recharging my batteries.

Seated on the couch, I darkened the room and remained alone with the light of some candles in the background, preparing for another attempt to contact Monika.

Again that feeling of muffled presence and nothing more. After several failed attempts I decided to try with a new approach: instead of looking for the association of emotional elements that were distinctive of her, I decided to use the function of the Translator that stemmed from an act of will of the bearer to generate the ensemble of operations on reality finalized to reaching a result. In a few words, the function which automatically produced spells from the root of desire.

So I focused my attention to see where Monika's body was, transmitting the visualization and the order directly to the Translator and activating the corresponding geometry with my hand.

Suddenly, all around me, I had the feeling of going back in time at reckless speed remaining in my apartment.

Then I saw Monika in that same room making some gestures in the air. I saw she was holding a sharp knife in her hand – surely taken from the breakfast tray – and with that blade she cut a long scar on her left forearm.

The blood began to flow and she dipped her finger in it and used it to trace signs on her body and face.

Her mouth moved, like I had seen Amelia's mouth move in the middle of the interrupted Incantation. Then she disappeared from the room like in an explosion of atoms.

The Translator had allowed me to follow her; the scene around me changed and now I was in a big room with dim lights from an undefined source where a group of completely naked people with painted bodies were standing in three concentric circles. Monika materialized right in the middle.

Even though their bodies and faces were painted I was able to recognize Amelia in an inner part of the circle, exactly in front of Monika when she had disappeared.

A heavy feeling, viscid, of coarse power could be felt in the atmosphere, even though I was living this episode only as a transmission of the past.

The eyes of the participants to the ritual were completely dark except for a deep light which animated them and were far from human looking , even for the members of the Caste.

They were all in physical contact in each one of the three circles through the palms of their hands yet the circles themselves were not in contact.

On the floor instead, there was a strange design similar to a circuit that crossed the circles of bodies and converged to the center, exactly where

Monika had just appeared.

Everyone repeated a six word formula that will not be reported in this chronicle in that they are cursed and belong to the dark and degenerate world of the Potentiae.

Even though I was aware that this was only a projection of the memory of the past, mindful of the experience in the Sarcophagus, I didn't want to risk attracting attention and therefore tried to interrupt the contact. I was able, though with some difficulty, but not before looking at Monika's face which seemed to be prey to a mad trance.

With a gesture of apprehension I looked at her eyes and saw that light which meant she had become the dwelling for one of the Potentiae and her soul was lost forever.

The Translator brought me back to my time and I realized I had difficulty breathing. My heart beat was too quick and strong: I had lost Monika too.

She wasn't dead, sure, but I hadn't been able to rescue her from something that for her was much worse. Yet, I still couldn't understand why the Translator wouldn't allow me to contact her directly. Maybe the integration process with the Potentia had made her sufficiently different that I wasn't able to recognize her in the image I had of her in my mind.

It was time for me to understand what this could mean: the Potentiae had used her to arrive to the Gathering and now they would certainly have the acquired knowledge to penetrate the Fifth Emanation and find the mechanism that would have brought them well beyond, to the refuge of the Lords of the Guardians.

X

I immediately informed Shen who urgently sent for the War Council formed by all the resident Eternals and by the Generals, or in any case the highest in rank or in experience to be spokesperson for the armies.

Everyone agreed that it was necessary to act quickly and after having obtained a map of the presence of the Caste on the Second Emanation from the Guardian set on Moon-2, decided for a massive attack to the base of the Headquarters of Temporal Archives. The residents of the Fifth Emanation would have to be evacuated to Earth-7 leaving on the Fifth only Shen and his army to keep the Caste busy in battle, in case of an attack to Amn'el'Tyr.

The armies headed by the Eternals, which had on their side the fact that time on the other Emanations passed about ten times faster, would have marched towards the second emanation in two days of Earth-5, also but not only, counting on the benevolent protection of the Second Guardian and as for Shen and his army, of the Fifth Guardian which was at the bottom of the ocean in front of the city.

No one asked me what my next moves would be and I understood that this didn't depend on an unnatural absence of curiosity but for reasons of security so that in case they were captured by the Caste or the Potentiae, no one from the Gathering would have been able to reveal more than what had been decided at the War Council.

Truth is, that even if they had asked me, in that moment I wouldn't have been able to answer given that complete information of my task had not yet been deposited in my mind. It was as though there were a clockwork mechanism that released information with a dispenser, in the right amount and at the right moment in which I needed it.

All I knew was that I had to attack the Potentiae directly and the only way I knew to reach such purpose at that moment was to directly attack one or more members of the Caste.

Until then I had met few: Amelia, Icarus and now Monika too, without counting the scientific personnel on Moon-2, but I didn't remember them much.

Of the main three, Amelia and Monika were surely the most vulnerable because their feelings for me contrasted with the aims of the Potentiae.

At least this is what I wanted to believe.

I counted on the fact that they would have opposed resistance to any attempt of the Potentae of destroying me, if they actually wanted to destroy me.

To reconcile their feelings and the purposes of the Potentiae they would have to transform me into one of them, a dwelling and instrument for those damned entities.

It was then that I realized that since the beginning the Potentiae had probably manipulated the events so that Amelia and Monika would act on their own will just to reach this objective.

And it was then that part of the mission I had to undertake came to my mind like an illumination: I had to go along with this line of action of the enemy in that it was the only way to come close enough to them to do what I had been prepared to do.

What I still didn't know was what I had to do after that: should I give in to their attempts of possession, and then? Should I count on the accuracy of the clockwork mechanism? And as they say: 'last but not least' to have a line of action, suicidal as it may seem, is better than nothing at all?

I remembered the words, like many other times in my life, 'fortune favours the bold', and I considered that, given the situation, I had to become the luckiest man of all the Emanations!

In any case, being well conscious of the situation and the final result expected, I instilled in my Image on this side of the Mirror the principle of Sacrifice or of Martyrdom carried out in the Name of the Great Dream and to protect the Transient Souls on their way home. The container of power connected to this principle was put at my disposal to serve me on the coming task.

Nothing to do with martyrdom as conceived by men on Earth, mostly a way to escape from Life hoping for a reward and above all a tool of the Potentiae to use as power on the flesh.

There aren't adequate words to describe the principle of Sacrifice because it is done by the Eternals and by their Images who have everything or can have everything, but give it up for the Grand Design of the Makers.

The container of power which came with this new quality integrating with my Image caused a strong emotion which shook me inside. I allowed this emotion to fill me and ravage any shadow of mechanical doubt or residual fear, then I slowly smoked a cigarette, enjoying every moment before plunging into action.

I went on the balcony sitting on the usual couch and with the setting sun, began.

XI

First of all I had to find a place far from Amn'el'Tyr; in case something didn't work I wouldn't have allowed direct access to the city.

There was only one problem: I had never been outside of the city and therefore didn't have a place in my memory to visualize.

I could have also imagined one built by my imagination, but I knew it wouldn't have been a wise move: I could have ended on another planet or in another time or anywhere the conditions I had imagined were real. I would have almost certainly reached a real other Reality of the Great Dream and this maybe meant leaving the history of this World. This would have also brought me out of range of the Potentiae which instead completely belonged to it.

So I used the projection function of the Translator and visualized the furthest place from the city that I could see from the balcony. There was a little hill on the horizon to the left covered by thick vegetation.

I projected myself there then activated the Translator to transport myself there. I made another three leaps getting further away until I arrived to a clearing on a little island in the middle of a great lake with water that seemed dense like petroleum but was the color of lapis lazuli.

It was a tranquil place, probably much more suitable for meditating than for what I wanted to stir up, but the tranquility of the atmosphere that surrounded it helped, first of all me, not to have other distractions.

I found a tree, sat down with my back against the trunk and then started to empty my mind to make space for one image: Amelia.

This time I used the function of the Translator which called a person or an object and brought it to the caller: I was sure that whatever Amelia and the Potentiae were ready for, they never would have imagined I had the power to tear them away from their space and bring them to me, and from Amelia's expression when she appeared in front of me I deduced I was right.

She wore a gym suit and running shoes as if I had caught her while she was jogging. It took her some minutes to realize what had happened; she felt her body, looked around and then looked at me with a cocktail of astonishment and fury in her eyes.

"Hello Amelia, how are you? Did I disturb you?", I said smiling.

"What...? How...? What did you do to me?", she said in a shaky voice. It seemed she wasn't able to overcome the astonishment.

There was no sign of the Potentia in her eyes and I therefore deduced it hadn't realized what had happened yet.

"I wanted to see you. Sit and chat with me for a while", I said smiling.

She didn't move and I saw astonishment in her eyes but also fear.

"Sit!", I repeated, but this time in a stricter tone.

She slowly sat on the grass with her legs crossed.

"Don't be afraid. As I've told you before I won't hurt you if you don't force me to", I said.

I saw she was trying to appear relaxed but her breath was quick and uncertain, even if she was rapidly recovering control. She looked around, the ground, the vegetation, the profile of the mountains on the horizon, the waters of the lake, the sky. She didn't recognize anything.

"Where are we?", she asked.

"I'll ask the questions if you don't mind. What did you do to Monika?", I asked.

She smiled a challenging smile.

"She has become one of us now. The dwelling of her Master", she answered.

I knew the answer but something in me was looking for different clues, maybe because hope is always last to die.

"Has she been possessed by one of the Potentiae?".

"Yes. She too now has a Master and like us, once she has tasted its touch, has become its slave. It's not a bad thing, you know. You should try it. It's like being chosen and it gives you a great power asking only the use of your flesh in return. I wanted you to join us too, but you fled. But it's not too late. You can still give yourself to our Masters and then we can be together... forever", she said

"Why instead don't we do the opposite? Say good-bye to your Master, free yourself and come with me", I said.

"I'm afraid that the way of the Potentiae is a one way choice. Even if I wanted I wouldn't be able to free myself. The touch of a Potentia changes you and from that time on you can't live without it", she said.

I thought I perceived a sadness in her voice while she spoke.

"Therefore to free yourself you must die?", I asked.

"There is no death for us", she answered.

"So, if I wanted to kill you now your Master would stop me?", I asked.

"It would be useless. A new Amelia would be awakened and my essence would be transferred to the new body through my Master", she answered.

I remembered the words of the First Guardian relative to the Caste and to how they were prevented from returning to the Great Dream when their body died.

"Where are the cloned bodies of the members of the Caste kept?", I asked.

"In a safe place", she said smiling.

"I could imprison you now and prevent the Potentia from establishing a contact with you", I said bluffing.

"So this body would die suffering in an excruciating way for the absence of its Master. In the end he would find me a new vehicle and I would reawaken. But I doubt you are able to. Join us and help us destroy our enemy and your future will be glorious", she continued with a mad light in her eyes.

My objective wasn't Amelia and the now lost Monika or the members of the Caste; I had to find a way to reach the Potentiae and strike at them directly. By striking Amelia I would have obtained the meager result of creating a nuisance and nothing more to the Demons behind her.

Yet, the only way I had of communicating with them was through their slaves in the Caste .

"In a while you will be able to ask my Master directly whatever questions you have. He is coming", said Amelia with an almost mystic fervor.

I observed her well. Her expression seemed lost for a moment and her eyes rolled back. Then she returned normal, calm, controlled and the light behind her eyes, more intense than the other times, confirmed to me that it was no longer her I had in front of me.

She pierced me with her eyes that were now ice-cold and remote, vibrating with an abysmal hate. Eyes used to looking at Life like a disease, like something to crush and control. Only one command was engraved in the original code of this entity: the absolute control over everything.

"Fool. You have opened the way I so much searched for", it said with Amelia's voice.

"What are you looking for?", I said enunciating each word very clearly. I had to take time.

She stood up and I imitated her. Then I saw her eyes settle on the

Translator around my neck. The smile that sprang from her face told me it wasn't the first time she saw it.

"I see that you have effectively become a part of that group of deplorable insects that would like to contrast us. You disappoint me! I expected more from someone like you".

"I have always been a part of the Gathering and as you see now you are just where I wanted you to be", I answered. I had to take time, keep her occupied as long as possible.

"And what have you obtained with this? For thousands of years we have been looking for your refuge and you have served it to me on a silver platter. Or do you have the delusion of striking me? Or of getting away from me", she said in an imperious tone.

"Striking you? I can try. Getting away from you? I think I've already done it at least once. Give up and realize that it is you who has lost control of the situation", I answered calmly.

"And where would you like to run to now? Listen! It's not too late for you. Many of the human species have joined us through the centuries and still today enjoy the Power. But you... You are unique and you still don't remember it. Our strengths together can change everything. You don't belong to all this. You are more similar to us than you can imagine", she said as though she were a tempting devil. And she was convincing. She used the trick of the corrupters of always, telling an incomplete truth so that the Soul would recognize it.

My instinct gave me an inspiration and it was too late now to be prudent.

I visualized Monika and then activated the shape on the Translator that would have brought her to me.

I made her appear by Amelia's side. She was dressed in her black Temporal Archives suit.

Amelia and the entity which governed her displayed an evident amazement, but not as much as that of Monika.

"She is your last acquisition. Which temptation did you use to corrupt the integrity of someone like her?", I asked the Demon inside Amelia.

In the meanwhile I saw a Potentia appear in Monika's eyes too.

Amelia took a step towards me.

"No temptation Eternal", She had pronounced this last word very slowly with a tone which vibrated between hate and respect.

"All it took was our touch. The human flesh and soul are very receptive to Us. And once she tasted the Power she could no longer do without. Do you think you are different? Try it! Open yourself to Us. Join Us. Prove that you are superior, incorruptible", said Amelia in a challenging tone.

I continued to stare at her in silence. She took another step forward.

"What have you got to lose? If you think you are so strong you won't risk anything. If instead you are not able to oppose resistance you won't care anymore. But I know it will be different for you. You will inebriate yourself at Our fountain and We at yours", Amelia continued.

Then Monika spoke.

"She is telling you the truth, why don't you understand? I am still your Monika, yet I can no longer imagine my life before the touch of my Master", she said. Her eyes were hers now and there wasn't the demon behind her glance. A way of the Potentiae of telling me that they didn't need to put words in the mouths of their hosts in that they were like in love. This shook me.

"How can you speak like that? You, more than anyone else, should remember the darkness that these entities represent", I said to Monika.

"I remember what I felt but it was only ignorance. An ignorance that brought great emptiness inside of me which I tried to fill with fleeting and transitional ideals. Only the contact with my Master awakened me from this sleepwalking condition which afflicted me. And there is no other way to discover this glorious new world if not to abandon yourself to them. Then everything will be clearer, every doubt will be dispelled and you will fear no more and we will be together forever", she said almost imploring.

"I am still Monika. The same Monika who made your heart beat fast. And I'm also much more. I have been transformed into a bigger container. More powerful. More ancient. What filled me before is only a small drop in a container as big as the ocean. And of course, I still remember everything of my life before the Potentia. Now we know of the Nine Emanations. And you have opened the door to the refuge of the enemy. Maybe, inside of you, you are looking for us and your resistance will be inevitably abandoned to make space for the gift. We want you and we will have you!", she said and in the end the Demon returned in her eyes.

My purpose was to take time and I had to create a stalemate which would keep their attention concentrated on me. Without Amelia and Monika and the two Potentiae which dwelled in them, Earth-2 was vulnerable and, if everything went according to plans, the Temporal Archives base would be attacked and destroyed before the Caste could realize it and without being able to count on the protection of their Masters.

Yet their words disturbed me at a level that was still submerged in the waters of my subconscious. They had to know something about me that I myself didn't know and were using it.

I decided to use their tactic; I had to use the Potentiae's obsession against them, the origin of their eternal suffering.

"You want to return, more than any other thing. And as big as your power on the flesh is, you will never be granted to return from exile", I said.

A grimace of ire shook their face.

"We have all eternity and we will never stop! Not even those who have exiled us have the power to destroy us and they fear us, otherwise why would they hide? Time for us is not important and we will continue to strike until our enemies are subdued to us as it should be, and then all that exists will be submitted to us. You and our enemy are the only natural obstacles, a physiological inconvenience in the path that has already been traced and where our role has already been written", said Monika with fury and blind hate on her face.

"You speak as if you were creatures of Destiny. But do you remember your origins?", I asked.

There was a long moment during which Amelia-Demon and Monika-Demon examined me attentively.

"We have never revealed the mystery of our origins. In a faraway time further than any history can remember, We Were, and since then have always been the equal to Ourselves. We are, so that life in anywhere shall be at our service. We are your real Gods",

"But you know you didn't always exists. Someone or something wanted you and created you, did you know that?".

Silence. Then Monika interjected.

"In time the dilemma was faced and we reached the conclusion that the answer was irrelevant. If you hypothesize a superior Authority than us, know that this has never manifested itself and even if it did exist, it created us with an awareness and a common spur: control over everything!".

"And yet someone successfully opposed your control. Therefore this authority didn't want you to be omnipotent. Or it couldn't", I said.

"Irrelevant inconveniences that will be resolved in time. And now, thanks to you, we will be able to return", answered Amelia.

"I will not allow you to act through me", I said.

"We will find out very soon", retorted Amelia smiling.

Now Monika was coming closer too.

I had to act quickly in that I wasn't sure how long I would have been able to hold the stalemate for. I confided in a sign that my Equals and their armies had started the invasion of Earth-2, yet I had no idea as to how this sign could arrive to me.

It was Monika who continued with that alien, ice-cold, mad light in her eyes. "Isn't it you who believes that to know something means having canceled all distance, every difference? Isn't this the most complete Love? Joining us transforms the flesh into something bigger, so big you have never created a word to define this state. Our touch has not destroyed or driven away the slightest thing that occupied it; it transformed it, made it evolve, bringing it to such a height that the return to the former state was inconceivable. And for all this, we ask so little in return".

Listening to a Potentiae speak of love made me want to laugh and I would have if I hadn't been a little worried for the trouble I had evidently put myself into.

"Of course it depends on your point of view", I rebutted feigning indifference.

"Which point of view?", asked Amelia.

"Of course, I forgot that you can't even conceive of someone who is not one of you or your slaves. What you give is not greatness and unity but a dependence without return. Those whose bodies you own are not united with you but chained and tainted beyond hope to the most powerful addictive: power. In fact I doubt that you share the real end that moves you with your hosts. What will become of them when you succeed in returning?".

Just for a moment I was certain I saw confusion through their eyes and their bodies like a wave in total absence of control coming from the center of the deception brought forth by the Potentiae. But it was only for an instant. I was able though to plant a seed, even if I wasn't sure how much it would sprout. Now Monika and Amelia, in the silence in which they had taken shelter in the shadow of the Potentiae, would have asked themselves what would become of them if their Masters had been able to finally return from their exile.

At that moment I decided to bring there also the third member of the Caste present on the Second Emanation.

I concentrated on the image of Icarus and he, by the power of the Translator, appeared right behind Amelia and Monika. Useless to say that his reaction was very similar to theirs.

For the first time they all looked at each other questioningly and then turned all their attention on me.

Icarus didn't even have time to utter a word when a moment of absence seized all three representatives of the Caste, as if they had been called to a faraway place. After a while they were all present again and what they expressed was anger and frustration.

"It was a diversion! You brought us here to allow your Equals to attack our outposts", said Amelia coldly.

"Surely not to have a conversation", I said ironically. At last the signal I was waiting for came and from the enemy!

"So be it", Amelia said and I saw all three absent again for a few seconds.

"Now its war and we have to go. We'll come back to get you", she concluded.

I didn't answer and was ready to activate the Translator in case of rash movements on their part. They came close to each other uniting the palms of their hands to form a circular circuit, then, as I had seen Monika disappear, so did they.

All the atoms of their bodies seemed to lose adhesion and explode until they disappeared.

I imagined their destination was inside the Circles of Power created by the other members of the Caste which, evidently, were not on the Second Emanation.

Now that I had finished with the diversion, I wanted to see how the campaign was going on Earth-2 and visualized the Temporal Archives headquarters.

The vision arrived almost immediately and I saw it had all been razed to the ground, destroyed by the knights and other forms of warriors of the Gathering which occupied that space now full of rubble.

Among the warriors on foot and on horse, some standing looking at the sky, others guarding strategic positions and many injured which were escorted away from the battle grounds to be cured, I also recognized many Eternals who interacted with the attack forces or observed their work of destruction. I was struck by the old man who had intervened at the Council perceiving my ghostly presence who, leaning on his long wand, looked at a chasm so deep that darkness concealed its bottom. It had been the most important building of the base, the one with the countless underground levels in which, Monika had told me, were concealed the greatest secrets of Temporal Archives. It seemed to have been hit by a meteor, so big was the Power stirred off by the Eternal who now observed his work.

The stables had been saved and the horses escorted away from the battle grounds while a little further away I saw what remained of the airport Terminal: a heap of rubble with its fuel deposits burning, darkening the sky with columns of dense, black smoke and what remained of the airplanes smashed to the ground as if a huge foot had stepped on them. There were casualties everywhere, some with uniforms I had never seen and weapons similar to small guns which, by their look, must have struck with high energy particles. They were most surely troopers of the Empire at the service of the Caste and their appearance was perfectly human.

I also saw Khalid who was giving instructions to a little group of men and a little further Julia, with her eyes and her arms to the sky pronouncing a Conjuration sequenced towards an object that was taking off. A few moments later there was an azure explosion and the object became a strip of smoke.

On the Second Emanation the Caste could not use the big starships in that the presence of the atmosphere was not compatible with their propulsion systems and therefore could only count on the means of transport imported from Earth and opportunely modified, like the plane which had brought me to Moon-2.

I moved my senses away from the battle field in the direction taken by the line of wounded and prisoners and saw that at a few hundred meters away from the perimeter of what had been the headquarters, the army was already at a good point in raising a big camp complete of a hospital tent.

I then discovered that the prisoners were transferred to the Third Emanation to an island temporarily used as a penal colony.

Satisfied, I canceled the vision.

I felt a strong sense of urgency after the last words of Amelia and Monika and wanted to have a free mind before my next move or that of Amelia.

I decided to verify that Shen too had everything under control at Amn'el'Tyr and had to hurry because I felt that, sooner or later, the Caste and the Potentiae would have devised something.

There was at least one incomplete truth in what I had been told, and that is that calling them to me I had opened the door for them to the Fifth Emanation and maybe in time they would have even learned how to reach the realm of the Anantrya, custodians of the secret the Potentiae so much yearned for.

I found Shen in a camp not far from the city in the middle of a forest. I updated him on the latest events which had engaged me and he told me that, so far as the success of the invasion of the Second Emanation went, he had already been informed by the Eternals who had participated in the campaign. He told me that with the help of the Second Guardian they had also occupied the scientific base on Moon-2, this time with the least amount of bloodshed in that almost all the residents surrendered immediately with the exception of the resident security guards, entirely composed of soldiers of the Empire. We entered his tent where he offered me some hot tea made with local herbs which, according to him, helped focus the thoughts.

"So, they could arrive any time now", he said referring to the Potentiae and the Caste.

"I'm afraid so. They will attack the city, of course", I said.

"Amn'el'Tyr is not the only city on this world, although I guess it's the only one they're interested in. The evacuation of the residents has been completed and now they are all on the Seventh Emanation as guests of the fortified city of Yshmaal. My army instead has been dislocated around Amn'el'Tyr and are waiting for the forces of the Caste. Unfortunately we are not on the Second Emanation. Here, they will be able to attack us from land, sky, sea and above all from the stars. One of their star ships would suffice to raze the entire planet to the ground in ordinary conditions. We have evoked a protective shield against their weapons and I hope it will hold for sufficient time in that we have never experimented it before", said Shen.

"They'll raze the city to the ground", I said with sadness for the beauty and antiquity of this place which would be sacrificed for the common cause.

"It is very probable. But when they arrive they will find a nice surprise.

The entire area has been strewn with Power traps and when they start to realize it their numbers will have been considerably reduced. In any case, a city can always be rebuilt", said Shen with a sinister smile.

"They won't find anything useful in the city nor in any part of the Fifth Emanation. We have been preparing for this possibility for a long time and we are ready. And above all, the armies are very motivated. When will the possibility of canceling the darkness from the World happen again?", continued Shen.

"Very well", I said satisfied by our first move.

"Even if we didn't have an ace up our sleeve, in any case it would take centuries for the Caste to reorganize after this war", said Shen.

"An ace up our sleeve?".

"Sure! You are our ace! All this is only to weaken the Caste. But the Potentiae are out of our reach. We count on you for their elimination. If you fail it will take centuries before the right conditions would allow us to try again and by then we would not be able to count on the surprise effect", said Shen.

"Right. I was afraid you'd say that!", I said dispassionately.

I finished the tea and smoked a cigarette which he offered me from his reserve. It was a local product and didn't taste like tobacco. Shen said it would have helped keep interior peace and in fact it was very relaxing. I asked myself how many other local bad habits had such healthy effects on mind and body!

Shen asked me what my plan of action was and I answered I had to rely on improvisation until the proper knowledge was revealed to my mind.

It was only a half truth. I knew what I would have done initially. Then I would have had to improvise, also because I had no comparison for this experience.

I felt my sixth sense ring like an alarm bell. Something was happening and I thought I knew what: I had to go away from that place. I said good-bye to Shen wishing him a good battle and left the tent dislocating myself in the clearing where I had called Monika, Amelia and Icarus a while before.

I found the tree against which I had sat and sat back down again with my back against its trunk; I felt something come near me in waves more and more frequent, more and more violent like the labor pains of a pregnant woman.

I opposed a passive resistance visualizing with my internal eye an endless emptiness in that I didn't want to make it easy for them.

The appeal became stronger and stronger and time passed like in a viewer, very slowly.

My thoughts were more and more confused, as though my mind were shaken by a gigantic barman preparing a cocktail of thoughts and emotions.

I kept my passive resistance which was about to give in, though. I started seeing images of arid desolation and death, to be shaken by strong emotions, at the limit of madness, then the voices came, many voices calling me until all my world was a cold desert populated by voices.

Finally, all around me, the world began to take shape again.

I was in the middle of the circles formed by the Caste who were naked and with their bodies painted, each one of them expressing a different aspect of the Potentiae and each one wore that effigy on their bodies.

From that moment on I only remember that everything became confused and in the end I lost my senses.

XII

I don't know how much time passed until I woke up and found myself lying on a hot and humid stone bed and thought I heard a heavy liquid drip somewhere behind me.

The surroundings were so weakly lit, probably by tongues of fire coming from big torches, that I wasn't able to distinguish any details.

I was immobilized.

Some people that had the terrible light of the Potentiae in their eyes, were tracing geometrical shapes with their fingers on my body.

My thoughts were still confused and Amelia's face appeared on top of me. Her hand closed my eyes without me being able to oppose the least resistance.

"Calm down and don't fight what has to happen. It would be useless. It will soon be all over".

I found the strength to say a few words.

"What... are... you... doing... to... me?".

"When you wake up you will be one of Us and in that moment all doubts will disappear and all conflicts inside you will be resolved", said the Potentiae with Amelia's voice.

What I wanted was happening and I was very careful not to show what I really aimed for in that nothing had to give away my Task.

I had only one moment of fear, fear of no longer having the strength to free myself from the Potentia which wanted my body, the entity which had agreed to use me as its dwelling for the time being.

Then I let myself go: it was too late to have second thoughts and I stayed there, with my eyes closed to allow the people present make me one of them.

And again I was swallowed by oblivion.

THE FOOD OF THE GODS

I woke up in a hospital bed, the sun weakly lit the room from the window. The memory of the last events came back to my mind very slowly, in pieces, in vivid and dense fragments and at last I remembered everything. What was I doing in a hospital?

"Good morning", came the familiar voice from my right.

I slowly turned and saw Amelia with her smile. No one else looking out from her eyes.

"Good morning", I said with a pasty mouth.

"Rest now. I'll tell the nurses you have regained consciousness", she said getting up.

I felt strangely peaceful. No fear, no apprehension. My sustained emotion was that of superior serenity, as if I were conscious that nothing could harm me and that I had all the time in the world for whatever.

"What happened?", I asked.

"I'll explain everything calmly when you are completely recovered. Don't be in a hurry, time is no longer a limiting factor. Your body is adapting to the new condition", she said.

"New condition?".

"Don't wear yourself out", she said pushing a button above my head.

"Where are we?".

"This is Earth. The original one. This is our Base in Chile, where all the work of the Caste and the Potentiae come together", she answered.

I had never heard about a Base in Chile. In fact I knew the Organization had to have other establishments; though security reasons had always refrained me from asking myself inconvenient questions.

"What kind of work?", I asked. Of course I was interested in increasing my knowledge since I had been brought to that place.

I felt the world muffle around me and feared I would lose

consciousness.

"Here we complete the research programs on Eugenics for the Empire. And supplies for our Mother System leave from here. You'll learn everything about your new family, don't be hasty".

Eugenics... supplies... Right at that moment a nurse came in.

Amelia spoke briefly with her getting whispered answers. I tried to listen to their words but felt my senses leave me. Then it was dark again.

II

I fell in and out between consciousness and sleep to "adapt" before finally waking up. Once, I even thought I had awakened, not in hospital, but in another dark place doused in a hot, viscous liquid, naked and with a lot of people around chanting litanies in a language I didn't know.

Then I woke up once and for all.

It was night judging by the darkness, broken only by the paleness of the full moon visible from the broad window. The bed was king size and didn't seem very hospital like. In fact I was sure that place, was anything but a hospital.

I remained still for a while, even to allow my eyes to verify if there were anyone else in the room: it actually seemed as though I were alone.

I felt different, to begin with from the fact that between unconsciousness and being awake there hadn't been the typical transitional state of drowsiness. I was strangely full of energy and in particular felt a taste for anger, for violent movements and the feel for adrenaline that took over my body.

I had a curious desire to go out and look for a fight and someone to beat to death.

I sat up and tried to see inside myself.

Besides the taste for these strong and violent emotions, I didn't feel very different. If they had managed to make me become a container or window for one of the sleeping Potentiae I didn't feel its presence at the moment.

I also asked myself how much of my memory was accessible to the Caste and the Potentiae and if, among the various treatments which I had undergone, they had tried to access my deepest memories.

Then I found the door which had been opened to the Potentia.

The access wasn't in the mental sphere but the bio-neural one. In other words, the Potentia had access to me through my nervous system, governing, among others, its biochemical functions, but it didn't have connections that I could perceive with the compound of extra-corporeal components which together constituted my mind.

This seemed somewhat strange. I tried to put together what little I knew of the symbiosis between humans and Potentiae to understand how such a crude connection could generate the heavy transformation I had observed, for example, in Monika.

I concluded that I was surely missing something and that it would probably be clearer in time.

For now I had to take note that, at least in my case, all the sensations that the Potentiae were able to control, the needs, the desires, the drives were all regulated through the biochemistry of the body. I realized this made their touch more and more similar to that of a powerful drug.

Having access to the biochemical switches of the brain and of the body could in fact cause any type of emotion and drive starting from the bottom, that is from the body, to arrive to the mind and to the living center of the individual. Of course, the individual in question, had to have a center, what religions had always called the Soul, and I had already learned that not all human bodies had one. Most could be compared to sophisticated machines with no one looking out to the world through their eyes.

I got up keeping the lights off and found my clothes folded and clean on a little table in the middle of the room.

I continued feeling clear-headed and full of energy, maybe even too much. I hadn't lost the memory of the Gathering at all, nor had the preoccupation for their fate in the ongoing war been substituted by anything else.

So I asked myself what really was this control by the Potentiae which abated all will and transformed people in ruthless members of the Caste.

I considered the possibility that the Potentia which had been chosen for me was behaving in a different way from usual, giving me a way to adapt without opposing resistance or imposing its powerful Will.

Or they just wanted me to believe that the possession wasn't so bad, that it didn't deprive one who was touched of their freedom of choice.

Or the Demon was simply prudent considering me an unknown factor; they had known the humans of the Empire and of Earth for centuries but didn't know anything about the Eternals, who for them, were a kind of Terra Incognita. So maybe it proceeded prudently as not to risk stirring up a conflict of wills, but acquire my trust as a host more slowly and shiftily.

Then there was this powerful sense of hunger, as though it were a long time since I last ate. It wasn't just any kind of hunger. I wanted something particular but couldn't understand what.

Outside the window the night showed only reliefs in the distance and avenues dimly lit by lampposts, with numerous little houses which extended as far as the eye could see. I could imagine, with a reasonable approximation, that this was a standard base of Temporal Archives, in all similar in its structure to that of the headquarters on Earth-2 (though it seemed much vaster), before it was destroyed by the Gathering in the attack to the Second Emanation.

I noticed that the victory of the Gathering did not evoke in me a positive emotion, instead I felt a sense of anger and a desire for revenge.

I had to quickly learn to distinguish between my emotions and those brought about by the biochemical domination of the Potentia or I would have soon lost myself in a disassociated condition which would have been difficult to recover from.

I waited in front of the window until dawn, when a nurse finally entered the room.

"Sir! You woke up. Why didn't you call us? We were waiting".

"I wanted to be alone for a while", I answered.

"The Lady Amelia asked us to call her when you woke up. Can I bring you something?", she said in a respectful tone.

I had that great hunger but decided to resist until I had understood more about it.

"Only coffee for now. I'll wait for Amelia".

"As you wish, Sir".

And saying this she slowly closed the door leaving the room.

Dawn showed me the details of what I had guessed to be; I was on a typical Temporal Archives base. It seemed really vast, maybe many kilometers in all directions. The sun was rising slowly and the sky was partly cloudy.

Amelia had said we were in Chile, in a place where everything came together and we were on Earth Prime. I intended asking more details, like for example, why choose Chile for this type of Base.

In the meanwhile, the feeling of hunger and the adrenaline in my body made it difficult for me to fix my thoughts and control myself. My head started to fill with images of outrageous violence and in that moment I realized how difficult it had been to control the impulse to jump on the nurse and beat her wildly to then bite her flesh as a hungry predator would have done.

Something inside me said I should have felt a repulsion for these instincts, but I wasn't able to. Instead I felt a sense of excitement and pleasure. I felt a moment of admiration for Amelia. If she had had to live with all this for centuries, she was able to govern it with mastery.

I found a mirror and looked at my reflection looking in my eyes for any trace of the Demon that had tuned in my body.

I didn't see anything except the coldness and anger I felt. I had a million questions for Amelia but she was taking her time to arrive. I tried regaining control vigorously walking about the room and thinking about the Gathering, trying not to feel the emotions through my body; it was a very arduous endeavor. So I thought about the task which had been revealed to me. I felt it didn't entail doing something but in becoming, transforming myself into something new and that this experience was fundamental for the transfiguration I had to undergo; nothing more. Access to further information was prevented in that moment. So I decided to do the only thing I was sure would have given a result: if the Potentia was tuned in with my body then I too could communicate with it.

It took some moments, then I felt something move deep down inside, like some huge bulges entering my nervous system bringing a cold feeling which, through the brain and the spine, filled my body until it was completely diffused.

I completely lost the sense of touch and an image started to materialize around me. At first it was a cold void, neither of darkness nor of light, then a landscape which started to take shape from that substance as if it were the negative of a photograph being developed.

It was primordial and breathtaking: in the distance, huge volcanoes spewed smoke and lava from their mouths while the high and distant horizon made one suppose it was a much bigger planet than Earth. In the sky above me the sun which looked huge gave off a weak and dull red light.

My point of view was the top of a majestic overhanging of a canyon which sank for kilometers; the stars were visible in the sky in spite of the sun and enormous creatures hovered over that land scourged by eruptions and earthquakes.

The sky above me suddenly broke and a light came out totally engulfing me.

It was blinding, not only visually but also emotionally and it transmitted a feeling of the remote superiority of what had evoked it. It was directed to me. In that moment I understood the reason for the name "Potentiae".

The feeling transmitted by the light seemed so alien and immeasurable that, had it not been for my former memory, had I just been a common man, I might have thought it was God himself. Then I felt a force manifest itself like a beacon to the eye of my mind, descending towards me and then inside of me.

I felt that strange ecstasy I had only heard described by who had mystical experiences then rationalized in a thousand ways; at that moment I could have died and I would have been, in any case, happy. I wasn't able to think, see or hear anything else beyond that light and the feeling of Power it released.

"Who are you?", I asked.

"I am your Lord, your Master and you will live only to carry out my plan", thundered a voice in my mind.

At that moment it seemed like a sensible answer and I felt that strange shame of who hesitated, who doubted what he was in the presence of or to sin for the lack of faith.

As if it were reading my mind, the voice thundered again.

"I am the Source. I am the Origin. You were reborn in me; what you were up to this instant no longer exists and is no longer important. Everything that you have done up to the moment of your awakening no longer means anything. You are my son. Everything has been forgiven".

I felt a strong emotion and a sense of intense gratitude fill all my being. If I had had a body in that moment I would have bowed down, crying ceaselessly, thanking the source for the grace I had been given.

Then everything suddenly disappeared and I felt my body again which shivered, shaken by uncontrollable convulsions, saliva overflowing from my mouth.

I was laying on the floor and no longer sitting and when I opened my eyes there was Amelia in front of me observing me with an almost cohort smile, holding my head slightly above the floor with one hand.

She signaled to the others present and several hands lifted me, bringing me to the bed in a semi-seated position, supported by some pillows behind my back. Amelia ordered everyone to leave and everyone silently obeyed.

I still felt my body prey to adjustment convulsions, as if I had been struck by lightning which instead of killing me or burning me had overcharged all my nervous circuits.

Amelia was seated beside the bed with a strange face, as if she had just witnessed a divine manifestation which aroused her devotion. She held my hand tightly between hers. All the scene made me think of the image of a nun taking care of a saint after a mystic experience or right before his martyrdom.

Anyway, besides the convulsions and the muscle starts which were rapidly abating, I was strangely clear-headed and present, aware of Amelia's longing eyes on me, but ignorant as to what would have been appropriate to say in this situation; so I said the first thing that came to my mind:

"I'm a little hungry".

Amelia held my hand tighter and, I noticed, with the so called lump in her throat; her lips trembled and her eyes trembled and filled with tears, afterward she started sobbing for some seconds gripping then letting go of my hand to quickly wipe her eyes.

"Right... I'm so sorry... ".

She got up and went lightly to the door, opened it and gave some instructions to someone. Then she came back by my side.

In the meanwhile my body had substantially normalized. She continued looking at me and it was becoming really embarrassing.

"What is it?", I asked her.

"You saw him, didn't you?... Did he speak to you?...".

It was a statement more than a question and seemed incredible to me.

Apparently the great and terrible Amelia considered the experience I had, as very special if not unique and for the first time didn't make any effort to hide her most intimate emotions. It was evident by the way she spoke to me that she had never had this kind of experience with her Master.

I considered this very interesting and for a moment felt pity for her who in all the centuries of sharing with the entity had never had a vision. Probably none of the members of the Caste had ever bothered or been curious to mentally contact the Potentia or maybe she wanted to tell me, once more, that she considered me special.

But Amelia had recognized the exterior signs of the contact, so similar to an epileptic crisis. This could only mean that in the centuries of association between the members of the Caste and the Potentiae, it had already happened that some of them directly communicated with the Potentia that governed them. I deduced that this event, besides being rare, was considered a great honor, a sign of distinction even among them. But all this didn't tell me how I would have to behave now and therefore I continued to improvise.

"I had a vision, an experience, but I don't know if I could find the words to describe it. Ah yes, it spoke to me", I said.

"You're lucky", she said with a hint of envy mixed with ecstasy in her voice. "It's rare for them to take us to their world and speak directly to us".

"It never happened to you?", I asked already imagining the answer.

"No. He never spoke to me", she said bitter and sad. "I served him for a long time and yet I still haven't deserved his vision. He will do it whenever He considers it right. It's already a great privilege that He has chosen me as his dwelling".

"You could try calling him and beginning a communication yourself ", I said.

"No, no, no! I absolutely couldn't do it only for a futile curiosity", she said in a respectful tone.

I didn't want to diminish the experience in her eyes and in fact there wasn't really anything to diminish in that the contact had really deeply shaken me.

"It was an incredible experience. Impossible to describe. And I have only you Amelia to thank for this", I said.

"I have only performed my task, but you had already been chosen by them", she said.

"I understand... ", I said feeling at the same time a disturbing grumbling coming from my stomach.

"Now, you know, I'm really, very hungry".

This seemed to break the reverie in which Amelia had plunged, who immediately shook at my words. At that moment the same nurse came in with a big cart full of many steaming dishes which made me forget everything except the emptiness in my stomach.

I got up, took Amelia by the hand and helping her up went towards the armchairs around the table by the cart. My mouth was watering.

I couldn't recognize the dishes and Amelia told me that for the first days I would have to eat exclusively cereals and fruit to regain energy and prepare my body for the nourishment used by the members of the Caste.

To my question about this nourishment she was evasive telling me only that I would have discovered it at the right moment. She told me that the hunger I felt was in reference to this nourishment that the contact with the Potentia made me feel, like an imperious need, but I had to resist until I was ready or I could have suffered serious neurological damages.

I ate everything in silence and with the voraciousness of a piranha, rinsing my throat with boiling, black coffee. She had told the truth. As much as I ate I continued feeling this hunger for something different. I stopped only when the food was almost finished and I started feeling full.

"And now?", I asked.

"Now I will show you around our little citadel. Then you will know what you have to do from your Master, like all of us", she answered suddenly formal.

III

The Chilean base was exactly a citadel, so much so that we used a strange vehicle, probably electric, to move around.

As the Earth-2 base, this one had small building complexes too, surrounded by vegetation and a big number of rooms underground; the civilization of the Empire of the Caste had probably developed a town plan projected underground. I remembered the landscape evoked by Amelia in the vision produced by the contact of our minds: then, she had told me I had brought her in her world of birth which in reality was only a projection of her mind. I remember that desolation she called "home" and at that point it wasn't difficult for me to imagine why they preferred being underground.

We were in the southern hemisphere of Chile and the area was protected by the same authorities which governed that nation of Earth, authorities which had absolutely no jurisdiction in the vast area of the Base but guarded its periphery from curious or rash explorers.

Many on Earth thought that was a mysterious place and various paranoids and conspiracy theorists had built myths and legends around it: some said there were German Nazi party officials and doctors who had escaped after World War II hidden there and that they performed horrifying experiments on human beings; others said it was a concentration camp of desaparecidos, and others that the good old CIA governed that base to conceal new generation war technologies. Of course, none of the hypothesis could have ever competed with reality.

Inside there was only Empire personnel and as Amelia told me, advanced eugenic research was made to improve the bodies of the members of the Caste and to increase the efficiency in their interaction with the Potentiae and performed genetic experiments on earthling specimens. Moreover, the base had been one of the very few functioning spaceports for connections with the Empire, for centuries.

The security systems were the best in terms of technology with agents armed with particle guns at every corner and in front of every building. Along the border there were surveillance towers and Amelia told me there were guards disguised as tourists even outside the perimeter of the base besides snipers and orbital surveillance.

From time to time there were curious people, tourists or journalists who tried to approach; when it wasn't possible to send them away, they were captured and used as specimens for experiments. I asked her information regarding the battle on Earth-2, given that the Translator had been taken away from me.

She told me that the enemy had completely destroyed the Temporal Archives base and that they had been forced to evacuate. She revealed to me that nothing had been lost though in that the main archives had been redounded on another base, inaccessible to the Gathering.

She also said that from the point of view of the Potentiae and the Caste there was no perception of loss in that they had obtained the result they had hoped for, that is, my capture and conversion; I wondered why I wasn't able to feel honored by this revelation.

Yet, until that day, there still wasn't anything new or unexpected, so I asked where the spaceport was and how they were able to dodge Earth's satellite surveillance.

Amelia answered that substantially the area of the base was not covered by satellite routes and agreements made with the administrations of the main countries and with the security council of the United Nations made it so that any signaling was readily destroyed together with eventual dangerous witnesses.

"Therefore the information that the members of the Caste cannot leave this planet is essentially false", I said.

"Exactly. It's true that the residents of the Caste in this system have been here for about twelve-thousand years", she answered.

"And you never wish to be relieved? I mean, it must be boring to stay here all the time considering all that you could do in the Universe... ", I said.

"Wrong. We are not forced to stay in this system. This planet and everything connected to it are the real power center of the galaxy. There is nothing in our empire, before the Potentiae, that can equal the uniqueness of Earth. We never want to go away from here", she said.

"You are, of course, referring to the presence of the Potentiae and the Emanations of Earth", I said.

"Sure these are unique aspects. But the Potentiae and the Caste, now that we have found each other, could keep their connection anywhere and we wouldn't need to stay on this planet", she answered.

"Are you telling me that there are other aspects of the uniqueness of Earth I don't know?", I asked really amazed.

"Exactly!", she answered.

"And are you going to tell me?".

"I'll do better than that. I'll show you everything in a few minutes", she answered.

In the meanwhile we had arrived near a big structure which looked like a hangar or a huge airport hub, so high and extended it could have had clouds and climactic perturbations. We stopped right in front of the little entrance of the huge structure.

I followed Amelia, without asking any questions, beyond the door where there was a little foyer with two armed security guards on both sides of another door. They must have immediately recognized her because they stood at attention, their arms crossed on their chests, a gesture which I supposed to be for the hierarchies of the Empire. Her rank must have been really high even among them.

When they saw she intended crossing the door they were guarding one of the two lightly touched a sensor on the wall and the door opened sideways.

Beyond that, at the end of a narrow hallway, there was another foyer with three descenders. We entered the one on the left. Inside there was a keyboard with a little screen.

When I was at the Base on Earth-2 I hadn't noticed these details, or they were different due to the presence of humans from Earth among the personnel, in Chile instead no one was from Earth and the exceptions represented by Monika and me didn't count. Amelia keyed in three symbols I didn't know on the keyboard and the descender gently moved .

"Aren't we going in the hangar?", I asked.

"When we come back up. You must see things in the right sequence to understand what we were talking about", she answered.

"We're about to visit the offices?".

"No. This is our work and stocking structure for the nourishing resources destined to the other bases of the Caste scattered around the Empire and of course the Mother planet", she calmly said.

"It's the second time you call it 'Mother planet'. Does it have a name?".

"Of course! The name is Maarhab. It's the place from where we set off for the conquest of the stars some thousands years ago, after having defeated such powerful races you can't even imagine. At first we devastated all the surrounding reigns and created a big Confederation of systems. The great peace that was determined gave way almost immediately to a long period of well-being. Yet, without wars, illnesses and with a life span equal to almost one thousand years the population continued to increase until the resources started to become scarce causing an economic crisis we were not prepared to face. So we moved beyond until we reached this solar system. I was commander of one of the ships of the first exploration fleet which arrived here; this system was outside of the usual routes and showed signs of ancient battles fought by civilizations which had apparently disappeared a long time before. The Earth then was populated by many types of life forms and we discovered that there were outposts of the human race. We initially thought they were exiles of the great Confederation driven by the search for new worlds rich in resources, but it wasn't so. The origin of the humans on Earth was a mystery to us which we haven't solved to this day. We also noticed that many humans or humanoids were living the very first dawn of their development, while other small groups were so advanced in a science unknown to us, who located us in orbit and asked us, more or less nicely, to go away. It was then that for the first time we felt the Potentiae, which taught us how to bring them back to life through us. They helped us contrast the most powerful human groups on Earth, to occupy it and at last to reform the Confederation creating the Empire of the Caste".

I was engrossed in thought trying to absorb all that incredible story and Amelia must have noticed.

"If you want, our historical archives are at your disposal to study in depth all the aspects which interest you the most".

"I'll surely do it. The symbols on the keyboard?", I asked.

"This is our language, that is, the language of the Empire, pretty much the same as the one of the old Confederation. It's natural that you don't know it given that it never had any relation with the development of the languages on Earth. Also our numerical system is different and not based on 10 like yours, but this is irrelevant. Besides I was never interested in mathematics and neither were the Potentiae".

But there was another line of questioning I wanted to pose instead...

"Are you telling me that the food resources for the Empire all come from this place?", I asked in disbelief.

"Not for the Empire, but for the Caste installations in the Empire. There's a big difference! You must know that one of the scarcest resources in the known Galaxy is food. The population of the Empire is organized in a stratified social system according to a specific hierarchical code. The food resources are synthesized and destined to the population according to their level of social relevance", she explained.

"Therefore the less relevant social layers are starved to death?".

"Absolutely not. All the human resources below a specific mark are recycled", she answered.

"Recycled??".

"Exactly. They are transformed in food resources. This is one of the great solutions to the global problem, shown to us by the Potentiae. They enabled us to survive, to be powerful and feared again and above all to form once more the old social system that allowed anyone to consume resources, living without giving anything in return", she said as if it were the most normal thing in the world, without bothering with my astonishment.

"Therefore, let me see if I've understood correctly... In this Empire the dead are transformed in food for the population and if someone isn't sufficiently useful he is killed and transformed in food?? But don't you have agriculture, animals, oceans, fish... well, natural resources?", I asked while the descender stopped. We walked out into a completely white room with a single door. Amelia stopped in front of me and continued with her explanation.

"I can understand your astonishment; you are used to a rich world where the resources are still intact, without counting the other Emanations with as much resources available. There is enough for everyone, even for those who don't contribute with their work to the survival of the group. But in the galaxy these conditions are very rare. The planet I come from was similar to Earth a long time ago. Despite our colonization of other systems, the population increase, also due to the lengthening of the life span, at some point reached such a critical mass that the available resources were no longer sufficient".

There were some structures similar to little sofas along two of the walls which seemed lit from the inside. Amelia sat and invited me to do the same. She took my hand and continued like a tutor who is explaining something to a child.

"As it always happens, while there was abundance everything went well but scarcity of resources and the economic crisis made the political situation fall. Revolutionary disorders started everywhere and those who occupied areas arid of resources tried to take them away from those who had an abundance. I am naturally giving you the summary of a situation which degenerated in the course of dozens of thousands of years, in a territory as vast as several hundred solar systems. The Confederate government was first taken by the military who established what you would call a police state, authoritative and regulated by fear of weapons. In the meanwhile several military expeditions were sent to look for systems rich in resources and We were part of one of these expeditions. We found Earth and then there was the miracle of our contact with the Potentiae. Almost all the members of the fleet that reached Earth decided to submit to the

Communion with the Potentiae and so We became the Caste. It was decided that the power center should be Earth, the only place found rich in food resources. Therefore, while a part of Us remained here to build and consolidate the power, the others brought the fleet to the center of the Confederation and, through the Potentiae, created a new order and founded an Empire where law and peace reign. The Potentiae showed us the access to the second emanation and showed us the glory we would have reached if we had helped them return to this space after having been deceitfully exiled thousands of years ago by their enemy".

Amelia paused examining me.

It all seemed extremely logical. A cold, calculating, terribly inhuman logic, but still logical. I could have acted indignant, or exhibited a crude critical dissertation of their work, but what good would it have done? Besides, the Potentia in me kept me from feeling strong emotions in relation to what I had heard.

"This is very interesting but you haven't answered my question yet", I said.

"You want to know if in the Empire those who don't reach the usefulness criteria are transformed in food? Look...", she said without waiting for my answer, "in our society, to feed on human flesh, or if you prefer, cannibalism, is considered a normal practice in the high and well-off social layers, as it is normal to have and use slaves. The Potentiae have shown us this way of survival and it works! The low social layers have always fed themselves on animals, vegetables and when these finished, on synthesized food. A small part of the Empire can feed itself on good quality human flesh and blood that is, not coming from the recycling of cadavers. And the biggest and richest reserve known is Earth. For thousands of years, every twenty-five days there has been an expedition which leaves right from this base towards the capital of the empire".

"So that's the solution to the mystery of what happens to all the people who have disappeared!", I said.

"Well, surely many of them, but we don't want to take credit for all the disappearance cases!", she said jokingly.

"I suppose you don't send butchered cadavers, but live human bodies", I said keeping an impassive expression.

"Of course! We don't feed on cadavers!", she said as if I had cursed.

"But how are you able to keep the bodies alive?", I asked. She looked at me as if I had asked the dumbest question in the world. Then she sighed resoundingly.

"Well, if there is something we know how to do perfectly, that is preserve food! Seriously, the bodies are kept in living stasis by a substance injected in their circulatory system and kept vacuum-packed until they reach destination", she said.

The incredible thing is that I wasn't able to rationally elaborate the information Amelia was communicating to me and no emotion of rejection or imminent danger was activating.

Such was the modification given by the influence of the Potentiae! In a few words Amelia was telling me that Earth was a thriving breeding of food resources destined to a faraway Empire and it had been so for thousands of years before the official history recorded on Earth.

Nothing. No emotion activated. Only the remote and rational feeling that I should have felt horror, or at least indignation, but I inexplicably elaborated what I was being told as pure and simple information. In fact I felt my curiosity increase.

"And how long is the trip to destination?", I asked.

"This is an interesting question. In time relative to the ship, about six hours. In time relative to Earth, about six days, give or take a day. But don't ask me the physics details or anything else because these topics have never fascinated me. The technology for interstellar travel has been the same since the times of the Confederation before the Empire and, of course, there are two particular types of knowledge we keep from the humans that live on Earth. One of these is of course the one relative to travel outside the planet. In fact, we encourage everything that will keep the population tied to the surface. The Potentiae, besides tying the population, let's say, biologically, to the Planet, have asked us to also tie their mental emanation and guided us into developing the necessary technology for this purpose. This means that when a human being is sent to Earth, it will continue to give life to bodies on Earth without ever being able to leave the field of this planet. We don't know why the Potentiae want this but we don't see the point in questioning their will. Even we, of the Caste, are subject to this law wanted by the Potentiae, with the difference that we are allowed to keep the same body and our complete memory, while the humans of Earth lose their memory in the process of installing in a new body: what in some religions is called 'reincarnation'. The suppression and reprogramming of the survival imperatives are indispensable also for the control of the resident population, of course".

"But wouldn't it just be simpler to produce only bodies?" I asked.

"For reasons we ignore, the bodies would not be alive without the installation of the conscious component. What religions call 'Soul'. Genetics alone produces an imperfect and inadequate growth for our purposes. Of course a human body can lead a long and autonomous life even without a soul, like for many animal species. A big part of the population on Earth doesn't have a soul. Yet, when the members of the Caste nourish themselves they also nourish the Potentiae and if the body isn't or hasn't been 'vitalized' They obtain no benefit. It has to do with something that changes in the biochemistry or the magnetic structure of the body but we are not allowed to study this topic in depth. We know because we tried it, that this nourishment considerably strengthens our ties with the Potentiae and their ability to interact with the surrounding environment through us", she answered.

"So, wouldn't it be easier to let 'nature' vitalize the bodies as it probably always did in the universe?", I asked.

"You are asking difficult questions now. Maybe your Master could reveal this secret to you. So far as I know, first of all they don't want who was imprisoned on Earth to leave for reasons of... let's call it 'public order'. The Empire is now a neat aggregation and the conscious units which could constitute a chaotic variable are all exiled on Earth inside the field of influence of the planet. The Potentiae and now the Caste and therefore the Empire have the technology to keep the vital conscious units chained to the influence of this planet. When the conscious unit leaves the body, normally at the moment of biological death or, as in the case of the food resources we send outside, when we induce the impulse which separates the conscious unit from the body, this instinctively tries to transfer itself to the original source, or to transfer itself somewhere else according to a plan we don't know. Yet the Earth is surrounded by a containment field and transmits an impulse which suppresses the memories and impresses a tuning-in imprint with the new body forming still deprived of its vital element, or with a body, already adult with its own amount of knowledge. All this takes place automatically from bases built by the Caste as instructed by the Potentiae", she explained.

"Therefore, not even the members of the Caste can leave the planet?", I asked.

"The members of the Caste are not subject to the containment field. Only the exiled. When a human being is sent on Earth an imprint from the containment installation is impressed on him. From that moment, the conscious unit of the subject cannot leave the planet and the cycle of rotation from one body to another on Earth begins", she said.

"And so the Eternals of the Gathering?", I asked

She smiled and shrugged.

"No system is perfect. And the Potentiae, our Masters, have powerful enemies, the same who lived and protected the planet when we arrived. In some way there were fallacies in the system, caused by the enemies of the order of the Potentiae. I know it's inconceivable to think or even imagine of such powers who would oppose the Potentiae, but it was so. We are only instruments in the hands of our Masters; which is why your arrival among us is so important. You don't come from the ordinary framework channels on Earth but from the great enemy of the Potentiae itself. Your conversion will grant us unhoped for progress", she said.

Everything seemed extremely logical, as though I already knew the essence of what she was communicating to me.

"And the only inconveniences you had were from the Gathering?", I asked.

"Yes. The so called governors and the dynasties which govern the Earth are individuals faithful to the Caste or servants of the Empire. None of the Earth's government agencies are autonomous or untied from Our control. The only variable beyond Our control is the infiltration by one of the Gathering in the system. But we are also perfecting the identification techniques of its members; when we identify one of them we immediately take steps to suppress him. Of course, also the Gathering has found ways to make the identification process of its members difficult", she said, bringing to my mind my conversation with the First Guardian, then she continued.

"We obviously also had to modify the genetics of the bodies on Earth to shorten their life and to allow the development of biological suppressants of their mental capacity. We have used the technology of what you know as retrovirus for this purpose. Of course these modifications don't influence their nutritive properties".

I didn't ask her the other knowledge to which the population on Earth was denied because I already knew the answer: Eunos Art, known on Earth as Magic or the art of connecting with the One mental sphere to influence the continuum. Amelia stood up and beckoned me to do the same.

"Come, let me show you", she said leading me towards a door: beyond, as far as the eye could see and bagged in a transparent material that looked like plastic there were hundreds of thousands of white blueish colored bodies , probably an effect of the lighting and the substance they were injected with to keep them in stasis. The material which covered them seemed to keep them vacuum packed and they were aligned on shelves, one on top of the other. The oldest must have been from thirty-five to forty and there were men, women, children and newborns. A disturbing sight, infernal in the normality in which it was proposed.

"Are they all still... alive?", I asked in an uncertain voice.

"Of course. But the conscious unit, what on Earth is referred to as the 'soul', as I've already told you, was expelled from the body during the procedure of putting them in stasis and inserted in other bodies on the planet".

"But here there are bodies of all ages and races. What selection principle do you use?".

"It's a question of tastes. Even on Earth there are animals which are sacrificed at an early age or as adults and according to their age their taste changes. We too operate this type of selection", she simply answered.

I felt a shiver down my spine thinking about the years I had spent in the Organization and the period spent at Temporal Archives.

As if she had read my mind, Amelia smiled putting her hand on my shoulder.

"Don't worry. Only those from the Empire and the members of the Caste follow this diet. The people of Earth are nourished differently. By the way, that hunger you felt when you woke up and that you surely still feel. Guess what it's for?", she said smiling.

A part of me shivered but unfortunately the other part was really hungry. I imposed myself to resist and not to finish my period of nutrition adjustment until I had driven out the Potentia I had inside me. I didn't want to add the culinary experience to my resume.

"And all these bodies are sent away?", I asked.

"Yes. Now I'll show you some cargoes that take them to the base on the Moon", she answered.

We returned to the descender/elevator, Amelia keyed in other three symbols on the keyboard and we began to go up while in the background my mind elaborated all that I was learning.

Once back on the surface, Amelia guided me towards the door which led to the heart of the great hangar I had seen from the outside; inside there was a big metallic rectangular structure, about five-hundred meters long by two-hundred meters in width and about fifty meters high. It was suspended in mid air and I could hear a constant hum, probably coming from one of its engines.

"This is a storage deposit which, together with the others, will be loaded on the cargo which will leave in three days", she said perfectly imitating a tour guide.

"So, this isn't the actual ship?". I asked.

"Of course not! The ships are much bigger and could never leave or land from the surface of a planet. Each ship, loaded with about twenty cargoes like this one, leaves from a base orbiting the Moon", she said. "Before you ask... ", she immediately continued, "... the base used for interstellar connections is behind the Moon, not visible or detectable from Earth. It's stationary above the equator of the so called 'dark side'".

It really seemed as though Amelia wanted to let me in on every part of the life and operations of the Caste. My tuning in with the Potentia was probably considered sufficient, in her eyes, to make me in fact, a member of the team independently from what my personal thoughts might be.

As for me, I felt strangely excited, like a kid with a new toy or a researcher who finally solves an important scientific problem. I didn't want to contrast this feeling, as rationally illogical it seemed, in that I had to learn as much as possible of the Caste and the Potentiae and everything was going too well to cause them any suspicions. Given that this objective wasn't in contrast with the Gathering or the Caste, it was easy for me to keep my curiosity active. But there was more. I didn't have any way of comparing how I felt inside, but was really excited to discover these new aspects of the History of the World, as if they were unexpected and therefore full of allure and attraction.

"I would like to see the Moon Base and one of the interstellar ships", I said without hiding the excitement I felt.

"Of course", she said, clearly satisfied with how I was reacting, "... I had already planned an excursion to the Moon; also because, even there, on the hidden hemisphere there is a pyramid structure all in all similar to the one you saw on Moon-2... and given that we can no longer go to Moon-2 at the moment... ".

"Very well. But I would also like to see a ship and I would really like to make a trip to your world. I have no memory of interstellar trips and I would consider it a unique and unforgettable experience", I said more and more enthusiastic.

"I suppose we could organize a trip, compatibly with the time available and the war in act. I'll see what I can do but don't forget that now you are one of us and time is no longer a problem; you will be able to make all the trips you want in the eternity ahead of you".

We left the giant hangar and got on the standard electric vehicle on the way back.

"There are many other things I have to show you, but first let's have some lunch", she said.

I felt a cold shiver.

"Speaking of food... ", I said.

"Don't worry. You'll be able to cross over to our diet in a few weeks and when your body will have adapted to the new condition you won't see anything strange about it, believe me. In the meanwhile you can eat the usual things you are used to without forgetting a lot of fruit and cereals", she said.

"I think bread, eggs, cheese and fruit will be good for now", I said fearing that if I'd asked for a steak or a hamburger I would have never known its origin.

She laughed nodding her head.

"Don't worry, we don't want to poison you", she said.

And then we arrived to the mess hall, one of the many in the city, in a one storied building. Amelia and I were alone at the table and ate in silence. I thought about Monika and made a mental note to ask about her when I could.

Even though, as promised, it was a meatless meal, just the same I tried not to look at what Amelia was eating.

III

After our meal we remained in the area of the mess hall, in a little park where we walked a little, followed at a distance by two security agents.

"This is really a quiet place", I said.

"Yes. It's far from everything and really safe. There aren't such beautiful landscapes within the Empire anymore, nor such wild nature", she said, and by her entranced tone I understood she felt not only lucky but even privileged to be in that place.

"What has become of Monika?", I asked taking advantage of her moment of ecstasy.

"She has become one of Us as you have seen. A Potentia considered her worthy and chose her. They came into communion and since then, like you now, she is one of the Caste", Amelia answered.

"I understand. But where is she?", I asked.

"How impatient. You still worry about her!", she said a little touchy.

"I think it's natural. We were colleagues... and friends", I answered.

"Friends? Right! Anyway, jokes aside, now she is up there", she said pointing to the Moon which was visible in the daylight "... she is on the base we have called ISIS. A base similar to the one on Moon-2 but adapted to the moon's gravity and the absence of atmosphere, besides the danger of impact with asteroids", she said.

"And how did she get up there? With one of the transports or in the same way you brought me here?", I asked.

"You were brought here using a procedure sacred to us, or if you prefer, a sacred rite revealed to us by the Potentiae. It's similar to the dislocation that you do but not as efficient and it doesn't work on long distances. It obviously works between Emanations in that the emanated spaces are intertwined. We need you to gain that technology. Monika went to the ISIS base with a transport; there is one taking off and landing every night, sometimes in connection with the food shipment", she said and added, "... we will reach her tonight. The sooner we put you in contact with the lunar Pyramid the better, while we prepare the counterattack".

"Counterattack?". For a moment I had forgotten about the ongoing war, taken as I was by all the new information being revealed to me.

"Don't think we will passively endure what the Gathering has done to us! We would have already reacted but the design of the Potentiae is much more complex", she said.

We walked for another little while when I suddenly felt my head fill with something that was halfway between a liquid gust and a deafening noise. I saw that Amelia too was hearing something similar and in her eyes there appeared the light of her Master the Potentia. Without a doubt the same thing was happening to me and despite myself I had opened up to the possession now that I was playing in their territory. I felt my consciousness move aside to make room for the entity. A feeling of power filled my every cell together with a tremendous, total hate.

"The base has been compromised: they are here!", said the Potentia to Amelia.

I heard some distant explosions coming from the center of the citadel and instinctively, or because I was in communion with the entity that had occupied my body, I knew that my Equals were attacking here too and at the same time I knew that the Second Emanation was completely in the hands of the armies of the Eternals.

I felt my identity remaining intact; yet, independently from my own will, the Potentia had taken possession of my body. Its possession was domineering, irresistible. I saw Amelia quickly go towards the origin of the apparent battle and I found myself following her in spite of myself.

The nearer we came the louder the noises became and now we could also distinguish voices and harrowing cries on top of the noise of the explosions.

We turned a corner and found the first rubble and then blood and bodies in pieces in Caste forces uniforms. With each passing moment I perceived a totally alien energy diffuse in every cell of my body, as if it were becoming an accumulator for a force that was getting ready to strike. In front of us there was a crossroad and more bodies and rubble burning. I could hear the sound of blows of particle weapons and excruciating cries.

Another explosion shook the air and made us lose our balance for a moment and then we turned another corner. The noise of the conflict came from the street on the left; there were two warriors from the Gathering. They probably already knew of this place and had transported themselves with the Translator I saw hanging on the chest of the Eternal facing me. He was dressed as an ancient Druid with a very long beard as white as his hair. He was back to back with a woman with long blond hair of which I could only make out her movements and the devastating effects of her attacks. The Druid had a long cane lit at the top and seemed busy extending a protective shield while the witch attacked. Amelia and I stopped about five-hundred meters from them, I felt an imposing emanation of energy exude from me and almost immediately the Druid's face contorted in a grimace of pain and folly. He lost his grip on the cane while his hands went to take his head. He cried so loudly that for a moment his voice surpassed the sounds of the battle. I felt Amelia getting ready to strike at the woman in the same way but the woman was already aware of the attack and quickly put her hand on the Druid's shoulder, already on his knees, with blood trickling down the cavity of his eyes which had exploded and also from his nose, mouth and ears. I saw the witch resist, close her eyes and activate the Translator. Almost instantly they disappeared while the mad expression of pain started to appear on her face too.

Amelia and I were side by side. The armed security men came out from their shelters going to the place where the two attackers had been to verify if they had really disappeared.

I felt the presence in my body withdraw until it became a point inside my brain. The presence of the Potentia had disappeared from Amelia's eyes too while the recovery groups mobilized to isolate the area beginning to extinguish the fires. In a moment, the alarm which had rung all that time and which I hadn't noticed before, went off.

Amelia went away reaching a security officer and I saw her give instructions. The officer saluted her and said something to a transmitter and a few seconds later we were reached by an electric vehicle. Amelia motioned me to get on and she got on too. Our tour for the day was obviously over. The priorities had changed: we had to go to an emergency meeting.

"First we will go get the dislocating device you had around your neck when we evoked you. Sooner or later you will of course have to explain to us what it can do and how it works", she said.

"Why is it so important?", I asked.

Amelia made an eloquent grimace to my obvious question, snorted and lifted her eyes to the sky. The answer could have been obvious, of course, yet with experience I had learned that sometimes what we think we know has nothing to do with reality.

"Because it could be useful in a counteroffensive and more important, you have to wear it before it spontaneously transports itself far from us. We have already seen in the past that after a number of days, if the device isn't with or comes in contact with its owner, it automatically dislocates to a place inaccessible to us. You will have to wear it again", she said.

Very interesting: they had already had one or more Translators but hadn't been able to work on them because of the recall mechanism.

"It's a great test of trust", I said smiling.

"There is no question of trust since you have been transmuted. And a while ago, it was thanks to you that we were able to stop the attack. If you had the strength or the willpower to oppose, that would have been a good moment", she said looking at me with pride.

"Amelia, I don't want to lie to you saying I understand and suddenly share the mission of your Empire and the objectives of the Potentiae. The understanding is making its way inside of me. One of the really important factors is that you are here by my side", I said knowing I couldn't risk deceiving her or the entity that was able to manifest itself inside of me. After all I had told her a truth and my emotional sphere had surely conveyed the real nature to her as to the Potentia at the bottom of my mind.

I saw her lightly blush and lower her eyes.

"But... I thought you were here for your Monika", she said as her eyes met mine.

"I experienced something unique with you and you know it".

"The same for me". And her eyes turned glossy.

After so many thousands of years a being like Amelia was still able to feel strong and real emotions.

Maybe even she marveled at her being able to feel them after an eternity of ice and barenness. Maybe she was finding inside herself a fertile area where it was possible to plant and grow something worth.

This made me hope for her race and all those who came from that decadent and arid empire, whether possessed by a Potentia or simple humans.

Or maybe she was a beautiful exception. I would have never known.

IV

My Translator was kept in one of the underground rooms inside a transparent container.

Amelia took it, not hiding her relief in finding it still in its place, gave it to me and I put it on.

I immediately perceived the entity inside me curious to know how the contact with the device made me feel, to then immediately retreat to a remote point inside my mind when it realized that such contact didn't cause any kind of reaction.

Amelia led me to a big room where three other components of the Caste in flesh and blood were present and four others encamped on a three-dimensional screen which largely occupied a long wall. After a few seconds Monika appeared and even through the screen I could see the light of the Potentia which was by now indivisible from her. When she came into the room I saw Amelia observe me, out the corner of her eye, as if looking for a reaction from me. Not seeing anything, she turned her concentration towards the screen. We were all standing side by side and Icarus was with us too.

I was told that the present members of the Caste, with the exception of Monika and myself in that we were newbies, were part of the Emergency Council, a sort of executive committee which took control of all the operations in the Terrestrial system in case of crisis. I felt the Potentia in me take control of my body and I saw the same happen to the others; a real Summit Meeting!

The Potentiae communicated through us in a strange way, extremely essential and synthetic. They decided for my trip to the Moon base and the preparation for an attack on Earth-5. The entity inside of me, whose name I won't repeat in this account to avoid an involuntary evocation, wanted to make some dislocation experiments using my Translator to observe the effect on himself and evaluate its tactical value.

When the meeting ended we knew exactly what we had to do.

ISIS

The Potentiae would have liked me to try to transfer to Moon-2 with the Translator and it took me a while to convince them that the instrument would work only if the destination could be visualized. In fact I could have used the Translator to arrive first as a projection on the Moon, but tried to hide this information to the Potentia; I don't know if my attempt worked or if the entity was indulging so as not to run the risk of physically losing me in an unfortunate accident, fact is, I was able to convince everyone it was better for me to travel on board of one of their carriers. The departure was programmed for that same evening.

In the meanwhile I found out that the attack I had witnessed by the Gathering had not been an isolated case; there had been numerous others, thwarted in a similar way by the Potentiae, but had, in any case, produced heavy damages to the structures of the Caste.

A little before sunset Amelia came by to get me; she had a uniform of the Caste brought to me to wear for the trip and a couple of changes in a black handbag.

We reached the hangar we had visited that morning with the same electric vehicle, entered the same door, crossed the reception hall and the guards and reached the ship.

A round opening was visible on the side and after positioning ourselves on a platform directly underneath the opening we were permeated with a whitish blue light which lit us, giving the air around us a florescent quality. Almost immediately we began to rise together with the platform and after a while we were inside the cargo in a big weakly lit room. I followed Amelia down a long corridor and couldn't help thinking that beyond those walls, left and right and on the top and on the bottom, we were surrounded by human bodies in the form of foodstuffs, destined to feed the elite of an alien race, but at the same time still human in structure. The corridor ended in a spacious hemispherical room. On the right and on the left, adjacent to the walls forming a semicircle there were what looked like some perfectly rectangular cabins, about two and a half meters in height, from the middle of which came a gentle blue light. Amelia invited me to access one of these cabins; I overstepped what seemed like an electrostatic field and felt myself being pulled by the back towards the bottom of the container; I yielded to the pull until I lay completely against the internal wall which was at the bottom.

From inside, the walls were transparent and I saw Amelia position herself in the cabin on my left. I had the feeling of entering into a state of altered consciousness, very similar to a half-sleep or one of those first stages of the hypnotic condition. My skin progressively lost sensitivity but my mind remained alert.

After a while I felt a light vibration, after which I felt slightly nauseous and for a few minutes felt I was no longer standing but laying down even if the alcove container in which I was positioned hadn't moved. Shortly after I felt the pull change direction: now, instead of pulling me by the back, it pulled me to the ground. Amelia left her cabin and signaled me to do the same.

I briefly fought against the electrostatic field which gave me the impression of moving inside a dense liquid, then got out and followed her along the same corridor we had walked to get to the room of the alcoves, only that now the floor was lit. We arrived to the room where the white-blue light had led us.

A little jolt. Shortly after a lighter one, and in the end the door opened and two guards welcomed us.

"Welcome to the ISIS outpost", Amelia said, motioning with a wide gesture of the arms everything around us; we had arrived on the Moon.

"Where are we going?", I asked.

"First of all to a scenic site from which you will be able to see the great lunar Pyramid. The sight is breathtaking if you like that kind of nature".

We arrived to another big hemispherical room, with the only difference that the ceiling was completely transparent, so much so that there seemed to be nothing between us and the open space.

From there we could see in the distance the huge structure which was the Pyramid and its four cornerstones which rose on each one of its sides. Above, the sky was black, filled with stars, while on the left there was an artificial structure shaped like a flattened "eight" which Amelia told me was the interstellar ship about to take off on its way to the heart of the Empire with its cargo of 'food'. A little above the horizon a geostationary orbiting station could be seen which was so big and near that it could have been mistaken for a little moon had it not been for the lights it was studded with. It overlooked the desolate rock landscape, regolith, rubble and moon dust and thinking of Earth, which couldn't be seen from the dark side of the Moon, I was assailed by a great sadness, which even now, from this far away future, in my memory, pollutes the ink of my pen from which the inadequate words of this account derive. A deep sadness remembering that big prison of flesh and mind where no Soul would have peace, the return Home and the communion with the Great Dream from which everything had come from. I briefly envied those who had no memory of this in that the awareness of the prison would have probably taken the will to live away from anyone. Then I felt anger for those entities which were the Potentiae, which had created this prison and that, without any pity at all, used that power which had been given them to oppress and butcher every creature they laid their eyes or their attention on. Fortunately the Potentia inside of me didn't seem to notice these feelings which devastated me, maybe because they originated from a part of my conscience far away from the biology of my body.

My inner eye filled with images of life on Earth and of how the regime of amnesia established by an abusive dictatorship, which went far beyond human imagination, generated a never ending cycle of sacrifices. I saw the infernal carousel of horrors of the prison of the senses created to give life to an illusion, but used for slavery in suffering and deprivation.

In that moment I felt the desire to cancel everything, to turn into a purifying channel so strong as to cancel history itself, a desire I had to control for a long time. I felt the corrupt Potentia at the back of my mind experiment that desire indirectly, and at its touch feel a shiver of fear. It was in that moment that Monika came in, together with other two members of the Caste; our eyes crossed for a few seconds under Amelia's vigil scrutiny.

I noticed then that there was a huge difference between the contamination I had been subjected to and that which instead tainted the other members of the Caste, Monika included.

I could in fact see that the presence of the Potentiae in them had become an indispensable component, a fundamental element. The contamination effect was especially visible in Monika, maybe because it was such a recent event for her and she still hadn't learned to manage the external effects. She almost seemed exalted, with a crazed expression even though her Potentia wasn't there; I realized that freeing her from her Master would be a difficult endeavor, extremely difficult, even if I hoped it wouldn't be impossible.

"That structure should, of course, be familiar to you", Amelia said pointing to the Pyramid complex with its cornerstones or monoliths.

"Of course. It looks like an exact copy of the one on Moon-2".

"Exactly. We hypothesized that it is also in a position exactly symmetrical to that of Moon-2. That is, we hypothesize that all the Emanations of Earth and of its Space have that complex in common, which evidently must also be on the Original Earth. We also think that those structures participated in the generating process of the Emanations", Amelia continued.

"I understand. It could be a logical deduction but impossible to prove", I said, "... and anyway, even if it were so, I don't understand how this kind of information could be useful".

Amelia looked at me closely as if for a moment she had thought I was still trying to sidetrack her. Then she evidently discarded that hypothesis.

"If the structures of the Pyramid and of the Cornerstones are responsible for the existence of the Emanations it means that this is the first great work together with its twin on Earth. Another one must be on the final destination Emanation, that is on the last Emanation. All the other ones are reflections or harmonic reverberations of the tension generated between the first and the last. Therefore, through this structure revealing its secrets, we should be able to directly interact with its twin in the Emanation which hosts our enemy; up to now, only your proximity to its surface produced important reactions. Given that we don't know where the structure on Earth is, nor did we find it on Earth-2, is why we brought you here", Amelia concluded.

I knew then that the Potentiae had not had access to my entire memory, nor did they have it now; otherwise they would have known of the First Guardian, that is, of the one they considered a buried spaceship in Corsica which was, in fact, what they were looking for. I was curious to discover how they would have put me in contact with the structure in the Moon's environment without an atmosphere, and in case, what the reaction of the Guardian would be given the presence of the Potentia in me. According to reports, other members of the Caste, possessed by the Potentiae, had tried a physical contact with the Guardian on Moon-2 but without results.

In the meanwhile, while I was at it, I asked Amelia again if it were possible to take a trip on the interstellar ship to its destination and back just to experience the feeling of a trip in space to such a faraway destination. Predictably, she told me that at the moment that wasn't a priority and that if everything went well I would have many opportunities of traveling through the stars if I wished. I seemed to understand that she didn't share this kind of wish.

"How will we arrive to the Pyramid in the absence of atmosphere?", I asked. Amelia was about to answer but in that exact moment we saw a star, or what in that moment looked like one, appear and break lose from the vault of the dark sky.

It seemed to move towards us. I looked first at Amelia and then at Monika but didn't see signs of worry on their faces who instead seemed to observe the phenomenon almost as an entertainment.

It wasn't a star, of course, and at every passing second it became bigger and bigger. It could have been a space vehicle, or an asteroid or a meteor which was approaching dangerously. I then thought that none of the present were alarmed in that the big ship in orbit would have intervened. But seconds passed and this didn't happen. No one seemed to be bothered by the phenomenon except me. I looked at the people present again. Instinctively my hand reached for the Translator and Amelia, in seeing my gesture stopped me with a motion of her hand.

"Stop. Don't worry and observe. The show can be very nice", she said.

My hand slowly moved away but I was sweating cold. The Potentia at the back of my mind was there, but not reactive.

The object suddenly became discernible as a big meteor and in a few seconds struck something that surrounded the pyramid and exploded. The ground shook and I only managed to see a flash of light spurt from a dome, invisible to the eye, which surrounded the Pyramid and then everything darkened. The dome we were observing from was probably reacting to the light and to the variation in the radioactive field thus protecting our bodies, I thought. Amelia confirmed my thought.

"As you can see, this base and the site of the Pyramid are completely contained in an energy field inside of which there is a breathable atmosphere at the right pressure".

"Of course", I said. I should have known that Potentiae or not I was dealing with the science of an ancient Empire which mastered technologies beyond the imagination of the exiled on Earth.

I decided there was no time to waste and broke the delay.

"Whenever you're ready, I'm ready to go to the Pyramid for the physical proximity experiment", I said.

I felt the Potentia inside me stir at the idea.

"Are you impatient?", Monika asked.

"You know me. You know I'm never able to wait", I answered.

"And neither can we. Our expectations are very high. We have planned for the experiment to take place in about four hours. Enough time to put our bags down and allow our bodies to get used to the new environment. Oscar will take you to your lodgings and we will come to get you in about two hours", Amelia said pointing to Oscar, one of the resident representatives of the Caste.

"If you or Oscar don't mind I'd like to be taken by Monika", I said without expression.

"No problem", Amelia said. "Monika?".

224

"Absolutely no problem. Follow me", she said, cordially cold. I followed her while she moved with great ease between the corridors of the lunar base as though she had lived there for years. I noticed that she tried to avoid my eyes even if she was surely aware that my attention was entirely concentrated on her. While I observed her my thought formed a question never expressed as sound and words: was it possible that she had so completely and suddenly abandoned the person she had been before the touch of the Potentia?

We got on what seemed like an elevator and Monika keyed in a code on the keyboard showing me she completely understood the alphabet of the Caste.

Finally we were in front of each other, and she didn't escape my gaze. In fact she stared at me with challenging eyes and with a slightly teasing smile.

"Does the Monika I came to know in the Earth-2 forest still exist? Has she ever existed?", I asked her.

"In the end you too ... even you had to surrender", she said instead of answering my question. The Potentia wasn't in her eyes and I perceived a shadow of disappointment in her tone of voice as if she had thought that I was above that power that had instead overcome her so easily and she had expected a ferocious resistance besides a refusal to the bitter end to submit.

"You know, I couldn't believe it until I saw it with my own eyes", she continued emphasizing that strange disappointment, near contempt, in her voice.

"What did you expect exactly?", I asked.

"What did I expect?? You had made me believe certain things ... you used me, deceived me, to try and get me away from ... this!". And so saying she made a movement with her hand as if to want to include her body and everything around her.

"Isn't it a bit too late for useless accusations?", I asked, hinting to the fact that by now, from her point of view, we were both on the same team.

In fact, what she was saying and her tone of voice were completely out of place now that, at least in theory, we were both 'enrolled' in that new world we had wanted to fight. I asked myself if her anger was genuine or induced by the Potentia.

"You're right", she said, but the light of her emotion took a little while longer to go away and disappear from her face and her eyes. I couldn't help feeling a weak hope for her too. She left me at the door of my room warning me not to leave my room in that someone would have come to escort me to the meeting place. I mentally asked myself if she had already conformed to the horrifying diet of the Caste but didn't want to openly ask her for fear of an affirmative answer.

After exactly one hour, an anonymous attendant in uniform came to get me and so I discovered that the meeting place was the 'restaurant' of the outpost. We ate, for the most part, in silence and my attention was focused on making sure that my meal was completely vegetarian. Then I was led to what looked like a little station of shuttles which were similar to little carriages which ran by magnetic levitation, and I learned that the ISIS base was divided in compounds all linked to each other by a network of underground connections. Amelia, Monika and other components of the Caste, which I wasn't introduced to, arrived and then we boarded a little coach which looked like a big elevator from the inside; there was nowhere to sit neither handrails to hold on to. I imitated the others who leaned against the walls and almost immediately, after the door closed, perceived a light movement. According to an approximate calculation I had made from the panoramic dome, we were a few kilometers from the great Pyramid. The trip lasted maybe a little over a minute after which a subtle sound impulse signaled our arrival to destination and soon after the automatic door opened and we walked out into the arrival station.

"What depth are we?", I asked while getting out of the shuttle.

"About three hundred meters under the surface. As you may have learned, our bases are always prevalently underground", answered one of the people present to whom I hadn't been introduced and who didn't bother to introduce himself in that moment either. I followed the committee inside an elevator.

"As you already know, the entire space around ISIS and the Pyramid is surrounded by a domed force field with a breathable atmosphere where the concentration of oxygen is more than normal, as in all our bases", continued the nameless man.

In the meantime, while we went up, I felt the pressure variation in my ears, immediately after the crossing of a membrane which seemed to be made of pure static electricity.

We arrived at the top and got out in a little lobby with a single door. On the right and the left there were two wide windows from which you could see we were on the surface.

"The force field also filters a great deal of the solar and cosmic radiations, and as you've been able to see, it's also impact proof by any object of any size coming from space. Briefly speaking, it's a completely safe place", Amelia concluded.

"Shall we go out?", I asked.

"Of course. That's what we're here for. You only need to wear this around your wrist... ", she said handing me a kind of bracelet with colored symbols along the entire surface.

"It's a remote terminal that will allow our researchers in the observation room to monitor your bio-magnetic reactions in proximity of the Pyramid", Amelia explained.

I put on the bracelet without asking any questions. As soon as it closed around my wrist it adhered perfectly and seemed very light. It immediately switched on and a series of lights lit up on its surface. I wasn't able to make out its symbols though.

"One last thing ...", Amelia continued, "... outside that door the gravity will be that of the moon and therefore your movements will have to correspond to the gravitational ratio you are used to. We'll go out first so you can observe our movements. I advise you not to make sudden movements or impressive experiments with gravity to avoid that your body lose control and come in contact with the force field. It doesn't distinguish the difference between Asteroids and human bodies!".

I nodded. In fact, the lunar gravity might have probably led me to playful deviations from my mission.

The door opened and as we had agreed I waited for everyone to go out carefully observing them from the threshold; every step was executed almost in slow motion to measure out the strength exerted. A little step separated me from the ground outside and I finally moved. I remained standing still for almost a minute. The lower gravity acted also on the rest of my body loosening the hold on the internal organs which almost seemed weightless. My blood circulation underwent this effect too and I felt my legs almost lose their sensibility; only then did I perceive the spacesuit automatically adjust the adherence points on my body compressing around the buttocks and thighs, almost wanting to restrain the blood to the lower body. I started to move rather awkwardly measuring every step. My breathing rhythm had changed too. The higher concentration of oxygen had, fortunately, suggested to me to immediately breath slowly and not deeply but even so I felt a sense of euphoria widen my thoughts. The approach of the researcher automatically came to my aid: I observed myself and the effect of the environment in a detached way avoiding, as much as possible, any emotional involvement. But there was also another source of environmental 'diversity': the Pyramid itself. It almost seemed immaterial in that environment. It didn't reflect the light in a stable way.

Sometimes it seemed transparent, liquid in its structure, sometimes completely black and at other times it looked like gleaming metal; the fluidity of the metamaterial was a hypnotic sight in itself.

The committee had stopped near one of the monoliths to wait for me.

"What do you want me to do?", I asked when I reached them. My voice was distorted in that environment, with an echo and a deepness similar to that of a big and empty cave.

"We are here to monitor the activity of the structure in your proximity. Feel free to do what you prefer", answered one of the present, speaking for the first time since we had met. He was holding a little instrument which completely captured his attention.

I felt the embarrassing responsibility of having to entertain the whole committee.

Actually, I could have made fun of them and I must say that I had been tempted, yet, besides their concentrated attention I also had to deal with the increased presence of the Potentia that had tuned into my body; at that moment it was no longer a faraway point in the background of my awareness and I could perceive its attention; I was still in control of my body and likewise of my thoughts, yet he was there, paying attention, full of a curiosity that had the taste of obsession.

I stopped delaying and headed straight for the closest monolith. The Potentia moved as if in anxious anticipation, with the slightest aura of reverential fear of that forbidden object of desire, maybe symbol in existence of the power that such a long time before had defeated its race. Despite the different environment, the entire structure of the Pyramid and its four cornerstones looked like an exact copy of the one I had encountered on Moon-2.

The monolith, which was one of the four cornerstones, seen from the human point of view, was huge: almost as high as the Pyramid with a broad base maybe more than one hundred meters.

As I came closer I felt a tension growing inside me that didn't stem only from the Potentia but, as I realized, also from the Pyramid complex; its casual behavior had modified, taking on a stable external configuration rather than chaotic, and apparently – also judging by the others' reaction, including Amelia and Monika – this behavior had never been observed before.

The great Guardian seemed to be made of liquid mercury in slow motion and the surface of the Pyramid like that of its Cornerstones, in front of which I had arrived, seemed crossed by geometrical shapes which formed at the bottom and rose. These shapes were perfect figures in three dimensional projections and black. I felt the reverential fear of the Potentia increase equal in size to its excitement. I was sure that they too felt such emotions.

I brought my hand near the surface of the Cornerstone and, as though in conformity with my movements, the gliding of the geometrical shapes towards the top stopped while in front of my hand the shape of a black sphere appeared which started to apply an irresistible attraction to my body. I was allowing this force to take my hand when, a few centimeters from the surface, I felt the Potentia take complete control of my body and stop the movement opposing a mighty resistance. I felt it fight against the attraction of the Cornerstone until it was able to move my body away from its surface. At that moment the 'liquid mercury' effect disappeared and with it also the rising geometrical shapes and all four cornerstones and the Pyramid took on their apparently chaotic movement again. The Potentia still had control of my body and directed me towards the elevator. The others followed me. Finally the entity receded (but only when we were on the shuttle which brought us back to the heart of the base), leaving me with a residual feeling of dread and hate, as if it feared the touch of the Cornerstone as much as it desired its control.

No one spoke a word the whole trip back and by their silence I realized their distress. Maybe deep down they didn't expect relevant effects and therefore the ascertainment that it hadn't been so took them by surprise. Everyone, Potentiae included.

As a matter of fact, the Potentia had certainly ascertained that whatever controlled the cornerstone I was about to touch, not only didn't fear the contact but in fact wanted it. The burning memory of their defeat thousands of years before must have been a continuous torment for those minds used to total power.

I was taken to my room where I undressed and lie down on my bed feeling suddenly tired; all those new experiences, all that information to elaborate and the new emotions and sensations I had felt, were too much even for me.

My eyelids became heavy lead sheets and in no time I fell asleep like a narcoleptic.

II

I suddenly found myself with my back against a tree, above me a starry sky and around me the smell of the forest in Corsica. A familiar human figure, of which as usual, I perceived only the outline, appeared from the darkness. As it had already done in the past, it sat in front of me on the other side of the dying fire.

"Everything is proceeding according to the pattern", said the familiar voice of the Visitor.

I was surprised. I never would have expected of being brought to this long forgotten place once again.

"Why have you contacted me?", I asked.

"You are near me and more and more embedded in the heart and the mind of the enemy", it said.

"But aren't you on Earth?", I asked, but didn't need to receive an answer in that the knowledge of the Guardian was already in me and in that moment it started to surface.

In fact, only two Guardians existed, the one on Earth and the one on the Moon and the multidimensional structure of the metamatter made it possible for the structure to manifest itself on all of the nine Emanations at the same time.

Even the definitions of "First" and "Second" Guardian were only conventions used to distinguish the two different coordinates in which the structures manifested themselves on Earth and on the Moon; the guardians were in fact governed by a single artificial mind, generated by the science of the Anantrya and animated by the touch of the Messenger.

"Can you explain to me what happened today when we almost came in contact?", I asked the Visitor which I knew at this point to be the Guardian. He didn't answer right away, while I continued the immersion in the environment, induced in my mind, of the mountain forest in Corsica. The experience was really complete: I could feel the breeze, the pungent odors of the vegetation and the earth, the songs of the night animals, the stars, the moon, the gravity, and the feeling of the tree trunk behind my back. There was everything that defines a reality as such. Only one thing was missing: the presence of the Potentia. It had disappeared, yet I knew my body was elsewhere, in an unconscious state, but I couldn't help thinking that, wanting or being able to choose, I could have stayed in that place, which wasn't only a place in my mind, and if it were, relentlessly defined any perceived reality as a 'place of the mind'.

I felt peaceful even if it was the Guardian that had called me and not I to be in control.

"This is a very delicate moment. Your intense proximity to the darkness of the Potentiae is a fundamental component of the Grand Pattern to cancel them from the History of the World. Yet your nearness to them also entails unknown variables which could favor the Potentiae themselves", the Guardian said.

"Are you afraid I could fall victim of their power? I was able to notice that the control of the Potentia essentially concerns the biological sphere. The body can forcefully be tuned in by a Potentia which can therefore take total control. This is what happened when I was about to touch you. The entity tuned in with my body, took control and stopped the contact. I also perceived a conflict inside its mind, between the desire to go beyond and the ancient pain of those who defeated and exiled them", I said, more to repeat everything to myself than to update the Guardian who surely already had all the information from my mind.

"I must remind you that when a door is opened an entrance and exit flow become possible. You have opened the door and you and the enemy are now at a standstill on the boundary between what lies on this side and the other side. You are the Door; the knowledge you have could weaken and even destroy a Potentia that came in contact with you. In this way the entire foul collectivity would come out weakened, in that the bigger the power of a mind the bigger is the fear it can express. Yet, my Creators and I don't have sufficiently complete knowledge of the enemy to foresee an unambiguous result. You must not allow the enemy to delay at the threshold and observe what exists beyond the door, but force him to come in. The more time it has to observe the more danger there is that it can devise a way to violate Our integrity", said the Guardian.

"I need to know what was happening today that forced the Potentia to stop the contact", I said, renewing my original request.

In the moment of silence which followed I saw two eyes approaching on my right and then a wolf showed up in the weak light of the fire almost reduced to cinders.

It stopped for a second with its eyes fixed on me. It was surely a projection of the Guardian and its presence was strangely reassuring. It came closer until it arrived by my side and sat and then lay down right next to me in physical contact with my body. I couldn't resist and stroked it feeling its smooth fur between my fingers.

"If your body, with the Potentia present, had come in contact with the surface of my structure, the entity would have endured an attraction to which it wouldn't have been able to resist therefore embedding deeper into you", it said.

"And... this would have been good... Right?", I asked a bit dubious.

"The enemy wishes to possess the secrets of my creators and then control them, as is its nature. You are the means the enemy thinks of using to reach this purpose and we have stimulated it in believing that this is its only access way", it answered in a soft tone.

"But it's not the way", I concluded, thinking it was logical this way.

"On the contrary. You are an access and contact way to spheres that go beyond even my own creators. You can even reach the Messenger who animated my consciousness and maybe even beyond that, even if my ability to understand the phenomena of existence cannot go beyond the spheres of who animated me", it said.

"I need to understand... ", I said with a touch of frustration in my voice.

"And don't you understand?".

"Maybe you expect too much of me".

"I did not call you to measure your abilities".

"Well, then you can explain this too; which is why I'm here. But now, let me understand!".

"What may seem to you as reserve on my part is in reality only a precaution. All the knowledge you need has already been transmitted to you in the Ninth Emanation but will be made available to you in due time. As I have already told you, this is a delicate moment and we do not want to run the risk that the enemy discover our plans in advance".

"So you fear that the Potentia might acquire delicate and crucial information from me?".

"The more the enemy is allowed to remain in observation at the door the more the danger that it realize the Design and prepare a countermeasure. You must make it cross the Door as quickly as possible", it said, conveying to my mind a sense of urgency.

"And what will happen when it crosses this Door which, if I've understood well, means giving it full access to my mind?".

"This will become evident when it does so".

"Okay, so this is one of those things you prefer not to reveal to me now", I said, thinking out loud while continuing to stroke the wolf lying by my side, perceiving its reassuring rhythmic breath.

"In what way can the Potentia cross this threshold?", I asked.

"It can do it at any time, but it evidently prefers to remain waiting and observe. You must force its entrance", it answered.

"And how?".

"A sure way is to come into physical contact with my structure".

"Like what was happening today!".

"Exactly. Though the enemy stopped you. You must find the way to touch me, overcoming its resistance or in alternative with a scheme", it said.

"Clear".

"Now you must go back", said the Guardian getting up and beginning to walk away.

The wolf turned its head and looked me in the eyes. I felt drawn into its gaze and the sound of its heart became pervading. Everything turned around me, then nothingness.

III

I opened my eyes in the darkness of my room and felt completely awake. I felt the presence of the Potentia which was restless as if it had perceived something of what had happened to me. Maybe it had felt something but had certainly not understood its nature in that it wasn't present in that place of the mind where I had met with the Guardian. I smiled to myself thinking that even these ancient Demons were the same as the humans in fearing what they didn't understand. Something was lighting the ceiling with weak intermittent lights of various colors. I lifted my head and saw that the lights came from the bracelet I had on and it was unusually active. I had forgotten I had it and this meant that someone from the Caste was still monitoring or interacting with my nervous and biomagnetic system.

I became conscious of a rhythmic and agitated noise: someone was knocking at the door and they must had been there for a while by the energy and insistence of the blows.

"One moment!", I said in a loud voice. Another three knocks at the door. "I'm coming, I'm coming. Just a moment!", I exclaimed getting out of bed and searching for the door in the dark.

I opened the door and beyond the threshold there was Monika. The teasing contempt which had ruled her expression towards me lately was now blemished by an obvious nervousness.

"Well, couldn't you simply come in? You've never had reserves about that!", I said surprised. She shrugged and continued looking at me nervously.

I guessed she wanted to come in and opened the door all the way inviting her to come into the big room I was staying in. Being one of the Caste had its positive sides. She slowly came in and remained standing in the living room area with her hands in a fist along her hips.

"Please, have a seat", I said pointing to the standard little couch and armchairs positioned around a rectangular glass table.

"Let me put something on and I'll be right with you. If you're thirsty, you undoubtedly know better than me where everything is". So saying I went to the bathroom and found a light black bathrobe which I put on. I rinsed my face a little to dispel the sleepiness, feeling my curiosity increase for Monika's presence and for her obvious shaken emotional state.

The Potentia in me had calmed down but was positioned closer to the surface of my awareness. Looking at myself in the mirror I noticed I was still wearing the Translator which I had continued wearing ever since I had regained it at the base in Chile. It was heavy when it wasn't worn, yet once worn it became a part of the body without friction or weight. I quickly ran my fingers through my hair to groom them a little and went to the living room sitting on an armchair exactly opposite Monika who was sipping something from a can.

"Well, here we are!", I said to break the tension.

She set the can on the table and looked at me underhandedly.

"What is it? Are you afraid of sitting near me now?", she asked.

My expression was a question mark for her.

"I was joking... ", she said with a forced smile. "... to break the ice", she concluded.

"I understand", I said without having understood. "Well, will you tell me to what I owe the honor or the pleasure or whatever it is?", I asked impatiently.

She lowered her eyes to her hands which were clenched to one another. I remained in silence giving her time to choose her words. In the end, without lifting her eyes she said:

"I'm sorry about before".

"There's no need. You're not the same person you were before and... I understand how you feel", I answered.

"You! You... have no idea how I feel", she said confusing me even more.

"Well, I'm sorry to contradict you but I must say that you and Amelia or better yet, thanks to you, now I'm one... how did you put it... one of

233

you!", I said happily.

"No, you aren't", she said lifting her eyes.

My expression continued to appear like I had no idea what she was talking about. She looked more and more tense and worried as if something was seriously disturbing her.

"Tell me what's wrong", I told her serious. She sighed.

"I'm... still getting used to my new... condition", she said slowly.

I was about to say something but she stopped me lifting her hand.

"It's a feeling... strange. Sometimes I feel... powerful... invincible but sometimes I'm assailed by a feeling of uncontrollable restlessness... like a drug addict. And my drug is the Entity with which I now share my body and... my mind", she continued.

"I'm sure that every new condition requires a period of adaptation. Your body and your nervous system are reacting to the new situation. Give them some time", I said.

"I'm still here", she said referring to herself and pointing to her body. "I remember everything... even what I felt. But my point of view is changing. Many things that I would have considered horrible or unethical are now beginning to seem... normal, as if I were above them. But the Monika you knew is still here, at least for now", she said.

I still couldn't understand why she was telling me these things and why she had felt it necessary to come to me.

"I understand", I said waiting for her to come to the point.

"No! You don't understand!", she said suddenly raising her voice. "You... can't understand", she concluded.

"So, explain yourself! I don't understand what you're trying to tell me". She took a deep breath.

"What separates my condition from that of... Amelia, for example... is only... time. She has known her condition for thousands of years and... has come to an agreement... she accepted it and her cohabitation with the Entity is now... normal for her", she said choosing her words. Maybe she didn't want to say or think anything wrong or compromising. She leaned against the chair and crossed her legs breathing deeply.

"I instead feel like a drug addict on my first trip... where the drug is very special. After the first dose, you can no longer do without... its touch changes you, irreparably transforming you. You once used the word 'corrupts' referring to the Potentiae, I'm no longer so objective and therefore no longer feel free to use this term. But the result is the same: a one way path; not even the death of the body can put an end to it and... in this period of adaptation I sometimes feel the desperation of the impotence of no longer being able to... choose a different path".

Her voice was apparently tranquil in spite of the terrible profoundness of what she was saying. I tried to grasp what she was trying to communicate and especially why now but couldn't.

"As you have said, it's only a matter of time. And then, we are together, right?", I said at last.

"You... are not like me... you will never become like Amelia... You... are really special. Even They know it", she said pointing with her eyes to something indistinct above her.

"Well... thanks for the compliment", I said getting up to get something to drink from the refrigerator. "Yet I'm sorry to disappoint you. As you have noticed... and even because of you... I am here, like you, in your same condition. The Potentia has already taken control of my body in at least two occasions and I felt its irresistible touch", I objected.

"You just don't want to understand, do you? Or do you enjoy teasing me?", she said irritated.

"Listen, it might be better if you explained yourself, don't you think?".

"Don't you understand? Not even They treat you like one of us! Don't tell me you didn't realize it! Before, when you were about to touch the object, each one inside of us was alarmed. They... for some reason... are afraid... of you. Even the Entity which should have taken you like I was taken, takes its time", she said.

I thought of the words of the Guardian which had just recently called upon me. It had defined me as a "Door" and the Entity as waiting on the threshold. Monika's reasoning was becoming interesting but I had no intention of confirming her words at this point.

"It seemed to me that on the surface, even at the base in Chile, during the attack, the Potentia had no difficulty taking control of my body and acting through me. I can assure you that even if I had wanted to I wouldn't have been able to resist", I answered.

"This is the point! You can only share your body. But for some reason it doesn't take over your mind. Why?". I couldn't deny the evidence.

"Look, I admit I perceive a sort of cautious reserve by the Potentia or the Entity, if you prefer. But I don't have anything to compare it to because I don't know what kind of bond it has with you or with the other members of the Caste. As far as I know its behavior with me is standard, normal. I thought the communion process should be gradual and that it was this way for everyone", I explained.

"I suppose you have nothing to compare your experience to as I was able to do", she said thoughtfully.

"Can you mentally communicate with the others of the Caste?", I asked.

"Yes. But only at a symbolic and emotional level. It's not like reading someone's thoughts. Sometimes the Entities communicate with each other through images and symbols and all of us perceive this in that we are tied to

Them. Except you, that is. This is further proof of what I was telling you".

"And why do you think that is?", I asked.

"Why what?".

"Why do you think they behave differently with me?".

"I have no idea. I feel caution and fear but I don't understand it. I didn't think They could fear something or someone. They are studying you but I don't know why. They are so powerful that... I can't believe They see you as a possible threat", she answered.

"But if I were a threat They could have simply killed me just to be safe. I'm not invulnerable". For a moment she seemed to consider what I had said.

"According to logic, yes. They probably also consider you an opportunity. In this case, They will sooner or later make their move and take you too. Or They will kill you!".

"And you say there's no way out?", I insisted.

"Absolutely. You can't understand now and neither would I have understood before".

"Understood what?", I asked.

"The effects of the touch of the Entity. It's like a powerful endorphin cocktail that makes you feel the Power skin-deep. A pure Power beyond good and evil. A feeling that cannot be produced by any psychotropic substance nor by an episode of mystical ecstasy. Now, if I no longer had this... I would rather die. Can you understand?".

"I understand your words but not what you're saying. So you're telling me you can't be saved?", I said gloomily and she looked at me as if I had just said the funniest thing on earth.

"Save me? And who should save me? You? A bit late for that, don't you think? And anyway, I don't want to be saved! Didn't you hear what I just said?".

"So, why are you here?", I said. She gave me a dirty look.

"To understand... to talk... But, you're right. I better leave". She started to get up.

"Wait!", I quickly said. I didn't want to believe that her condition was hopeless.

"What?".

I got up. A crazy idea crossed my mind and without a second thought I made my decision.

"Forgive me", I said, "... I didn't want to send you away. Please sit down. I'll get dressed and come with you". She seemed to hesitate.

"Please", I insisted.

"Okay, but hurry up", she said nervously sitting down again.

"No problem. Only a few minutes".

I had also had time to think while we spoke. As if I needed it, I had further proof that the Potentia didn't have access to my mind but only to the biological dimension.

Well! During those minutes I had elaborated a plan to force her to cross the famous Door which the Guardian had spoken of. I had to move quickly though and in that moment, against all logic, wanted to bring Monika with me too.

I dressed in no time. Monika got up from her armchair and headed for the door.

"Wait!", I said, standing in the middle of the little sitting room.

"... Can I express a wish?", I asked.

"Which is?".

"Come here a moment. Close to me. Like when you brought me back to the headquarters of Earth-2 on horseback...".

She slowly came close. "Please, turn around", I told her.

She turned around and I went up to her, coming in contact with her body. She tried to turn around but I restrained her.

"Listen", she hesitated, "... it's a bit late for these little games".

"It's a surprise", I whispered. "Close your eyes".

She closed her eyes; I embraced her with my right arm while my left arm reached for the Translator. I visualized the surface of the moon near the Cornerstone. I felt the Potentia getting restless but I was sure it wouldn't have understood until it was too late. I activated the Translator and in no time we were in front of the Cornerstone which immediately took on the proximity configuration with its mercury surface and the geometrical figures rising from the base. Monika opened her eyes frightened and tried to free herself but I held her tight.

"No! Let me go! You are mad!", she said screaming and her voice came out distorted in that environment.

I felt the Potentia coming on: I had to be quick or everything would be lost and I wouldn't have another opportunity like this one again. In an instant my hand was on the sphere symbol of the Cornerstone: I completely lost sense of my body and total darkness fell all around me.

NEMESIS

In the place where I had arrived, time was not linear, but rather, an abstract concept of existence. I couldn't distinguish seconds from thousands of years and had only a feeling of falling speed. The Mu shape had turned into an essential symbol, a glyph, which is how I perceived Monika too, as if in this encoded space shapes didn't exist and everything was reduced to a basic symbol.

Monika, next to me, looked like a lily sparkling of non-light in more dimensions.

I felt that my impulsive decision to bring her with me had not been foreseen and therefore her presence requested adapting to that strange dimension and then my attention turned to the Potentia inside of me that was dazed and in chaos not knowing what was happening to it: it was reduced to total impotence there where we had arrived and it was conscious it couldn't do anything about it. Something forced me to direct my attention to Monika's glyph. I saw that among the simple lines and curves that defined her there was also something different, clinging in some parts and stuck to others. Like a tumor of great proportions of which metastasis permeated all her essence. I perceived that, like a cancer, it was a process in the making; only that the new substance which polluted Monika's essence was changing her, transforming her and the process was still ongoing. I knew then that when this process was finished, that which defined her and the 'cancer' would have become indistinguishable. That alien substance that was transfiguring her was the Potentia.

In that peculiar environment, if it could be defined as such, I could only perceive myself and the glyph of my essence as if it were an object which belonged to me but through which I wasn't identified.

I saw that I was represented in a completely different way from Monika. I don't mean in the shape of the glyph which, by logic, had to be different for each individual, but in the architecture, in its fundamental configuration. It was as though there were two different orders of symbols: an obvious one and a concealed one, occult, underlying but substantially real. Real because it is unchanging and eternal and from this fundamental icon an infinite number of expression glyphs could have been emanated; the image I saw represented was one of the possible infinite unexpressed and underlying aspects of the icon.

I had already seen this design in the dream I had at the outpost on Moon-2: it was the nine pointed star that in this place out of time and space appeared like a multidimensional object, projected in spaces, in times and in the expressions of reality: fixed but at the same time in perpetual motion. It was one of the sublime experiences which had marked me even if I hadn't realize it at that time.

Then, I also saw what the Guardian had meant referring to the Potentia which had tuned into my body and what, with great confusion, Monika had tried to explain: the entity wasn't, like with her, clinging and stuck to my Glyph, but barely leaned on it and the expressed glyph in its shape contained it like in a cage. The Potentia seemed sometimes an octopus with countless tentacles which looked like hair and sometimes a spider with legs everywhere. It was restless and I could hear its simple symbolic thoughts: it was overwhelmed by anxiety and deep fear. It found itself in an unknown environment in which its great powers had no game. From that precious point of view, perceiving the configuration of my glyph, I perfectly understood what the Guardian had wanted me to know: my expression was a natural antibody for the Potentiae, a cure, a sort of natural enemy, their perfect nemesis.

My touch on them acted as a virus, an acid, a solvent and now that, thanks to the Guardian, it had crossed the threshold, it was enclosed and was about to be dissipated.

I first wished to take care of Monika and try to free her from her terrible condition. I approached her Glyph through an act of my desire, extended myself towards the substance which represented the Potentia in her and touched her.

I heard like a scream in my mind and immediately the filaments or dark tentacles withdrew as if they had come in contact with something which caused them a terrible pain. I did it again and the substance of the Potentia continued to withdraw to my touch: I saw it start to dissipate as though eaten by countless little invisible insects or melt away by an acid which affected only the gray form of the entity and not Monika's martyred Glyph. Yet I saw that in the parts which had been touched or pierced by the Potentia her Glyph remained modified, like wounded and bleeding. So, through an act of will, I completely threw myself on the Potentia that polluted Monika and saw it dissolve in a thousand spasms and convulsions.

Every single bit of it was consumed like by an invisible fire, drying up and then disappearing in what seemed like dust that at great speed broke loose from her Glyph, dispersing upwards like smoke. It was impossible to determine how much time had gone by, but the moment came when Monika was completely free of the parasite even if the wounds caused to her Glyph remained. So I asked myself what this could imply in the world of shapes we came from.

I turned my attention to the Potentia that was imprisoned in my Glyph; its grayish and oily substance kept itself away from my essence. Through my desire I reached it and closed myself on it perceiving a tremendous terror while it dissolved, consumed by my touch.

In the end, the impression of the eternal fall seemed to reduce until it completely stopped. Some shapes appeared all around: the first were trees suspended in a vacuum, then the earth, then the sky; I realized that our glyphs had once again taken on the shapes of our human bodies.

I was still holding Monika who, by the way she was falling from my arms had to be really in bad shape. I deduced that my task in that dimension of symbols was finished for the moment and something had brought me back.

Now I knew. I had finally learned what my task was and the exact operative procedures. The weapon which had been put to my disposal was my own essence.

The environment around me looked familiar and even if it was daytime I recognized the tree against which I had leaned my back and the smell of the forest: I was in Corsica, in the same place where, at nighttime, I had met the first Guardian a long time ago and to where I had been recalled in my dreams just a few hours before. But this time I wasn't there only with my mind; Monika and I were really there.

She had lost consciousness but her body was strangely tense and she was shaking. I delicately loosened my embrace and laid her down; her eyes were open and circled as if she hadn't slept in days. She was pale and her lips were white with many little cuts; she continued shaking. I tried speaking to her but she didn't seem to hear, as if her mind were in another place. I was invaded by a great sadness remembering the injuries and deep wounds I had seen on her Glyph, and I remembered also what she had said about the way of the Potentiae being with no return. Actually I had just proved that it wasn't so, but the consequences of the damage caused by those immortal parasites could have been irreparable. I felt her heart beat very weakly. I quickly thought of what I could do to help her.

I visualized Shen and activated the Translator. In a moment I was on Earth-5 inside a tent where Shen was in council with what looked like his generals. I could hear confusion, shouted orders, horses, people running and explosions in the distance, coming from outside. Shen turned around and saw me.

"Heylel. Have you come to help us?", he said.

"It's a long story. I think, or rather, I'm sure I've killed two Potentiae, but now I need your help for my friend", I said pointing to Monika who I was now holding. He looked at me serious.

"You have given me some good news bringing me up to date on your accomplishment. But now is not the right moment. The army is mobilizing. We have found some fractures at the entrance points to the Fifth Emanation and our agents are telling us that the Caste has rounded up its forces and is preparing a massive offensive. All the doctors are on the front line".

I thought quickly. I couldn't hinder the preparations for the defense. Regardless of my feelings for Monika I had to consider the greater good.

"Okay. I'll soon be back to help you and bring you up to date. Now I know my task", I said and at the same time visualizing my apartment at the Palace in Amn'el'Tyr. I barely managed to see Shen's big smile to my last statement and activated the Translator.

I delicately laid Monika on the bed and got her out of the uniform she was wearing despite the stiffness of her body: she was still alive even if her breathing and her heartbeat were very weak. I found some pajamas and dressed her with those, then gently picked her up again. I visualized the entrance of a hospital in which I had been in Portland, Oregon then activated the projection function with the Translator and was immediately mentally there. I reached a little area, between the parking lot and the entrance where there was no one and activated the dislocating function of the Translator. We were immediately physically there and holding Monika I approached the emergency room entrance where I found two paramedics near an ambulance.

"What happened?", one of the two asked me.

"I found her this way on the corner of the road", I explained.

They brought me a stretcher and I gently laid Monika on it. The two paramedics quickly performed the conventional check-up looking at her eyes, her mouth and listening to her heart.

"She seems to be in a state of shock", said one of the two.

"Do you know if she is under the influence of drugs?", the other asked.

"I don't know anything... I only found her", I answered.

"Okay, we'll take care of her now".

They brought her inside and started yelling at the people in the hallway to let them pass. I felt my heart tighten in my chest seeing her in that condition but there was nothing I could do about it.

I stopped and slowly started to move back until I saw the stretcher and the paramedics disappear down a hallway to the right, then went out and started walking towards the parking area followed by sadness and resisting the impulse of going back to Monika to be with her.

Unfortunately the procedures were clear: they would have asked me for my name and address and I had no documents and therefore couldn't remain even if I had wanted to. So I reached a sheltered place, behind a big pick-up.

Once again I visualized my apartment at Amn'el'Tyr and immediately dislocated myself there. It was late afternoon on Earth-5. Given the temporal differential, ten hours had already passed there while I had been away only some minutes.

I saw some blinding flashes and some objects in the sky. Wide smoke columns rose in the distance: the Caste's attack had begun. I sat in the lotus position on my bed and breathed deeply mentally going through the line of action I wanted to follow, then I visualized Amelia and activated the projection function: she was there on the Fifth Emanation.

II

Amelia was standing in her black uniform monitoring Earth-5 from orbit.

In front of her, a huge transparent panel took up the entire wall of the big room. The floor shined weakly of a blue light signaling that the artificial gravity had been activated. She was on one of the big starships of the Caste Empire.

Seen from that perspective, Earth-5 was an exotic sight. Even from that height it was different from the Earth Prime, as for color and geography. The orbit seemed geostationary and therefore I guessed that underneath there was Amn'el'Tyr.

If the Caste was ready to use its powerful and ancient technology and had been able to cross the boundaries which led to the Fifth Emanation even from space, I asked myself what could, an apparently archaic army, like that of the Gathering, do against such a massive deployment of forces. The battle on the Second Emanation had been fought and won by the Gathering thanks to the use of the Power of the Eunos Art and of the dislocation technology, therefore there was some chance that the power these ships could release be contained.

At that time I didn't have sufficient information for an objective evaluation in that I had never seen the two armies fight, nor the Caste's fleet attack. I decided I had to see Shen as soon as possible and inform him of the threat from the sky.

I had used the projection function of the Translator to find Amelia; her face held no expression. Her eyes did not exhibit the light of the Potentia which must have been therefore hidden in the depths of her being. For a moment I thought of Monika and the damage she had to endure due to the removal of the Potentia and I imagined that for Amelia instead, killing the Potentia and removing its influence would have surely killed her.

Nevertheless, I still felt bound to her which would have made me hesitate before causing her any damage or pain. I wondered what she was thinking about at that moment, what was behind her undisturbed expression. Her hair was tied in a bun and she was still incredibly beautiful to my eyes.

While I tried to elaborate a plan of action, I decided to take a look around the ship which was of no use: I saw the obvious: a lot of people and work posts which activated instruments unknown to me, while speaking their language which I didn't understand.

Not understanding their written or spoken language made it impossible for me to gather specific information which could be of any use to my companions. The only card I could play at that moment was Amelia and I had to discover as much as possible from her before going back to Shen.

I went back to the panoramic window and found her in the same position as if she were observing everything that was happening on the surface. I found a good position behind her to the left and activated the symbol which operated the dislocation function and was instantly there.

She was immediately aware of my presence and her hand automatically reached for a little device hanging from her belt. A rhythmic buzz was heard which I imagined being an alarm. I instinctively reached her and held her arm but the alarm had gone off.

"It's you!", she said almost relieved when she saw me.

"Who did you expect?", I asked a little surprised.

"You could have been one of the others", she said surely referring to one of the Eternals of the Gathering.

Someone else in my place would have surely struck her.

She looked intensely into my eyes.

"You have been able to free yourself! Now I understand the meaning of what we felt", as if she had finally got the answer to the question that tormented her.

"What did you feel?", I asked. I was curious to know the effect of the death of a Potentia on their collectivity.

"A great emptiness and a weakening of the collectivity together with a river of alarmed emotions by our Masters. A terrible feeling in that whatever strikes Them instantly reflects on us. How were you able to free yourself?".

"I annihilated the Potentia that had taken me. And Monika's too".

Her face paled as if I had given her some terrible news.

"You killed them? But it's impossible. How?".

"The 'how' is not important".

"How were you able to survive?".

"I don't count. But Monika is in bad shape. I hope she recovers but don't have high hopes".

"What do you want to do now? Are you here to kill me?". Her expression moved me. She seemed ready for her fate so long as it was I who determined it.

While we spoke, the big window darkened and the artificial gravity was turned off, probably as part of the security system, while waiting for the guards to arrive. The Potentia didn't appear in her eyes and I thought that after the death of two of them it simply feared the contact.

But in that moment my problem wasn't the Potentiae but the conventional weapons the guards could have turned on me. Still holding Amelia with one arm I visualized my apartment in the Palace at Amn'el'Tyr.

I activated the dislocator just as the doors opened and the guards entered the panoramic room. As soon as we reached our destination, Amelia freed herself from my arm and hastily moved a few steps away.

"What did you do? Where are we?", she asked yelling.

"Don't worry. We're at my place, in my apartment in the city you want to attack".

"Why did you bring me here? What do you think you'll obtain by keeping me prisoner?", she said nervously crossing her arms.

"You didn't leave me much choice! If you hadn't given the alarm...", I said calmly.

"The alarm is automatic. I didn't do a thing. And now? What do you want from me?".

"We're at war, right? What could I want?". She seemed to relax just a little. The Potentia still didn't surface to her eyes as though it were afraid of an eventual ace up my sleeve.

"Tell me exactly what you did to Monika...", she asked. For a moment I thought she wanted to be informed to see whether or not to subject herself to the same procedure.

"I freed her. And I freed myself", I said quickly.

"Where is she now?".

"She is safe in a hospital. As I've already told you, freeing her has unfortunately caused her some consequences".

"But don't you understand? We cannot, as you say, 'be freed'. We are one thing with our Master. And that's fine with us. It's the source of our power. You had the privilege of becoming one of us, but your plans were evidently different", she said.

"It seems obvious and natural that a war be fought with all means available, don't you think? Now you know that the Potentiae are not invulnerable and... can be destroyed. How do you feel about this new awareness?", I asked without hiding the satisfaction I felt.

"Damn you...", she said in a broken voice. "... damned the moment I met you, in which Monika brought you to us... I... really wanted to be with you forever and you deceived me from the beginning".

"It's not true Amelia. You and your Masters knew I represented a risk and, for whatever it's worth, for reasons beyond logic, I... wanted to be with you and still desire it so much. As I've already told you, I don't want to hurt you. I feel a great pain because we are formally enemies, but neither one of us can do anything about it", I said. I was tempted to confess to her the deep and irrational feeling I had for her but decided not to worsen the situation. I had already said too much. She turned around and headed towards the glass door that led to the panoramic balcony.

"And now? What do you want to do? Prevail over my Master? Am I your prisoner? You'd be better off killing me right away. You know I would be back", she said nervously. In the distance, through the glass door, I could see the flashes that must have been signs of the battle underway. I sighed and approached her.

"I honestly don't know Amelia. Prevailing over your Master, as you said, could kill you and I don't want to lose you. And I can't keep you prisoner and allow you to evaluate our forces. Lastly, I don't think your companions would hesitate striking at this place even knowing you are here".

I had brought her to my apartment exactly because I didn't want her, able strategist with twelve thousand years of war experience and the Potentia in her, to evaluate the forces of the Gathering and transmit tactical information to other members of the Caste; something which would have surely happened if I had brought her to Shen's camp, a mandatory stop for the penal colonies of the Third Emanation. She turned around facing me with an intense look.

"So you are really worried about me", she said, suddenly turning into a real woman.

"Yes. Yes, I am", I confessed without thinking.

"Be careful. I could consider this emotion a weakness to take advantage of at the right moment", she slowly said keeping her eyes fixed on mine.

"I'll take that risk", I said shrugging.

She seemed to consider my answer for a moment, then turned her attention outside, to the flashes of the battle.

"You don't stand a chance in an open conflict with us. Do you have any idea how many battles we fought against hostile races in thousands of years? We have never been defeated, never! Why don't you advise your Equals to withdraw with dignity and disappear? You know We don't take prisoners, and the few who survived and those who didn't become food supplies would be selected by our Masters that would want to extort their secrets. You know, beings like the Eternals are considered rare delicacies in our menu... ". An icy smile tainted her ancient beauty as she spoke.

"Thanks for your worry... Well, I don't think my Equals would follow my advice if I proposed anything other than a mortal battle", I said. "Don't forget I can reach your Caste colleagues one by one and destroy each one of their Masters and if this should happen, I can assure you that eating would be the last of your worries. You just might want to retreat with dignity while you still can. You have many worlds to go to without having to worry about Earth", I added in a threatening tone.

"Can you really do it?", she asked without taking her eyes off mine.

"Are you challenging me?", I asked.

"No. Of course not. But I think that if you could do it, it's strange that you haven't already done it or that in any case you haven't begun doing it. How do you plan to defeat us? With swords and pitchforks? Without counting the power of our Masters, with just our weapons we could cancel the whole planet without effort. Maybe with Monika it was a lucky strike", she said following a challenging line of reasoning. She was evidently playing for time and trying to extort as much as possible from me, or it was her way of saying she didn't want me to die in battle and was alerting me.

"I know your Masters would never want you to try to destroy their only hope of returning from exile. You don't need to bluff with me, Amelia. Anyway, to answer your question, I haven't done it yet because I know you wouldn't survive. You're right, it's a weakness and I'd prefer... there were another way".

She seemed stunned by my last words.

"Tell me what you want from me", she said seriously.

I thought about it for a moment.

"Let's see. So long as you're here there's a chance your ships won't bomb the city so they don't risk killing you. After all, you are in enemy territory", I said, revealing to her a possible line of reasoning.

"Don't worry. The city won't be bombed anyway because we need it intact".

"Ah, right, I forgot... Your endless search for findings and your maniacal attachment to archeology".

"Right. Speaking of which", she said, "... how did you manage to get rid of the bracelet we had made you wear at the ISIS outpost?", she asked.

I quickly looked at and felt my left arm. It was true, somehow the bracelet was no longer there. It had probably happened during the experience in the symbolic space induced by the Guardian. My amazement was obviously noticed by Amelia as well.

"Are you telling me you hadn't noticed? That you don't know how it happened? Interesting!", she said with satisfaction. She had just realized I didn't have full control of my abilities.

For an answer I approached her and took her in my arms. I knew that eventually I would have had to face the Amelia problem but didn't want to do it just now, and she had unintentionally suggested a line of action that would have helped the Gathering. I had to try to remember each one of the members of the Caste I had met and strike at the Potentiae one by one, weakening them collectively.

"And now, what do you want to do?", she asked a bit frightened but not opposing resistance.

"Turn around please", I said.

She obeyed. I embraced her again from behind with my right arm and her body fell back against mine letting me know she wasn't afraid. I visualized our destination, activated the Translator and the world around us became my favorite corner of the forest in Corsica. Maybe, leaving her in the sphere of influence of the Guardian would have kept her from returning to the battle too soon.

"Where are we?", she asked. "... This is not Earth-5!".

"I'm leaving you here for now, to find out. I advise you not to go in that direction", I said pointing to the mountain. "And remember that there is nowhere I can't find you. You would do well to stay here and enjoy the nature for a few days. If you do, I'll come back to get you", I said.

"Where will you go now? What do you want to do?", she asked evidently confused; I pretended to think about it.

"I'll put an end to this conflict in one way or another. Or at least to this battle".

"Even if you were able to win this round, the forces and the means of the Caste are huge. We would always come back. So far as the Potentiae instead, even if you were really able, you would never be able to kill them all. Should they perceive you cannot be overpowered, they would retreat for some years waiting for your natural death. The next generation of children on Earth would be monitored to prevent your rebirth. In brief, whatever you did, you would never win and we would never be able to be together as long as you refuse to fight for the Potentiae", she said as if begging me to think about it.

I had her sit with her back against the big tree I had leaned against some time before. I took her hands and kissed her lips. She closed her eyes letting herself go to my kiss and freeing her hands she sighed embracing me. I kissed her hands as I stood up.

"Won't you wish me good luck?", I asked smiling at her, but she just looked at me.

I turned my back to her and started walking activating the Translator. I didn't want her to see how I used it, just to be safe.

"Good luck!", I heard her cry behind me.

"See you soon", I whispered and after a moment I was in Shen's tent.

III

The tent was empty. I had preferred that place instead of appearing near Shen in the middle of a battle to avoid distracting him in a delicate moment and also to avoid being hit by a beam of stray particles. I went out and the guards at the entrance, alarmed, moved to stop me but then they recognized me and greeted me.

"Where is Lord Shen?", I asked one of them.

"He left with other Eternals towards the forest front", the guard answered in a military way.

The camp was almost empty. There was only a small logistic garrison and personnel from the camp hospital, besides the security guards.

Far away explosions could be heard, the only hint of the ongoing battle. I looked to the sky. The big ships orbiting could not be seen from down here. Amelia's words came to my mind: they could have destroyed the entire planet and massacred the entire Gathering force with a few blows if they had wanted to. But she had been even too clear and detailed, so much so, I realized she probably had wanted to give me useful indications on the tactics of the Caste.

According to her words, their aim was to capture the greatest number possible of Eternals to extort their secrets and afterward feed on their flesh which had been touched by an authentic power.

They surely also wanted to try to preserve places and findings, in fear of destroying something that could have led them to the space of the Anantrya, their real all time objective.

So the ships were there for precaution, as a last resort. If things had taken a negative twist for them, they could have swept away the entire continent in a few minutes from space.

"Don't let anyone in", I said to the guards going back into Shen's tent.

"Yes Eternal", they answered in unison.

I sat on the ground and crossed my legs. I looked for Shen with my mind while I activated the projection function of the Translator.

I saw a mixed troop of Knights and other armored and masked warriors with painted faces together with three Eternals, in an elevated position overlooking the ocean, filled to the horizon with Caste ships, probably from Earth-2 and from Earth Prime. Inside the influence of the planet they preferred using the conventional means in that they were surely more accustomed to battles in and from space. Shen and the other Equals were observing, in a big mirror stuck into the Earth, in the middle of a Power circle marked by a series of stones and icons, the landing units which spewed men on the shore underneath. I observed too and saw that the soldiers being used by the Caste were humans from Earth, army, marines and special units, probably lent by the various governments controlled by the Empire. Yet, their weapons didn't look like the regular ones with bullets. These soldiers' destinies had been marked the moment they were selected. Even in case of victory, they would have probably been turned into food, even just for reasons of security. In the meanwhile, those who came from the dark empire, remained sheltered, among the armored starships in orbit. Up there, at least, they thought they were safe. I activated the symbol which would have transported me and appeared behind Shen and my Equals. As a reaction, the hands of some of the Knights went to their swords, immediately relaxing when they recognized me.

IV

"Heylel! You're still wearing the enemy uniform", Shen told me with a smile which expressed all his happiness in seeing me. Actually, the last time I had got dressed was at the ISIS outpost. I shook his hand and those of the other three Eternals who looked like two Englishmen from the 19th century and a high ranking Archimandrite from an Occult order, whose names will not be revealed here.

"It's a long story. A story I have to share with you before the battle takes all our attention", I said with urgency in my voice. Shen nodded vigorously and exchanged understanding glances with the three Eternals.

"Of course. Let's retire to a more tranquil place", he said at last signaling me to follow him.

The Archimandrite stopped to give orders and instructions to the officers of the troops with masked faces which later disappeared among the trees leaving only the guards on the spot.

We reached a small open space, protected only by the foliage of huge trees. Shen took a dark metal scepter from his belt on which top there was a little jade sphere, marked with power symbols. He pronounced some words and traced some geometrical figures in the air in front of him. The scepter vibrated emitting an acute sound that peaked with a crack similar to the one produced by lightning when it hits the ground; a big tent with armored guards, who looked like Samurai from ancient imperial Japan, appeared in front of us. Shen noticed my inquiring expression.

"What's the point of having the Art if one does not use it? My tent was concealed in the Shadow to protect its content from the enemy", he explained approaching the entrance.

Once inside he had us sit on some pillows laying around a low octagonal wooden table, covered by a big map which probably represented our part of the continent.

There wasn't time for other greetings and I immediately addressed them. What I had seen in the mirror of the vision had given me a few scruples which I wanted to rid myself of immediately.

"I saw that the forces that are landing come from 20th century Earth. They are human, terrestrials and equipped with explosive weapons which are definitely superior to a sword", I said referring in particular to Shen and the Archimandrite.

"You mustn't worry for our warriors. They have all been blessed and strengthened through fragments of the Eunos Art. And if the Caste has learned something from the defeat it endured on the Second Emanation, they didn't arm the soldiers or the ships off the coast with chemical reaction weapons. The planet has been enveloped in a special formula, a temporal spell which cancels all the chemical reactions triggered off by the will to kill or destroy. The conventional terrestrial weapons will not be able to function. Instead I fear the soldiers have been directly equipped by the Caste, in which case our preoccupation has been useless and the warriors will have to make do with the new operative possibilities granted them by the Art".

"The Caste uses soldiers coming from the nations of Earth. None of them probably knows why they're here and who they're fighting against and they surely won't survive even in case of victory", I said coming to the point. Shen sighed.

"I understand your hesitation. Unfortunately the only way to resolve the situation is to win the war once and for all. And, as in all wars, there will be blood sheds on both parts. Our warriors are ready to win or die and I want to believe, the enemy too, in whichever way it manifests itself", he said placing a hand on my shoulder as a sign of understanding.

I sighed too and decided to go on.

I started to tell them all about what had happened from the time I had confronted Monika and Amelia on Earth-5 up to my awakening in Chile, the description of the discovery of the eating habits of the Caste, where they came from, their tie with the Potentiae and whatever else I had discovered, omitting only personal details and my last encounter with Amelia.

I concluded detailing the plan to destroy as many Potentiae as possible and on the layout of the starships of the Empire in orbit. At the end of my report everyone remained silent for a few minutes in which, I was sure, each one present was evaluating the new information projecting it in the strategic scenario or in a tactical battleplan.

"The good news you have brought us by far exceeds the more critical one", said one of the present. "You have run great risks but the result has been enormously greater than anyone would expect. Many of us were starting to think there wasn't Power in the World that could destroy those devils. For a long time we have waited for an answer from above and now that your task has been revealed to you, we know that our prayers have been heeded. In the battles which followed the invasion of the Second Emanation, many of our Equals found themselves confronting members of the Caste possessed by the devils and, according to their reports, I don't think it was a pleasant experience".

"Their powers on the mind are terrible, yet the Potentiae must necessarily be at the surface for me to bring them to the dimension where I can destroy them", I explained. The Englishman nodded vigorously.

"Concerning what you called starships deployed in the skies above the city, you say they will attack only as a last choice?", Shen asked.

"Not exactly. They want to preserve as much as possible to then continue their search for the Ninth Emanation. Therefore the destruction of Earth-5 is excluded, whichever way the battle goes. They could use them to strike at our warriors in battle or the camps outside of the city. Amn'el'Tyr instead will be preserved even in case of their defeat in that they don't want to hit the Vortex and eventual other Anantrya technologies. The enemy has time on its side and therefore will try again until they get what they want. Therefore it's important to strike at the Potentiae first of all; once they are out of the scenario the entire Caste would disappear and their Empire would fall in such a deep and extended crisis they wouldn't think about Earth for thousands of years", I explained.

"How could we be sure that all the Devils are dead?", the Archimandrite asked.

The question wasn't only legitimate but it was exactly the only real unknown factor in the whole equation. We could win the battle with the Caste and kill hundreds of Potentiae but there was no way of knowing how many they were and therefore to have any certainty there.

"I can't answer that question. But I do know that their collective group is weakened becoming more and more vulnerable each time one of them is erased from the World. They could retreat much sooner before giving us the time and the opportunity of killing all of them but they will probably be weaker and their ranks thinner. They can't reproduce or generate Life, therefore, when I will have killed the last one of them, they will no longer exist".

"Then begin right away. Only destruction will be able to stop the Devils and there could be entire legions to kill!", the Englishman said as if wanting to cheer to victory already.

A gust of hot air hit us and the Druid and the Witch, who had attacked the Caste base in Chile, appeared in the tent. His name was Siegraad and she was Nausicaa and I finally recognized them as old adventure companions, from a faraway time, when I had another image-body and my Task was very different.

The eyes of the Druid were no longer tortured and in fact he looked completely regenerated. Surely thanks to the doctors at Amn'el'Tyr, experts in the Art of Healing.

"Siegraad! It's been such a long time", I said opening my arms.

"Too long, as usual", he answered embracing me tightly. He looked the same, so much so, that I imagined him being one of those people who used dark spells to remain the same as the day when he was Anointed as an Eternal of the Gathering, thousands of years before. But none of us, as a matter of convention, asked an Equal to reveal their own Art. Yet, I had a burning curiosity: his long hair and beard, white as snow, which framed his ancient face on a vigorous warrior body, in a long dress with a braided rope belt around his waist. Only the Translator around his neck stood out, and of course, the Staff of the Art which he handled with mastery. The Staff was a unique object for those of his race but Siegraad's had always seemed special; its shape was that of a serpent with constellations of Eunos symbols which filled its surface. A pearly pink sphere was set on its top, which emanated a constant golden light from its center. I had seen Siegraad do any number of things with the aid of his Staff, which now vibrated of the color of a recent battle.

"Heylel! It's a pleasure to see you, even if you should be careful with those clothes!", Nausicaa said holding out her hand which I kissed bowing.

In the past and more than once, Nausicaa had saved me from definitely difficult if not lethal situations. I was very fond of her because she was gentle and sweet in spite of the Power she was able to summon, showing a highly discordant aspect of her position. She too had kept her same appearance as the day of her Anointment, with long straw colored hair which framed her delicate face and very pale skin on a minute and graceful body like that of a court lady.

She had always got me out of trouble like an older sister would do with a mischievous little brother, in times when I was much more restless and would have given my life to protect her. I remembered her with a long light purple dress. That day instead she was covered by a metal and leather armor. She wore a different ring on each finger, two big bracelets of a dark metal with arcane inscriptions and symbols engraved which, even from that distance, emanated Power. She also wore a band, like a crown, around her head of the same metal. Everything she wore was engraved with those symbols and inscriptions of Power and I knew that nothing that Nausicaa decided to wear on her body was just for esthetics. They were surely all powerful defense and offense weapons. And even her arms had magic marks, that were not tattooed but drawn in the flesh, probably with a hot blade, in that they were like deep scars in the skin filled with appropriate colors and substances. In her left hand she had a thin dark metal rod, but of a different metal from that of her accessories. At the two ends of the rod there were geometrical shapes of an opaque but bright metal: on the south pole a sphere and on the north pole a little pyramid.

When she moved it, shadows seemed to move in the texture of reality. She had probably just used it in battle and the Power lingered before obeying the call of its mistress. It was impossible to guess little Nausicaa's age, as was for the other Eternals of the Gathering which wore image-bodies treated by the Art.

"The Demons are organizing to block our interventions. With each attack they come closer to us and relentlessly force us to retreat", Siegraad said facing all of us.

"Their mental fluid cannot be contrasted. We have tried every possibility that our knowledge of the Art allows us but to no avail on the Demons", Nausicaa followed worriedly. "They will soon be everywhere we might attack".

"Please, have a seat", I said, then briefly repeated my story for Siegraad and Nausicaa without omitting anything essential.

"Therefore the Demons can die! This is probably the best news you could give us since the day of our Anointment. This will give real meaning to our battle. Without this possibility all our actions would have served only to delay the inevitable", Siegraad said passionately.

"Exactly. I intend to start the genocide of the Potentiae as soon as possible, but not before synchronizing with all of you. I could need some baits!", I answered. Everyone present smiled at each other in a sinister way at the prospect.

"And the bodies they possess, even if they come from another world, have no power of their own and therefore can be easily overpowered or captured", Nausicaa added.

"Not exactly. When the Potentia dies, the body it possessed may follow a similar destiny", I said and I couldn't hide a note of sadness thinking of Amelia.

"Better still! Therefore we would then be able to concentrate on striking at the big ships in the sky", the Archimandrite said.

"They are surely protected from impact with objects and from weapons and are probably surrounded by a force field similar to the one I met on the Moon and I don't have sufficient information to foresee the effect the Art could have against it", I said.

"You are the key to kill the Demons and you surely have a plan. What line of action do you suggest?", Shen asked.

I waited a few seconds to recompose my thoughts.

"I suggest using the army and a few of Us to contain the invasion of Amn-el-Tyr. In the meanwhile the surprise attacks by the Eternals to the outposts on Earth should continue. I equally suggest using this type of attack against the starships in that they are not protected from the Translators. Yet, the alarm against outside intrusions is rapidly triggered off and therefore every attack will have to be brief but devastating", I said.

"In this way the Caste will soon be able to strike us with the fluid of the Demons as soon as we reach one of the places controlled by them. We know where to appear, but we count on the surprise effect and if this doesn't happen we risk leaving ourselves open to attack... almost suicidal",said Nausicaa.

I had forgotten that none of them knew all the functions of the Translator. The Anantrya had not found it necessary to reveal the complete potential of the instrument but neither had they asked me not to diffuse, if the need arose, portions of this knowledge. I quickly decided that the safety of my Equals in this war was fundamental and therefore explained to them how to use the projection function to allow everyone to be in the right place during the attacks. After the explanation, no questions were asked, but I saw everyone fumble with their Translators, surely attempting to test this new information: I then saw them, one by one, smiling with their eyes.

"We thank you Heylel for sharing this knowledge with us. I will see about diffusing it to as many Eternals as soon as possible", Shen said bowing his head slightly.

I continued explaining my plan.

"The conflict with the army here on the Fifth Emanation and the attack by our Equals to the enemy outposts will serve as a diversion for me to reach, with the aid of the Translator, all the members of the Caste I remember and destroy them with their Potentiae, as I've already done twice. When I'm finished with those I can visualize, I'll follow each one of You in battle, observing until a member of the Caste arrives, which at that point, will follow the same destiny as the others. There will be a moment in which no one else will come so we have to try to strike rapidly and repeatedly to kill as many as possible before they perceive the trap. At the same time you will have to strike at the ships in orbit from the inside and understand how to prevent them from striking at us or how to protect ourselves from their weapons. There will be a moment in which the enemy will retreat to a safe place which will only mean that we have won this battle", I concluded.

There was a brief silence, finally interrupted by Shen:

"Very well", he said, "... we will organize ourselves to follow this line of action. Heylel, the sooner you begin killing the Demons the better". He stood up and everyone else followed.

As soon as they left the tent, everyone – including Shen – dislocated somewhere else. Siegraad and Nausicaa remained together. I gave one last glance to the sea and the sky and dislocated once again to my apartment in the Palace at Amn'el'tyr.

It seemed like a good starting point. From that moment on, speed would have been fundamental. I couldn't give the Potentiae time to imagine the hunt of which they were prey.

I started with Icarus which I found on board of one of the ships and then took the members of the Caste which I remembered from Moon-2, from the base in Chile and from the ISIS base. The procedure was always the same: I dislocated behind them, then brought them to the Guardian on the Moon which transferred us to the symbolic space. Once there, one by one, I destroyed them. In the end the bodies fell in a strange coma and I deposited them all in the forest in Corsica: all together, twenty two Potentiae died in a few hours. When I brought Icarus's body, I realized Amelia had left. I hadn't expected her to still be there even if I had hoped so... In the end I went back to Shen, who I found in the Council amphitheater at Amn'el'Tyr.

He had probably just finished updating the Council on the progresses of the ongoing war and now was answering questions. Everyone fell silent upon my appearance.

"Heylel! Welcome back. Do you have any updates for the Council before we close the meeting?", Shen asked formally.

"Twenty-two Potentiae have been destroyed", I told those present. There followed a long uproar of excitement. Shen, who in the meanwhile had come next to me, updated me on the ongoing war of which explosions could be heard in the distance.

The fleet off the coast of the ocean had been swept away by a super hurricane created by my Equals, masters in the creation of natural phenomena. If some ships were able to escape the tremendous fury of the "natural" phenomenon, they surely returned to the Second Emanation or even to Earth Prime.

The starships in orbit had not acted yet, and in the meanwhile, a little group of four Eternals, inspired by my description of the force field I had observed on the Moon, was creating the magical equivalent above the city. The losses had been considerable but contained and prevalently due to the intervention of the Potentiae, which had also killed the body-images of four Eternals during some attacks to the base in Chile, the one in Antarctica and the one in Greenland. Meanwhile, the knowledge of the projection function of the Translator had been passed on to all the Eternals who could now use it for more targeted attacks and at a safe distance from the Potentiae.

Everything seemed to proceed according to plans, even if I still didn't know how to win the war, or progress, that great battle. No one knew how many Potentiae there were and besides the ones on Earth there were also those connected to the members of the Caste in the Empire together with those not in communion with a human being. The possibility that every victory was only a temporary event was frustrating. Not only: even the possibility that the Potentiae could adapt, in time, to anything the Gathering could generate against them. Every single representative was of course willing to make the biggest sacrifice to ultimately free the Earth and the human race, yet the uncertainty and the impossibility to make forecasts didn't positively influence morale and the unity of intentions, important factors for the Eternals servicing on this side of the Mirror, in generating the Sacred movement in unison, driven by the collective connection. I had looked for inspiration in the infused knowledge I had received on the Ninth Emanation but to no great avail. At that time all I knew I had to do was to eliminate the biggest number of Potentiae possible, and the time had come to ask for volunteers among my Equals to act as baits carrying out attacks exclusively finalized to killing Potentiae in the symbolic space.

I made this request to Shen and he expounded it to all the present.

"So long as a definitive line of action is not revealed to us, the destruction of the Potentiae remains the fundamental priority, even if we don't know how many there are, and we must prepare for a reaction from the Empire, from the Stars they control", Shen concluded.

A big bearded Oriental man stood up and started talking pronouncing clearly and rhythmically every word in the ancient language shared by the Gathering which we all knew innately.

"We should then try to obtain the most advantage from any tactic operation. We now know that the dark Empire governed by the Potentiae uses the Earth as a prison but also as a food source. I propose that every attack finalized to the destruction of a Potentiae also try to interrupt, through sabotage, the main supply installations".

"Wise proposal. And so be it!", said Shen.

"Everyone get ready. In an hour we will meet again in this hall and we will complete a series of multiple and contemporary attacks to one outpost at the time in order to allow Heylel to perform his task. We will also be provided with maps of Earth and the Moon with the positions of the known bases of the Caste", concluded Shen and made a movement that had the effect of making everyone stand up and head for the exit. They had to prepare their weapons and divide in groups of two or four for attack.

I intercepted Shen who was himself leaving the big hall.

"Thank you my friend. I'll be ready in an hour and until that time I'll be in my apartment", I said.

Shen waved me off with a nod while I was already dislocating directly to my place.

I looked for something light to wear and found a long black kimono of a shiny material with oriental pants of the same material. The kimono was particular, it had a high collar and draped almost like a cape; it fit like a glove. Each hem had a design embossed – in black – with symbols which instinctively seemed appropriate. Then I saw that each sleeve had half of the nine pointed star I had seen in my dream and in the symbolic space, and I noticed that when I moved my arms a halo of shade and light, visible on a different plane from the material one, moved the fabric of reality around it.

I thought I had never before seen that piece of clothing in my wardrobe.

I suspected this garment had not been made for me by the dressmakers of Amn'el'Tyr and therefore that others had had access to my spaces. I wasn't able to be alarmed though and this seemed strange to me. I reached a big mirror about two meters high by one meter in width, surrounded by a frame of dark metal similar to Nausicaa's rod or Siegraad's staff. All the frame was engraved with symbols I didn't recognize. Come to think of it, it was the first time I had seen that mirror!

But the surprises weren't finished. Positioning myself in front of its reflecting surface, I noticed that it interacted with the energy emitted by my attention. A little after I had started observing my reflection something changed: the background seemed that of my apartment but it was moving, as though trying to change into something else, but only within the space of the mirror.

My image instead was fixed but more colorful and brighter than the light in the room allowed.

I perfectly distinguished every embossed inscription on my garment in the mirror and one symbol in particular distinguished itself from the others: it was the symbol of the contrasting double arches cut in half by two diagonal lines, as it had been described by Monika and as I had perceived it during Amelia's incantation on Moon-2.

That woman, who had appeared for a moment, showing me how to escape the incantation, had been here or had somehow brought those garments and the mirror. Maybe she was a guardian angel and that was the sign she was watching over me. Or, it was someone watching me in the shadows. I wasn't able to feel alarmed, but only to think that that Entity surely acted with the only intention of protecting me.

I approached the mirror and noticed that my distance from it had no influence on the size of the reflection of my body which I realized to be full size even from a distance. I asked myself what other reason there could be for this "gift" from an entity which I thought unknown to me, but I knew I had no time to explore or experiment the possibilities.

When I came very close to the object nothing of the definition of my image had changed nor of the shady fluidity of the background; I slowly reached out to touch its surface and saw that something was changing: the matter near the area my hand was about to touch began to move as though it were of a fluid metal and I began to feel a tingling spread along my arm and a feeling of attraction as though a growing gravitational force springing from the mirror were attracting me inside it. I pulled my hand back.

I didn't perceive a threat but I didn't really have time to experiment. I made a mental note that at the end of the battle I would have had to come back and discover what that object concealed. As soon as I took my attention away from it, it went back to being a normal reflecting mirror.

I wanted to collect myself before the battle with the Potentiae and therefore sat on the couch in front of the big window which faced the balcony, in a particular variation of the lotus position, which was supposed to produce a rapid regeneration of the psycho physical energies.

I emptied my mind and closed my eyes entering the limbo of my essence which I felt fluid and kept similar to a nucleus of pure Space.

Suddenly, I don't know after how long, I had a terrible feeling: a chill crossed my body like an Arctic wind and I felt a turmoil in my mental fluid as if it had been torn.

I opened my eyes alarmed and still felt the chill going through me. I looked around but didn't notice anything. As I was about to go back to my former position, thinking I might have been influenced by the experience with the mirror, I saw a movement in a near corner, in the shadow beyond the door that went to the bedroom. I slowly got up keeping my left hand fixed on the Translator and slowly approached the half closed door. The room beyond was almost completely dark. I slowly opened the door and saw it: it was a human shape dressed in what looked like veils of a material which seemed to be made of light and shadow.

She was standing sideways and so I recognized her.

"Monika!", I said opening the door.

I barely managed to see her face, slowly turning towards me, outlining a smile, when a strong gust of cold air came out of the room running over me and moving everything that could be moved in the room.

But inside, I knew it wasn't so and intuitively knew what had happened: Monika had died.

When a person connected to us leaves the dominion of the bodies by dying, residual effects manifest themselves near all the people who had mental and emotional ties with that person.

All living beings have, through their non-physical vital component, a connection with a force field which is the sum of their memories, of their ties and relationships, and of the uncountable aspects which are components of the consciousness, whether these come from an experience lived through the totality of the body's sensors which underlies contact with other realities, in that something that never existed cannot be imagined. Normally, the human mind can turn its attention to gather, read or observe, but it cannot create something from nothing.

Well, when the mind definitively leaves the body at death, a tear in the connective tissue which connects all the minds occurs, and this doesn't only happen at the human level but of all Life connected and related, including the animals.

At every death an adjustment in the relationship system of the local (planetary) collective force field occurs and the same happens for every birth which, on the contrary, causes a new system of relationships. When the relationship system includes the emotional aspect, a death causes such a strong interruption of the connections to recall near each one of the related minds a phenomenon which manifests itself like a dream, a vision, an apparition, a premonition or other important emotional experiences, which in any case mean only one thing: the death of the person. And this is why I knew that in that moment Monika had left this World. I felt a deep sadness while images of her and of moments spent together ran through me; sadness then substituted by a powerful anger towards those that had killed her, infecting her with the germ of power.

I went back to the couch and slowly recomposed the position, but it took a while before I was able to find the mental focus.

Had it been necessary, from that moment on, I had a new reason to wish for the destruction of the enemy, but I knew that the fuel of anger, hate and vengeance was not suitable. In fact, it was unsuitable in the operations with the Art and was a weakening element. I didn't therefore restrain my emotions, nor push them deep down inside, but lie in wait, as an external spectator, and observed them pass through me with their destructive energy until they extinguished themselves. Then I focused on the visualization which, in that moment, I felt most natural: the nine pointed star.

After a while I lost control of my reactive system which the visualization was evidently generating: first I lost sensitivity on my skin, while the light shined and revolved in every direction and yet remained motionless and centralized.

My mind's eye was filled by a brightness that canceled everything then at last, light left room to the primitive scenario of a great desert of white sand under a sky that looked like open space without atmosphere.

Above there was a big nebula, studded with stars which colored it and the sky was full of constellations I had never seen. My body was still in the lotus position.

A group of shining stars to the left attracted my attention; they seemed brighter and brighter with each passing moment, as if they were coming closer; then I saw that they were really moving, approaching my position, as though engaging in a configuration and from them I saw the contrasting double arched Sign arise which, a little after, turned into the woman which in this same way had announced herself to me during Amelia's terrible incantation. In an instant she materialized in front of me.

She was a superb Being which barely contained itself in the Image of the human form, outfitted for war, with a luminous opaque silver armor and a thin crown around her head of the same material as the armor. On her belt she had a sword and a scepter of a quality which looked like a stable evolution of the metamatter of which the Guardians were made.

Living waves of energy flowed all along her body and I saw electric discharges travel from her body towards the ground. Her dark hair was held back by the crown and her smooth white skin looked like that of an adolescent. She smiled at me.

"It wasn't an easy endeavor to contact you!", she said in an arcane language – known as … – which I discovered I understood perfectly well. Her voice seemed to come from everywhere. I remained still, in position, not knowing how to behave. I had to wait for her to declare her intentions. She seemed to notice my unease.

"Do not fear, I didn't summon you to harm you. Your memory will be of no use to you now so I only ask you to trust me and what I am about to tell you". It seemed reasonable and anyway, I had no other choice.

"I am listening", I said simply.

"I had great difficulty coming in contact with you in your World. A strange force prevented me from finding you and then also your choice of body-image in History made the contact difficult. But now something has changed".

"Excuse me but I understand very little of what you are telling me", I said sincerely.

"I suppose you have no memory of your origins", she said as if waiting for my approval.

"I only remember my Task as an Eternal of the Gathering".

"I understand... ", she said articulating the word. "Surely you must have had your good reasons. I will try to explain without violating your wish to be without memory and awareness", she continued.

"You could begin by telling me who you are! And while we're at it, who I am", I said realizing that this was the information I wanted most of all. She nodded.

"You will have to discover who you are as History discloses itself. My Name is Yanil of the Makers of the Ring of the Worlds".

While she spoke the texture of the space itself seemed to quiver, calling the great contrasting double arched sign. Now I knew what Her Name was.

A shiver like a shock ran all through my body when I heard that Name. The energy became emotion and it was so strong I thought I'd lose my senses. I felt I could only allow the tears to run down my eyes which freely fell to the ground producing crystalline sounds. When She declared her identity something powerful moved inside me, something real, ancient and I could see the reason for this: I was in front of one of the great Beings from whose dreams Worlds were created. All the possibilities, the spaces, the Laws on the other side of the Mirror, including the Mirror itself, proceeded from them and the Life itself contained in the Great Dream was the Substance of their creating and destroying.

She patiently waited for me to take control of myself and I felt an emanation of deep affection come from her heart. She slowly continued to communicate.

"For reasons you will remember when this is foreseen to happen, you are my favorite, and I can't hide my preoccupation for your safety now that you are vulnerable to forces you don't understand".

"Please... Tell me what's happening", I said with a shaky voice. I wasn't able to pronounce Her name without feeling that devastating emotion at just the thought of it.

She seemed to sigh.

"A few other Brothers and I have discovered that a dark alliance was created among some of the Great Makers. Their identity is unknown to us. It appears that their aim is to take possession of the Ring of the Worlds and in this way generate a new order of Reality, contrary to the Desire of the Great Dream. Knowing that they cannot directly strike another Maker, they have devised a plan to determine the end of every generated World of those who do not adhere to the new order.

Unfortunately what they want to create is, in theory, possible. Their united forces could absorb the Worlds of the other Makers into Theirs, creating one single dark Reality directed by a Collectivity that would constitute a hierarchy of command inside the New World itself, undermining in this way the Principle of the Ring issued by the Great Dream.

"Simply put, it is an attempt to take over the Power and the direction of everything, from the bottom, that is, from the inside of the mutating Realities, banishing the Fountain of Life, which is the Great Dream, to the position of a pure container of elemental Substance and enlivening Essence.

"When the rebels discovered the possibility of acting together, first they united their Worlds creating an imbalance of forces in the Great Ring and then they generated dark entities, endowing them with great Power and injecting them in the World you come from. These Entities have been molded with two imperatives: to dominate everything and serve their creators! And also to look for a door to the top, towards the Great Ring which can only be reached through the mind of a Maker. These entities are known as Potentiae in all the Worlds in which they have manifested themselves, in that the one you come from is not the only one infected".

I felt alarmed.

"Are you in danger too?", I asked.

She smiled, surely at the thought of my worrying for her safety which she, contrary to me, understood.

"No. Not yet at least. I am probably not perceived as an imminent threat to their design, or the process of infecting the Worlds has simply not reached me yet. Though, it is only a question of time", she answered.

"I have met these Potentiae and, in some way, I have been provided with the tools to cancel them", I said.

"Who has provided you with this Power?", She asked.

"I think it was the Messenger". A flash of understanding crossed her eyes.

"I understand. The Origin has become aware of the rebel alliance", she said more to herself than to me.

"What do you mean by the term Origin?".

"The Great Dream of course. The Messenger stems from the Origin and sometimes from the Makers themselves. I have come to show you the nature of the threat, that is, where it started, how it was created and why. Maybe this knowledge will be able to help us efficiently contrast the design of the rogue Makers. Where you come from now, no one has the power to destroy these forces in that their origin is not local. They were created by the Makers and can only be contrasted from our dominion", she said.

"The contrast action I have started with the help of the Messenger seems to be efficient. Many Potentiae have already been canceled", I said.

"We have perceived this new Power at work. As long as I am able, I will help you in every way. Yet, if we are not quick and effective, sooner or later the infection will touch me too and at that point it will be impossible for me to help you", she said.

The situation seemed really very serious and from her tone I perceived we had just enough time to put a definitive end to this problem. There was one big unknown factor that could make a difference in the present.

"The Power that was given me to destroy the Potentiae allows me to act on one Entity at the time, and to do it I must be near its host. Do you know the total number of them? Do you know a way to be more effective than what I am now?".

"Their number is not known and knowing it would be of no help. I fear it will be impossible to stop the threat if we don't discover who it originated from. These Entities can be replicated to infinity and if we don't find those responsible sooner or later the rebels could unveil a way to act on the connection with the Ring itself and on the real substance of everything", she said with an urgency I hadn't perceived in Her before.

"So far as the efficiency of your work with the Power given you, only the Messenger has the authority to instruct you on its use".

I thought about it for a moment. As much as I wanted to prolong this meeting I couldn't allow myself any further delays. I already knew what I had to do. I could contact the Messenger after the battle and so prepare for the next one, which could be the final one.

"Thanks for your help, now and in the future. I must go back now to insure the victory of this battle or else many Eternals will be needlessly sacrificed. I will look for you when we will have won", I said effectively. "By the way, how do I contact you?", I asked.

"I left you my Mirror of Substance. You will be able to call me whenever you want with it and you will also... be able to do many other things that you will remember in time", she answered.

I recalled the Mirror that had appeared in my room and Yanil's symbol on it.

She had thought of everything.

"You have also left me some clothes. Do they have a secret use as well?", I said smiling.

"I've always liked you in black", she said smiling back.

I took her hand and kissed it.

"My heart aches at the idea that I must leave you now", I said once again invaded by that emotion I wasn't able to understand.

"To the Great Awakening!", she simply answered disappearing; right after the light returned, consuming everything, and then the darkness from my closed eyes.

I opened them and was once again sitting on my couch with the impression that not even a second had gone by. It was useless to delay any further. There was much to do and I had a strong feeling that there was too little time.

I stood up, visualized Shen and appeared in front of him in the Council hall of Amn'el'Tyr.

The hour was not up yet, but the hall was slowly filling up while the present were all evidently concentrated and focused on the coming events.

"Heylel!".

"Shen", I said greeting with a bow.

"Do you have any news for us?", he asked.

"Nothing relevant for now. I am ready", I said unsparingly.

"Very well!", he said staring at me with intensity.

"This may not be the day of reckoning, though for the first time the Potentiae will tremble at the mere thought of the new Power that will be able to consume them".

"It's time!".

So saying he approached a blood red crystal sphere and drew a sign on it with his finger. I heard like the sound of a bell in my mind and knew it was the recall signal for all the awakened Eternals of the Gathering.

The great battle was about to begin.

A BITTER VICTORY

The counteroffensive by the Gathering had been going on for almost three days of the Fifth Emanation.

During a quiet moment, Shen found time to quickly update me on the progresses of the war on Earth-5, transporting me to the numerous battlefields, so that I could see for myself the offensive and defensive capabilities of the enemy, and of course, ours.

The warriors fought heroically, protected by the arcane Power of the Art, cleverly unleashed by those Eternals with well developed and powerful operative abilities, yet the army of the Caste had reorganized and was now making heavy use of particle weapons and antimatter which reaped victims among our warriors in definitely greater numbers than our expectations.

The wounded and the prisoners were respectively escorted to the Seventh and Third Emanations by way of the Translators. Fortunately, the hospitals were organized to manage great numbers of wounded. The prisons instead, were simply fences put up quickly, mainly to protect the prisoners from the hostile and extreme environment of the Third Emanation.

"With our remaining forces we will be able to drive back their attacks for only a few more days. Yet, we must be faster in the two main missions: kill the Potentiae and destroy the starships. If they don't withdraw, we will soon be without an army and we could lose this battle. Unfortunately their weapons are superior to everything our warriors are used to", Shen said to me and to a group of Eternals present.

"I'm afraid that when they're cornered, they will use the firing abilities of the orbiting starships to sweep everything away. We have to allocate more Eternals to the forces that will shoot them down from the sky and at the same time, it is indispensable to devise an escape plan in case even one ship remains to strike at us", I said a little worried.

"We have a way to escape a definitive attack", Shen said indicating his Translator, "... but I have no intention of abandoning our warriors. I will assign other Eternals to the legion in charge of the ships".

"It won't be an easy task but neither should it be suicidal. I suppose the simplest way would be to take their energy away or drive them into the atmosphere towards the sea", I said.

"Its not so simple given that none of us has ever seen them nor do we know the principles of how they work. Yet, some of our Equals, masters of the Art are already confronting the problem", he said.

"If I can be of any help... ", I said.

He gave me a pat on the back. "Who is working on it has much more experience than you have now. And the task you have been given is equally important, if not more", he said.

"Do we know the amount of the losses that they and we have had?", I asked with some apprehension.

Shen's face, furrowed by tension, wrinkles and lack of sleep, became thoughtful.

"Their losses cannot be determined and even if it could, this information would be irrelevant to us in that I fear the Caste has unlimited forces it can set off against us. Our legions instead have been reduced to almost half. We have about twenty thousand warriors distributed on four main battlefields. Unfortunately we don't have time to fuel the army with new recruits from the eras of Earth or from other allied Emanations in that there isn't the necessary time to prepare them for this enemy and its weapons".

In the meanwhile, I could see the flashes from the particle weapons strike and wherever they struck, explosions of light precede the destruction of the target. Knights with big swords, shields and armors were in the melee, reaping heads like wheat, protected from the flashes of the weapons by a great Legis Cantio, which didn't save them from the radiation, though. One after the other, the great knights which were struck, after a sufficient time to grant them an honorable death, would collapse, their bodies consumed.

"We don't have sufficient knowledge of the weapons used by the enemy to totally protect our warriors. It seems that their proximity to the soldiers of the Caste causes a fatal and unknown disease among those who fight", Shen said.

"It's not a disease. It's the explosion of the matter caused by their weapons. It would be too complicated to explain now and in any case I don't know how to prevent it", I said.

I thought that if the Caste had Antimatter weapons and decided to use them, we would not have time to leave Earth-5.

"Shen. Trust me. We must transfer all the Eternals on Earth Prime with the exception of those who will remain here with me and do the same with the army. We'll keep a small garrison of volunteers to defend the palace of Amn'el'Tyr, to give me time to kill as many Potentiae as possible. The important thing now is to contain the enemy as long as we can, given the circumstances, without sacrificing all the army and the Eternals", I said.

Shen stared at me profoundly considering my request.

"What are you not telling me, Heylel?".

"I promise I'll explain everything when the battle is over. Now please, trust me and do as I've asked".

"All right. I will give the necessary instructions".

He put his hand on my shoulder and we transferred once again to the Council hall.

He summoned some Eternals and explained the situation to them: no one objected and after a few hours eight great masters of the Art were left in the Council hall: four men and four women, while the others had dislocated to Earth Prime, after having recovered the remaining legions and having organized the detachment of volunteers to defend Amn'el'Tyr.

II

In pairs, the remaining Eternals explored the areas occupied by the enemy army on the Fifth Emanation and the bases on Earth using their projections and started, two by two, to dislocate to attack. I followed them, projecting myself in the places they had chosen, waiting for the appearance of members of the Caste.

Each one of the Eternals who had remained was a master of extremely operative aspects of the Art and therefore qualified to summon devastating destructive Powers or to alter the fabric of reality, in mystical or physical battles, where necessary. The origin of their Power was their connection to the Great Dream, reawakened in them the day of their Anointment, through the entities and the laws which represented the fundamental principles of the World. Each one of them, as with scientists, knowingly used the specialties of the Art which were most in tune with their individual vibration and magnetic qualities. There were also great expressive differences among Eternals with male or female image-bodies: the women preferred operating through being possessed by entities coming from the subtle boundaries of the surface of the Mirror, such as Principles and Gods, or by living beings from the cosmic order like Stars or the Earth itself, regardless of the fact that these represented light or darkness, order or chaos.

This aspect of their line of operations made it more difficult for the Potentiae to use their terrifying mental fluid on a woman expert in the Art, when she was possessed by such an entity. In this way the men could handle aspects of the Power from more sources at the same time, while the women could manifest the power of one single entity, totally, as if this were temporarily incarnate and present in the image-body of the Eternal who had summoned it.

The men of the Gathering were therefore more vulnerable to the vile fluid of the Potentiae.

My attention was attracted by the couple who had attacked the secret base of the enemy in Greenland: I saw four human figures, three men and a woman, with the Caste uniform, who were about to reach them from each side, while they evoked enormous destruction to the base through a lightning storm, a devastating tornado and a local earthquake which produced fractures from which lava from the depths of the Earth oozed.

They had made the firearms unusable with an enchantment which inhibited the explosive chemical reactions in their range and the Caste soldiers approaching them were struck down by the lightning bolts which fell like rain in Summer.

The woman's image-body was dark complexed, probably from North Africa or the Caribbean, dressed only with the essential and on her bare abdomen, under the Translator, she had a mystical Pattern, colored and elaborated which she probably used to call into herself the entity to which she was devoted.

She was probably the one who was causing the great earthquake and her eyes were bright in their depth and wild by the power which was possessing her.

The man instead, probably originated from the Indian subcontinent, slender and dressed in a simple white and orange tunic and a turban like that of the Sikh was composing geometrical shapes and forms in every direction, with his hands, in the air and an absent gaze as if he were immersed in his inner sea, governing its movements. I couldn't exactly understand what he was doing but it didn't matter: the four representatives of the Caste were dangerously approaching and they were unfortunately too far, one from the other, for me to be able to take more than one to the symbolic space. I couldn't even dislocate too far from the two Eternals to avoid finding myself involved, in spite of them, in one or more of the phenomena they were stirring up and neither memorize the appearance of the four Caste members. I therefore decided to immediately materialize near my Equals.

The sound of the forces summoned dominated everything, and the wind and the heat were barely tolerable even there, by their side.

I wasn't a master of the Art as they were and even if the knowledge which had been instilled in me on the Ninth Emanation had contained my ancient heritage, this was not available to my awareness. All I had at my disposal was the possibility of using the technology of the Translator based on the dislocation secrets of the Anantrya and my mind, impermeable to the fluid of the Potentiae. The great Black Amazon and the Indian seemed totally absorbed in their task.

I had to find a way to tell them to go away before the arrival of the four Caste members, but it was too late: two of them were already visible and even at that distance I saw the light in their eyes and in their expressions which revealed the presence of their Masters.

They didn't seem to experience the consequences of the surrounding phenomena and I therefore thought they had a way of protecting themselves from that type of mystical aggressions. Their minds were already striking the two Eternals and the destructive natural phenomena they were managing started to waver. The Indian was sweating and his hands tried to reach the Translator.

The Amazon instead, seemed to resist, but she too showed signs of her superhuman exertion. I tried to attract their attention signaling them to go away immediately, but they were elsewhere with their minds: I had to improvise.

I used the Translator and appeared exactly in front of one of the two visible enemies, but as my hand was about to touch him, his attention was entirely directed on me and I felt the cold penetrating touch of the fluid of the Potentia which tried to paralyze me: my hand was blocked and I saw him smile while the other one approached. I wasn't able to move and only hoped that my Equals had been able to flee, taking advantage of the moment.

Through their human puppets, both Potentiae had concentrated their devastating fluid against my mind and I could feel the invisible tentacles of their frightening touch enter me, occupy my thoughts and my emotions like a terrible scream which covered the sound of everything.

I understood in that moment that I was immune to their possession but not as much to the destructive power they could bring about. My whole body started to ache, inside and out. My heart beat wildly, I gasped for air and a piercing pain in my head was making feel as though my eyes, ears and teeth were about to explode. I would have lost control of my thoughts, before dying, but then I remembered the divine Yanil who had inspired me.

As though driven by an intuition, untouched by the darkness of the Potentiae, I had the strength to visualize the nine pointed star as I had seen it in the symbolic space. The star, as though animated by a life of its own, appeared in front of my interior vision without having to apply myself with any willpower or energy.

The pain immediately began to recede and a little after I felt the touch of the Potentiae tremble and perceived them as struck by an ancient shudder of fear. Through their fluid, they were trapped inside of me, and while the power of the star increased, their desire to flee became stronger and stronger. Their human hosts of the Caste in front of me had distorted expressions, a mix between disbelief and fear. The star began to give off a series of blinding lightning bolts at the end of which I knew that the Potentiae had been destroyed in my mind as well as on the far away shores of the intergalactic space, where their bodies slept.

The two men of the Caste fell to the ground and started shaking: the death of their masters would have killed them too in no time.

And this was how I had discovered another way of striking at the enemy, without always having to go to the symbolic space. That strange sign had in itself the Power to trap and kill them, in any space. I was so taken by that new discovery that I didn't realize that the third member of the Caste had reached us and was standing about ten meters in front of us.

He had seen everything and looked at me sternly, with an incredulous expression. Before dying, the Potentiae had surely been able to share with their collectivity, what had happened. He was looking at me but didn't have the least intention of attacking me with its lethal fluid. Taken by a moment of mad rashness, I took a step towards him, while the heat and the smoke – a by product of the the attack of the Eternals - was all around us and even in the air which separated us (I had a sudden thought: the Caste members that were converging on my position were four. Where was the fourth?). My movement seemed to shake my opponent from the numbness of disbelief and I saw the Potentiae recede from his eyes. Once, back in charge of his body, he pulled out a particle weapon from his belt and pointed it at me. I felt my blood freeze inside, I knew I was physically vulnerable! As a reflex, my left hand went to the Translator while I began to visualize my room at Amn'el'Tyr.

But it was too late: my fingers still hadn't reached the colored geometrical shapes of the Translator when the man activated his weapon releasing a flash of light towards me. And right at that same moment the missing member of the Caste appeared on the scene.

She threw herself in front of me, on the line of the lethal ray, and just before being hit, her voice – that of Amelia – shouted.

"Nooo!!!".

She was struck in the chest, intercepting the ray destined to me, which by itself would have put an end to all the sophisticated preparations that had been necessary to turn me into the Potentiae's nemesis; she fell back and I caught her in my arms, while the weapon which had stuck her emitted a sound which indicated that it was recharging to strike again.

But it was too late: I activated the Translator and in no time we were in my apartment. I delicately lay Amelia on the floor; her left breast had been completely consumed by the blow but the wound was much deeper, even if the concentrated band of radiation of the weapon had cauterized it with its heat, blocking the inevitable hemorrhage.

She was pale and her body was trembling, but she was still conscious even if I couldn't have said for how long. My emotions blocked my throat.

We were technically enemies, but I just couldn't see her as such, and she, despite the Demon which possessed her, had not hesitated to putting herself in the line of fire to save me.

I was about to be struck by a strong emotion that immediately turned into tears while I rocked Amelia caressing her hair.

"You... are... safe", she said feebly, looking at me.

"Yes. Thanks to you", I answered, smiling at her through the tears.

She slowly extended her hand which I took, holding it gently.

"Why did you do it?", I asked, even if I already knew the answer and perceiving in that moment, deep down inside, that I would have done exactly the same stupid thing, if the situation had been the other way around.

"Because I understood there is only one thing I fear more than death... to live without you".

She answered in agony and a tear rolled down from her left eye. My mind was quickly elaborating a way to save her. Potentia or not, I didn't want her to die.

"I will have you taken care of now and in no time you'll get better until you're well again", I said trying to let go of her hand to activate the Translator, but she restrained me.

"No... it's... useless. Maybe you could heal the wounds, but the radiations would get me shortly after", she said in a weak voice. Her life was inexorably leaving her.

"And what will become of you? I don't want you to die".

She weakly clenched the hand which I was holding.

"It's... inevitable... but... I'm not sorry... ".

"Call the Potentia... your Master... have it save you! I swear on my Heart that if he saves you I won't do anything to harm it", I said.

"It has already left me... maybe I wasn't an obedient enough slave... and also for this reason, I will die... ".

"What can I do? Tell me!".

She smiled weakly.

"Hold me tight one last time... give me one last kiss... and when... you win the war... don't forget me...", she said.

I embraced her and kissed her while our tears mixed, while I felt an acute anger rise from the depths of my being, out of the range of intensity of human emotions.

Revenge!

"I swear I will bring you back to me, as a free being, when my task is finished. I will hunt for the Caste and the Potentiae to the most remote corners of the universe, until I am sure you have had justice. I swear this on my Heart", I said, trying to remain calm.

She held me tighter.

"I know... ", she said, dying shortly after in my arms.

I wanted to scream. I wanted to destroy. I wanted to kill everything.

I held her tightly a while longer, then I closed her eyes and lifted her, bringing her to the bed where I lay her down.

II

The Council hall at Amn'el'Tyr was enveloped in a buzz of ongoing activities, with Eternals who, in turn, dislocated to areas to sabotage or to help other troops which had remained to protect the city.

Shen was busy in the coordination and updating operations for the Eternals which had left the Fifth Emanation: many of them had already started to rebuild the army in anticipation of another big battle.

I was furious and didn't try to hide it; I wanted to carry out a slaughter. I slowly approached him and he saw me.

"We feared for you. The last news we had was that you were facing two Demons at the same time", Shen said without hiding the relief he felt.

"Two Demons which no longer exist", I said coldly.

"You can't imagine how glad we all are. During your absence we intensified the attacks and recalled some operative Eternals to cover the troops defending the city. Half of our warriors have fallen and we are now withdrawing more and more internally", he said worriedly.

"I hope the enemy has come off worse", I said.

"With all the energy we are using, for each one of ours twenty of theirs fall. But their resources seem to never end and we are, at all effects, under siege".

"Let's begin right away then", I said, rubbing my hands.

"Heylel... is something bothering you?", asked Shen with the eyes of who has already read inside of you.

We stared at each other for a moment, Shen with a worried expression and I with a fury which boiled my blood.

"Nothing", I answered, "... I just want victory for all of us, now! And now I know how to do it more quickly", I added.

Before answering, Shen worriedly looked me straight in the eyes again for a few seconds.

"Let's go then! We don't have much time".

He made all the Eternals present leave, still in pairs, towards the destinations they had chosen for the sabotage attacks.

I oversaw them with the Translator and as soon as I felt a Potentia approach I immediately dislocated there. I realized that the two Potentiae I had destroyed before Amelia's sacrifice had been victims of the Power of the the nine pointed star - and a part of the hidden knowledge in me revealed itself, revealing to me that I didn't have to have the Demon's tentacles in my head; I could project the symbol in the direction of the Potentia and this would have simply canceled it, and this I did everywhere I came across one. Together with two volunteer Equals, we also attacked one of the ships in orbit which was destroyed together with the Potentia which commanded it, unfortunately with the image-bodies of the two Eternals who were not able to escape in time.

From the beginning of the battle for the Fifth Emanation, more than fifty Eternals had sacrificed their lives.

The destruction of the ship in orbit was decisive for the battle on the Fifth Emanation: all the ships withdrew to Earth's standard space, but not before sparking off a little inferno against Earth-5, bombing the entire continent which housed Amn'el'Tyr with antimatter, transforming it into a radioactive desert with vitrified craters and contaminating its atmosphere.

Only the city went untouched. Amn'el'Tyr was abandoned almost immediately after the beginning of the bombing and the remainder of my Equals and I reached the stronghold city of Hatesh, in the Third Emanation, with our Translators.

While the ships of the Empire devastated Earth-5, numerous Eternals followed the event in projected form, to learn more about their weapons and of the capabilities of the Caste in that the outcome of the war for Earth would not have touched, for the moment at least, the faraway stellar Empire from which they came. Sooner or later the Gathering would have had to face them again.

In the meanwhile, a group of eleven Eternals and I attacked the base in Chile and that in Antarctica, razing them to the ground and killing seventeen more Potentiae, and above all, destroying the flourishing food supply industry, therefore interrupting, at least for the moment, the capturing and shipping of live human bodies destined to restaurants and cafeterias of the Caste in their far away capital. Even the clone deposit in Antarctica was destroyed, so blocking the possibility for the members of the Caste to transmigrate to new bodies in case of physical death. The lunar base was easier to destroy, but it cost the lives of three Eternals. The Potentiae and the forces of the Caste withdrew to the external margins of the Solar System.

This war had not been won, but no one harbored illusions of giving up the riches and the mysteries of Earth: sooner or later they would have come back stronger and more determined and by that time the Gathering would have been ready to inflict a new defeat to the enemy.

III

Before leaving Amn'el'Tyr, I returned to my apartment and took Amelia's lifeless body to the refuge that had meant so much for my awakening: the forest of the Guardian in Corsica, which I had prayed to preserve her from nature and predators until my return.

And so it was.

I returned at sunset on a cloudy day and remained near her until the middle of night.

Then, in a little clearing, I built a pyre with dry branches and leaves and lay Amelia's body on top. I gave her one last kiss and, as by ancient tradition, put a coin on each one of her eyes.

I watched the fire consume that ancient body until the end with my mind full of memories of the time we had been allowed together. Too little maybe, but enough for her to sacrifice herself for love.

Then, while I observed the eastern sky lighten, signaling the oncoming dawn, I thought that maybe all wasn't lost for this human race from another world, soured by time and by hunger.

Maybe one day they too would have fought against the Potentiae and returned the Earth and its prisoners to the stars to which they belonged to from time immemorial.

ABOUT THE AUTHOR

Fabio Ghioni was allegedly born in Milano, Italy, sometimes in the 20th century. He majored a PhD in Clinical Psychology and is recognized as one of the major pioneers of the digital age although most of his work for public institutions and governments cannot be disclosed or even mentioned.

Amongst his many activities as writer, essayist, journalist and lecturer, he founded in 2012 the Evolution and New Order Civilization Project that he later developed in Psychogony, a new technology exploring the depths of human ability and the Philosophy of Apotheosis.

10814525R00167

Printed in Germany
by Amazon Distribution
GmbH, Leipzig